PALM BEACH COUNTY
LIBRARY SYSTEM
3650 Summit Boulevard
West Palm Beach, FL 33406-4198

DEAD IN A
WEEK

DEAD IN A WEEK

ANDREA KANE

ISBN-13:   9781682320297 (Hardcover)
               9781682320303 (Trade Paperback)
               9781682320310 (ePub)
               9781682320327 (Kindle)

LCCN: 2018952251

DEAD IN A WEEK

For questions and comments about the quality of this book, please contact us at CustomerService@bonniemeadowpublishing.com.

www.BonnieMeadowPublishing.com

Printed in USA

Publisher's Cataloging-in-Publication

Publisher's Cataloging-in-Publication

Names: Kane, Andrea. | Kane, Andrea. Forensic Instincts novel.
Title: Dead in a week / Andrea Kane.
Description: Warren, NJ : Bonnie Meadow Publishing LLC, [2019]
Identifiers: ISBN 9781682320297 (hardcover) | ISBN 9781682320303 (trade Paperback) | ISBN 9781682320310 (ePub) | ISBN 9781682320327 (Kindle)
Subjects: LCSH: Students, Foreign--Germany--Munich--Fiction. | Kidnapping--Germany--Munich--Fiction. | Nanostructured materials industry--United States--Fiction. | Undercover operations--Fiction. | Forensic sciences--Fiction. | LCGFT: Thrillers (Fiction)
Classification: LCC PS3561.A463 D43 2019 (print) | LCC PS3561.A463 (ebook) | DDC 813/.54--dc23

DEDICATION

To Laci, our tiny miracle who's instilled in my heart a new and unconditional love, the depths of which I could never have imagined. You're a blessing beyond compare, my precious little granddaughter.

1

Munich, Germany
20 February
Tuesday, 4:00 p.m. local time

Normally, Lauren Pennington loved the sound of her combat boots clomping across the cobblestone apron. But right now, all she could think about was the growling of her empty stomach, urging her to move faster. She was oblivious to everything else—the couple on the corner sharing a passionate, open-mouthed kiss, the guy puking up his overconsumption of beer into the storm sewer grating, and the man watching her every move as he talked into his cell phone in a language that Lauren wouldn't have recognized had she been paying attention.

She walked into Hofbräuhaus' main hall, took a seat at one of the wooden tables, and placed her order. Minutes later, the waitress came over and brought Lauren's food and drink. Barely uttering a perfunctory "*Danke,*" Lauren bit into a pretzel the size of her head and took a healthy gulp of Hofbräu.

The semester had ended, and she was entitled to some carbs and a dose of people-watching at the historic Munich brewery. Pretzels and beer were addicting, but people-watching had always fascinated her.

Despite a whole winter semester of her junior year abroad studying art history at the Ludwig Maximilian University at Munich, she still enjoyed playing the tourist. Not at school, but every time she strolled the streets, studied the architecture, chatted with the locals.

Hofbräuhaus was less than a mile from campus, but the brewery's main hall had a reputation all its own. With its old-world atmosphere of wooden tables, terra cotta floors, painted arches, and hanging lanterns, how could anyone not feel a sense of history just being within these walls?

Maybe that's why Europe called out to her, not just here, but from a million different places. Museums. Theaters. Cathedrals. She wanted to experience them all, and then some. She'd be going home to San Francisco in July, and she hadn't been to Paris or London or Brussels. She'd gotten a mere taste of Munich and had yet to visit Berlin.

When would she get another chance to do all that?

Not for ages. And certainly not with the sense of freedom she had as a college student, with little or no responsibilities outside her schoolwork to claim her attention.

On the flip side, she felt terribly guilty. Every February, her entire family traveled to Lake Tahoe together. It was a ritual and a very big deal, since her father rarely got a day, much less a week, off as a high-powered executive. Her mother usually began making arrangements for the trip right after the holidays. In her mind, it was like a second Christmas, with the whole family reuniting and sharing time and laughter together.

This year was no different. Lauren's brother, Andrew, and her sister, Jessica, were both taking time off from their busy careers to join their parents at Tahoe—no easy feat considering Andrew was an intellectual property attorney in Atlanta, and Jess was a corporate buyer for Neiman Marcus in Dallas.

Lauren was the only holdout. Lauren. The college kid. The baby. The free spirit who always came home from Pomona College to nest, especially for family gatherings and rituals.

Her parents had been very quiet when she'd told them about her plans. Lauren knew what that silence meant. After the phone call ended, her mother would have cried that she was losing her baby, and her father would have scowled and written off her decision as college rebellion.

Neither was true. But no matter how she explained it, her parents didn't understand. They'd traveled extensively in Europe, and to them, it was no big deal. But it was Lauren's first time here, and to her, it was like discovering a whole new world—a world she felt an instant rapport with. It was like discovering a part of her soul she'd never known existed. And she had to immerse herself in it.

She'd entertained the idea of flying to Lake Tahoe for the week and then returning to fulfill her dream. Her parents would definitely pay for that. But given the long international travel, the flight changes, the time differences, and the jet lag, Tahoe would put too much of a crimp in the many plans she had for her break between semesters. She'd had invitations from school friends who said she could stay with them during her travels—friends from Germany and so many other countries.

The world was at her feet.

No, despite how much she loved her family, she had to do things her way this time. There'd be other Februarys, other trips to Tahoe. But this was a once-in-a-lifetime opportunity.

She was still drinking her beer and lamenting her situation when a masculine voice from behind her said, "*Hallo. Darf ich dich begleiten?*"

Turning, Lauren saw a handsome, rugged-featured guy, gazing at her with raised brows. He was asking if he could join her.

"*Bist du allein?*" he asked, glancing to her right and to her left.

"Yes, I'm alone," she answered in German. "And, yes, please join me."

The man came around and slid onto the bench seat. He propped his elbow on the table, signalling to the waitress that he'd have the same as the lady. The waitress nodded, hurrying off to get his refreshment.

He turned his gaze back to Lauren. "You're American," he noted, speaking English that was heavily accented.

"Guilty as charged," she responded in English. "Is it that obvious?" She gave him a rueful look.

He smiled, idly playing with the gold chain around his neck. "Your German is quite good. But I picked up the American...what's the word you use? *Twang*."

Lauren had to laugh. "It's my turn to take a stab at it, then. You're French? Slavic? A combination of both?"

"The last." His smile widened. "You have a good ear, as well."

"Your German and your English are excellent. I guess I just got lucky."

"Speaking of getting lucky, what's your name?" he asked.

His boldness took her aback, but she answered anyway. "Lauren. What's yours?"

"Marko." He held out his hand, which Lauren shook. "I'm in Munich on business. And you?"

"I'm an exchange student. I'm on break, and I'm looking forward to enjoying some time exploring Europe."

Marko looked intrigued. "I can give you a few tips." A mischievous glint lit his eyes. "Or I could travel with you for a few days and give you the best taste of Munich you'll ever have."

Lauren felt flushed. She was twenty years old. She knew very well what Marko meant by "the best taste." She should be offended. But she couldn't help being flattered. He was older, good-looking, and charming.

Nonetheless, she wasn't stupid. And she wasn't in the market for a hookup.

"Thanks, but I'm tackling this trip on my own," she replied. "I'm meeting up with friends later, but I'm good as planned."

"Pity." The glint in his eyes faded with regret. "Then at least let me give you some pointers about the best sights to see and the best restaurants and places to visit."

"That would be fantastic." Lauren rummaged in her purse for a pen and paper. Having found them, she set her bag on the floor between them.

She spent the next twenty mesmerizing minutes listening to Marko detail the highlights of Munich and other parts of Bavaria, as she simultaneously scribbled down what he was saying.

"Thank you so much," she said when he was finished. "This is like a guided tour."

"Once again, I could do it in person."

"And once again, I'm flattered, but no thank you." Lauren signaled for her check, reaching into her bag and retrieving a twenty euro bill when the waitress approached the table. "The rest is for you," she told her.

"I'll take care of that," Marko offered, stopping Lauren by catching her wrist and simultaneously fishing for his wallet. Evidently, he was still holding out hope that she would change her mind.

"That's okay. I've got it." Lauren wriggled out of his grasp, leaned forward, and completed the transaction. "You've been a tremendous help," she said to Marko as she rose. "I'm glad we met."

This time it was she who extended her hand.

Reluctantly, he shook it. "I hope we meet again, Lauren. I'll look for you the next time I'm in Munich."

Still smiling, Lauren left the café and walked through the wide cobblestone apron outside. There were little tables with umbrellas scattered about, with patrons chatting and eating. Sated by the beer and pretzel, she inhaled happily, and then, walking over to the sidewalk, began what she expected to be a thoughtful stroll. Maybe she'd text her parents this time, try explaining her position without all the drama of a phone call.

She was halfway down the street when she heard a male voice call after her, "Lauren!"

She turned to see Marko hurrying in her direction. "Here." He extended his arm, a familiar iPhone in his hand. "You left this on the table."

"Oh, thank you." How could she have been so careless? She protected her cell phone like a small child. "I'd be lost without that—"

As she spoke, a Mercedes van tore around the corner and came screeching up to them.

The near doors were flung open, and a stocky man jumped out, his face concealed by a black hood. Before Lauren could so much as blink, he grabbed her, yanking a burlap sack over her head and tossing her over his shoulder.

"*Merr në makinë,*" he said in a language Lauren didn't understand.

By this time, Lauren had recovered enough to struggle for her freedom. Her legs flailed in the air, kicking furiously, and she pounded on the man's back as he carried her and flung her into the back of the van.

Marko jumped in behind her, slamming the doors shut and barking out something in the same dialect as the other man—neither French nor Slavic—as the stocky barbarian held her down.

Finally finding her voice, Lauren let out a scream, which was quickly muffled by the pressure of Marko's hand over her mouth. She could taste the wool of the sack, and she inclined her head so she could breathe through her nose.

A short-lived reprieve.

Marko fumbled around, then shoved a handkerchief under the sack, covering her nose and mouth. Lauren thrashed her head from side to side, struggling to avoid it. The odor was sickeningly sweet and citrusy.

Chloroform.

Tears burned behind her eyes. Shock waves pulsed through her body.

Oh God, she didn't want to die.

Marko clamped his other hand on the back of her head, holding it in place while he forced the handkerchief flush against her nose and mouth, making it impossible for her to escape.

Dizziness. Nausea. Black specks. Nothing.

"*Shko*," Marko ordered his accomplice, shoving him toward the driver's seat.

The van screeched off, headed to hell.

2

Another late night.

Aidan Devereaux leaned back in his office chair for a brief moment of peace.

There weren't many of those at Heckman Flax. He was responsible for troubleshooting the labyrinthine communications infrastructure at the largest investment bank in the world. The company relied on its operations to extract billions in profits by trading everything from stocks and bonds to options and commodities. Virtually nothing in the world was traded without flowing through their book of business. They would take any side of any transaction if there was a buck to be made. With trillions of dollars on the line, nothing short of perfection in its communications network was acceptable. And it was his department's sole purpose to guarantee that perfection.

No one understood that better than Aidan. As a former Marine, he had seen men live or die based on communication failures of all types—equipment, procedures, and people. And he had learned how to prevent all of them. Uncle Sam had taught him well.

Most of his time was spent in meetings or on the phone, putting out fire after fire. No sooner would one "near miss" end when the next one would flare up in another part of the world. Last week, it was the loss of a critical data circuit in Singapore that placed the Far East operations at risk of slow transaction processing, or worse, a complete halt of trading operations. Aidan knew the drill. He'd immediately awakened the IT director in Japan, telling him to mobilize his team and bring on extra capacity in Tokyo should it be necessary. Fortunately, the worst hadn't happened, as his team quickly resolved the Singapore issue.

Frankly, Heckman Flax nauseated Aidan. Talk about a sharp contrast to his days as a Marine on active duty. In the military there had been a sense of real purpose, a common goal of annihilating the enemy, doing good, forming a brotherhood. And Wall Street? It was the worst of the worst. There was nothing decent or patriotic about individuals attacking their own team members—and all for the almighty dollar. It was screw or be screwed. Friendship was for losers.

Working in this jungle made Aidan's "other" life that much more appealing, and a hell of a lot more rewarding.

But he had personal responsibilities that he couldn't—and *wouldn't*—walk away from. He needed this job for the obscene amount of money Heckman Flax paid him, for the "cover" it provided, and for the advantages his position gave him to pursue his ideals.

Thinking of his primary responsibility, he picked up and studied the only personal item in his entire office. It was a photo of a four-and-a-half-year-old hellion. She was the one who had transformed *all* facets of his life and turned it totally upside down.

Abby. His little girl. His daughter.

He hadn't known of her existence until social services showed up at his door, with the necessary proof and documentation, and placed her in Aidan's arms. He'd been shocked to the core. But none of that mattered now. Abby's mother, Valèrie, was dead, and Aidan was all Abby had.

Nothing in his life had prepared him for becoming a single dad. There was no field manual. No Special Operations Parenting training. Just his instincts, wits, and anything he could read from supposed experts. And talk about losing a battle—he was losing this one each and every day in every possible way as little Abby wrapped him around her tiny little finger.

It appeared that former Marine Captain Aidan Devereaux was suddenly not so tough anymore, at least where his precocious daughter was concerned.

A smile curved his lips. Abby could wreak more havoc in an hour than a cave full of Taliban fighters or a conference room packed with corporate lawyers.

His tender musings were interrupted by the ringing of his secure cell phone.

His smiled vanished. "What's up?" he answered.

"I need to see you." Terri Underwood had an unmistakably author-itative tone to her voice. A former analyst for the National Security Agency and now a freelance security consultant, she had no time for bullshit small talk. She knew more about PRISM—the US government's not-so-secret data collection and spying efforts—than the people running it. She knew every nuance of the massive information-gathering behemoth, and even where a trap door existed so she could sneak into its vast repository of information without being detected.

Aidan relied heavily on Terri's clandestine genius to use PRISM for a secret purpose—ferreting out variations in human communi-cation patterns, variations that were the precursors to tragic or even catastrophic events.

"We've got a high-risk situation," she told him now.

Aidan glanced at his watch. "Give me a half hour to wrap things up. Then I'm on my way."

Los Altos Hills, California
23 February
Friday, 7:45 p.m. local time

"Vance, there's something wrong. I know it."

Susan Pennington was pacing anxiously around Vance's massive walnut desk, which seemed diminutive inside the expansive, well-appointed study.

Vance didn't answer. He was deep in concentration, squinting at his computer screen and studying an Excel spreadsheet that Robert Maxwell, the CEO of NanoUSA, had just forwarded to him. As VP of Manufacturing, he was pressed to review the data tonight. That way, he and Robert could have their closed-door meeting in the office at seven a.m. tomorrow.

"Vance!" Susan repeated, this time more adamantly. She might have her husband home, but his mind was still locked into the round-the-clock work schedule that comprised his life. He'd be at it till way past midnight. And she needed his attention *now*.

With a resigned sigh, Vance removed his glasses and eased back in his leather chair, studying his wife's stricken expression.

"Susan, it's only been three days since she called. She's pissed. She didn't like our reaction to her grand announcement that she'd be blowing off our annual family gathering. She's still been texting us every day at the same time to let us know she's okay. So what is it you're worried about?"

"It's not like Lauren to hold a grudge," Susan answered. "She's always about making up and moving on. This time's different. Even when I call her, my calls go straight to voice mail. She's clearly ignoring me. And her texts are cryptic. They sound more like a travel guide than like our daughter."

"Like I said, she's pissed at us. Maybe there's a guy in the picture," Vance suggested. "You know how Lauren is. If she's `in love' yet again, she'll be totally consumed with God knows who. It would explain everything—including why she wants to stay in Europe rather than joining her family for our once-a-year vacation. Hormones trump skiing."

Susan rubbed her hands together and considered that. Vance wasn't wrong in his assessment. When Lauren fell for a guy, it was hard, it was fast, and it overshadowed all else. After numerous failed relationships, Lauren had stopped sharing the details, waiting until the love affair was over and then defaulting to: "It didn't work out."

Could that be what this was about?

She blew out her breath. "I suppose that could explain it."

"Of course it could." Vance slid his glasses back on his nose and returned to his work. "Why don't you make yourself a cup of chamomile tea to unwind and then go upstairs? I'll join you as soon as I can."

"Okay." Susan left the room and headed down to the kitchen.

But she couldn't get rid of the nagging feeling that something just wasn't right.

The Zermatt Group Offices
West 75th Street, Manhattan, New York
23 February
Friday, 10:55 p.m. local time

Aidan went straight to his apartment building, greeted George the doorman, and then took the elevator up to the seventh floor.

He unlocked the front door and strode in, locking it firmly behind him.

This was home to him and Abby, and often to Joyce Reynolds, Abby's middle-aged nanny, who spent many an overnight or a late night—such as tonight—in the guest room while Aidan traveled or worked. Joyce had twenty years of experience, an enormously long fuse, and a genuine fondness for her little charge. She cooked, straightened up the apartment, and accompanied Abby to preschool and to all her other activities and playdates. She was a lifesaver.

The apartment was well-appointed and huge, with tons of rooms and a loft-like area that Abby loved to play in. Right now, it was quiet, which meant that Abby was asleep.

He'd check in on her later. At the moment, enjoying his home's amenities was the farthest thing from his mind.

He headed directly for the windowless room at the rear of the apartment, which served as the strategic command center for the Zermatt Group, a.k.a. the home base of Aidan's "other life." They called this space "the Cage" because the entire room was a Faraday cage. It didn't allow electromagnetic waves to enter and thereby protected all the sensitive electronic devices within its walls from electronic surveillance. All communications to the outside world were hardwired, heavily monitored, and protected with multiple firewalls. When someone tried to reach either Aidan or Terri on their cell phone when inside the Cage, the call could be routed instead to the desk phone in the room.

He paused in front of the solid steel door and the Hirsh keypad controlling access to it. Adjacent to the keypad was a small red light. When it glowed, Aidan was inside and not to be disturbed.

Spotting a crumpled candy wrapper on the floor, he squatted to pick it up and pocket it, a smile tugging at his lips as he thought of Abby repeating to her little friends, "Unless there's fire, flood, or blood, do *not* disturb my daddy 'cause he's working." So very Abby-like. She defended her daddy's unusual and über-private work space with absolute loyalty, even if she did have a million questions about it when she and Aidan were alone.

Right now Aidan could see that the red light was glowing, which told him that Terri was already inside. Only the two of them had the combination to the Hirsh. Aidan entered the access code and pushed the door open when he heard the lock click.

"I'm here," he announced, tossing his jacket on the nearest chair and striding over to Terri's desk, peering over her head as he did. The entire wall was a panorama of LED monitors partitioned into smaller screens that displayed everything from international news broadcasts to PRISM to computers monitoring events all over the world.

As a former NSA analyst and a sought-after computer security consultant, Terri was an expert on finding people who were trying to stay anonymous. From her stint at the NSA, she knew what worked and what didn't. Friends and foes quickly learned that she was quite the force to be reckoned with.

Physically, she was also a formidable woman, almost six feet tall, with a figure that rivaled Wonder Woman's. Her eyes were intense and dark, her hair was wavy and shoulder-length, and her skin was a light golden brown, the product of an African-American father and a Caucasian mother. As head of intelligence for the Zermatt Group and Aidan's right hand, she'd been an integral part of it since its onset.

Now she glanced up from her laptop, then rose and walked over to the printer, where she retrieved a handful of pages and passed them to Aidan. "Take a look at what Donovan found."

Donovan, Terri's artificial intelligence system, had been named by Aidan after "Wild Bill" Donovan, head of the OSS during World War II and regarded as the father of modern intelligence. Terri's Donovan would sniff out examples of corporations stealing from each other, criminal enterprises working with terrorists, and governments spying on everybody. The Zermatt Group didn't have the time or the resources to address all of them, only those that were really serious and that they might be able to do something about.

Clearly, this one was really serious. It would be interesting to see if they could impact it.

Frowning in concentration, Aidan flipped through the pages, noting the key briefing points in his hands.

He returned to page one.

"Vance Pennington," he said, without reading the details he already knew. "He's NanoUSA's Vice-President of Manufacturing. They're in the middle of something very big."

Terri nodded. "Our intelligence tells us that NanoUSA is about to commercialize a breakthrough manufacturing technology that will turn the electronics industry upside down. The Chinese desperately need this technology—to protect the status quo of their electronics dominance. Over the past few months, my analysis shows increased chatter from Chinese companies about stealing the technology—including hacking attempts targeting NanoUSA, heightened communications between known spies for the Chinese, and Chinese-sponsored agents looking to bribe or blackmail company employees into leaking details."

Aidan pursed his lips. "I assume that, to date, all attempts on the part of the Chinese have failed."

"Yes," Terri replied. "Let's move on to Pennington's personal life. Turn to page ten." She waited and then pointed at the page Aidan had flipped to. "He has a wife, Susan, and three children—Andrew, twenty-seven, Jessica, twenty-five, and Lauren, twenty. Lauren is an exchange student in Munich. She just finished up her winter semester. She's on her break now, supposedly touring Europe."

"Supposedly?"

"My system has detected a statistically significant shift in the communication flow from Lauren to her parents. Upon further analysis, I don't believe she's the person who's been communicating with them for the past three days."

Aidan's brows lifted. Terri never failed to impress him. "Go on."

"Lauren hasn't returned any of her parents' calls, nor has she initiated a single phone call to them," Terri replied. "That's the first anomaly. As for her text messages, they've diminished in frequency from many times a day to one per day, delivered at precisely the same time. I'm also seeing a marked change in linguistic patterns. Up until three days ago, the language pattern suggested a US-educated, college-aged female."

"And now?"

"Now the words are more typical of a Balkan male, in his thirties—a person who's trying very hard to appear female and American."

"So two different people composed the messages."

"Yes." Terri folded her arms across her chest, looking troubled. "I took it upon myself to contact Philip in London. I asked him to do some local reconnaissance on Lauren in Munich, using his former MI6 contacts. Philip confirmed that she was last seen having a beer and pretzel at the Hofbräuhaus, flirting with some Euro trash. Her apartment's been empty for days. Every piece of her matching set of luggage is accounted for. Her backpack is hanging on a hook. Her birth control pills, makeup, and pharmaceuticals are still in her medicine cabinet. Philip and I agree. Lauren's not traveling in Europe. She's been kidnapped."

Aidan nodded. "It's no coincidence that the victim is the daughter of NanoUSA's VP of Manufacturing. All that's required now is a simple barter transaction—NanoUSA's trade secrets in exchange for Lauren."

"My guess is that the Chinese aren't even doing their own dirty work." Terri sank down on the edge of her desk. "They've hired a Balkan crime group—probably the Albanians—to handle the kidnapping. This is now a High Priority."

Aidan didn't miss a beat. "I'll set up a meeting with Vance Pennington."

He reached for the phone on the desk and dialed his office. He knew that his personal assistant was still at her desk at this ungodly hour, addressing a situation with the Far East. Then again, a quarter of Heckman Flax's staff was still in the building, hard at work.

"Melissa, sorry for the hour and the short notice. I need you to book me on tomorrow's six a.m. flight to San Francisco, returning the following day. Have a rental car ready for me at the airport. I need to drive down to Santa Clara for a meeting in Silicon Valley." A pause. "Good. Also, I need to speak to John Reams. Right, our analyst who covers the technology space. He was there when I left. Phone is fine. Thanks."

Aidan hung up and turned to Terri. "I'm going into my home office for a teleconference," he told Terri. "I'll contact you tomorrow after I meet with Pennington. Lock up on your way out."

* * *

Aidan's teleconference with John Reams had been illuminating.

Heckman Flax's technology expert had explained that the breakthrough electronics technology NanoUSA had developed would significantly reduce labor required for electronics assembly. Implementation of the technology would result in massive unemployment in the Asian electronics industry.

To make matters worse, Robert Maxwell, the CEO of NanoUSA, was a patriot and was determined to revitalize electronics manufacturing in the US. In a seismic shift, cell phones, tablets, laptops would all be made in the US. The Chinese leaders were running scared. Millions had migrated from rural China to urban areas in order to fill factory jobs. If NanoUSA had its way, those Chinese factories would be empty. For the first time, Chinese workers would experience what their American counterparts felt in the Rust Belt as Chinese manufacturing eviscerated their manufacturing jobs. Now the tables would be turned.

John made the call to Vance Pennington's secretary and got Aidan an appointment on Pennington's calendar for tomorrow. So everything in California was set.

John deserved a huge thank-you. Aidan planned to give him one—something that Terri would relish arranging.

He texted her, asking her to finagle a table for two at Rao's East Harlem restaurant for John and his girlfriend. Then, he chuckled, thinking of what her reaction would be. She'd wallow like a pig in shit. Terri loved nothing more than to screw over a rich, entitled SOB. She'd hack into Rao's computerized seating list with great relish and replace the name of some Hollywood diva with John Reams.

You couldn't just get a table at Rao's. Tables had owners. Owners let you sit at their table.

Well, some asshole or other wouldn't be eating at Rao's tomorrow night.

Aidan had one last task left to complete the arrangements—an imperative task, since he'd given Joyce the rest of Saturday and Sunday off.

Abby would be thrilled.

He couldn't speak for her Uncle Marc and Aunt Madeline.

Farmhouse
Slavonia, Croatia
24 February
Saturday, 10:00 a.m. local time

Lauren paced around the bedroom, pausing to stare out the windows that overlooked nothing but acres and acres of lightly snow-covered land punctuated only by the occasional ice-glistening tree. Flat. Barren. It was the same in every room of the house—windows with views of nothingness. No signs of life or roads or activity.

Even after four days…God only knew where she was.

She still couldn't get rid of the faint odor of chloroform in her nostrils. It made her retch unless she breathed through her mouth. Between that and the paralyzing terror she felt, she'd barely eaten or left this room, although she was allowed to move freely through the one-story house and offered three full meals a day. The only people she saw were Marko and a terrifying-looking man who Marko addressed as Bashkim, whose powerful build told Lauren he was probably the man who'd grabbed her. He was in his mid-forties and balding, and the receding hairline of his light brown hair made his forehead and nose look all the more prominent. But it was his piercing light blue eyes that were the most frightening to Lauren. They were like lasers, pinning her to the post with a stare that made her insides clench with fear.

He never spoke to her and barely looked at her. She was a commodity to him, a pawn in whatever game he and his associates were playing. And she desperately tried not to imagine what role that was.

Someone higher level than Marko and Bashkim was running the show. She could hear snippets of phone conversations—too muffled for her to decipher through the wall and spoken in a language she didn't understand. But she picked up on a definite tone of deference and respect. Lauren was smart enough to realize that this was no random kidnapping. It had been carefully planned with her as its target.

Why? *Why*?

She kept trying to stifle her sobs. Showing weakness around these monsters would only bring them pleasure and give them more ammunition to torment her with.

Were they going to kill her?

She sank down on the bed, shivering as she curled up in a tight, self-protective ball.

The bedroom door opened, and Marko walked in, shutting the door behind him. He sauntered over to the bed and sank down beside her—way too close for comfort.

It wasn't the first time.

Lauren stiffened and, instinctively, shifted her weight to put a bit more distance between them. She loathed Marko joining her. Normally, he was somewhere else in the farmhouse, either conversing with Bashkim or talking quietly on the phone in what he'd proudly told Lauren was Albanian. But periodically, he'd pay her a visit, during which he managed to touch and taunt her. He hadn't taken it beyond that—yet—but the very sight of him turned Lauren's stomach even more.

Now, she fought back another gag as he put his hand on her thigh, gliding it upward, simultaneously caressing the gold chain around his neck in a blatant show of what he wanted to do to her. "You haven't eaten a decent meal since the pretzel at Hofbräuhaus," he said. "Starving yourself isn't going to help."

"I'm not hungry," Lauren said.

"Of course you are." He caressed her hip. "What would you like? I'm sure I can supply it."

Die and go to hell, Lauren thought with a shudder.

Marko smiled, arrogant enough to assume she was shuddering with desire. "We did have a connection, didn't we? I saw the look in your eyes when I asked if I could join you. You wanted me. I wanted you, too."

Lauren didn't answer.

"You were so taken by me that you didn't even notice when I slipped your cell phone out of your purse." His teeth gleamed in a face that Lauren couldn't believe she'd ever thought was handsome. "We didn't have time to enjoy each other then. We do now." He reached up and rubbed his knuckles across her breast.

That did it.

Lauren couldn't help herself. She sat up and slapped him resoundingly across the face. "Take your hands off of me!"

Hot color suffused Marko's cheeks and the furious glint in his eyes made Lauren cringe. Dear Lord, what had she done?

Abruptly, the door opened, and Lauren felt a wave of gratitude for the intrusion—until she saw who it was.

Bashkim. Oh God, did he plan on joining Marko and raping her? He was carrying something in his hands, and Lauren lifted her head to see what weapon of torture he'd brought to intensify her pain and add to their pleasure.

To her surprise, it was a tray of food—a bowl of Bavarian potato soup, a slab of bread, and a bottle of water.

He stopped halfway across the room, seeing what Marko was doing.

"*Mjaft!*" he barked, with an adamant shake of his head. He set the tray down on a chair, reached into his pocket, and peeled off a one hundred euro bill, tossing it at Marko. "*Merrni këto para dhe për të marrë veten një lavire.*"

Still glowering, Marko released Lauren, picked up the one hundred euros, and rose.

"I'm being told to get laid elsewhere," he told her icily. Lowering his voice, he added, "But we're far from done, my wild little Lauren."

Lauren squeezed her eyes shut until Marko's footsteps had vanished down the hall.

Bashkim picked up the tray and continued toward her.

"Thank you for sending him away," Lauren said weakly, fully aware of the irony of thanking this man, and equally aware that he couldn't understand a word she was saying.

"You're welcome," he replied in excellent, only slightly accented English. "Marko has the manners of a pig."

Lauren started. "You speak English."

He nodded, setting the tray on the nightstand.

"You're weak. You must eat," he said. "I know you're frightened. But soon we'll get what we want, and this will all be over."

"What is it you want?" Lauren couldn't control the tears any longer, and they spilled down her cheeks. "Money? Call my father. Please. He's very rich. He'll wire the ransom to you today."

"It's being taken care of. I have no doubt that your father will cooperate." Bashkim gestured at the food. "Enough talk."

Lauren fell silent, scrambling into a cross-legged position and placing the tray on her lap. The food smelled good. The knot in her stomach eased just knowing that her father was being contacted. He'd wire the money to them in an hour.

She'd be free.

With a resurgence of hope, she tasted the soup. "This is delicious." She hadn't realized how hungry she was. "Thank you."

"You're welcome."

She uncapped the bottle of water and began to greedily drink. It was the first substantial amount of fluid she'd drunk in four days. She was badly dehydrated and her body was desperate for renewal.

"Slowly," Bashkim cautioned. "You want to keep it down."

Lauren nodded, placing the bottle on the tray. He was right. The taste of choloroform was beginning to fade, but her body was protesting the large onslaught of fluid.

She paused for a moment. Then, she took a small bite of bread, chewing slowly and thoroughly before she swallowed.

"Good." Bashkim nodded. He stood, feet planted apart, waiting patiently while Lauren made her way through the meal.

Fifteen minutes later, she'd eaten most of the bread and half the soup.

"That's all I can manage," she said.

"It's enough." He set aside the tray. "Next time you'll come to the kitchen. There's more food there."

Lauren wiped the streaks of tears off her face, trying to come to terms with her violent abduction and her now less-than-barbaric treatment. "You're being very kind. I'm grateful. Because you're right. I'm scared—terrified. Please call my father as soon as you can. I beg you." She started crying again.

"I told you, it's being taken care of." Bashkim didn't elaborate. "And don't worry about Marko. He won't bother you again."

He turned to leave.

"Thank you," Lauren called after him. "Thank you so much."

She listened to his retreating footsteps, bowing her head in relief. Her father was being contacted. It would be okay. Soon she'd be home.

Suddenly she had the strength to take a shower and resume being human.

* * *

Bashkim paused in the hallway, listening to the sounds of her preparing for her shower.

She was a nice girl. He hoped her father would cooperate. He hoped she wouldn't have to die.

He didn't normally feel pity. Normally, he didn't give a shit if or how he slaughtered the people he killed. But this one reminded him of his youngest sister. He'd make the next few days as easy on her as possible.

If death became necessary, he'd kill her in a kind way.

3

Aidan settled himself in the rear seat of the limo as it pulled away from his apartment building.

He punched in a secure cell phone number that rang in Lyon, France. When the other party answered, he said, "It's Aidan."

"I assumed so. *Patience.* I just sent you the email," Simone Martin responded in her lilting voice, her speech laced with that particularly sexy French accent. That, among other things, had been what drew Aidan to Simone from the start. Their relationship was a complicated and torrid one—on-again, off-again at the beginning, very much on-again now.

Ironically, it had been Valèrie who'd introduced them when Aidan was, once again, overseas, having been called back to active duty by the Marines for a specified period of time. Valèrie and Simone had studied together at the Paris-Sorbonne University and gone on to remain friends. As for the introduction, it was classic Valèrie. She'd bid a fond *adieu* to the month-long sexual marathon she and Aidan had shared, and had become immersed in some intensive journalistic assignment that consumed all her time and energy. As a result, she was unbothered by the obvious and electric attraction between Aidan and Simone.

Life worked in strange ways. At the time, Aidan had dismissed the affair with Valèrie as a pleasant diversion. But that had been before he'd known Abby had been the result. Now? He could never regret a liaison that had given him his precious child.

As for him and Simone, it turned out that, at the time, she was working for Thales, a military contractor, giving the two of them the opportunity to work—and to play—together. She'd moved on to McKinsey and Company, and Aidan's military assignment had ended, at which time he'd headed home to the States and begun working with Heckman Flax. But their fire still burned, even now, when they continued to live countries apart and saw each other so seldom.

"Aidan?" Simone prompted.

"I'm here." He cleared his throat and checked his iPhone. "I don't see the email yet."

"*Un minute, chéri.* I included a brief summary of the skills I felt were necessary, plus a list of those people best suited to address a European kidnapping with an industrial espionage component. You'll find dossiers on each individual attached, as well as a few alternate selections in the event that you disagree with my assessment of the mission."

Aidan felt himself grinning. "When have I ever disagreed with your assessments?"

Simone was what Aidan affectionately referred to as a "people whisperer." She knew more about human beings than they knew about themselves. Based out of Lyon, France, she spoke five languages fluently. In her current "real" job as a managing partner for McKinsey, she was head of recruiting. Her role was to find the best people in the world and convince them to join the firm. As the Zermatt Group's human capital expert, she applied the same skills in recruiting talent for them.

Aidan relied on Simone to not only find new talent but, when a project presented itself, to scan their talent pool and develop a short list of professionals with the skills and team chemistry to be successful.

She'd never let him down yet.

"Here it is," he said, opening the email. "Great. I'll review it all on the plane."

* * *

Two hours later, Aidan's flight took off.

First class on United flight 303 to San Francisco was quiet this morning. Probably because it was Saturday and all the business travelers were already home for the weekend.

Aidan sank back, enjoying his morning cup of black coffee. He needed it after the night he'd had. Poor Abby had woken up at two a.m. really sick. Aidan had prevailed upon their pediatrician, explaining his business dilemma. The compassionate man had met them in his office and diagnosed Abby with strep throat. The twenty-four-hour drugstore had filled the doctor's prescription. Still, Aidan had been in a major bind. He had to take this trip. But Abby's fever was high and her throat was horribly sore. Not to mention she was probably still contagious. The nanny had left at midnight and was now visiting her daughter in New Hampshire for the weekend. He just didn't know how he was going to manage.

So he'd called Marc and Maddy to come over quite early. God bless his brother and sister-in-law. They were dressed and ready before Aidan hung up the phone. Madeline was an ER nurse. She'd assured Aidan that she'd take care of Abby. And Marc would love being the entertainment committee.

Abby had woken up from her feverish sleep as soon as she heard her uncle and aunt arrive. And she'd forgotten all about how sick she was. Not only were they here for what she viewed as a two-day playdate, they'd brought gifts: a gallon of cotton candy ice cream, her favorite, and a get-well present of a brand-new princess doll they'd saved to give her. The doll had flowing golden hair, a pink satin gown, and a crown with tiny colored rhinestones on it. Abby collected princess dolls like baseball cards. This was another beauty to add to her prized collection.

So Aidan had blown out of there with an enormous hug from his own little princess and, just as importantly, peace of mind.

"Mr. Devereaux, can I bring you anything?" the flight attendant was asking. "Breakfast will be served in an hour. Would you like something in the interim?"

Aidan glanced at his near-empty cup. "Just some more coffee, please. I need all the caffeine I can get."

She smiled, having seen more than her share of business travelers. "I'll get it right away."

Aidan spent the next few hours reviewing everything Simone had sent him. All spot on—as usual.

He glanced out the window. The morning was new and clear, and he found himself staring down at the beauty of the Rockies. Just seeing them brought back vivid memories of the Swiss Alps, the formation of the Zermatt Group, and the events leading up to the coalition that had taken on a life of its own.

It started five years ago in the small Swiss town of Zermatt. Three amazing professionals from Aidan's previous life—Terri, Simone, and former MI6 agent Philip Banks—had arrived at the mountain resort at Aidan's invitation. Over wine and raclette, they came together as a loosely formed group and adopted their meeting location as a *nom de guerre:* The Zermatt Group.

Aidan had met each of them during his overseas military career in communications and intelligence. They had worked together on different projects, under the auspices of different organizations and governments. Aidan had selected them for the unique talent they brought to the table—leadership, information technology skills, investigative abilities, even the assessment of human personalities and capabilities. But most important was each team member's strong network of contacts and innate skill at recruiting others to serve as a secondary circle of operatives.

With the same respect that he'd shown in naming Zermatt's AI system, Aidan had modeled the group after the actions of his own childhood hero, World War II intelligence leader "Wild Bill" Donovan. Donovan's outgoing personality and business skills afforded him access to key European leaders in both industry and government. His skill in recruiting others to help him, both domestically and internationally, made him the ultimate master spy and the founder of the OSS, the precursor of the modern-day CIA. Aidan had been fascinated with Donovan. It was that fascination that led him to enter military service, become a Marine, and choose a specialty in communications and intelligence that allowed him, like Donovan, to travel the world, working with many talented people on difficult missions.

Over the past decade, Aidan's international exposure had afforded him a unique view of global geopolitics and business. And it had turned his stomach. The world was taking an alarming direction. With the lines blurring between legal and illegal, moral and immoral, the Zermatt Group would be there to remind the transgressors that they had gone too far.

Utilizing his Marine training and Donovan's intelligence methods, Aidan had founded the Zermatt Group like a special ops military strike force, with himself, Terri, Simone, and Philip—who served as the group's lead on-the-ground investigator—as a force multiplier to help the good guys, above or below their radars. They relied upon the respective networks of contacts they'd cultivated over the years.

The Zermatt Group members lived and worked in their local communities. Their jobs and business contacts gave them critical access to people, technology and financial assets. That allowed them to operate in the shadows. Terri made sure of it.

That's how it started, and that's how it had stayed.

And now, the Pennington kidnapping and industrial blackmail crisis loomed over them, begging for a swift resolution without sacrificing Lauren's life in the process.

* * *

Aidan picked up his rental car and drove the fifty minutes from San Francisco to Silicon Valley, and directly to Santa Clara. It might be a Saturday, but it was no surprise that Vance Pennington was at work. Like Aidan's, Pennington's job required a seven-days-a-week, twenty-four-hours-a-day commitment.

Pulling around the bend, Aidan drove up the private road that led to NanoUSA. At first glance, he thought he was at a top-secret military base rather than a corporate headquarters. The entire building complex looked as if it were on lockdown.

He was stopped at the main checkpoint, where, as a visitor, he was required to leave his vehicle, plus just about everything else. All his personal belongings, including electronic communication devices, were placed in a steel box and locked away for safekeeping. He had to submit to a body scanner, which could check for any hidden weapons or embedded devices—swallowed, implanted, or otherwise.

The security procedures were similar to those Aidan had experienced at FBI Headquarters, only heightened to the nth degree.

When he'd stepped into the security office, he could see that his cell signal died instantly. So the windowless building was lead-lined, blocking any and all signals from entering or leaving.

These people were definitely serious about keeping their secrets secret.

Aidan was transported in a company vehicle from security to the main building and reception area. Since it was Saturday, a security guard was on duty, instead of a receptionist. Aidan gave him his name, and the security guard called Vance to tell him that his visitor had arrived. The security guard attached a Bluetooth bracelet to Aidan's wrist and told him to make sure he was always with his escort. The bracelet would keep track of his physical whereabouts at all times, and any attempts to leave authorized areas or to tamper with the device would be immediately detected and dealt with harshly.

A second guard arrived, advising Aidan to accompany him up to Mr. Pennington's office.

They rode up to the tenth floor and exited, walking past frosted glass walls to the rear corner office that flourished a brass plate with the name *Vance Pennington, Vice-President* on it.

The guard knocked. "Mr. Pennington? Mr. Devereaux is here to see you."

"Come in," came the reply.

The guard pushed the door open and gestured for Aidan to enter. Then he quickly made his retreat, shutting the door behind him.

Glancing around, Aidan crossed over the threshold and onto the thick pile of cream carpeting. The office had classic mahogany furniture, plush leather sofa and chairs, and an expansive, horse-shoe-shaped desk. It was a good thing that the place was so huge and well-appointed, since there wasn't a single window to look out of or to make you feel connected with the outside world. In short, it was a luxury coffin. Given the number of hours Vance Pennington worked, if this office were anything less than it was, he might succumb to claustrophobia.

Aidan's gaze quickly scanned the few personal items on Pennington's desk. Photos of his family. An expensive fountain pen and ink well. And on the wall behind him, a framed US Marine Corps Good Conduct Medal.

Not a surprise. Terri's intel had told him as much, just as John's information had informed him that Robert Maxwell hired patriots. But the fact that Pennington had served in Aidan's own division of the military was a nice bonus. It might be a bonding mechanism that would swing the pendulum in Aidan's favor.

"Mr. Devereaux." Vance Pennington rose from behind his desk, reaching across to shake Aidan's hand. Saturday or not, he was wearing an expensive suit and tie, as if it were a weekday.

Then again, so was Aidan.

"Please." Vance gestured at one of the buttery-soft leather chairs across from him. "Have a seat."

"Thank you." Aidan sank down into the chair. "And I'm not big on the formalities. It's Aidan."

"Vance," Pennington replied. "Can I have someone get you something to drink? Coffee? Tea? Something stronger?"

"I'm fine," Aidan assured him. "Although I am intrigued by the extent NanoUSA has gone to ensure its security. The grounds and the building are a veritable fortress."

A hint of a smile touched Vance's lips. "It's the only way to ensure the level of secrecy we require."

"Does that apply to the executives, as well? Do you also have to forfeit your cell phones at the door?"

"Absolutely." Vance nodded. "The cell phones we use outside of this office complex are quarantined in a special facility. Phone calls and texts are forwarded to our *red phones* that are only used within this facility." He held up his red phone for Aidan to see. "This way, we can stay in touch with the outside world, but because the devices are quarantined, any potential for hacking, spying, industrial espionage is eliminated."

Aidan found himself fascinated. "How can you be so sure? There's always the next virus or Trojan horse that someone manages to sneak by even the best of systems."

"Very simple," Vance replied. "We change the form of each type of communication and then change it back. Say, for example, that you receive a text message. Let's assume that somehow, the text message had a nefarious payload along with it. The first step in the process would convert the text message into speech, preventing any payload from being delivered. In the second conversion step, the now audible words of the text message would be converted using a speech-to-text algorithm in a separate system. We do the same kind of conversion for phone calls, as well. The process is just reversed."

A corner of Aidan's mouth lifted. "Got it. It's like having my Siri talk to your Siri."

"Exactly. Photos and videos are handled in a similar but different fashion. Incoming images are displayed on a high-resolution LCD screen. In the second conversion, a high-resolution video camera aimed at the computer screen captures a still picture or video of the incoming visual information. In this way, the form of the picture remains the same, but the air gap isolation keeps any potential computer viruses from entering Nano. Soundtracks from videos are played through studio-quality speakers, where they're picked up by the video camera during recording."

"I'm impressed. And I don't impress easily." Aidan cleared his throat and got down to business. "We're both busy men. I'll get to the reason I'm here."

"Please do." Vance's brows drew together and he sat back, inclining his head. "Your assistant at Heckman Flax said this meeting was of an urgent nature."

"It is." Aidan didn't mince words. "But it has nothing to do with Heckman Flax."

A start of surprise. "I don't understand."

"Let's just say that I work independently of Heckman Flax, as well, with some very well-connected, one-of-a-kind professionals all over the world. Our job is to identify high-level crises and to stop them before they get out of hand."

Pennington took a moment to digest all that. "Is Heckman Flax aware of this enormous additional job you have?"

"No. But now you are."

"Why tell me?"

"Because you're in the middle of a crisis that you're completely unaware of. It involves the new manufacturing technology that NanoUSA is about to commercialize."

Vance's eyes narrowed. "And you want to hear all the details of the technology in order to fix my problem?"

"It's not what *I* want that matters," Aidan said. "It's what *others* want—and what they'll do to get it. We already have a significant amount of data. We need more."

"What is it you think you know?"

Aidan relayed all the information John had debriefed him with.

With a dubious shake of his head, Vance rose. "None of that is news to us, Mr. Devereaux." It didn't go unnoticed by Aidan that Vance had reverted back to the formal address. "I'm surprised that you'd come all this way to ask something of me you know I can't reveal. If you're right and the Chinese are stepping up their game to try to obtain our technology, we'll handle it on our own. Now, if there's nothing else—"

"They've got your daughter."

Vance froze. "Pardon me?"

"Lauren. She's been kidnapped. The Chinese hired an Albanian crime group to take her—which they did four days ago. They're going to offer you a trade—the technology for Lauren. And they're going to kill her unless we act now to prevent it."

Vance gripped the edge of his desk. "What proof do you have of this?"

Aidan went on to provide some of the intel Zermatt had gathered, including the unreported kidnapping outside Hofbräuhaus.

"I wouldn't be here if I didn't believe this," he added. "Have you noticed any change in Lauren's behavior over the past couple of days?"

The expression on Vance's face told Aidan he'd struck a nerve.

He started to speak and then abruptly halted as wariness interceded. He stared at Aidan, his long, hard assessment a clear indication that he was waging an internal battle over whether or not he should trust a total stranger, compelling or not.

Aidan remained silent, keeping his own gaze steady as he waited for Vance to reach the inevitable conclusion that trusting Aidan was his only choice.

Sure enough, Vance gave a hard swallow and an almost imperceptible nod.

"My wife . . . I didn't think anything of it at the time, but my wife has been concerned," he said at last. "Lauren's phone calls have stopped. So have her texts, other than a once-a-day, same-time-every-day check-in." Vance shifted from one foot to the other. "In her last text, she told us that she was having a problem with the reception where she was. Also, that her cell phone was fading in and out. She was taking it in to be checked out, so we shouldn't worry if she was out of touch for a day. She said she'd call soon."

"Did her tone sound different?"

"You're saying you don't think she's the one who sent those texts."

"That's exactly what I'm saying." Aidan went on without so much as a blink. "I've given you more than enough data to convince you of what's happening. Do you want to bring me into the loop so we can help you and Lauren? Otherwise, I can promise that you won't be seeing her again—at least not alive."

Vince winced at Aidan's words. "I can't divulge company secrets," he replied on autopilot. "There has to be another way. We'll call the police. The FBI. The damned White House if we have to."

"And tell them what? There's no tangible proof. And there won't be until we're out of time and Lauren is dead."

Vance rubbed his hand over his jaw. He was clearly waffling.

Aidan rose. "I'm leaving town in a few hours. What's your decision?"

Before Vance could reply, his red phone vibrated.

Aidan's gaze shifted and he gestured at the phone. "Go ahead. See what that is."

Reluctantly, Vance looked down and took his phone out of sleep mode. He was greeted by five successive *bings*.

"Texts," he murmured.

Each of the five texts appeared in a balloon message on his phone, all of them in rapid succession.

"Oh my God," Vance whispered, sinking back down into his chair.

Aidan came around and read the texts over Vance's shoulder.

You have: Seven days to comply.

You will: turn over all the details of your manufacturing technology.

You won't: contact the police, the FBI, or make any changes in your routine.

You should: Wait for our instructions.

You must: do everything we ask or your daughter will be dead in a week.

4

Seven days left...

Silence permeated Vance's office as he stared down at the texts, rereading them one at a time. At the bottom of the last message was a photo of Lauren, unconscious, stretched out on her back in what looked to be the rear compartment of a van, her face angled in such a way that there was no mistaking her identity.

With a hard swallow, Vance's fingers traced his daughter's face. "They really do have her," he said in a strained, hoarse voice. Abruptly, he twisted around to look up at Aidan, his expression guarded. "You said you're part of a well-connected group that resolves crises, but you've shown me no tangible proof that your group even exists—or that you're not in on this somehow yourself! How do I know I can trust you?" His hand tightened around the phone. "I should call the FBI right now."

"But you won't," Aidan replied quietly, returning to his chair. "Because, based on the information I gave you and your own gut instincts, you know I'm telling you the truth. Just as you know that one wrong phone call could incite a pack of criminals to kill Lauren." He leaned forward, elbows propped on the desk, fixing his hard gaze on Vance's rattled one. "I understand your ambivalence. But you're a former Marine. So am I. Integrity is part of who we are. That should go a long way in eliminating your doubts."

A heartbeat of a pause. Then Vance set down his phone. "It does."

"Good. Now until we understand exactly who and what we're dealing with, any blatant disregard for the kidnappers' orders would be playing Russian roulette with Lauren's life."

Vance dropped his head into his hands. "I can't give them what they want. But Lauren is my child, and I can't sit still and do nothing."

"I didn't suggest doing nothing. I said that violating their instructions would be a huge mistake. The steps you need to take must be strategic and under the radar, taken with proper direction. My group and I will provide you with that direction while we're simultaneously searching for Lauren. We'll bring her home. As for who we are, I've told you what you need to know. We don't exactly carry business cards. If you're wondering about our skills, don't. We're all former military, former government agents, former specialists in more areas than I can enumerate. All exceptional. Trust me, we're more than qualified. And unlike the FBI, CIA, and MI6, we have no limitations, rules, or hidden political agendas. We just resolve situations like Lauren's."

Vance blew out a breath. "I don't see that I have a choice."

"Yes you do. You can tell me to leave your office and then follow the conventional route."

"Which you think will get Lauren killed."

Aidan didn't mince words. "I do. Any FBI involvement will be discovered. And while I think highly of our country's law enforcement agencies, I think more of us. Your decision. One thing you should know up front. If you opt to work with us, we'll be taking the lead and you'll be following it. That's unconditional."

Per usual, Aidan's certainty and confidence struck home, and Vance nodded.

"Okay." His eyes were glazed and he was clearly still in shock. "Tell me what to do."

Aidan sat back in his chair. "Your family is going to Lake Tahoe tomorrow for a family vacation."

Vance didn't even bother to ask how Aidan knew that. "Yes. But of course, we'll cancel that now."

"No. You won't. As per the kidnappers' conditions, you need to stick to business as usual, and that includes taking your family's annual vacation. Any deviation in your behavior will be noted and acted upon."

"How the hell am I supposed to go skiing with my kids when their sister is being held captive in some godforsaken place, enduring Lord knows what kind of hell?"

"Because, as I said, you and I are former Marines. Marines don't quit. And we don't leave team members or family behind." Aidan plucked a Post-it from Vance's desk and scribbled down a name and phone number. "With regard to Lauren's physical condition, my experience tells me they're not harming her," he said as he wrote. "That would be contrary to their end goal. They need her alive and well to get what they want." Aidan handed the Post-it to Vance.

"What is this?" Vance glanced down at it, seeing the name and the international dialing code +33. "Who is Simone Martin and why am I calling her in France?"

"Lyon," Aidan clarified. "Simone works there as a managing partner for McKinsey. I want her out here ASAP. Use the guise that you need to reorganize your division, given all the pressures on growth. McKinsey will gladly send her to develop, explore, and implement ideas—for a healthy fee. She's the best there is at recognizing and enhancing current talent and determining the criteria for hiring future superstars."

"But you're intimating that that's not why she'll really be here," Vance deduced aloud. "She's part of this team of yours."

"She's both, but yes. Simone is extraordinary at sniffing out friend from foe. She'll be our inside person. We have to make sure there are no moles right here at NanoUSA who are being paid to find and leak information to whoever is trying to steal your technology—most probably the Chinese. An internal conspirator is always suspect in situations like this." Aidan's brows drew together. "I assume your relationship with your CEO, Robert Maxwell, is good?"

"Very good," Vance confirmed.

Something in Vance's tone told Aidan there was more to that answer. "What aren't you telling me?"

The briefest of pauses. "This isn't public information yet. It hasn't even been released inside the company, and it won't be until after the new technology has been rolled out. Seeing this achievement to completion is Robert's dream. After that, he plans to retire."

"After which you'll be named NanoUSA's new CEO," Aidan concluded.

Vance had ceased looking surprised at Aidan's perceptiveness. "Yes."

"Congratulations." Aidan tucked that tidbit away for later. Even though no announcements had been made, that didn't mean someone didn't know about this. There were no such things as secrets, not in corporate America. "Is Maxwell accessible today?" he asked.

"He's in his office," Vance replied. "I came from a meeting with him just before you arrived."

"Good. Then, right after I leave, find a way to cut through corporate bullshit and hire Simone as a management consultant, scheduled to start on Monday. That'll not only get her in place ASAP, it'll explain the daily morning flights you'll be taking from Tahoe to here during the week. You'll be in meetings at NanoUSA until noon. Then, you'll be making return trips to your family. It'll satisfy the kidnappers and keep you in the loop."

Vance gave a hard swallow. "I'll take care of it."

"Once Maxwell is on board, call Simone at that number." Aidan gestured at the Post-it. "Fill her in on NanoUSA. As for the rest—I'll have brought her up to speed by then."

Vance was still staring at the Post-it. His head was obviously spinning and he looked like he was going to be sick. "What do I tell my family?"

"Tell your kids nothing," Aidan replied. "They need to be kept completely in the dark for their own protection and for Lauren's. As for your wife, it will be hard to keep this from her. I'm sure she'll continue asking why Lauren's communications are odd and/or absent. She's her mother." Aidan studied Vance carefully. "Tell me about Susan. Will she be able to hold it together and keep this between you? And will she accept the route you've chosen to take or will her emotions demand that you call the FBI?"

"She'll do this." Vance didn't hesitate. "She'll be a wreck. But she'll pull herself together. She'd do anything for our kids. And in this case—it's Lauren's life we're protecting. So she'll accept and work with my decision."

"Good." Aidan hoped Vance's assessment was accurate. But it was a risk that had to be taken. If Susan made the wrong move because she was uninformed, everything could blow up in their faces. This way there was a fighting chance that she'd cooperate and not get in the way of Zermatt's ability to do its job.

"One last thing," Aidan said. "I need to know if you have a photocopy of Lauren's passport."

Vance nodded. "I keep copies of all our important papers, including passports, in my home safe."

"Good." Aidan wasn't surprised. Vance was meticulous and thorough, much like Aidan himself. "I need you to take pictures of that photocopy and text them to me." He scribbled down another phone number. "We'll be providing you with secure cell phones. In the interim, here's an untraceable number that is routed directly to me. Lauren's passport has long since been discarded or destroyed. We'll need to replicate it to get her home."

"You have people who can do that?"

"We have people who can do anything."

"I'm beginning to believe that."

Aidan glanced at his watch. "I've got to get going and set things in motion. You'll be here for a good part of the day, I assume?"

"Till at least dinnertime. Unless you want me to stay longer."

"No, that works. I'll arrange for secure cell phones to be delivered to your office this afternoon. Use them for all your communications to me and my team. Make sure to give one to Susan. That way, she'll feel connected, which will prevent her from feeling uninformed and isolated. Let me know the moment you receive any further contact from the kidnappers. And Vance—" Aidan extended his hand. "Semper Fi."

Vance rose from behind his desk and met Aidan's handshake. "Thank you, Aidan. Semper Fi."

* * *

Aidan waited only until he'd driven out of the parking lot before he accessed his own secure line. It was Saturday evening in France. Simone would be working.

She answered on the first ring. "*Oui?*" None of the Zermatt team used names until they were certain it was one of their own at the other end.

"It's me," Aidan said.

"I assumed it would be." Yes, Simone had clearly been working— Aidan could hear it in the intent sound of her voice. Instantly, she stopped whatever project she'd been handling and switched into Zermatt mode. "You've wrapped up your meeting?"

"Yup."

"And?"

Aidan proceeded to fill Simone in on what had transpired, adding that Vance Pennington would be calling her soon to request her assistance on revamping his department.

"My alleged role." Simone had that voice that said she was mentally running through her plans. "I'm assuming Vance Pennington's phone call to me is a *fait accompli*. I'm also assuming you want me in Silicon Valley tomorrow so I can hit the ground running on Monday, no?"

"Can you swing it?" Aidan asked, even though he already knew what her answer would be.

"I'm at home. So I can begin packing now. There'll be no obstacles. McKinsey will be delighted to acquire Nano as a client." She paused, and Aidan could hear her unzipping a suitcase. "I'll take the train from Lyon to Paris—"

"Not necessary." Aidan cut her off. "I already dispatched Zermatt's Gulfstream to you. It'll arrive at Lyon-Bron Airport by morning."

Simone had a smile in her voice. "*Merci*. I'm honored. Such royal treatment after you just flew commercial. Or was leaving the private jet in New York a strategic move on your part?"

"You know the answer to that. I wanted you out here. I wasn't going to waste time making that happen for my own personal convenience. The jet will arrive in Lyon by five a.m. You should be in San Francisco tomorrow afternoon Pacific Time. A car will pick you up and drive you to the Four Seasons Hotel in Silicon Valley. There'll be a reservation in your name."

"Will you be there in my bed to welcome me?"

Aidan heard the half-teasing, half-seductive note in her voice and responded ruefully. "Unfortunately, no. I've got to get home to Abby and put some other pieces in place. I'll probably be flying to Munich for an overnight. But not to worry. I'll be back in California ASAP."

"I'm very glad to hear that. *Au revoir, mon amour*."

Aidan stared at his phone for a long time after disconnecting the call. His mind was racing in an entirely different direction, rethinking an idea that he'd been toying with for some time now. His network was vast. But there was one avenue he had yet to tap—a strong and accessible one. This would be the perfect opportunity to reach out and see what it would be like to work with his brother in a hands-on way he'd never done. Plus, his brother's own investigative team—a team Aidan had helped out more than once—had a few key members who'd be very helpful here in both a professional and personal capacity. The fit was good.

He'd make the call and start the ball rolling.

Offices of Forensic Instincts
Tribeca, Manhattan, New York
24 February
Saturday, 3:00 p.m. local time

Casey Woods, president of the successful and high-powered investigation agency Forensic Instincts was seated at the brownstone's main conference room table, reading an update on their current case. It was still in its infancy—preliminary interviews and computer searches being conducted—and Casey didn't expect it to burst into full swing until all the intel had been gathered. For now, the urgency was moderate. Her gut told her that would change. By then, she and her team would be ready.

She'd just poured herself yet another cup of coffee when her cell phone rang.

She glanced down at the blocked number and frowned. She didn't like anonymous calls. Still, she couldn't ignore them. Sometimes they were important. So she settled for answering in an equally anonymous manner.

"Hello?"

"Hi, Casey. It's Aidan."

Casey's brows rose in surprise. Aidan Devereaux was the older brother of her right-hand man, Marc Devereaux. Both brothers were forces to be reckoned with. Marc was former Navy SEAL, former FBI, former FBI Behavioral Analysis Unit, and an original member of Forensic Instincts. Aidan was a former Marine communications and intelligence officer and current bigwig at Heckman Flax—plus something larger that Casey wasn't privy to but suspected was huge. Aidan had consulted for FI on several significant cases. Still, she wasn't accustomed to him calling her—not unless they were working on a case together. Which, right now, they weren't.

"Hi, Aidan," she said. "This is unexpected."

"I hope it's not a bad time." He didn't wait to ensure that it wasn't. "I need to ask you a favor, and at the same time, I need to request that you not ask why."

Casey's lips curved. "Now that sounds intriguing. Surprising, too. You've never asked us for a favor, although we've called on you more than once." She sipped her coffee. "You've saved our asses and our lives. Whatever you want is yours, no questions asked."

"What I want is to borrow three of your team members. My brother, Emma, and Ryan."

Whatever Casey had been expecting, it hadn't been that.

"That's an interesting request," she replied. Marc was an obvious choice for whatever Aidan was doing. As FI's techno genius, Ryan made sense, too. But Emma? She was the youngest and newest team member—a former pickpocket, now reformed. Invaluable, but still…

"Did I promise not to ask any questions?" Casey tried.

"Yeah, you did."

A sigh. "Okay, consider it done. When do you need them and for how long?"

"Immediately. And for a week. Marc and Emma will be traveling and away full-time. Ryan will be on call twenty-four seven from New York."

"Does this mean we'll finally learn about the secret life of Aidan Devereaux?" Casey asked lightly but with genuine curiosity.

"It means that you and your team members will be given information on a need-to-know basis."

"Understood." Casey didn't press. "The rest of us are available to you, as well. However we can help, we will."

"I know. And thanks. I hope you're not in the middle of a critical investigation that I'm interrupting."

"I'll handle things."

"I'm sure you will." Aidan didn't miss a beat. "Do I have your permission to call your team members directly or do you need to speak with them first?"

"Clearly what you're working on is urgent. There's no need to stand on ceremony. Call them. Tell them I gave you the okay. They'll know to check in before they take off."

"Good enough." Aidan paused. "I appreciate this, Casey. I know it's tough as a leader to give an unconditional yes without knowing what you're saying yes to."

"I trust you," she replied. "And I respect you—two things I don't offer easily or often. Good luck with whatever this is."

5

Aidan was in a foul mood. He'd arrived here early only to find that his three p.m. flight had been canceled and he'd been rebooked on the next flight to JFK, scheduled for a six p.m. takeoff. That meant he wouldn't walk into his apartment until some ungodly hour nearing dawn. Great. He didn't give a damn about sleep; he could catch some on the plane. But Abby—he wouldn't be able to give her even a quick kiss on her forehead. His little firecracker was the lightest of sleepers and required nothing more than several hours of slumber before she was refreshed enough to get up and go. One muffled footstep and she'd snap into wakefulness, ready to plunge into full active morning mode. And with her strep throat just under control, there was no way Aidan was rousing her before her little body clock went off.

He'd stay in New York long enough to spend the morning with Abby. He could hardly wait to see her face when he told her his plans for the upcoming week. She'd probably shriek and run around in circles, grabbing her favorite dolls and stuffed animals—not to mention her Minnie Mouse ears—to pack. While she was doing that, he'd fill in Joyce, who he'd frantically called to return home from New Hampshire. The blessed woman was already on her way, having perceived this as one of Aidan's true emergency situations. She'd be arriving soon—but not simply to relieve Marc and Maddy, as she undoubtedly expected.

A grin tugged at Aidan's lips as he contemplated Joyce's reaction to the spur-of-the-moment vacation he'd be springing on her. As amazing a nanny as she was, the woman was past fifty and not about to jump up and down about spending a week in a can't-catch-your-breath amusement park. But she'd be vastly relieved when he told her that Emma—who was young and energetic—would accompany them. It would all work out fine.

Still, he'd have to double Joyce's weekly salary—not out of necessity but out of guilt.

Once all his plans were in place, Aidan would grab a late-day flight to Munich, arriving there first thing in the morning, revved and ready to go. Marc would be flying there with him, even though he didn't know it yet.

Despite the superb dossiers Simone had provided him with, Aidan was looking forward to working with his brother, as well as Forensic Instincts as a whole. Over the course of working together on several cases, he'd developed both trust and respect for them. Tapping into their expertise was a smart move.

Aidan made all three phone calls in rapid succession.

"My fucking flight was canceled and I won't be home until almost dawn," he announced when Marc answered the phone. "Also, how's my princess?"

"She's great," Marc reassured him. "The penicillin kicked right in. Fever's down. She's in her room, reading a first-grade-level book to Maddy. She's frighteningly brilliant—must take after Valèrie. Oh, and your apartment is still standing, but barely."

That rare tender smile reserved for Abby curved Aidan's lips. "She is amazing—*and* Mensa material. How are you and Maddy holding up?"

"Like soldiers."

"Good. I'm glad you're up to par. Because I need you to fly to Munich with me tomorrow. I'll be there for a day. But I need you, boots on the ground, for the good part of a week. I just talked to Casey. She approved all this."

Marc digested that thoughtfully. "Care to share?"

"Not on the phone. We'll talk when I get home. After that, you and Maddy head out and catch a few hours of sleep. You and I will take off tomorrow afternoon. I'll find a way to tie the trip to Heckman Flax business. Melissa will make the reservations."

"You need me, I'm there."

"Thanks. I also need Emma and Ryan and am calling them next. Ryan can do his job from New York. Emma's another story. She's going to Disneyland with Abby."

Marc chuckled. "Sounds like fun. I hope you're paying Emma for the week's vacation she'll need from her vacation."

"I'll pay for the next vacation she takes. Destination of her choice, taken with the guy of her choice. Five-star all the way."

"Do Maddy and I get that, too?"

"Sure. Tell Maddy to start researching her dream spots. She can take the guy of her choice, too."

"Very funny. I'll let that fly because you're in a piss-ass mood."

"Is that Daddy?" Abby's voice called out from Marc's side of the line.

"It sure is," he called back. "Wanna talk to him?"

"*Yes!*" The sound of her racing feet reached Aidan's ears.

"Here's your little genius," Marc told Aidan. "See you soon."

Aidan heard muffled sounds as the phone was transferred.

"Daddy?" Abby sounded giddy with joy, as if Aidan had been away for weeks rather than a day.

"Hi, princess." Aidan was getting used to that tight feeling in his chest whenever he had to speak to his daughter long-distance—which was far too often to suit his tastes. "Are you taking good care of Aunt Maddy and Uncle Marc?"

"'Course. I hate my medicine. But Aunt Maddy gives me ice cream afterwards. My favorite flavor."

"Let me guess—pink cotton candy?"

"Uh-huh. It feels cold and nice in my throat. It makes it stop hurting. It's so pretty. And it tastes so good. I saved some for you. The container's kind of messy now because Aunt Maddy let me use the scooper and I dripped. I wanted to lick the sides, but she said I couldn't 'cause there might be germs." Abby barely paused to catch her breath. "When are you coming home?"

"I'll be there when you wake up." Aidan was grinning broadly by now. "And I have a surprise for you." He heard her whoop with excitement. "But only if you promise to get a good night's sleep."

That gave her pause. "How long a sleep?"

"Until I come in and tickle you."

Abby gave an indulgent sigh. "Okay. But I can't help it if I wake up before that. If I do, I'll keep my eyes closed."

"Do that. And not just to fool me. To rest. Because you're going to need lots of energy for my surprise."

Abby was still squealing and Aidan was still grinning when he hung up.

Next call was to Emma.

"Aidan?" She sounded more surprised by the call than Casey had. Then again, she was the most junior member of Forensic Instincts and the least likely for Aidan to reach out to. Having been orphaned at a young age, Emma had survived the foster care system only to hit the streets as an all-too-successful pickpocket. When she decided to get her act together, she'd applied for a job at FI and Casey had given her the chance of a lifetime. Now Emma was a far-more-mature, full-time team member.

"Why are you calling?" she asked, her blunt candor almost as refreshing as Abby's.

"Because it's time to pack," he replied. "I need a week of your time and a ton of your energy. You're going on a trip—if you're willing. Casey's given her okay."

"A trip?" Emma was audibly stunned. "To where? For what? Are you asking me to help with whatever secret thing it is you do? Am I going to be investigating with you?"

Aidan gave an uncustomary chuckle. "You sound like Abby. Which is good. Because if you agree to this trip, you're going to be spending a lot of time with her. To answer your questions, no, you're not going to be investigating anything and, no, I'm not sharing work details with you. I will tell you that my job is taking me to California. I'll be there for a week and I want Abby nearby. So I'd like to make provisions for her—along with you and Joyce Reynolds, Abby's nanny—to spend that week in Disneyland. Joyce will do the mothering, you'll do the theme park circuit. That work for you?"

"Wow." Emma sounded both excited and hesitant. "I'd love it. But with Abby…" She hesitated. "Even though I won't take my eyes off of her, I'm terrified she'll find a way to take off."

"That's why Joyce will be there. Two pairs of eyes. Besides, I have a feeling that you'll offer her enough fun things to do to hold her interest. And I'll have a long talk with her before you go. I'll also send Joyce with my credit card and a wad of cash for you to buy drinks for everyone on the flight out—a thank-you in advance for what they might have to put up with. I'll make sure there's enough money there for additional rounds if need be. Deal?"

Emma was laughing. "Deal. When do we leave?"

"Tomorrow, probably somewhere around dinnertime. I've got a quick international trip to make first, and I want to spend the morning with Abby before she and I take off in opposite directions. Once I've made the necessary arrangements, I'll text you everything you need. You'll meet Abby and Joyce at JFK. Abby's recovering from strep throat, so I'm hoping she'll sleep through part of the flight. I'll be winging my way to California immediately following my meeting. And Emma? Thanks."

Aidan's third call was a piece of cake. Ryan McKay, who rivaled Terri in his technology genius, was thrilled to be brought on board. He and Aidan had worked together before, but always on FI cases and never including any of the Zermatt team members other than Aidan himself. This was new and intriguing terrain for him. So, in his customary way, he asked question after question, all of which Aidan evaded, promising that his own brilliant IT colleague, Terri Underwood, would fill him in as needed.

"What's her background?" Ryan asked.

"She's the best. That's all you need to know."

Ryan snorted. "You're not going to tell me shit, are you?"

"I won't keep anything from you that could help you work on this investigation," Aidan replied. "But you're going to have to curb that nosy personality of yours. And you're also going to have to learn to share. Terri is in charge here. You're second-in-command on this. Think you can handle that?"

"To work with you again, yeah, I can handle it."

"Good. Terri will contact you soon."

* * *

Six days left…

Munich, Germany
25 February
Sunday, 3:00 p.m. local time

Philip Banks didn't look like the retired MI6 agent that he was, nor like the crackerjack investigator who now comprised one of

Zermatt's core four. No, this afternoon, dressed in his well-worn jeans and half-zipped parka, messenger bag slung over his shoulder and cell phone poised for candids, he looked like a tourist visiting Munich, totally fascinated by Hofbräuhaus, the city's largest and most historic pub.

Precisely the image he was going for.

Brows knit in apparent concentration, he refocused his phone, appearing to be snapping pictures in a Snapchat frenzy. In fact, he was actually running a special app that Terri had created, which mapped the visual, telemetric, and Wi-Fi data of the entire area around him. The data was captured and streamed real time to Terri in New York. At her end, Terri would be watching her computer systems as they analyzed the data and began to immediately search for nearby businesses, Wi-Fi networks, and security cameras. Philip was well aware that the process would take hours, but by penetrating the local networks, accessing the security and router logs, Terri would be able to tell exactly who had been present when Lauren was kidnapped.

He'd spent the past day and a half conducting fieldwork—casually engaging employees, patrons, and even passersby to see if any of them remembered his "daughter" who'd been at Hofbräuhaus Friday afternoon with friends. No luck. And he had to be careful to keep his questions light and offhanded. He couldn't come off as a creeper, and he couldn't tip his hand and alert anyone to a "missing girl" scenario. Other than Zermatt and the Penningtons, no one knew about Lauren's kidnapping, including and especially law enforcement. Philip intended to keep it that way.

From the brewery, he'd trekked the mile to Ludwig Maximilian University, where Lauren was attending school during her junior year abroad. The campus was quiet, since winter break had just begun, but Philip was determined to check out some of the names Terri had plucked off Lauren's cell history—names of friends she'd texted who wanted her to visit them during her hiatus from academia. If any of them had yet to leave campus, Philip would find them. And if any of them were already at home, he'd find them, too.

After two hours of searching…nothing.

The sand in the hourglass continued to trickle downward. And Lauren Pennington's time was running out.

6

Terri was hunched over her computer in the Cage, concentrating on the wall of video screens facing her and analyzing the stream of NSA data that her back-door access provided. Aidan had long since left for JFK and his quick trip to Munich. That left Terri in workaholic solitude—save for Windsor, her black and tan Cavalier King Charles chilling out in his dog bed nearby. He was one of her four rescues, all of whom had a special place in her heart, and each of whom occasionally accompanied her to work. Dogs were worth opening your heart to. People? No.

Right now, Terri was relishing what she was doing. She'd donned her other Zermatt hat as the group's chief revenue officer. Wealthy as he was, Aidan couldn't fund all their investigations himself. So it was up to her to find other sources of income. And her back door never let her down. She always enjoyed the irony of hackers—in this case the NSA—being hacked by her. Nothing better than being the mouse chasing the cat.

Tuning her filters to analyze the information stream, she searched for new sources of illegal money that Zermatt could tap into to keep their operations going. She knew what to look for. Patterns in communications that suggested illegal transactions. Drug dealers. Shady businessmen. Equally shady corporations. Corrupt politicians. All of them ripe for the plucking.

It took a while, but Terri found what she needed. Some slimy businessmen who were dodging US taxes by wiring money to an account in the Cayman Islands. Well, it was time for the SOBs to bid farewell to their ill-gotten gains.

This was Terri's favorite part of the process. It allowed her to indulge in her one mundane pleasure: playing Wheel of Fortune. A game she'd taken to a whole new level.

Smiling, she clicked on a specific icon on her desktop and the Wheel of Fortune game she'd created filled the entire wall of computer screens. She clicked on the spin button and watched as the wheel went round and round, numbers whizzing by amounts ranging from one to five million with everything in between. With Zermatt's checking account balance on her mind, she was hoping for big money because their Gulfstream G550 had just gone through a major overhaul. Paying those bills had depleted some of their reserves and she was eager to replace them. Even though the plane was obscenely expensive to operate, its ultra-long range allowed Zermatt to reach almost anywhere on the globe without refueling. That tactical advantage had proved invaluable again and again.

Impatiently, she waited for the wheel to stop spinning and point to the sum of money she was going to help herself to.

As it came to a stop, slot machine bells began to ring, fireworks flashed across the screen, and Donna Summer's "She Works Hard for the Money" burst forth. Terri grinned ear to ear. Jackpot. She hadn't seen five million come up in ages.

The Gulfstream would get a full tank of aviation fuel and those tax-cheating bastards would get screwed.

She hacked into the Cayman Islands account, entered five million as the wire amount, and ran it through her normal money laundering protocol: bouncing around the world like a steel ball in a pinball machine through a dozen shell companies all around the world. Moments later, it arrived in Zermatt's secret bank account. The funds had been cleaned, sterilized, and were now untraceable. The scumbags not only couldn't report it or recover it, they'd never even know where it was or who took it.

* * *

Outside the Cage's steel door, Abby fidgeted, staring at the intercom button. She knew that Aunt Terri was inside the room and that Windsor was with her. She also knew that Aunt Terri was working, and that Abby was never supposed to interrupt that. But she was so excited about Disneyland and she and Joyce weren't leaving for the airport until Joyce packed what she called "essentials" into Abby's suitcase. Her daddy had kissed her good-bye ages ago, and she had to wait to get to the airport to see Emma. So Abby was bursting with energy and she needed someone to share it with.

Giving in to her impulses, she did what she didn't do too often— not unless she wanted to get scolded.

She dragged one of the hall chairs over to the Cage, climbed up onto it, and pressed the intercom button.

There was no sound from inside, but there never was. Her daddy said the room kept all sounds in and let no sounds out. It sounded like a boring room to her, but she guessed that all work was probably boring. Except art. She loved painting pictures. And since that was homework, it counted as work. She counted it as fun.

A minute later, Aunt Terri's voice sounded through the intercom. "Yes?"

"It's me, Aunt Terri. Can Windsor come out to play?"

There was a long pause. "I thought you and Joyce had left," Aunt Terri finally said in that serious voice of hers. But Abby wasn't fooled. She'd heard Aunt Terri talking to her dogs before, and her voice sounded soft and sweet.

"We're leaving pretty soon. But I wanted to show Windsor my Minnie Mouse ears. Just for a minute. *Please*?"

She heard the lock turn and eagerly jumped off the chair.

An instant later, the door to the room swung open. Terri stepped out, calling to Windsor to follow her.

He shot out like a bullet, running straight for Abby. She giggled and plopped down on the floor, hugging him as he licked her face.

"I'm taking medicine so I can't give my germs to Windsor," Abby assured Terri. "I'm not"—she wrinkled her nose, searching for the word and brightening as she found it—"c'ntagious anymore. And my throat doesn't even hurt."

Terri folded her arms across her chest. "Strep throat isn't transferable from humans to dogs. And your antibiotic is keeping your bacterial infection under control. So I'm not particularly concerned about Windsor."

Abby had understood only half of what Aunt Terri had just said. Aunt Terri was really smart and always used big words.

"Okay." She settled for that, pulling out her Minnie Mouse ears and waving them at Windsor. "Look, Windsor! Mouse ears! I'm going to Disneyland!"

The little dog was beside himself by this time, bouncing around and trying to snatch the ears with his teeth.

Abby held them out of reach. "You can't have these, 'cause Daddy gave them to me. But I promise to get you your own when I'm at Disneyland. I'll get Mickey ears since you're a boy."

Terri sighed. "Now Windsor is overstimulated. I'll have to take him out to urinate before I can get back to work."

"I'm sorry, Aunt Terri." Abby scrambled to her feet and hugged her. Aunt Terri was way tall, so all she could reach were her knees, but she gave those a huge squeeze. "You can walk Windsor. Joyce and I will be gone when you get back. Then you can work." Abby tipped back her head and gave Aunt Terri a hopeful look. "And you won't tell Daddy that I bothered you, right? Because I'm sick and it wouldn't be fair to punish me. Right, Aunt Terri?"

Terri hesitated, then gave Abby's shoulder an awkward pat. "All right. I won't say anything. You enjoy your vacation."

"Thanks!" Abby was all smiles. "Bye, Aunt Terri. Bye, Windsor." She raced off to get her suitcase.

Terri shook her head, her brows drawn in puzzlement. She didn't understand children. They were little people and should have all the negative characteristics thereof, but they acted more like puppies. It was an inexplicable combination. And she didn't quite know what to do with it.

On that thought, she got Windsor's leash and snapped it on, closing the Cage's door behind her as she left.

Munich Airport
26 February
Monday, 7:25 a.m. local time

The plane was slowly descending as the tops of the airport terminals came into view.

Aidan glanced at his watch. Only twenty-five minutes late. Not bad for an international flight. Of course, now came customs, which was a royal pain in the ass. All he wanted to do was to quickly anchor the investigation at this end so he could fly back and manage things at the US end—close to the client and close to Abby.

Marc watched his brother thoughtfully. He'd learned more about Aidan's other life in the past day than he'd been privy to since the formation of Zermatt five years ago. In fact, he hadn't even known the group's name—only that it existed and that Aidan was at the helm. Having been filled in on the big picture—and sworn to secrecy—he was impressed but not surprised. Aidan was a natural leader, a skilled and brilliant man, and a fighter for the greater good. Marc got it. He also got that bringing him in, including him in his inner circle, was a huge step for Aidan—one he could have made sooner but had chosen not to.

Marc was better aware of the reasons for that than his brother was. Although they were both deeply private people, Aidan had always been an island—until Abby. Since he'd become a father, there'd been a slow metamorphosis in which emotional ties and personal sharing had become part of who the impenetrable Aidan Devereaux was. In letting down his walls a bit, Aidan was now able to turn to someone he trusted—rather than just a skilled but strictly professional colleague—for help.

It was all good.

"So we're going directly to meet Philip at his hotel," Aidan said. "We'll be holding a videoconference with Terri and Simone from there, after which you can check into your hotel room, shower and change, and hit the ground running with Philip. I'll be heading back to the airport, with a stop at Hofbräuhaus to do some of my own reconnaissance. I'll check out the place inside and then do a line-of-sight check outside, acting as a second pair of eyes to Philip. I want a plan in place before I board that plane. I'll contact you before my flight to California takes off."

Marc rolled his eyes. "You gave me that entire speech three times since takeoff. You're getting senile, Leatherneck. I guess that's to be expected, given your advanced age."

Aidan arched a brow. "I've only got three years on you, Frogman. And I've got a kid to keep me young. So don't get cocky."

The good-natured Navy SEAL vs. Marine banter had been part of the brothers' lives since their respective military careers had begun.

"Besides the fact that he's one of your key guys and former MI6, what do I need to know about Philip?" Marc asked, his years at the FBI's Behavioral Analysis Unit compelling him to get as complete a picture of Philip as possible. He'd ask questions about Terri later. But Philip was first up.

"Before he was MI6, he was SAS," Aidan replied, referring to the Special Air Service, one of the British Army's Special Forces units. "He worked primarily in covert recon and hostage rescue."

"Impressive. What about personally? What's he like?"

Aidan considered the question, looking somewhat amused. "He's not what you're expecting."

"I'm not expecting James Bond, if that's what you mean. That's why I'm asking you."

"Fair enough. Philip is like two sides of a coin. When he's entrenched in a Zermatt mission, he's singularly focused. He works round-the-clock, is razor sharp, and won't rest until we've brought things to a successful resolution. We call him the bloodhound—nothing and no one exists that he can't hunt down. When there's no mission to focus on, he's settled comfortably into his new life as a dedicated retiree who loves life, wealthy, willing women, and more than a little fine wine and single malt whisky."

"A kept man—nice." A corner of Marc's mouth lifted. "He sounds like a fascinating guy."

"He thinks so." Despite Aidan's sarcasm, deep respect laced his tone. Philip's personal life was immaterial. His commitment and skill when it came to Zermatt were all that mattered.

Marc didn't ask any more questions—not then. The plane was about to land. And he was about to get his personal initiation into Zermatt's way of doing things.

San Mateo, California
25 February
Sunday, 10:45 p.m. local time

The man left his California ranch-style home as he always did—through the side door—and walked up the brick driveway toward the mailbox. As per usual, his suburban neighborhood was all tucked in for the night, with just a few lights from bedroom windows filtering into the darkened street. He wasn't worried about detection. Anyone seeing him would assume he was making his routine mail check. Given his line of work, late-night business dinners were the rule rather than the exception, and arriving home at this hour was standard operating procedure. None of his neighbors would bat an eye if they happened to spot him.

Reaching his destination, he pulled open the mailbox door, reaching inside to find the small box he'd been told to expect. He then retraced his steps, going in through the side door and locking it before heading out to the garage.

He hit the remote control on the garage door and lit a cigarette while it slid open. After climbing in the car, he turned the ignition and backed out, shutting the door behind him.

He drove to his customary spot—the diner that was a mile and a half away. He left his car only long enough to go around back and throw his old burner phone into the dumpster. He hesitated as he reached his car door and thought about grabbing a slice of pie and a cup of coffee. He'd wolfed down a sandwich three hours ago, but a shot of sugar and caffeine would be great about now. Nope. No time.

Sure enough, just as he settled himself in the driver's seat, his package began to ring. He tore it open and removed the new burner phone.

He listened carefully to the instructions provided in perfect English.

7

Marc gave a dry chuckle as he and Aidan walked down the elegant hallway and approached Philip's deluxe hotel room. "A five-star hotel," he commented, stating the obvious. "Nice. Your guy has good taste."

Aidan grimaced as he checked his iPhone—for the third time—to read Philip's text so he could ensure they had the right room. "I told you. Philip is a connoisseur of fine… everything."

With that, he walked up to the door and knocked. "It's me," he said just audibly enough for the occupant inside the room to hear.

A muffled burst of activity and a "hang on" was his response.

"Great," Aidan muttered under his breath.

Two minutes later, the door opened partway and Marc had to bite back a smile as he realized the reason behind Aidan's comment. The tall man leaning against the doorjamb—who actually *did* look like a fiftyish version of James Bond with his chiseled features, penetrating dark eyes, and hard-muscled body—was wearing nothing but a bath towel that was knotted loosely around his waist. His dark hair had droplets of water clinging to it, and rather than apologetic, he looked distinctly annoyed.

"You're early," he said, his clipped English accent definitely Bond-like.

"Ten minutes," Aidan replied. "Customs was efficient and traffic was light. We can talk while you get dressed. Unless you have company?"

Aidan's words were more a statement than a question.

Sure enough, the door opened wider and an attractive woman, clearly just dressed, slithered out the door, head lowered. With a muffled "bye" to Philip, she hurried down the hall and disappeared.

Philip glanced briefly after her, his expression saying that he could have made good use of those ten minutes. Then, with a shrug, he swung open the door and gestured for Aidan and Marc to come in.

"Next time hang a sock on your door," Aidan advised, tossing down his coat.

"Very amusing." Philip's gaze shifted to Marc. "Definitely Aidan's brother. I see the resemblance." He extended his hand. "Good to meet you, Marc."

"Likewise." Marc met Philip's handshake. "Sorry we interrupted."

"I stand corrected," Philip replied. "You have better manners than Aidan."

"That's because this is Marc's first exposure—if you'll excuse the pun—to your private life," Aidan retorted. "Give him time."

"He won't be seeing my private life. He'll be seeing me do my job." Philip's entire demeanor had changed. Gone was the lighthearted banter. Abruptly, he was all MI6, a total professional, bath towel or not.

"I never assumed otherwise." Aidan was surveying the room. Philip had brought their special rig that allowed them to assemble six iPad Pros into a frame that formed a large video screen. The three of them would sit in front of this while Terri took them through the debriefing.

"Bring us up to speed from your end while I set this up and you throw on some clothes," Aidan said to Philip. "Then we'll connect up with the rest of the team."

Philip pulled out a sweater and slacks, dressing rapidly as he spoke. "You know as much as I do," he said. "I've got nothing solid. From my interviews with the waitstaff at Hofbräuhaus, Lauren arrived alone and enjoyed a beer and a pretzel. Some guy chatted her up at the table. They left separately, but he followed quickly after her. She paid in cash. Her credit card hasn't been used since her disappearance. Terri had me digitally surveil the surrounding area outside the restaurant. Last I spoke to her, she was still doing analysis."

Aidan nodded as he completed his task. "We'll see what she's come up with at this videoconference."

As Marc and Philip pulled up chairs and settled themselves in them, Aidan whipped out his own iPad Pro, positioned it on the desk, and fired it up. With a few clicks of the mouse, he opened a Facetime-like app that Terri had written. The big difference was that this was fully encrypted so that prying eyes and ears were locked out.

Instantly, both Terri's and Simone's faces appeared on individual screens of the panoramic setup.

"I'm early," Aidan began. "Sorry."

"No earlier than usual," Terri replied. "I signed on five minutes ago."

"As did I," Simone said.

"Good." Aidan shot a meaningful sideways look at Philip, who ignored him.

After clearing his throat, Aidan continued. "Marc, meet Terri and Simone, the other two members of my team. Ladies, this is my brother, Marc. As you know, he'll be staying on in Europe to work with Philip."

Marc, Terri, and Simone exchanged greetings.

"Terri," Aidan instructed, "please record this video chat and have Donovan transcribe it all. Place all info on a secure hard drive that everyone on the team has access to and notify us when there's a meaningful update. We're racing the clock and we don't have time to write reports and summaries. We'll have to let Donovan do this for us."

"Already done and in progress," Terri replied.

"Then the ball's in your court. We're listening."

Nodding, Terri clicked her mouse and a new image appeared on her screen—the image of a man. "This is a cell phone picture of the guy who went up to Lauren in the restaurant."

Marc looked startled. "How did you get this?"

The rest of the team sat back and let Terri do her thing, although they'd heard this explanation so often they were bored.

Clearly, Terri was not. "By knowing the Wi-Fi networks in the area from the scan that Philip did for me, I was able to find traces left by the devices that had connected to the various Wi-Fi networks," she said. "Once I had device-specific information, it was just a matter of hacking into the T-Mobile systems and coming in over their cell network to the people and devices who were in the restaurant at the same time as Lauren. I just used the device trails I found on Wi-Fi networks to find those same cell phones on T-Mobile's cell network."

"Why T-Mobile?" Marc asked. He wasn't surprised by Terri's enthusiasm over her tech work. Ryan practically embraced his computer when he came up with major discoveries. So this was business as usual.

"There are four main cell carriers in Germany," Terri reported. "T-Mobile is by far the largest."

Marc nodded. "Go on."

"After that, it was just a matter of looking into the requisite photo history around that time. We got lucky. Someone had taken a group photo of their friends, all of whom were totally inebriated and celebrating who knows what. In the background were Lauren and the guy she was talking to."

"Okay, technology lesson over," Aidan said. "Tell us where you went from there."

Terri was clearly unbothered by Aidan's abruptness. They were all painfully aware that time was their enemy here.

"I found a hidden video camera installed by the restaurant owner to spy on the employees. Evidently, there have been a number of inside thefts, which they were checking out." Terri displayed the video clip. "From this time-lapse video, you can see the kidnapper pocketing Lauren's phone." A quick shift and another video clip appeared. "Finally, thanks to a local ATM camera, you can see a black Mercedes van with the back of a woman with a sack over her head being forced into the side of the van and the guy—who's the same guy we see Lauren with at the restaurant—doing the pushing. I'm running facial recognition on him."

"It's a long shot that he'll be in the system," Philip commented.

"I realize that. I won't be restricting myself to legal or governmental channels."

"Okay." Aidan knew Terri's tone. There was more to come.

"I hacked into the security system of the bank across the street from the restaurant," she said, her face reappearing on the screen. "There were two kidnappers. The first was the man who made contact with Lauren inside the restaurant. He was approximately one hundred seventy-eight centimeters tall and weighed about seventy-five kilos."

"Five ten, hundred sixty-five pounds," Marc muttered to himself.

"The second kidnapper was stockier—approximately one hundred seventy-three centimeters in height and one hundred two kilos in weight."

"Five eight and two twenty-five," Marc murmured again, automatically making the conversions.

Terri took a sip of water, then continued. "Based on the limited audio from the bank's surveillance cameras, I can confirm at an eighty-seven percent confidence level that the two men were speaking Albanian. That piece of information, coupled with the comparison of his face using various facial databases that link ethnicity to facial features, take us to the ninety-eight percent confidence level that Albanian organized crime is involved."

"At least we can confirm that much," Simone noted aloud.

"Yes, but it's just a formality." Aidan was sounding impatient again. "We already knew who we were dealing with. What we really need is to identify the individual himself, not just his ethnicity and dialect." A quizzical look at Terri. "You said you're extending your ID hunt beyond searching law enforcement criminal databases. Elaborate."

"I'm hacking photos that have been uploaded to Facebook. I have to be very careful not to do too many in too short a time so I don't alert the Facebook security team to my intrusion. I've already enlisted Ryan McKay's help. He has some expertise in this area and together we need to launch a multipronged query of Facebook to stay under their security radar."

"Move fast. Even if you have to risk their wrath. Wrath can be soothed. Dead bodies cannot."

Terri sighed. "Aidan, trust me to do my job. Adding Ryan to the mix was smart. He's good and he's fast. We'll get it done."

"I know." Aidan rubbed his eyes as if to take himself down a notch. "I didn't mean to bite your head off."

"We're all on edge," Simone said in a calming tone. "But failure is not in our vocabulary."

Aidan's gaze flickered to her. "You arrived in Santa Clara on schedule?"

Simone nodded. "Yes, and I've already had a conversation with Vance Pennington. He's shaky but manageable, certainly by you. He'll be flying in from Tahoe for a few hours tomorrow morning to meet with me and to introduce me to the numerous areas within his department. All part of my cover." A thoughtful look. "Obviously, he's going to ask me more about what's going on. Can I share a bare-bones overview of our plans and our progress?"

"Use your judgement, but yes. You're better at people than anyone." Aidan looked concerned, but not about that. "Simone, make sure that Pennington flies back to Tahoe ASAP. Quick daily commutes to the office during family vacations are standard operating procedure for high-level execs. That won't raise any red flags. Prolonged visits will."

"Prolonged visits won't be necessary," Simone replied. "Once I'm in place, I can connect with Pennington by phone. You'll be the one to shuttle back and forth to Tahoe to manage him and his family."

"Yup. I'll get my frequent flier miles all filled up."

"What about the photocopy of Lauren's passport?" Simone asked. "Did Vance get it to you?"

"Yes. Thanks for reminding me. Terri, contact our guy about making a new passport for Lauren. Pay him extra. We need it yesterday."

Terri frowned. "He's off the grid. It'll take me a few days to track him down."

"We don't have a few days."

"Aidan," Marc interjected. "Let me handle this one. I'll call Ryan. He has a guy who's done this for Forensic Instincts before. He'll make it happen."

"Good." Aidan gave his brother the thumbs-up. "Then I'll text the photocopied pages directly to Ryan as soon as you give me the word that he's able to come through on a dime."

"I'll call him right after this videoconference is over."

"So things in the States are covered," Philip interceded. "Let's get to the European assignment. Marc and I need to know which physical direction we should be heading in to locate Lauren. Any insights, Terri?"

"Of course." Terri glanced down at some printed pages on her desk. "Knowing the starting point and the time of the kidnapping, I hacked into the Munich camera system and was able to follow the route of the van to A10 southbound."

"Not a surprise," Philip said. "They headed southeast—away from the densely populated areas of Germany. The good news is that they took toll roads, which means there'll be monetary records of their passage. Not to mention they have to have crossed country lines, at least from Germany to Austria."

"And probably from there into Croatia," Marc said. "A country with great isolated areas with low populations, plus law enforcement that's not as capable. I.e., they're poorly paid and easier to bribe."

"Precisely," Terri said. "I plan on accessing the transport records Philip mentioned. That will tell us where they were when. Given the size, model, and number of passengers in the van, I can estimate the driving range on one tank of fuel to be five hundred kilometers to six hundred kilometers."

Terri clicked her mouse and her face was replaced by a Google map of Europe. "The donut shape in yellow indicates how far the van could travel on one tank of fuel, hence the likely refueling area. Given the route they took, I've blacked out Germany, France, and Switzerland and grayed out Italy, Poland, and the surrounding countries that are unlikely given the route taken. Unfortunately, given that I agree with your assessment that Croatia is their ultimate destination, their most probable refueling area would be Zagreb."

"Shit," Marc said. "Zagreb is the capital of Croatia. So much for omitting densely populated areas."

"Nevertheless, I suggest you go there as your starting point."

"You're correct." Philip nodded. "It sucks, but it is what it is."

"I'll text this map to you both," Terri said. "That way you'll have it for easy reference. I'll also text you a detailed map of Zagreb, with local gas stations highlighted. Try the ones that are off the beaten path but not too far from the highway."

"Done," Philip replied.

Aidan jumped in right there. "I have a strong contact in the Croatian police. Danijel Horvat. He's a chief police inspector stationed in Zagreb. He's the head of the Organized Crime Division. He also served on a Europol Organized Crime Task Force. He's smart and well-connected, and I can always count on his discretion. I'll call and bring him up to speed. He'll be ready for Marc and Philip's arrival, and he'll be a vital ally."

None of the team members looked surprised, although Marc did look impressed. He knew that Aidan had contacts everywhere and in every area of expertise. Still, his brother's reach was even wider than he'd realized.

"Having inside help from high-level law enforcement is a great start," Marc said. "Now we need to figure out what additional resources we need to find Lauren."

"None of the dossiers Simone sent me are going to be useful," Aidan stated. "Excellent people, but not for what we're dealing with now. We're crawling into isolated areas of Croatia. We need a small, targeted number of specific assets." He turned to Philip. "Ideas?"

"Yes," Philip responded without hesitation. "Even though most Croatians speak English, we can't count on that being the case in some of the remote stops we'll be making. So unless Marc speaks fluent Croatian, we're going to need one or more people who do, to translate emails, cell phone calls, texts, and any wire-tapping we have to do."

"Nope." Marc shook his head. "Mandarin, French, and Spanish, yes. Croatian and Serb, no."

"None of us fits that category." Aidan's gaze shifted to Simone. "Can you help us with this?"

Simone was already scanning her dossiers. "Since Croatian is spoken by over ninety-six percent of the country, I'm focusing on that. I'm also looking for a woman, just in case it's necessary to have them interact with people. Marc and Philip come across as threatening. A woman will be less so. You'll get a lot farther with a softer touch." A hint of a smile. "And I'll make sure she's not model material so Philip won't hit on her."

Philip merely arched a brow.

Simone paused, glancing at her findings. "I have two possible candidates. Aidan, I assume you need this asset to start right away. For how long do you need her and how much are we willing to pay?"

In response, Aidan asked, "Terri, what's our financial situation on this?"

A rare grin curved Terri's lips. "Money is no object. I hit the jackpot on Wheel of Fortune."

"Oorah!" Aidan punched the air with his fist. A quick glance at Marc, and he said, "Frogman, that term means *charge*. A Marine thing, nothing you'd understand."

"I got the term," Marc returned dryly. "It's the game I'm lost about."

Aidan provided a quick explanation.

"Nice," Marc responded. "Share that with Ryan, Terri. He'll love it."

"Good idea." Terri looked proud and pleased. "He, of all people, will appreciate the intricacies of the app."

"Since the sky's the limit, I suggest we hire both women I've selected," Simone said. "One is more experienced in these types of operations, and the other speaks Albanian as well as Croatian. We have no idea the exact nature of the skills that will be required, or if we'll need one or both of these candidates. I don't want to take any chances by being short on resources in a crisis situation. Given that the kidnappers' deadline is less than a week away, I'll hire the two women for a full week."

"Go for it," Aidan agreed. "I need them to meet Philip and Marc in Munich ASAP." He turned to the two men sitting alongside him. "You guys are going to have to bring Simone's candidates up to speed and take it from there."

"Done," Marc replied.

"One last thing about what Philip and I need in addition to money—although we need plenty of that to grease the necessary palms," Marc said. "We need tactical support—weapons, transportation, communications. The Albanians don't play nice. Neither should we."

"Good point," Aidan responded. "Philip, can you arrange the transport and the weapons? Terri will wire the money to wherever you need it to go."

"Not a problem," Philip replied. "I have a weapons guy in Germany who can get us anything we want. As for transportation, I'll get us a BMW 7 series—nothing too flashy, but it'll handle well in a chase and move fast should we need it to."

"Smart thinking," Aidan said. "Marc, what are your current weapons of choice?"

"A Glock 27 nine-millimeter pistol and an H&K nine-millimeter MP5 submachine gun," his brother replied.

"Those are easy enough to get," Philip assured them.

"Good. Last thing up: communications," Aidan said. "We need to talk once a day as a team. Philip, you need to pick the best time for your European team to talk, since the rest of us have more flexibility."

Philip gave that a quick thought. "Let's go for zero seven hundred hours Central European Time, which is zero one hundred hours Eastern Standard Time and twenty-two hundred hours Pacific Standard Time."

"Seven a.m. in Croatia, one a.m. in Manhattan, and ten p.m. in Cali, respectively," Aidan automatically translated aloud. "Everyone on board with that?"

There was agreement from all screens.

"On that topic, I've already overnighted secure iPhones to everyone," Terri reported. "They're preprogrammed with everyone's cell numbers. I anticipated field operatives and included four extras for them, with only Marc's and Philip's numbers preprogrammed. They don't need to know about the rest of us."

"And that's a wrap." Aidan glanced at his watch. "I've got to make a couple of calls—one to Danijel Horvat and one to find out how my daughter's flight went. I'm sure she kept the passengers on her flight highly entertained. After that, I'm heading over to Hofbräuhaus to do a little recon of my own. I might get lucky. And FYI, I'll be taking off for the States later this afternoon. So I won't be reachable until I land. After that, I'm on call twenty-four seven, running the operation. Contact me in between our daily briefings as needed."

His mouth set in a grim line. "Experience tells me that Pennington will be getting new demands from the kidnappers soon."

Manhattan, New York
26 February
Monday, 4:25 a.m. local time

Ryan answered the phone on the fourth ring. "Shit, Marc, it's four something in the morning. And I'm busy."

"Then peel yourself off of Claire and get your head into work mode."

Marc was referring to Claire Hedgleigh, the Forensic Instincts team's claircognizant, as she termed herself. She hated the word *psychic*, although she'd resigned herself to being called that, since no one seemed to understand the difference. She and Ryan had a heated personal and work relationship, a love-hate thing that neither of them understood and had no desire to. It worked, it was hot, and it felt right.

What didn't feel right, at least to Claire, was the casual banter Ryan had with Marc when it came to her sex life. Unlike Ryan, who had zero inhibitions, Claire was reserved and private by nature. Just the thought of Marc knowing she was naked in Ryan's bed made her blush.

What didn't feel right to Ryan was being interrupted when he had Claire in his bed. In fact, it really pissed him off.

"This had better be good," he warned Marc.

"It involves the case we're working for Aidan."

Ryan was instantly and totally awake. "I'm listening."

"I thought you might be. This falls under the need-to-know. How fast can your counterfeiting guy make us a new passport?"

"If money is no object, probably a day, maybe two."

"Not good enough. You know the kind of deadline we're up against." Marc frowned. "Would it help if I had a copy of the girl's original passport and we want one that's identical?"

"Hell yeah. We're not setting up a new identity, we're recreating an old one. Text me that photocopy and I'll set the process in motion. A whole lot of cash and a little bit of arm-twisting—we'll have what we need within hours."

"I was hoping you'd say that. Call me when it's done. Oh, and hi, Claire."

Claire had the urge to dive under the covers and pretend she wasn't there. But who was she kidding? "Hi, Marc. Good night, Marc."

"You heard the lady," Ryan said. "Good night, Marc."

8

Five days left…

Susan Pennington stared out the window of their luxury suite, which overlooked the magnificent wonders of Lake Tahoe—the snow-covered mountains majestic enough to be the Alps and the water clear and blue enough to be Lake Geneva.

The exquisite scene was lost on her. She saw nothing but Lauren.

"Vance, I'm terrified." She turned, tightening the sash on her dressing robe, her gaze fixed on her husband as he packed up the laptop case he'd be taking to Santa Clara for his morning commute to NanoUSA.

Vance stopped what he was doing and walked over to her, gently gripping her shoulders. "I'm terrified, too," he admitted. "But I firmly believe we're going to get Lauren back soon and unharmed. I refuse to contemplate any other alternative."

Susan searched her husband's expression, her own tight with worry. "You have that much faith in Aidan Devereaux?"

"In him and his team, yes, I do. I realize that most of that faith comes from the gut. This group of theirs doesn't exactly have a website touting their skills and services. But I've been extremely impressed so far. Remember, they knew about Lauren's kidnapping before I was even contacted. They already had a plan in place before Aidan showed up at my office door. Just meeting with him—it's clear that he's a brilliant thinker and an equally brilliant leader."

"Not to mention a former Marine," Susan added quietly, fully aware of what that fact meant to her husband.

"Yes. That, too." Vance spoke with utter conviction. "I made a few phone calls to my guys in the Marines. They all came back with glowing reports on Aidan. So he's the real deal. I've also met with Simone Martin. She's insightful in ways that surprised even me. She'll handle both her feigned job and her real job without missing a beat. In a few hours I'll introduce her to my team. Then she'll be off and running."

"I'm sure you're right. But, Vance, time is running out." Susan gripped the lapels of his business suit, panic lacing her tone. "What if it takes Simone too much time to locate the mole at your company—assuming one even exists? And what if that discovery isn't soon enough to protect Lauren? She's somewhere in Europe—or God knows where. Aidan and Simone are here, thousands of miles away from our daughter and her kidnappers. What if—"

"Their European ground team must be in place by now," he interjected. "They'll be searching relentlessly for Lauren while Aidan runs the operation from our end. I'll get an update from Simone as soon as I get to the office. They've already coordinated a comprehensive plan that will cover every tangible scenario in every location. Lauren will be home with us within the week. You'll see."

Susan blinked back her tears. "And you?"

"What about me? I'll be wherever Aidan needs me to be."

"I never doubted that. But will you do whatever you have to? Including compromising your work ethics? What if it comes down to that?"

Warring emotions slashed across Vance's face. "According to Aidan, it won't."

"And if he's wrong?"

"Then there'll be no choice. As opposed as I am to disclosing details of Nano's most groundbreaking and confidential project, if it comes down to that or saving our daughter's life—there is no choice."

"Robert will never forgive you," Susan said, reluctantly bringing up Nano's CEO, his fierce commitment to his new technology, and his ultimate faith and future plans for Vance.

"Maybe not," Vance replied. "Maybe it will destroy my career and my relationship with Robert. But he's a father, too. I have to hope that, on some level, he'll understand. If not, it won't change my decision."

"Thank you for that." Susan knew how much that statement cost her husband. But all she could think about was Lauren.

She turned away, dashing tears off her cheeks. "In the meantime, I'm doing absolutely nothing but losing my mind. I can't concentrate. I can barely go through the motions of skiing and snowboarding. And I'm only doing that much for our other children."

"That's a *big* something. You're holding down the emotional fort."

"For now," Susan responded. "Jessica and Andrew aren't stupid. They're both picking up on my tension—and yours. I've implied that you and I are going through a rough patch. That certainly upsets them, but it's the only explanation I can give them without divulging the truth. Still, they're puzzled by the fact that Lauren isn't answering their texts, other than in cryptic snatches. How much longer do you think it's going to be before they put two and two together?"

"Not long," Vance said grimly. "We'll keep them out of the loop as long as we can. But I will discuss this with Aidan. We might have to tell the kids about their sister. They're adults. If they realize what's at stake, they'll stick to the script. But I don't want to do anything without running it by Aidan first. I might be a control freak, but I'm not an idiot. When I turned this over to Aidan and his team, I said I'd let them take the lead. I intend to do that."

He zipped up his laptop case and slung it over his shoulder, walking over to give Susan a quick kiss on her forehead. "I'll fly back right after I meet with Simone and give her center stage with my team."

"Find out as much as you can about Aidan's overseas efforts. Please, Vance."

"Count on it."

NanoUSA main conference room
26 February
Monday, 9:45 a.m. local time

Standing beside Vance at the podium, Simone scanned the cavernous room.

There were over a hundred very anxious people—executives, area managers, and workers—staring back at her as Vance outlined her credentials and explained what her role at Nano would be.

At the word *McKinsey*, the tension swelled to fill the room.

Simone got it. The employees were being told: "We're going to make this division even stronger and more efficient." But what they were hearing was: "Some of us are about to get fired."

She and Vance had discussed this prior to the meeting. Simone's advice to him was that he had to be the one who put his team's minds at ease. They needed to hear it from their boss, not some hired consultant. However, first they needed to know what this was all about. They needed Simone's direction regarding what was about to happen and what their roles would be. It was up to her to win them over and to make them think of her as an ally and not an enemy.

To that end, she'd chosen her outfit carefully. A deep navy Theory blazer with a standing collar and open front, over a matching wool-blend sheath dress that fell to just above her knee. Expensive but not intimidating. And the use of navy was no accident either. Blue was the color of loyalty and would inspire trust from her audience. And navy added just the level of professionalism and competence she wanted. Lastly, to compensate for her petite height, Simone had worn matching three-inch navy Tory Burch suede stiletto pumps.

The total effect would help her cause.

Smiling, she took the mike from Vance, thanked him for his introduction, and stepped up to the podium.

"I'm very pleased to have been invited to work with all of you to make NanoUSA even stronger than it already is," she said. Calming words chosen to inspire team spirit. Given the short time frame she had, she had to go for pointed words and a soothing presence to accomplish her goal.

"I know you're all very busy, so I'll start right out by sharing some results we've achieved for other clients. Simultaneously, I'll explain the process we'll follow, and after that, I'll be happy to answer any questions you may have."

With that, Simone dimmed the lights and switched to the first content slide in her presentation.

The slide appeared with a collage of word balloons emanating from a crowd of people in silhouette. *Productivity is up 20%*, the first balloon read. *Employee satisfaction is through the roof*, stated the second. The third balloon announced: *Gross margins are higher than ever*.

Simone read each one aloud in her lightly accented English. She then paused to mentally and physically assess the room. The vibes were mixed, and the tenor of the room was still clouded in suspicion. Given that, she made a tactical decision not to show the video testimonials behind each balloon.

Instead, she went straight to the methodology, a topic she hoped would divert their attention to something other than losing their jobs. She launched into describing End Products Value Analysis and the high-level concepts behind this diagnostic tool that would isolate inefficiencies in each area. Across the top of the page, she listed key deliverables in green, some in yellow, and others in red. She talked about how employees would be asked to list key end products/deliverables that they worked on and how much time they spent doing so. Other departments, executives, even outside companies—would be asked what they valued.

The obvious question raised by this value analysis was whether an area could stop doing a red item, saving those resources and redeploying them somewhere else.

"As you know," Simone continued, "your department has struggled to keep up with the demands placed upon it. Mr. Pennington has asked me to make sure that we are using our resources wisely before bringing anyone else on board." Her glance swept the room. "Questions?"

A hand was immediately raised, and Jim Baskin, one of Vance's senior executives, spoke directly to his boss, rather than to Simone.

"I'll be blunt," he said, "and ask what every person in this room wants to know. It's no secret that when McKinsey consultants like Ms. Martin come in, twenty percent of the employees lose their jobs. Is that what's going on here?"

Vance stepped up to the mike. "I really appreciate that honest and difficult question, Jim. And I'm going to give you an equally honest answer. No one is going to lose their job as a result of Ms. Martin's efforts. Let me repeat what I just said: No one is going to lose their job. Our goal here is to focus on identifying the inefficiencies and disconnects. There may be some changes in responsibilities, but all in the spirit of getting better."

Simone spoke up, reclaiming the position of power that Vance had hired her for. "I, too, am glad you said out loud what was on everyone's mind. And Mr. Pennington, I appreciate your candor in articulating the company's intent here."

She could actually feel the tension abate, allowing her to continue freely.

"Given the size of this organization, I'll be talking to each senior area manager. Those managers will be consulting with their teams. We'd like to make this entire process happen in two days, so I've broken up the next two days into forty-eight one-hour time slots. Please choose a time slot. I'll meet with you before work, during work, or after work to accommodate you."

Vance added, "And to kick off this process, I'll take the first slot available right after this meeting."

Simone penciled that in, then passed the sheet on to the twenty managers.

Phase one was underway.

* * *

Vance shut the door behind the last retreating employee and turned to face Simone.

"We barely had time to talk before the meeting," he said. "And we have only an hour now. So I'll get straight to it. I need a more thorough update than 'everything is in motion.'"

"And I plan to give you one," Simone replied. "I waited until after the meeting so I could include my assessments when I filled you in." She glanced down at her watch, her delicate brows drawing together. "I'll be thorough but brief. You must take off for Lake Tahoe by lunchtime."

"Agreed. But I also must know what's going on with the hunt for my daughter."

"To begin with, a European tactical team has been formed and is already on the move." Simone chose her words carefully—not too much, not too little. "They're following solid leads that will tell them where Lauren has been taken. They'll act accordingly. Aidan met with them while he was in Munich. He'll have more details for you. His flight is scheduled to arrive in San Francisco this evening, after which, he'll catch a quick flight to Reno and head straight to Lake Tahoe so he can bring you up to speed."

"Isn't that risky?" Vance asked nervously. "We know the kidnappers are watching my every move. Won't they spot Aidan showing up at my hotel?"

A small smile curved Simone's lips. "Aidan has a way of remaining invisible. So he'll be the one making all the necessary commutes between here and Tahoe when face-to-face meetings outside the office are necessary. I'll be available by phone or videoconference, as well. You know where to find me. I'll be a fixture at NanoUSA."

Vance nodded, absorbing Simone's detailed report even as his mind was fixed on results.

His next question came as no surprise.

"Is your tactical team close to finding Lauren?"

"I don't know their current status," Simone answered honestly. "But if they're not now, they will be. We're all aware that the clock is ticking. And *you* should be aware that our team doesn't fail."

"I pray you're right."

"I am. But while our tactical team is carrying out its overseas assignment, you and I have our work cut out for us right here. We have two days. When I'm finished talking to all the members of your staff, I'll have a clear picture of their level of integrity—where it comes to you and to the company. I'll need to expand that exploration further, to the senior leadership outside the manufacturing division. Can you get me on their calendars?"

"Of course," Vance replied. "I'll handle it myself. Although Ethan Gallagher, my personal assistant, could probably make it happen as fast as I can. He has a hotline to the PAs of all NanoUSA's top brass. He also knows me, my schedule, and my projects inside out."

"I'm sure he does or he wouldn't be your PA. Obviously, I'll want to talk to him, as well as the PAs of all the high-level executives—beginning with Robert Maxwell's. I assume he or she is exceptional?"

"She," Vance supplied. "Zoe Pearson. She's not just exceptional, she's indispensable. I don't think there's anything that woman can't do. Robert jokes that she's his unofficial CEO. I'll set up meetings for you with her, with Ethan, and of course, with the senior executives you've asked to speak with."

"Good," Simone responded. "Because those execs are internal customers of the outputs and services that your department provides and have important perspectives on the winners and losers. That info is essential to me. There's no question that, given how your technology threatens the Chinese electronics industry, Chinese agents have made multiple attempts to influence and infiltrate your company at this crucial time. The fact that your daughter was kidnapped is an indication that they were unsuccessful in their recruiting efforts or their successful recruiting efforts were stopped by the rigorous security measures your company has in place."

"Which leads us back to your theory that there's a mole inside our company and that ferreting him or her out could be crucial to finding the animals who have Lauren."

"Exactly." Simone nodded. "We suspect the kidnappers are European, not Chinese, for obvious reasons. A Chinese kidnapper in Munich, Germany, would stand out more. So my guess is that the Chinese are pulling the strings. They might be working with a mole in your company, but my experience tells me that they hired others to do the kidnapping for them."

Vance rubbed a palm over his jaw. "There are so many moving parts and so little I can do, other than lining up your meetings. What else?"

"You can talk to me about you."

"Pardon me?"

Simone walked over and poured two cups of coffee, handing one to Vance. "We're going to use the rest of this time for me to interview you. Starting with the personal. Who hates you the most?"

The question took Vance off guard and he started. "Now that's a tough one. Hates me? Resents me? Feels threatened by me? Which?"

"All of the above."

"That's a pretty complex question."

"It's an imperative one for you to answer."

"I understand." Vance's brow furrowed. "I'll need this cup of coffee—and the hour we've got."

"Fifty minutes," Simone corrected. "So drink your coffee. And voice your thought process aloud."

9

Aidan hopped into the town car that was waiting for him at the airport and leaned back in his seat, resting his eyes. He'd be videoconferencing with the team in twenty-five minutes. They wouldn't have a lot of time. He'd be at the Ritz-Carlton in an hour.

Not that he had a hell of a lot to report.

His last few hours in Munich had been a complete bust, other than ascertaining that Abby, Emma, and Joyce had safely arrived in Disneyland. Danijel had been unavailable all day and had yet to return Aidan's call. And his visit to Hofbräuhaus had yielded nothing. He'd hoped that by showing up there around the same time of day as Lauren had, he'd find some of the same employees and customers who worked and frequented the restaurant then. He'd managed that part just fine. After showing Lauren's photo around—casually saying she was his niece and he was here to surprise her—two male waiters and a table of college kids remembered seeing her. Unfortunately, that's all they remembered. Two of the kids had noticed a dark-haired guy talking to her, but they'd never seen him before and had no idea who he was. There'd been some curiosity expressed, which Aidan had immediately squelched by saying the guy was her boyfriend and they were vacationing in Europe.

That had been enough to satisfy the kids and the waiters, who were too self-involved to give him a second thought.

But he'd come away with zilch.

Given that, keeping Vance calm wasn't going to be easy. According to Simone's earlier phone call, she'd set the stage well, but there was only so much she could do. In addition, Aidan was now going to have to meet and size up the emotional state of Susan Pennington, who was doubtless experiencing the maternal hysteria she had every right to. He'd have to find a way to channel that energy into something positive. The filaments of an idea had occurred to him on his flight. He planned on implementing it ASAP—depending on the Penningtons' emotional and performance capabilities. That had to be assessed, and if all things checked out, it would be full speed ahead.

Aidan rubbed his forehead, fighting the effects of an overwork headache. It was going to be a long night.

His secure cell phone rang and he answered on the first ring. "Yes."

"You sound exhausted," Simone greeted him. "I can almost hear you massaging your temples."

A grin tugged at Aidan's lips. "Are you clairvoyant now?"

"No. I just know you. You're pondering how to deal with the Penningtons, which is going to be emotionally draining. And that's after putting in three days' work with little to no sleep, plus a full team videoconference in twenty-five minutes."

"Hey, I'm a tough guy. I'll be fine."

"I plan to make sure of that."

"Really? And how do you intend to do that?"

"Simple." Simone's tone was pure seduction. "I just had a bath and a long nap. I'm wide-awake. I plan to remain that way so I can greet you properly when you arrive at my hotel room—whatever time of night that might be."

"An invitation like that is like offering food to a starving man." Aidan felt his blood start to pump despite the impossibility of the situation. "But as much as it kills me, we'll have to wait for that heated reunion. I'll probably be with the Penningtons for a couple of hours. Car service will be standing by. But the drive from Tahoe to Palo Alto is four-plus hours. You'll be getting dressed to go to NanoUSA by the time I show up."

"*Au contraire, mon chéri,*" Simone replied. "I took the liberty of contacting our pilot and instructing him to set a flight plan for Lake Tahoe. The Gulfstream will be waiting at the airport whenever you finish up with the Penningtons. You'll be with me a short time later."

Aidan started to laugh. "And how did you pull that one off? I'm the only person authorized to commission the jet."

"What's that American expression—*so sue me*?" Simone sounded very pleased with herself. "I may have implied to our pilot that you'd instructed me to contact him and ask him to file the flight plan. Are you angry?"

"Furious." Aidan's headache was vanishing as he spoke. "After the videoconference, you'd better order up some late-night room service to fortify yourself. You're going to need all your energy for what I have in mind."

San Mateo, California
26 February
Monday, 9:55 p.m. local time

He lit his cigarette and took a deep drag, exhaling and watching the wisps of smoke vanish into the air. It was a disgusting habit. He'd promised himself, yet again, that he'd find a way to quit. Maybe he'd cave and try hypnosis. Nothing else seemed to work. They couldn't counterbalance his stress. He needed an outlet. And not one that piled pounds on his body. Maybe he'd double the amount of that tasteless, allegedly therapeutic gum he'd been chewing.

He'd concluded his work for the day and reported in. There'd been no red flags. Pennington had spent the morning at NanoUSA. No shocker there. He'd been told to stick to the script of his life, and so far, he had. Family time or not, there was no way he'd be in full-time vacation mode when his company was about to revolutionize the electronics world. He'd held a full department meeting, run by a high-level overseas McKinsey partner who had checked out. As had the purpose of the meeting. A divisional fine-tuning—boring but necessary. But a possible division overhaul? That had interesting connotations. It could be a coincidence. Or it could be Pennington's way of finding inroads in order to provide them with whatever they demanded in their next set of instructions. That would be a smart move on his part.

Lauren Pennington wouldn't have to be disposed of—yet.

Ritz-Carlton
26 February
Monday, 10:53 p.m. local time

Aidan had spent enough time in the hotel lobby to scope out the place for potential surveillance. He'd browsed his email, made a few staged phone calls, and acted like a typical businessman. Then he'd unknotted his tie, slung his jacket over his shoulder, and sucked in his breath—transformed into a businessman who was free to relax and unwind in a resort hotel. His instincts told him there were no eyes on him. Still, he played his part to the last—slinging his carry-on bag over his shoulder, going up to the front desk, and checking in to the room he'd reserved for himself in advance. That done, he'd taken the elevator up to the third floor, entered his room only long enough to chuck his jacket and tie on the bed and use the bathroom before exiting the room and purposely taking the stairs rather than the elevator up to the Penningtons' fourth-floor suite.

The team videoconference had gone well. He'd kept it short, partly because of his time constraints and partly because he was sitting in the back seat of a town car and, sound-deadening window or not, he wasn't thrilled by the lack of total privacy. Mostly, he'd listened. He'd put on his noise-canceling headphones for all the debriefings. Everything on track. He'd also had the opportunity to "meet" Derica and Ellie—the Croatian interpreters. Again, Simone had done an A-plus recruiting job. Two attractive women in their mid-thirties. Both from nearby towns in Germany, so they'd gotten to Marc and Philip ASAP. Both well-versed in the Croatian language, one from having lived there for a dozen years and the other from having been employed by a Croatian company for equally long. The former, Derica, had worked undercover cases such as these before, and the latter, Ellie, was fluent in Albanian as well as Croatian. Both women understood the meaning of the word *classified*. They'd been brought up to speed with all the information they needed to know and were fully prepared for the assignments ahead.

As for Aidan, he'd merely touched on the fact that he might have a specific agenda for the European team to follow, but that it was dependent upon the conversation he was about to have. No one asked questions. They knew why Aidan wasn't being more forthcoming. He'd give them the information once it was solidified and when his location was secure.

"Expect tomorrow to be busy," he'd said in closing. "I'll contact you as soon as developments occur."

Now, he made his way down the hall and knocked on the door of the Penningtons' hotel room.

"It's Aidan," he said.

Vance opened the door. He looked lousy and like he was about to jump out of his skin. The ashen-faced middle-aged woman standing behind him—obviously his wife, Susan—was peering around to see Aidan, imploring him with her eyes to give them something to cling to. Some good news. Anything.

He'd finesse this as best as he could. No bullshit. No lies. But progress. Things they could do. Collaboration. Hope.

"Come in." Vance looked nervously up and down the hallway. "Were you followed?"

"Nope." Aidan closed the door behind him. "Besides, I booked a room here, one flight down. I'm just a vacationer like any other—one who has nothing to do with you."

Vance's brows rose. "I didn't realize you'd done that. But I probably should have. Simone said you had a way of staying invisible."

"I've had years of practice." Aidan leaned forward and extended his hand to Susan. "I'm Aidan Devereaux."

She met his handshake, her fingers cold and trembling. "I'm glad you're here. Lauren is my baby. I need to know everything that's going on, please."

"I understand."

"I doubt you do." She inhaled sharply. "Forgive me. I didn't mean to be rude. I'm just coming apart at the seams. I feel helpless and terrified. But since Vance is convinced that you're our best hope of bringing Lauren home alive, I've stuck to your rules. I've spoken to no one, and I've gone about my daily vacation routine. It's killing me inside, but I'm doing it."

"That's essential," Aidan said, gesturing toward the hotel suite's sitting room sofa. "You need to keep doing exactly that. But you also need reassurance that there's been forward motion in the investigation. Well, there is. So let's all sit down and I'll fill you in on where things stand."

Susan led the way, perching at the edge of the couch. "I didn't order up food. But I can."

"Thanks, no." Aidan crossed over and sat in the upholstered chair across from the sofa. "I'd rather just get down to business."

He waited until Vance had taken a seat beside his wife, using that time to study Susan. Something in particular was on her mind. She was fidgeting now and her gaze had faltered a bit when she'd told him she was following his rules. He'd better find out what was going on—now.

"Is there something you want to tell me?" he asked bluntly.

Susan looked startled, then swallowed hard and nodded. "Jessica and Andrew—our other two children—they're asking questions and worrying about their sister's less-than-friendly texts. I've waylaid them as best as I can. But they're highly intelligent adults, Aidan. If they become any more suspicious, they're likely to start poking around on their own. That could be disastrous. I want them to know the truth. You can do all the talking; that's fine with me. But at this point it's more harmful to keep them in the dark than it is to be frank and ask for their silence, just as you did mine."

Aidan wasn't particularly surprised by the request. In fact, he was relieved that's all that Susan was withholding. Something like this he could and would deal with—*now*.

"I appreciate your position," he said. "But this situation needs to stay controlled. Including you is as far as I'm comfortable taking this. You'll have to keep your other two kids in the dark. It's the only way to ensure mistakes aren't made. Lie if you have to and tell them Lauren's contacted you and she's off having a great time in areas that have terrible cell reception. It's only for a few days. Please don't make me regret having brought you into the loop."

Susan bowed her head, grappling with her emotions. When she looked up, her cheeks were stained with tears. "Fine," she said. "I'll do as you ask."

"Will you?" Aidan searched her face, seeking the confirmation he needed.

"Yes. I will—for Lauren."

"Good." She wasn't lying. Aidan would have spotted that immediately.

Dashing away her tears, Susan leaned forward. "Tell us where things stand. Do you know where Lauren is? Do you have a rescue plan in place?"

"Susan, let Aidan talk before we start firing questions." Vance's rigid body language belied his gentle admonishment. He was struggling not to take control of this conversation. But he was clearly trying to be pragmatic—as pragmatic as a father could be under these circumstances.

"All right," Susan replied, although the barrage of questions was still flickering across her face. "Go ahead, Aidan."

"Start with your overseas team," Vance said. "I already know what's going on at this end thanks to Simone."

"I intended to do just that," Aidan replied calmly. He had to keep the Penningtons from erupting into panic. He'd give them everything he comfortably could—and then elicit their help. "My tactical team is in place and on the move. We've narrowed down the geographic area where the kidnappers are holding Lauren. We believe she's somewhere in Croatia."

This time it was Vance who couldn't contain himself. "*Somewhere*? Croatia is a country, Devereaux, not a neighborhood. How are you going to cover that vast an area in a matter of days?"

"Quickly and strategically," Aidan answered calmly. "Remember that, as of yesterday, we weren't even sure if she was still in Europe. The kidnappers could have flown her anywhere in the world. We've gone from global to a single country in a matter of twenty-four hours. If we can do that, we can go the rest of the way. As we speak, my team is preparing to connect with the right people and make its way through the various Croatian cities and towns."

"They're all fluent in Croatian?"

"Our contacts and translators are, yes."

Vance rose and began pacing the room. "It's not enough. There has to be more we can do."

"There is." It was time for the implementation of Aidan's idea. "I think I have a way for you to help us."

Vance jerked around to face Aidan. "Name it."

"It's been over two days since the kidnappers have contacted you. I'd bet money that you'll hear from them tomorrow. This time they'll provide you with a way to contact them so they can get what they need. They're going to want something as a show of faith—probably photographs from the specifications document."

"How am I supposed to deal with that?"

"Tell them you need time. Buy yourself as much as they'll allow."

"Even so, how do I get the photos to them? Nano is a fortress. I can't send out anything."

"I'm working on a solution to that. In the meantime, you call me the minute the contact is made. I'll have a plan in place. What's crucial—and the way you can help us—is in *your* demands. You're going to agree to give them what they want—under one condition. You're going to insist on daily communications with Lauren to ensure she's alive."

"I'm going to *what*?"

"You're going to demand to see and talk to your daughter on a daily basis."

Vance stared. "And why the hell would they allow that?"

"Because whoever hired these terrorists wants your technology. They don't want your daughter. In their minds, Lauren is just a means to an end."

"After which, what? What would stop them from killing her?"

"The fear of a huge international investigation. Right now, this extortion/kidnapping is under wraps. But if a major US executive's daughter was murdered overseas, and that executive started talking about it? All hell would break loose. Their entire purpose would be compromised, and their identities threatened to be exposed. Trust me. They'll agree to the proof-of-life demand. It gets them what they want and actually reassures them that you're playing along. My team will set things up, ensure you have a secure log-in link that only you and they will have access to."

"Oh, Vance," Susan said, tears gathering in her eyes. "If we could speak to Lauren, see her, know she's all right—it would mean everything to me."

"And to me," Vance replied. "All right, Aidan. Once again, I'll put my trust in you. I'll make that demand."

Aidan turned to Susan. "I'm sorry, Susan, but this has to be just Vance and Lauren. The kidnappers believe you know nothing about what's going on. We have to keep it that way."

Her face fell as she struggled with the fact that Aidan was right. "I understand . . ." she agreed at last, in a small, shaky voice.

"Vance, to ensure Lauren's safety, no stupid questions," Aidan warned. "No asking Lauren about her surroundings, her kidnappers, or her whereabouts. These animals might not be rocket scientists but they're not idiots. Subtlety is key here. You'll want to ask her if she's unharmed. If she's eating, sleeping, being treated well. All those things are normal parental questions that don't raise any red flags."

"Agreed," Vance replied.

"Also, don't be upset if she seems dazed. That doesn't imply drugs."

"You think they'll drug her?" Susan asked, alarmed.

Aidan shook his head. "They realize you'd pick up on that. What I'm saying is that she's most likely been inside the same dwelling for a week, with no access to the world and no sense of time or place. So she might seem out of it. Don't let that alarm you. Concentrate on what's important—the end goal."

Vance rubbed his jaw. "I sense you're going somewhere specific with this—besides just putting our minds at ease."

"I am," Aidan replied. "Croatia's regions often produce foods that are specific to that region. If we could zero in on one of those foods, it could narrow things down considerably. I want you to tell Lauren how worried you are about whether she's eating healthfully. I want you to insist that she tell you what she's eaten each day—breakfast, lunch, and dinner. It's a natural request from a nervous dad. With a modicum of luck, she'll name a food that will tell us what region she's in. The kidnappers probably won't even notice it, and if they do, they'd never think of it as a clue. You're supposedly acting alone, a terrified father, not a connoisseur of regional cuisine or a member of international law enforcement."

"It's a good idea, if it pays off."

"We won't know till we try. In the meantime, my team will work in tandem. They'll cover the entire country, until we tell them otherwise. Once they come up with something specific—with or without our help—they'll go after the kidnappers like hawks."

"Please find Lauren," Susan whispered. "Please bring her safely home to us. Please."

Aidan never blinked. "Count on it."

Ritz-Carlton
One hour later

Aidan had stayed with the Penningtons long enough to keep them calm, reassured, and on track.

Now he made a quick stop at his hotel room, intending to get in immediate touch with Terri.

The vibrating of his cell phone put a hold on that.

"Yes?" he answered.

"I hear you've been trying to track me down," a slightly accented male voice at the other end of the phone responded. "It was a long day and an even longer night. But I'm home now, enjoying my morning coffee and talking on a secure line. So tell me what you need."

"Good to hear your voice, *prijatelj*." Aidan hadn't talked to Danijel Horvat in months—not since he and his wife had visited Aidan and

Abby in New York last summer. Abby was already excited about the prospect of returning the visit and traveling to Croatia.

The two men went way back, having served together in the War in Kosovo. Aidan had been there doing Marine intel work during active combat. Danijel had also been doing intel work, in his case for the Croatian army. Aidan had received classified information saying that Danijel's base was in a target zone about to be bombed by the enemy. He'd gotten in touch with Danijel instantly. The base had been evacuated. Danijel was firm in his belief that Aidan had saved his life. He'd never forgotten. He never would.

Aidan shrugged off the rescue. But he never let Danijel forget the other time he'd saved his life. Danijel had gotten romantically involved with a beautiful Serbian woman who, unbeknownst to him, was married—and to a high-level politician. The politician had learned his wife was being unfaithful and was on his way to the hotel where a liaison was taking place to kill her lover. Aidan had gotten wind of that and had managed to whisk Danijel out of the hotel mere minutes before the shit hit the fan.

For *that* rescue, Aidan would forever rib Danijel.

"I'm in the middle of an investigation," he told Danijel now. "Two of my men are in Croatia. I need you to meet with them and help them. We're racing the clock to save a kidnapped young woman we believe is being held somewhere in your country."

"Then I'll be ready for them. I assume the details you'll be providing me will be only need-to-know?"

"They will be, yes," Aidan confirmed. "But I'll give you everything you require to make this rescue happen. My guys on the ground will add whatever's necessary."

"Fine. I'm listening."

* * *

As soon as Aidan had finished up with Danijel and emailed him photos and background information on Philip and Marc, he called Terri.

"Sorry it's the middle of the night there," he began. "But I need you to provide a way to transfer confidential digital files out of NanoUSA and to the kidnappers."

"It can't be done," Terri replied, clearly wide awake and working. "I've explored the NanoUSA systems. They're impenetrable."

"Get creative."

"I've tried. It would have to be done from the inside by someone who knows what they're doing. Even then, it would be next to impossible."

Aidan's mind was racing. "Can't you develop something that Simone can take in with her to use?"

"Simone has no knowledge of complex hardware and software security. And what do you mean by 'develop something'? I doubt C3PO is available, and he'd be far from invisible."

"It would have to be something more subtle."

Terri gave an exasperated sigh. "Aidan, I'm the best there is at big systems, complex programs, and firewalls. This would require a physical component to get around their format-variant systems. I don't do electronic gizmos."

A slow smile spread across Aidan's face. "You're right," he said. "But we both know someone who does."

Farmhouse
Slavonia, Croatia
Tuesday, 8:45 a.m. local time

Same endless acres of land. Same cramped room. Same praying to be rescued.

Lauren had moved past tears and terror and into a faraway, surreal place where only a hollow ache remained. She lay, curled up on the bed in her assigned quarters, staring off into nothingness, unaware if it was day or night and not really caring. She *was* aware that nearly a week had passed since she'd been taken. And she had no idea what that meant. Did they plan to return her or kill her? Had they contacted her father? Were there some kind of negotiations going on?

Did she dare to even hope anymore?

She'd fallen into a routine. Showering in the closet-sized hall bathroom and changing into some of the new clothes she'd been provided with. Forcing herself to go to the kitchen to eat—or try to eat. She couldn't choke down much, but she swallowed enough to sustain her. Twice, when the men who were holding her were locked away in another bedroom that was their meeting place, she'd tentatively walked around the small, starkly furnished farmhouse—with Bashkim keeping a close eye on her—and casually gazed out the windows, willing there to be some so-far-unseen landmark she could memorize to aid in her rescue.

If there ever was a rescue.

Eventually, she'd return to her room and crawl back into bed, lying there for hours. Solitude, which she normally despised, seemed to be her only friend. Any voices she heard made her heart start to pound and her body to shake. And when those voices moved away, she sagged with relief.

The lack of intrusion meant she wasn't going to be violated or worse.

Every evening before Bashkim turned in for the night, he'd respectfully knock on the door, coming in to make sure she was well and to see if there was anything she needed to make her stay here more comfortable.

Her stay? She'd almost laughed out loud. It sounded as if she were in a quaint bed-and-breakfast, free as a bird, backpacking her way through Europe. The truth was she was a prisoner and quite possibly a soon-to-be corpse.

Last night she'd asked him about Marko. She still had nightmares about him barging in and raping her. Bashkim's jaw had set and he'd said she didn't need to worry, that Marko wouldn't be back. He'd reached into his pocket, pulled out an all-too-familiar gold chain, and tossed it on the nightstand.

The message was clear. Marko was dead.

Relief flooded Lauren. She knew she should feel sickened by the fact that a man had been killed, probably brutally. She felt nothing but thankful. All she wanted was to never have to see Marko's smug, predatory face again.

Oh God, what were they asking for that her father couldn't—or wouldn't—give? Would he possibly be willing to play Russian roulette with her life?

No. Never.

She couldn't let thoughts like that creep into her head and sever the fragile threads of her prayers.

Please, Dad, she begged silently. *Please find a way. I want to come home.*

I don't want to die.

10

Four days left...

Aidan rolled onto his back and slowly opened his eyes.

The hotel room was cast in shadows, dimly lit only by the streetlamp just outside the curtained windows and the LED display of the clock on the nightstand. The sun wasn't ready to give way to dawn, so the skies were dark. And Aidan had only gotten an hour and a half of sleep. But his bio clock normally went off every morning at five thirty. It had since his military days.

Today he'd slept late.

He blinked away the final vestiges of sleep and pushed himself to a sitting position, trying not to disturb the sleeping woman beside him.

"No need to be chivalrous. I'm awake." Simone turned to face him, her dark hair disheveled and a soft smile touching her lips. "I'm flattered I tired you out enough to take even a cat nap."

Aidan returned her smile, reaching out to tuck a strand of hair behind her ear. "You did. I'm almost sorry. That's ninety minutes of a reunion missed."

"To be continued," Simone promised, propping herself on her elbow and leaning up to give Aidan a long, melting kiss. "But for now, we have much work to do. Do we have time to share a cup of coffee? Before I head into NanoUSA today, I need to know Vance Pennington's current state of mind. I must hear how your meeting with him and his wife went last night."

"I guess you and I didn't do much talking once I got here, did we?"

"None." Simone sat up and stretched like a contented cat. "I have no complaints."

Aidan kissed her bare shoulder. "I'll order us coffee and a light breakfast. Ladies first in the shower."

"First, yes—while you call room service." Simone climbed out of bed, letting the sheet drop seductively behind her. "Alone, no." She shot Aidan a teasing look over her shoulder. "In Europe, we conserve water. You Americans are so wasteful. Would you consider trying it my way?"

Aidan was already reaching for the hotel phone. "I'll be there before the water gets hot."

47th Street, Diamond District, Manhattan, New York
27 February
Tuesday, 9:20 a.m. local time

Ryan McKay shoved his hands into the pockets of his parka as he turned the corner and made his way down the sidewalk of the perpetually under-construction street. People were either striding rapidly along or halted at a dead standstill, ogling glittering diamonds in showcase windows. The result was sidewalk gridlock and a pedestrian collision course. The patches of snow from last night's two-inch accumulation didn't help.

The congestion and chaos were just what Ryan had counted on. Getting lost in the crowd would be a snap. Although, on the flip side, he'd made this trek in the middle of the night many times before, when his contact deemed the cloak of darkness necessary. Ryan didn't ask questions. He just followed directions. Henry wasn't the chatting type.

Ryan had been stoked when Terri called and asked him to run this part of the show—stoked enough so that he hadn't even minded giving up half a night's sleep doing prep work. The fact that Aidan and Terri had entrusted this part of their investigation to him, labeling him the expert, had fed his ego and kicked up his adrenaline level. Didn't matter that he wasn't privy to the why. He was part of the process, and that was good enough for him.

Ideas had erupted in his head like Mount Etna. The result was a solid go. Now all he needed was to meet up with the right person. Together, they'd get the job done.

Sloshing through a patch of wet snow, Ryan walked about halfway down the street and then stopped at the lackluster building that was lost amid the skyscrapers surrounding it. Clearly, this particular structure was an "original" and pre-dated World War II with only the most bare-bones of renovations. And what was waiting for Ryan inside was a real shithole.

He nodded at the security guard, giving him a fuck-you look that said, *I belong here.*

No questions were asked.

Ryan then took the elevator to the fourteenth floor, exited, and walked purposefully down the narrow hallway, stopping when he reached 1407.

He glanced up at the security camera and pressed the buzzer.

He got his return buzz, pushed open the door, and stepped inside. The outer door closed behind him, leaving him wedged between it and an inner door. A second buzzer went off. Ryan leaned against the inner door, gaining entry into the small dungeon that served as the jewelry maker's workshop. Given the value of the merchandise he handled, the owner made sure that no one was allowed in without him knowing them by sight.

Ryan was greeted by the usual stench of cigarette smoke, stale air, and the acrid smell of solder and flux. Piles of clutter were everywhere, and in the middle of the chaos stood a big, broken-down piece of furniture that resembled a cobbler's workbench. Behind the workbench sat the scariest-looking motherfucker Ryan had ever met. He was built like a brick shithouse, tattooed in every visible spot, with arms the size of tree trunks and a scarred face that would scare a kid at Halloween.

"Yeah, Ryan, what's so urgent that you woke me up at four in the morning? What do you need now?" Henry Lago didn't look up. He was peering at a large diamond through a jeweler's loupe.

"Hi to you, too, Lago," Ryan replied. "And I need a ring."

Henry sneered. "Getting engaged?"

"Nope. Getting creative."

That piqued Henry's interest. He glanced up, levelling his bloodshot stare at Ryan. "I'm listening."

"Thought you might be." Ryan warmed to his subject. He and Henry were dead alike in that they both loved a challenge. "I need a man's school ring, size nine."

"Any school in particular? Going straight for the top ten? Been there, done that. So have you. Not worth the money or the bullshit."

Ryan nodded. Another thing he and Henry had in common. Ryan had spent a couple of years at MIT before he decided he needed the freedom to fly on his own. Henry had spent less than a year there, realizing right away that his level of electronic genius was wasted in school.

The two guys had briefly crossed paths. It was enough to make Henry one of Ryan's favorite contacts when his role at Forensic Instincts required it. Henry was equally charged by their alliance—although his favorite jab was that he was the real deal, and that Ryan's success was rooted in the fact that he came across as a chick magnet.

Ryan countered that Henry's claim to fame was that he came off like a mass murderer.

Two egotistical geniuses. It was a partnership made in heaven.

"Let's flip the bird to the Ivies and the Little Ivies," Ryan replied. "Actually, I don't really care what school you choose, as long as it doesn't have a diamond or anything else transparent as its gemstone. Because a dark stone is what I need in the center of the ring."

Henry yawned. "Uh-huh. What goes with it?"

"A camera, for starters. I need you to plant one behind the stone. Also, somewhere in the ring you need to bury a flash memory. And there needs to be a capacitor that's charged by induction. We'll be using a wireless cell phone charger. I need the image capture to be triggered by a finger placed across two spots on the ring. And since the user has no way to frame the picture, I need control logic inside to detect the edges of the paper and capture the content within. It has to capture a full-size engineering drawing from a distance of three feet." Ryan raised his brows, although he knew his answer even as he asked the question. "Can you do it?"

"If you can think of it, I can do it—only better."

"I need it in four hours."

"Then it'll cost you four times the usual."

"Done." Ryan didn't flinch. Hey, it was Aidan's money. And Terri had given him carte blanche. "I'll be back at one thirty."

"Bring the cash."

"Do the job."

NanoUSA
27 February
Tuesday, 7:35 a.m. local time

Simone began her one-on-one morning meetings even before Vance's plane had landed from Lake Tahoe. Per her request, she'd been set up in a small meeting room, with only a round cherrywood table and a few matching chairs set up beside it, together with a sideboard containing a Keurig brewing station, a tray of fruit, and the appropriate plates and silverware. This setup had to be as non-threatening an environment as possible, given the delicacy of the situation. Despite Vance's reassurance, most of these employees would be geared up to protect their jobs. And Simone needed them to relax so she could accomplish what she was *really* here to do.

She crossed one leg over the other and read through her material for the fourth time. This wasn't just about preparedness. It was about insight, touching on just the right questions in the subtlest of ways, and gathering information without the interviewee realizing he or she was supplying it.

Simone was very pleased that Vance had set up her first morning of interviews with the VPs of other key departments, followed by meetings with his own area heads. Even Robert Maxwell had offered to give her a short time slot just before noon. All in all, this schedule meant she'd come away with a big-picture view of the Nano senior management team.

Her 7:45 interview—the first of the day—was with Lawrence Blockman, who was the VP of Engineering and, in her estimation, Vance's key competitor for the soon-to-be-named CEO position. According to what Vance had told Aidan in their initial meeting, no one in the company was aware that Robert Maxwell had already made his final decision as to his successor. Therefore, Blockman would still view himself as a fierce competitor, which would make him a prime suspect as the Chinese perpetrator's inside mole. Not only could Blockman keep an eye on Vance but—should Vance provide the kidnappers with any material whatsoever—Blockman could pin the crime of industrial espionage on Vance. It was a win-win for Blockman—*if* he turned out to be guilty.

Tapping her pen thoughtfully on the table, Simone did a once-over on the paper summary of Blockman. He was well-educated, highly qualified, and had twenty years of stellar performance reviews. In Vance's talk with Simone, he'd said that he and Blockman got along very well, although they didn't always see eye to eye on product designs. Not a red flag, given one engineering perspective and one manufacturing one.

Still, she planned on being extremely thorough with this man.

She re-scanned the list of today's interviewees, noting who had met the challenge head-on—signing up for the earliest slots—and who had dallied and delayed their meetings until the next day at the latest possible times. Those employees weren't just ostriching. They were waiting to pump info out of those who had preceded them, to be as prepared as possible, and probably to try calming their nerves.

Both Ethan Gallagher and Zoe Pearson, Vance's PA and Robert Maxwell's PA respectively, were scheduled for later today—Ethan at two thirty and Zoe at three thirty. Excellent. Each of them would be a fountain of information—the public and the not-so-public. The faster she spoke with them and won them over the better. She'd be interviewing Ethan right here in this meeting room and Zoe in her office—as requested. She'd made that request diplomatically, explaining to Simone that, given the rapid fire of phone calls and meetings that were leading up to Nano's huge announcement, she simply couldn't be away from her desk. Simone was fine with the arrangement. This way she could not only do her job, she could also scope out Zoe's work home.

A knock on the door interrupted her musings.

"Come in," she called out.

A tall man in his mid-fifties with a receding hairline, angular features, and a build like a blade of grass walked in. Contrary to his Poindexter appearance, he was wearing an expensive suit and tie, not to mention a stunning pair of gold cufflinks. Definitely a sense of style. Not the usual MO for an engineer. And definitely not the informal dress code she'd viewed thus far at Nano.

Unaware of her brief scrutiny, Blockman glanced around the room and then turned his attention on Simone as she rose and extended her hand.

"Mr. Blockman?"

He nodded, meeting her handshake. His smile was genuine. So were the dots of perspiration on his brow.

"Nice to meet you, Ms. Martin," he said.

"It's Simone—and it's a pleasure to meet you, as well." She gestured toward the sideboard. "Grab a cup of coffee and help yourself to some fruit. It's early. If you're anything like me, you've probably skipped breakfast."

"It's Lawrence. And I always seem to, yes." Looking at the table, he ascertained that Simone had her own coffee and fruit, just to assure himself of the protocol. Confirming that she had both, he went over, made himself a cup of coffee, and put some fruit on his plate, after which he settled himself in the chair adjacent to Simone's.

A healthy mound of sliced pineapple and cantaloupe covered his plate, Simone noted. Not the sign of a quaking employee.

She set up her iPad and began.

"I'm sure you're aware that I'm working with Vance Pennington to increase efficiency in his department."

"I'd heard, yes," Blockman replied. "I'm just not sure how I can be of any help in that process."

"I asked Vance to set up meetings with all the corporate VPs so that I could get a feel for what they do and how they interact with both Vance and the manufacturing department." Simone's delicate brows drew together. "I hope you don't mind. I won't take much of your time."

"I don't mind at all." Blockman swallowed some coffee. He looked a little tense but not alarmed. "Fire away."

Simone nodded, her fingers poised on the keypad. "For starters, who are your key customers and what do you do for them?"

It was an innocuous question, and an easy one for Blockman to answer.

"One of our prime responsibilities is to develop new product specifications so that manufacturing can produce them. So you're right, we do work closely with Vance's department."

"And how well do your departments work together? Are there any conflicts that might slow down productivity in the manufacturing area?"

Blockman shrugged. "There's always a certain amount of friction. Nothing serious. Sometimes our designs are difficult to manufacture, and manufacturing and engineering battle to compromise. It's a normal part of our business."

"You're right. It is." Simone edged a quick glance at him and then bluntly asked, "What about you and Vance? How do you two get along?"

Okay, now Blockman looked nervous and more than a little taken aback.

"That's an odd question."

"I'm just trying to establish if there are any potential interactions that could negatively impact the productivity of Vance's department. Remember, it's not your department I'm evaluating—it's his. I certainly mean no disrespect. So if you'd rather not answer…"

"I'll answer," he replied. "Vance and I respect each other as colleagues. We have for all the years we've worked at Nano. We don't socialize outside of the office, but we work well together. Does that address your concerns?"

"It does." *Testy*, Simone thought. *Very testy*. "And I appreciate your candor. Now let's get down to your department itself. How many products do you work on each year?"

Blockman relaxed. Definitely safer ground.

He speared a slice of pineapple and ate it before answering. "Three to ten. And sometimes we have revisions to existing products."

"Who else at Nano do you provide important services to?"

"Finance. We provide detailed cost estimates on new products, budgets for our research, product development, and support functions."

"Great." Simone typed that in. "How about people in companies outside of Nano?"

"I serve as Nano's representative to SIA," Blockman supplied, referring to the Semiconductor Industry Association. "That role takes me all over the world."

Time for a more personal angle—one that would be telling.

"So you must travel to Asia, with so many companies having facilities there."

Now Blockman looked distinctly uncomfortable. He took another belt of coffee and his response was terser than his others had been. "I'm a million-mile frequent flier many times over. Does that answer your question?"

Boy, did it ever.

"It does. And that's the last of them—except one." She smiled, simultaneously glancing down at his wrist. "Those are very handsome cufflinks. Just my boyfriend's taste. May I ask where you got them?"

"I'm not really sure." Blockman's response was stiff. "They were a gift."

Not a gift "from my wife," Simone noted, although her research had told her that he had one. Experience also told her that fashionable jewelry such as the cufflinks were usually purchased by a woman.

She went with her instincts.

"I'll be here at Nano for at least a week. Please ask your wife where she got them. I'd love to get a similar pair for my boyfriend."

An odd look crossed his face—discomfort and guilt—much as Simone had expected.

"I'll do that."

Simone pushed back her chair and rose. "Thank you for your time and forthcoming responses, Lawrence."

"You're welcome."

His coffee cup was drained, but most of his fruit was untouched. And he couldn't get out of the room fast enough.

Simone made a note to herself to text Terri as soon as she was out of Nano's eclipsing walls. It was imperative that Terri do an analysis of Blockman's travel and expense patterns for the past year.

And Simone knew just what she was asking Terri to look for.

An affair.

Simone didn't give a damn who Blockman was sleeping with.

Unless it was someone who worked at a Chinese tech company.

11

Vance paced around his hotel room, checking his watch every thirty seconds. Right before Aidan had left last night, he'd suggested that Vance take his time leaving for Nano this morning.

Gut instinct and experience made Aidan certain that enough time had passed. The kidnappers wouldn't wait another twenty-four hours. They'd contact Vance first thing today with their next set of demands. Aidan had assured Vance that he could still follow his routine of heading into the office for a half day. But sleeping in an extra hour—even for a VP—wasn't unusual during a family vacation.

Vance had argued that he shouldn't alter his routine even an iota, that he had his *red phone* at work for any incoming texts. Aidan had countered with the fact that, at this point, the kidnappers might choose another method of communication—a more tangible one like a package, and that the uber-secure NanoUSA would preclude any form of delivery. Vance had to be physically as well as electronically accessible.

Ultimately, Vance had gritted his teeth but agreed. To keep up the image that he was, in fact, making himself available to contact from the kidnappers—and that he was doing so without involving anyone else—he'd followed Aidan's advice and sent Susan out with Jessica and Andrew to have breakfast and hit the ski slopes.

Now he was losing his mind.

He was half-tempted to toss Aidan's advice to the wind and head out to the airport when a short, loud knock sounded at the hotel room door.

Vance strode over and yanked open the door.

The hall was deserted. But lying on the carpeted floor was a padded envelope with Vance's name typed on it.

Reflexively, he started down the hall to apprehend whomever had left it. Just as abruptly, he stopped. He was wasting time. Whoever had dropped off this package was a pro. He would have gotten in quickly and anonymously and left the same way. More importantly, if Vance stepped out of line and incited the kidnappers, the results could be fatal.

Amateurish reactions were bullshit. Lauren's life was all that mattered.

After retracing his steps, Vance shut his hotel room door and, with shaking hands, tore open the package.

Inside was a printed page, along with an empty, crumpled cross-body handbag and a Ziploc containing a lock of soft, wavy brown hair.

Lauren's handbag. Lauren's hair.

Tears gathered in Vance's eyes as he turned his attention to the letter.

Time for a show of faith, the words read. *We want a sample of the new technology—specifically a drawing showing one page of the specifications. Should you hesitate, please inspect the enclosed personal items that we've taken from your daughter so far. She has much left to be taken—including her well-being and her life. Get the data to us via a Tor browser. Type the following link in the address bar:* https://

mwt4wkynpe3f82ab.onion *and log in using the code name* baba. *You will then be able to send messages and files to a secure drop box that we will be monitoring regularly. Use a public Wi-Fi hotspot. We will be watching every move you make. We expect the file by the end of the business day today and we will acknowledge receipt in a message you'll find by logging in. Your daughter has four days left...*

Vance's hand was shaking so badly that he could barely hold the page, much less absorb the details of what he was reading. Sweat dripped down his spine. Almost in a daze, he put all the items back in the envelope, picked up his secure cell phone, and pressed Aidan's number.

"Yes?" Aidan's voice was already on high alert.

"You were right—it came," Vance heard himself say. "A package from the kidnappers." He proceeded to tell Aidan what the contents of the envelope were and then read him the note.

"This is nothing unexpected, Vance." Aidan sounded calm, reassuring. "What I need you to do is to get yourself to the Starbucks on Northstar Drive. It's about ten minutes away. You'll respond to them from your laptop. You'll be using Starbucks' public Wi-Fi, and I'll talk you through the Tor browser process as soon as you're settled and ready."

"Anonymity. Right." Vance felt like he was drowning. "The drawing—they expect this to happen instantly."

"You'll buy us a day. They'll accept that condition, since they're aware of the high level of security at Nano."

Vance swallowed, asking the same question he'd asked Aidan a dozen times already. "What I'm demanding of them in return—the daily video communications with Lauren—what if they say no? Worse, what if they take it out on her?"

"They won't. Just take me at my word."

"You still haven't told me how we're going to get a copy of the specifications out of Nano and into the kidnappers' hands."

"It's being handled. We'll have the tool we need in place and ready to implement within hours. It will be delivered to me along with a specialized computer I'll need you to use in your talks with Lauren."

Vance's panic was inciting a barrage of questions. "I thought this whole Deep Web thing makes it impossible to trace?"

"In most situations, that's true. But the special computer we're providing you with is enhanced in ways that will allow us to monitor your activity and also penetrate some of the anonymous layers of the Deep Web without raising red flags. In short, we have the tools and skills of the NSA. The kidnappers have no clue who they're dealing with."

"How—"

"We're losing precious time." Aidan cut off Vance's next question. "Explanations on how you're going to accomplish what they're asking can wait until I fly up to Tahoe tonight. Right now we need to worry about contacting the kidnappers and orchestrating your first video-conference with Lauren. So grab a taxi and get to Starbucks. Call me when you're in front of a computer."

* * *

Aidan disconnected the call and pressed Terri's number.

"Yes."

"It's me," Aidan replied.

"One sec." She said a muffled "Make it ten" into what was obviously another phone call and then ended it. "Sorry," she said to Aidan.

"Was that Ryan?"

"He's on his way here with his gizmo."

"Good." Aidan gave Terri a three-sentence update on where things stood at his end. "Did the two of you program the computer?"

"It's done," she replied. "Ryan did most of the work. He really is quite brilliant. He prepared the laptop specifically for Vance's needs. He started with a standard HP laptop and then replaced the entire operating system with a highly secure and customized version of Linux.

The user—in this case Vance—will be presented with a Windows login, but behind the scenes, every keystroke will be logged and forwarded to me. All audio and video signals will be mirrored and streamed to the Zermatt servers."

"So for all intents and purposes our team will be watching every-thing Vance does with that laptop in real time. He can concentrate on his communications with the kidnappers and we can pick up on any pertinent data he might miss. We'll get all content, body language, visual surroundings, nearby voices—the works. If there are any clues to lead us to Lauren, we'll get them."

"Precisely. Our courier service will be arriving here right on Ryan's heels. I'll have everything airborne within two hours—including a few other electronic items for you that might come in handy at some point."

Aidan made a quick mental calculation. "That means the package will arrive here after we've held our team videoconference, I'm guessing around midnight. Have it delivered to my room at the Tahoe Ritz-Carlton. I'll be there, tutoring Vance and keeping all the Penningtons in check. I'll break for the team meeting. Once the package arrives, I'll talk to Vance alone—no wife, no kids. I'll give him a bare-bones explanation of the computer. Immediately thereafter, I'll hop on our plane and get back to the Four Seasons so I can pass along the ring to Simone."

"Simone? But it's a man's ring. I thought that Vance..."

"Change in plans. Just talked to him—Vance is too much of a nervous wreck for me to trust him to successfully pull this off, espe-cially since all eyes are on him. He briefed Simone on where she'll find what she needs, but she'll be the one taking those photos. I'm not too thrilled about putting her in that position, but she'll come through for us." A pause. "As soon as I'm in Simone's room, I'll want an immediate videoconference with Ryan. Simone and I will both require a verbal instruction manual from him on the usage of the ring so that she can get those photos. Tell Ryan to be available."

"Already taken care of," Terri replied. "Ryan will be accessible all night. He knows what's expected of him." A pause. "As I said, he's really good, Aidan. Even I'm impressed. And he was amazed by my Wheel of Fortune app. It's gratifying to meet someone as young and savvy as Ryan—and someone who actually calls this work *fun*. I might have been dubious at first, but you were right to bring him on board. He's a strong asset."

Aidan bit back a smile. No surprise that Ryan's exuberance over Terri's app had won him major Brownie points. "I know he is. And I'm glad he's following your lead, since Ryan tends to like running the show." A quick glance at his watch. "Are we good? Because Vance should be calling me back any minute."

"We're good."

Starbucks
Northstar Drive, Lake Tahoe
27 February
Tuesday, 8:55 a.m. local time

Vance was a complete wreck when he called Aidan back. Discussing a procedure like this and actually carrying it out—with your child's life on the line—were two different things entirely.

"I hope you got yourself something to drink," Aidan began, hearing the familiar Starbucks sounds of complex beverages being ordered and customers arguing over who was first in the queue. "You have to look like everyone else. The Starbucks manager won't take kindly to freeloading their Wi-Fi with no purchase made. Not during prime breakfast hours."

"I got decaf," Vance replied. "I despise the stuff, but I don't need caffeine to rev me up even more."

"Smart." Aidan didn't waste time with small talk. He quickly and succinctly talked Vance through getting to where he needed to be using the Tor browser. Vance followed his instructions to a tee, which made the process go as painlessly as possible.

"Okay, I'm looking at a blinking cursor," Vance reported, having logged in and used his requisite password. "Why *baba*?"

"It's the phonetic translation for the Albanian word for father. The powers-that-be probably found it amusing."

"Well, I'm not amused. Nor do I know how to phrase this. Based on the note I received, I'm assuming these people speak English."

"Fluently. Despite the Albanian password, the communication you received, as well as all future communications, will be sent by whoever intends to steal Nano's technology, most likely the Chinese. The Albanians are just their muscle. So while the kidnappers' English may be broken, the head honchos will speak perfect English. No worries there."

"Right. No worries." Vance sucked in his breath. "Tell me what to say—verbatim."

Aidan dictated a response in succinct, straightforward terms—explaining the need for an extra day to get the drawing and to find a way to penetrate NanoUSA's ironclad walls to send it. The only time Aidan added some emotion was when, as Vance, he spoke of the need to see and hear his daughter daily, to ensure himself that she was indeed alive and well.

"That's it?" Vance asked.

"That's it."

"How long will it be before I hear from them?"

"Given their sense of urgency, I'd hang around Starbucks. You should hear back within an hour. Now read our response back to me." Aidan listened, nodding as he did. "Good. Post it."

"God help me," Vance murmured and pressed the Enter key.

* * *

The reply came forty-five minutes later, and Vance called Aidan back immediately.

"They agreed to our terms." He sounded shell-shocked.

"Read me their response," Aidan instructed.

Vance cleared his throat, and Aidan could hear him take a long gulp of his coffee. "We recognize your dilemma," he read. "You have until noon tomorrow, your time zone, to deliver the file. We assume you value your daughter's life enough to meet that demand. Therefore, your request has been approved and is being arranged. Return to your current location daily, beginning tomorrow morning, at seven ten a.m. Log in. We will be publishing a random Cyph link and you will have ten minutes to access it. You will be able to see and talk with Lauren. Five minutes per day. She will be watched at all times. If anything inflammatory is said, she'll be killed before your eyes."

Vance's voice broke on that last sentence.

"This is good news, Vance," Aidan told him. "They're willing to negotiate. They want that technology badly. They're *not* going to hurt Lauren—not when that would eliminate their only bargaining chip. You're going to talk to her and see her tomorrow morning. That gives us tonight to choreograph the entire conversation from your end and to reiterate the do's and don'ts that you'll adhere to. The computer you'll be using and the tool that's needed to get them the photo of that drawing should be arriving at the hotel around midnight, delivered to my hotel room. I'll explain the technical aspects of the computer to you and then head back to Silicon Valley to meet with Simone and pass the tool along to her. With the proper guidance from you, she'll be accessing and sending them what they want well before the noon deadline."

"And what do I do until then?" Vance asked.

"Exactly what you've been doing. Leave for Nano now. Check in with Simone. She's conducting interviews of your staff, supposedly to better your department. Have a quick catch-up meeting with Robert Maxwell. Get updates from Ethan."

"Business as usual? I'm not sure I can do this anymore."

"Yes you can. For Lauren. Now head out. You'll be back for lunch. Spend the afternoon with your family—calmly and in vacation mode—on the slopes or in front of a fire. I'll be flying to Tahoe tonight, probably by eight. I have a ten o'clock videoconference with my team, so I'll have to interrupt for that. You and I will have ample time to educate and orchestrate."

Silicon Valley, CA
27 February
Tuesday, 10:05 a.m. local time

Jia li Sung picked up her burner phone and punched in the country code eight-six, followed by the memorized number.

Several rings later, a man's voice answered in Mandarin. "Xu."

"I'm calling on behalf of my colleague," she replied, also in Mandarin. "I was told to inform you that waiting is no longer an option. Several months ago, when we all met in California, it was explained to you that we have a narrow window of time in which to accomplish our goal. That window is coming to an end and you have nothing to show for your efforts. My colleague is beginning to think that you are the wrong partner for this venture."

She paused, listening to the livid reply, punctuated by some unpleasant swearing.

"There is no reason to use that kind of language," she responded calmly. She'd been warned to expect this reaction. "Results are what we require here, not excuses or expletives."

The CEO at the other end of the phone sucked in his breath, clearly striving for calm. His reply, when it came, was terse. "Tell your colleague that in a week this will be done. Further, a sample of the data you're waiting for will be transmitted to you within two days—as a show of good faith."

"That's good news," Jia li said. "I will relay that information. But I was asked to remind you that your company was selected for this opportunity because of your resources and reputation. You are known as a man of your word and a force to be reckoned with. However, my colleague is a person of similar abilities and character. If you do not deliver on your part of the deal, your failure to do so will be made well known."

Her words were greeted by silence. Jia li could read the man's mind. The significance of a threat to be dishonored would be unthinkable.

"I will meet the deadline I just described," he said at last. "One week. You will have all you require."

"That would be wise. I'll pass your promise along."

Jia li disconnected the phone with a smile on her face.

Grand Californian Hotel and Spa
Disneyland, Anaheim, CA
27 February
Tuesday, 10:10 a.m. local time

Emma had just carried in the enormous stuffed Belle that she'd won for Abby in Mickey's Toontown when her cell phone rang. She glanced down, saw the private number Aidan had given her—along with instructions to always answer in private, out of Abby's keen earshot—and gestured to Joyce, silently asking her to take over with their exuberant charge.

Joyce nodded, managing to coax Abby to sit beside her on the sofa so they could look at the Disney map and plan out the next part of their day.

Scooting into her and Abby's bedroom suite, Emma answered her still trilling phone.

"Hello?" Again, no mention of names. That was an additional instruction on Aidan's part.

"Hello back." Aidan's tone was filled with dry humor. "You sound like you just lost a boxing match. I wonder why."

"Not *why*," Emma corrected. "*Who*. I have a knockout challenger." She smiled. "But she's worth it. It's so cool to be visiting Disneyland for the first time with Abby. I feel like I'm four again—except for my aching body. That needs some comedown time. I don't think that's on the menu though. We just got back to the suite with this morning's stash, and she's already planning out our next batch of rides and where we'll be eating." A pause as she listened to the background noises at Aidan's end. "You're at an airport. I won't keep you. I'll go get Abby."

"No, don't," Aidan replied quickly. "I don't even want her to know it's me on the phone. And you will be getting that comedown time. I should be there in an hour and a half. Abby's mine for the afternoon. We'll hit Fantasyland and do It's a Small World ride and the King Arthur Carrousel. After that, we have reservations at two o'clock for the Lunch with Ariel and Disney Princesses."

"Get out." Emma was duly impressed. "That character lunch is booked for six months or more."

"I'm resourceful. Especially since I know how much my little princess loves Disney princesses. Keep Abby at the hotel. Go to the Redwood Pool—that's where the Mickey Mouse kiddie pool is. That should keep her busy for a while."

"You're kidding." Emma stared at the phone, stupefied by Aidan's naivety. "She's been at that pool four times already and all she wants is to go to the big pool and ride the ninety-foot water slide."

"The... what?" Aidan sounded ill. "You didn't let her—"

"Of course not. But that's not going to stop her from asking. I think I'll convince her to eat a little something—maybe a few Mickey Mouse pancakes, and then tell her that since her tummy is full all she can do is wade in the kiddie pool. She won't like it, but once she sees her daddy, all will be forgotten and forgiven."

"Thanks, Emma."

"Thank you right back. I'll have four hours to work on my tan and sleep at the poolside. Joyce will probably go crash in the suite. We'll both be refreshed and ready to go by the time you take off."

"Who are you talking to, Emma?" Abby's voice emanated from the other room. "Is that Daddy?"

"Nope, just a friend of mine," Emma called back. "I'm hanging up now." She turned her mouth back to the receiver. "Bye, boss," she hissed.

"Hang in there, champ. Reinforcements are on the way."

12

Simone was escorted through glass doors and into Robert Maxwell's office suite by a twenty-something California girl who introduced herself as Jen and whose über-tanned skin announced that she spent long hours at a tanning salon. This was Silicon Valley, not LA. That meant a cool, often rainy February. Not exactly beach weather. So the tan was fake. The cordial treatment was real. Actually, her attitude was more than merely cordial, Simone noted. She was exuberant. And while the cordiality was directed at Simone, the exuberance smacked of something that had little to do with Jen's role at Nano. Simone recognized the signs. A sparkle in her eyes, a lilt to her step, not to mention the vase of fresh flowers on her desk—clearly Jen was in the throes of a new relationship.

With a glowing Jen leading the way, Simone shifted her focus, using this opportunity to survey the extensive work space surrounding Robert Maxwell's closed office door.

There was a teak sitting area that looked more like a living room, a boardroom that was currently empty but that could easily seat thirty, and an elaborate food preparation area designed to serve elegant cuisine to powerful people.

At the rear of the suite, there was one other closed-door inner sanctum—smaller, but stationed right beside Maxwell's—with a gold name plate that said *Zoe Pearson* on it.

The hierarchy here was crystal clear.

Jen knocked on Robert Maxwell's door.

"Come in," a strong voice responded.

Jen opened the door halfway and gave her boss a bright smile. "Ms. Martin is here to see you."

"Thanks, Jen. Send her in."

Robert Maxwell rose from behind his circular chrome and glass desk, walking around to shake Simone's hand. He was tall and broad-shouldered, a good-looking man who clearly worked out and paid attention to his appearance, as was evidenced by his neatly trimmed salt-and-pepper beard, his perfectly creased slacks—sans the jacket and tie, which were folded on the back of his executive desk chair—and his trim physique. He also had a ready handshake. But his demeanor and appearance belied the intensity that ran underneath. Maxwell had built this company with toughness and grit in a highly competitive industry. He was not to be trifled with.

Simone had done her homework and thoroughly researched Robert Maxwell. Professionally, he was highly respected throughout the industry. He was a frequent speaker at Stanford University, teaching and encouraging MBA students who had aspirations of working in the technology sector. He attended conferences and seminars worldwide to keep up with his ever-evolving world. And he worked tirelessly at his job, never asking more of his employees than he did of himself.

Personally, he was an avid golfer. He had a wide range of hobbies and interests, including bicycling, as was evidenced by the bicycle helmet sitting on the credenza behind his desk. And he had a family who was significant in his life.

All excellent motivations for a healthy sixty-three-year-old man to release groundbreaking cutting-edge technology and then move on to the next stage of his life. That, however, didn't mean he planned to totally bow out of Nano, not after all these years. The interviews of him that Simone had read reflected his fierce commitment to his company, as well as his total confidence in his staff—a staff he had vetted well and hired because they were the best. He demanded loyalty and gave equal amounts in return. And it wasn't BS. Simone could attest to that fact after spending half a day within these walls. Despite the more informal business attire and less rigid behavior she'd encountered—not a surprise, given that this was California and not New York City—NanoUSA had a small, tight-knit company feel—atypical for a high-powered corporation.

A culture such as that could only originate from its leader.

Simone knew in her gut that the idea of a mole would be unthinkable to Maxwell. Finding the culprit would be hard enough, but proving his or her guilt to Maxwell and then dealing with his inevitable sense of betrayal… Simone wasn't looking forward to that part of her job.

"Good to meet you, Ms. Martin," Maxwell was saying, his gaze flickering quickly over her. "Vance has spoken very highly of you."

"As he has of you." Simone almost laughed at the typical male once-over she'd just received. Why was it that men never realized a woman knew when she was being physically assessed?

Taking advantage of Maxwell's obvious approval of what he saw, she added, "Please call me Simone."

"Only if you call me Robert." He smiled, a charming and enveloping smile rather than a practiced one. It made him look years younger than sixty-three. Despite his awareness of an attractive woman, he wore his wedding band, and his enormous office was filled with family photos—his wife, his kids, and his two granddaughters, who looked to be about two years old and six months respectively.

"What can I get you?" he asked. "Coffee, tea, water?"

"Water would be wonderful, thank you," Simone replied. "I've been chatting with your staff for over four hours now and had more cups of coffee than I can count. Any more and I won't sleep for a week."

"I hear you." Robert strode over to a built-in fridge and pulled out two bottles of water. "Here you go." He handed one to Simone and then gestured at one of the two ivory-colored leather sofas that were situated adjacently in one corner of the office. "Please. Have a seat."

Simone sank down into the grained leather. She opened her bottled water and took a healthy swallow before settling herself, crossing one leg over the other. She opened her Louis Vuitton document holder and prepared to take notes as Robert took a seat on the other sofa.

"I hope my staff has been accommodating," he said with the certainty of a CEO who knew the answer would be yes.

"They most certainly have. They're an exceptional group. Very upbeat. Very excited about all the new developments happening at Nano."

"So how's the process going?"

"Exactly as I expected. I've only met with a handful of people, but preliminarily it seems as if there are some disconnects in opportunities to streamline and refocus efforts. I'll have a better-defined picture in a few days. Once I'm finished, Vance will have a clear action plan to get his organization ready for functioning without him when he succeeds you."

Robert's brows rose. "That's a pretty bold statement. No comment."

"Your deflection is all I needed to hear."

"I don't deal in rumors. Who's been spreading them?"

"No one. This is my interpretation of the emerging fact pattern."

Simone had rehearsed that part well. With Robert aware that she'd deduced the truth, he'd be less apt to be suspicious of her subsequent questions or the avenues she was pursuing.

"I see that McKinsey chooses its people wisely." That much Robert acknowledged. "I hope the results warrant the exorbitant fee we're paying you."

"Compliment accepted. I'll let my work speak for itself. And speaking of work, I requested this time with you so I could ask you a few questions that only you can answer."

Robert inclined his head and waited.

"Let's talk about the politics of your direct reports and how succession planning influences that. I know you're reticent to discuss change at the helm of the company, so let's approach this as a hypothetical and discuss succession plans that I'm sure are in place here, in the event that they're needed. Should you choose to retire, who in the company is in line to succeed you? Would the board prefer to appoint your successor from within the company or go outside? And since there'd only be one winner in this Tour de France, how would each one of the people on your list respond to losing?"

Robert didn't look happy. "Why are we talking about succession planning when the reason for your consulting engagement is to improve the functioning of the manufacturing department?"

"Sometimes dysfunction is intentional and orchestrated at the request of other department leaders. If someone wanted to undermine Vance and his department, they might use their department and its resources to make the manufacturing team seem less competent and capable."

"Okay." Robert eased up a bit, since he was unable to argue with Simone's logic. "I'll answer your hypothetical questions. *Assuming* I was considering stepping down as CEO, let's start with Vance, your odds-on favorite to win the race. He's been with me since the beginning. This company wouldn't be where it is today without him. I think he would be an excellent choice."

"And if the board disagreed with you, how would he respond?"

"That's a tough question," Robert said, stroking his beard pensively. "I think any candidate on the list would be hugely disappointed. As soon as word got out, the candidates not selected for the position would immediately be solicited by executive recruiters and competitors looking to upgrade their talent pool. As to whether or not my executives would jump ship would depend on how enticing those offers were. If one were offered the CEO slot at a good company, I wouldn't blame them for taking it. If this was a future promise, that's a more difficult call."

Simone nodded. "Whether it was Vance or someone else, would the board prefer to pick someone internally?"

"In this case, yes. The future of Nano is its technology, and having an intimate knowledge of it and its potential is critical. If the names on the successor list were weak, that might be less important. But all of my people are strong, capable, and worthy. So, yes, I believe they would choose an internal candidate."

"Can you tell me who those candidates might be—other than Vance, of course?"

"Sure." Robert shrugged. "It's hardly a secret as to who my top reports are. Lawrence Blockman, my VP Engineering, June Morris, my CFO, and Aaron Malcolm, my VP Sales."

Excellent. All people she'd spoken with—and formed opinions about—this morning.

"One last question and I'll be on my way," Simone said. "If Vance were to be your successor, who would be his?"

Robert sucked in a breath. "I'm very uncomfortable with this treason route you're taking."

"Treason is a very strong word. I'd call it politicking. And I understand your discomfort. But my tactics are rooted in necessity, not suspicion."

"Then I suggest you run that question by Vance, not me. It's his department and his choice. I'm just the final say."

Nodding, Simone rose. "I appreciate your time. If it's acceptable to you, I'd like to meet with both you and Vance in a few days once I've completed my interviews and had the chance to organize my proposal."

"I'd expect nothing less."

"Which of your employees handles your calendar? I'll set up an appointment on my way out."

"Talk to Jen. She'll be able to schedule it. But double-check it with Zoe when you interview her today. If there's a meeting I've forgotten about, she'll be aware of it since she's probably attending."

Simone silently noted that Robert was aware of her interviewing schedule. She hadn't mentioned that she'd be talking to Zoe later today.

"Do Zoe's professional responsibilities extend beyond being your personal assistant?" she asked instead. "Or does she attend meetings for note-taking purposes?"

Robert shook his head. "I'm working on coming up with a new title for Zoe. She's been with Nano for fifteen years and managed to earn an MBA despite the long hours she works here. She's sharp and she's smart, more of a junior executive—as well as my right arm—than anything else. I frequently elicit her input, so, yes, she does attend meetings for reasons other than note-taking. On the flip side, I doubt I could find the elevator without her."

"She sounds indispensable."

"She is."

"I'll keep that in mind," Simone said with a smile.

Her afternoon interview with Zoe Pearson could turn out to be more interesting than expected.

Sava River Walk, Zagreb, Croatia
27 February
Tuesday, 9:30 p.m. local time

The sky was overcast and the air was chilly, with snowflakes darting about and a fine sheen of ice shimmering on the bare trees that lined the Old Town side of the Sava.

Marc and Philip shook hands with Chief Police Inspector Danijel Horvat and joined him on a stroll in their prearranged location along the river walk. The Sava itself was unfrozen, smooth and serene, glistening in the darkness, and the area they were walking on was dark and shadowed, its benches deserted. Across the Sava they could see the newer side of Zagreb, lights illuminating the apartment buildings where many, including Danijel, lived.

It was clear why he'd chosen this spot for their meeting, especially given the sensitive information about to be discussed.

"Thank you for setting this up on such short notice," Marc began. "Not that my brother gave you much choice, I'm guessing."

A small smile played on Danijel's lips. He was a tall man, with Mediterranean coloring, dark brown hair, and Slavic features.

"Your brother is persuasive, yes," he replied. "But he's also one of the finest men I know. You resemble him. Being that he sent you here, I suspect that resemblance goes far deeper than the physical to the character beneath."

"I like to think so."

Danijel turned toward Philip. "And your dossier speaks for itself. As does your history with Aidan. I'll help you both in any way I can."

He cleared his throat. "I'm sure Aidan has filled you in on the fact that I'm head of the General Police Directorate's Organized Crime Division, or PNUSKOK, as it's called here in Croatia, as well as the fact that I worked on an Organized Crime Task Force with Europol. I have a wide range of contacts, both national and international—any of whom I have and will continue to reach out to with the utmost discretion, given the delicacy of your investigation."

"You've already put out feelers?"

"The moment I hung up the phone with Aidan, yes. I'm waiting to hear back."

"Just so we know, how much did Aidan tell you?" Marc asked bluntly.

Danijel looked unsurprised by the question. "He made it quite clear that my involvement is on a need-to-know basis. Therefore, I'm only privy to the international aspects of your investigation. I accept that. But if you want my help, you must accept that you're going to have to be as forthcoming with me as possible, as well as open to my taking the lead in any face-to-face interviews and questioning with confidential informants that might arise. I'm a native. You're foreigners. It becomes an issue of trust. In addition, while English is now taught as a second language in my country, that was not the case years ago. Few residents over the age of fifty can speak it. Even now, German, Italian, or Russian are often the second languages taught rather than English. Some regions teach no second language. So my translation skills will also be essential."

"We understand." Marc shoved his hands into the pockets of his leather jacket. "But in the interest of full disclosure, you should know that we brought two Croatian interpreters with us. Obviously, they won't be at the meetings you set up, but one of the two will be listening from the car and translating into our ears while you conduct the interviews. That will minimize how detailed you need to be in your back-and-forth explanations between your informants and us and allow you to concentrate on the nuances of the arrangements."

"I see." Danijel processed that and then nodded. "I can live with that. What about your other interpreter—what will be her role?"

Philip cleared his throat, thinking that while Derica was handling the CI meetings, Ellie could be used for less legitimate purposes—such as translating Albanian emails or texts that the team intercepted through whatever means they deemed necessary. "I think that's part of our process you'd prefer not to know."

"Very well." Danijel dropped the subject. "You just spoke of yourselves in the plural. Understand that it will be only one of you gentlemen who'll be accompanying me to each meeting. You can switch off if you like. That's your choice. The other can remain in the car with your interpreter. Informants either shut down or bolt when they're approached by more than one unknown quantity. They know me. They don't know you. So it's one at a time."

"Fine. When it comes to the CIs, you're in charge," Marc agreed, knowing he spoke for Philip, as well. Danijel had the expertise, skills, and contacts that were necessary to pull this off.

"Good. Then I'll have the necessary conversations with my CIs and we can move forward."

"As I'm sure Aidan told you, the young woman we're searching for has only a few days left before she's killed," Philip stated flatly as he trudged along, stones crunching beneath his feet. "The clock is ticking. We must fast-track this, through any means necessary."

"Yes, Aidan made that clear."

"Just so you know, we drove directly from Munich, where the victim was kidnapped, to Zagreb, where our computer data indicated was the probable refueling location before the kidnappers transferred the victim to her current place of confinement. Once we arrived in your city, we located a Lukoil station off the A2 whose owner remembered the Mercedes van we identified as the escape vehicle. So we confirmed that the subjects travelled through Zagreb. Now we need to figure out where the victim is currently being held."

"It's doubtful the kidnappers would choose an urban location for their place of confinement," Danijel said. "My suspicions are that we're looking into more remote districts."

"That's where we need your guidance," Philip responded. "Where would they go to remain undetected? And what specific Albanian organized crime groups would you narrow this operation down to? Is there one that's more apt to handle kidnappings?"

"That last question will send you down a blind alley." Danijel waved his hand dismissively. "Albanian crime groups don't restrict themselves to one line of work, or to one country. Drug, arms, and human trafficking—not to mention the trafficking of human organs—they don't care what their assignment is or who they work for as long as they get paid. They're mercenary and they're brutally violent. They're also widespread. They operate everywhere from the Balkans to England and the Netherlands."

"Really?" Marc's brows rose. "That's more expansive than I realized."

"Some of that branching out is recent, particularly in the Netherlands," Danijel replied. "As to the Albanian crime groups operating here in Croatia, those are greatly diminished after a large number of arrests that have taken place over the past several years. That doesn't mean they don't still exist. With regard to the groups that continue to operate in my country, I obviously have knowledge of their activities. But given we need particular specifics from an insider's point of view, I'm waiting to hear back from my *less legitimate* sources." His brows rose quizzically, seeking confirmation. "Aidan mentioned that you would be bringing cash to help them talk more freely."

Marc nodded. "The money is in American dollars. We couldn't risk raising red flags by converting large sums of money into Croatian kuna. Given your sources, we didn't think that would be a problem."

"It won't be."

"How much cash do you think will be needed?"

"Ten thousand is optimal, just to be on the safe side. A thousand American dollars is equivalent to over six thousand Croatian kuna. That will buy you a great deal of information—from one informant. There are several I have in mind, all of whom I need to meet with face-to-face—and alone—before I can set anything up with you. What I'm hoping is that those informants will lead to other informants until you close in on where this young woman is being held. Thus, the ten thousand dollars."

Marc unzipped the inside pocket of his jacket and pulled out two of the four rubber-banded packets of hundred dollar bills he was carrying. There were five thousand dollars in each. "Do you need this now?"

"No." Danijel gave an adamant shake of his head, shoving his hands deeper into his pockets as if to reinforce the adamancy of his reply. "You'll pay them directly. Any bribe money that's exchanged will not pass through my hands."

Marc nodded. "Understood."

"Good." Danijel came to an abrupt halt. "Then if we're all on the same page, I'll go follow up on my feelers so I can get things moving tonight. If I'm successful, I'll be setting up our first meeting for tomorrow morning. Once I have everything arranged, I'll call."

13

Ethan Gallagher walked through the meeting room door spot on time, a warm and congenial smile on his face. As Simone had expected, he looked just like his photo, since he clearly wasn't the pretentious, pose-for-the-camera type. Light brown hair and eyes, cool, trendy glasses, a navy sports coat—probably donned in honor of this meeting—khaki slacks, a white collared shirt, and boat shoes. Business casual at its best.

Simone rose from behind the table, primed to meet Vance's PA. She'd done her research. Ethan was twenty-eight years old, with all the traits of a millennial. Super tech savvy, intent on getting ahead, and striving for—and achieving—a tight relationship with Vance, for starters. He'd graduated from Berkeley with a degree in Information Technology Management, and Simone had no doubt that he had aspirations of moving up at Nano, maybe into the role of associate, either in the manufacturing or another department—but not before acquiring and capitalizing on the coveted role of PA to the new CEO at Nano. If he was smart, and Simone was quite sure that he was, he'd remain in his new position long enough to highlight it on his resume. And there wasn't a doubt in her mind that Ethan knew of Robert Maxwell's upcoming plans for Vance. If Vance knew, then Ethan knew.

Ethan also lived an above-his-means lifestyle—something Simone intended to address. It could be that he just racked up huge credit card bills. On the other hand, it could be that he was getting paid by another, more lucrative employer.

"Hi, Ethan. I'm Simone." She went straight for the casual, breaking down any walls Ethan might have assumed would be erected.

His brows rose in pleased surprise as he shook her hand. "It's a pleasure to meet you, Simone." He glanced down at her half-empty cup of coffee, simultaneously putting down his tan leather messenger bag. Clearly, he'd come prepared in case he was asked to pull up information on his laptop or iPad. "Can I get you a refill? I need a cup myself."

"That would be great." Simone handed him her cup, waiting to fully assess his demeanor when his attention was diverted at the coffee station.

He wasn't nervous. In fact, there was a self-assurance about him that spoke volumes. He knew his job was secure and that nothing but blue skies lay ahead. That could fare well for Simone; the more comfortable in his own skin Ethan was, the more likely he was to reveal something he didn't even realize he was revealing.

He brought over their coffee cups, handed Simone hers, and waited until she'd reseated herself before he pulled back the adjacent chair and sat down. A guy who'd been educated in the art of respect. Kudos to his parents.

"All set." He took the bull by the horns. "Anything I can do to help Vance and to make our department function more efficiently, I'm in."

Simone hid her smile behind the rim of her coffee cup. Ethan might be polished, but he was also a young man with a mission, not to mention a wealth of genuine enthusiasm.

"I appreciate that," she said. "Because from what Vance tells me, you're his right hand."

"I like to hope so."

"That means that you have a unique view of your boss and how he interacts with everyone in his world." Simone waved at his messenger bag. "You won't need that. My questions aren't data-related, they're personal instinct and knowledge related."

"Okay." Ethan propped his elbows on the table and waited.

"Let's start with: What does Vance's typical day look like? Where do you see him concentrating his energies? And in what areas do you see his major time challenges?"

Ethan proceeded to give her an accounting that was in sync with what Vance had told her, save the actual details of meetings and emails Ethan wasn't privy to. No hesitation. No faltering. No visible artifice whatsoever. And he seemed to be fiercely loyal to Vance.

Seemed to be being the operative phrase. How far would that loyalty run if he were promised a huge payout for the right information?

Simone took notes, even though they were unnecessary. But it was crucial that all her interviewees believed she was factoring in their input in order to better the manufacturing department.

"Who does Vance interact with most, both inside and outside the department?" she asked.

For the first time, a flicker of unease crossed Ethan's face. Clearly, Simone had touched a nerve. She remained silent, knowing that was the best way to increase Ethan's anxiety and to force him to start talking. And hopefully what he said would be the truth.

"Vance and Robert Maxwell work closely together." Ethan's wheels were spinning rapidly as he spoke—Simone could read his body language loud and clear. "And with the upcoming release of our game-changing technology, they've been in constant meetings."

An evasion tactic—one Simone wasn't about to let slide.

"Does Robert meet more frequently with Vance than with his other VPs?"

"I really can't speak to that," Ethan replied. "I'm only clued in to the other departments as they relate to ours."

"Then let's talk about the other departments—and their VPs," Simone said. "I had the chance to speak with all of them this morning. They're all smart and capable. Wouldn't you agree?"

"Of course." Ethan nodded vigorously.

Simone didn't give him time to feel comfortable. "Where do you perceive there to be conflicts between Vance and the other VPs?"

That one threw Ethan for a loop. He took a long belt of his coffee, then set down the cup with a bit of an unsteady hand. He licked his lips a few times, looking like a trapped rat who wasn't sure which direction to run in.

"Is that an uncomfortable question?" Simone asked bluntly. "Because if there's bad blood between high-level executives, I need to know that. It can affect the functioning of a department."

Ethan nodded again, this time with the resignation of someone who knew he couldn't extricate himself without providing information that could potentially get him in trouble.

"*Conflict* is a strong word," he hedged. "But there are often raised voices when Vance and Lawrence Blockman have their meetings."

"Has it been more frequent of late?"

"Yes."

"Do you think it's the nature of their job responsibilities or do you think it's personal?" Simone asked.

"Can I speak off the record?"

Simone had a pretty good idea what confidential information Ethan was about to disclose. And since none of it was news to her, it was easy to promise Ethan what he wanted.

She put down her iPad. "Very well. Go ahead."

With a deep breath, Ethan said, "There are rumors that, after the big technology release, Robert Maxwell is going to retire. Word has it that Vance has the inside track for his job. I believe it to be true, although Vance hasn't mentioned a word of it to me. Based upon the fact that Lawrence Blockman is not only high-performing but has been with Nano almost as long as Vance has, my guess is that he's the other major contender."

"And you think that fact is causing heightened tension between the two men."

"I do. I get the sense that Lawrence knows Vance is the favored child, and he resents it. This is just gut feel on my part—along with some information from trusted sources. But you asked, so I'm answering—off the record," he reiterated.

"Off the record," Simone echoed. She pressed a thoughtful finger to her lips. "What about June Morris and Aaron Malcolm? They might not have Vance's and Lawrence's tenure here, but I'd think that the CFO and VP Sales would also be prime contenders."

"Aaron loves his job. I don't think he has any aspirations of leaving sales and taking on the enormous responsibility of running Nano. As for June, I don't know. I don't interact with her much. When it comes to finance, I work with her direct reports. Vance deals with her directly."

"So there could be resentment there, as well," Simone pointed out.

"I have no idea."

A terse answer, she noted. And an interesting one. Nano was a tight corporate family. Ethan had provided a good read of both Blockman and Malcolm. And yet he had zero read on June Morris? That was odd. Simone had found June to be nervous and tightly wired, something she was sure Ethan would mention. Yet he said nothing.

Simone tucked away that factoid to probe later.

"Ethan, I see from your profile that you are fluent in Mandarin. That's fascinating. Tell me more about it."

"I always had a knack with languages—foreign and computer," Ethan replied. "At Berkeley, I decided to try my hand at Chinese. What I didn't know is that I'd be the only nonnative speaker in the class. The rest of them must have taken the class for an easy A to boost their GPAs. As for me, I worked unbelievably hard for a B. But I loved it and continued for two years." A grin. "I guess I was a glutton for punishment."

Simone smiled back. "And have you ever traveled to China to put that linguistic skill to good use?"

"Not yet," Ethan said ruefully. "It's on my bucket list."

"You're a little young for a bucket list," Simone said with a chuckle.

Ethan nodded, his grin widening. "Okay then, my want-to-do list. As soon as I save up enough money and vacation time."

Simone chewed that one over. Vacation time? Maybe. Money? Now *that* was an interesting topic. Ethan made a low six-figure salary. Very nice. But not enough to pay for his choice of "toys," particularly his lavish car. The Porsche 911 Turbo S Cabriolet had a ticket price of well over two hundred thousand dollars. Definitely out of Ethan's price range—unless he was up to his neck in debt or getting income from an outside source.

"I'm sure that amazing convertible I saw you drive in with must suck up a lot of your discretionary funds," she said lightly. "It's a beauty."

A red flush crept up Ethan's neck. "Yeah, she's my baby," he replied uneasily. "I went way out on a limb when I bought her. The monthly lease payments eat up a good chunk of my salary. That's why trips to the Far East will have to wait."

"I understand." Simone wasn't going to push it. If she did, he'd become suspicious. She knew he was bothered by her question. That was good enough for now.

Time to wrap things up. She'd gotten everything she needed out of this interview. "So, is there anything else you think I should know that would assist me in helping Vance improve your department?" she asked calmly.

Ethan looked like a man whose prison sentence had just been reduced. "I think we've covered everything," he said, already half out of his seat.

"Good." Simone handed him her card. "I'll be at Nano all week. If you think of anything else, please let me know. You're an invaluable member of Vance's team."

Ethan rose, pausing only to pocket her card and collect his messenger bag. His grip on the handles was tight and he didn't take the time to swing the strap over his shoulder. "Of course. Anything I can do."

Probably not *anything*, Simone thought as she watched him leave the room. Not only had he been thrown by her more in-depth questions, he also hadn't exactly oozed enthusiasm at her request to contact her. Nor had he responded in kind, offering Simone a welcome mat to keep the lines of communication open.

Loyalty to Vance aside, there was more going on with Ethan Gallagher. She just had to sort things out and figure out what.

But for now, it was time to move on to Zoe Pearson.

Ariel's Grotto, Disneyland
27 February
Tuesday, 2:55 p.m. local time

Aidan grinned, watching the wide-eyed, mesmerized look on Abby's face as she took in the wonders of Ariel's Grotto, which was indeed an under-the-sea extravaganza. The restaurant was drenched in deep ocean-blue colors, complimented by hanging lanterns and pillars entwined with greenery. There was a full wall mural that was straight from the screen of *The Little Mermaid*, and—most magical of all to Abby—there was the smiling young redheaded woman who was playing the part of Ariel, dressed in an exquisite, authentic mermaid costume and seated on her scalloped throne.

"Daddy, you promised that we could take a picture with Ariel," Abby reminded him, her mouth full of her Whozits and Whatzits Nuggetz. "There are already people in line."

"So I see," Aidan replied, taking a bite of his lobster salad. He'd better eat up. Abby had an agenda, and savoring lobster wasn't part of it.

He scanned the room in a quick assessment. "People are getting dessert, so the line is thinning out. I'd say you have just enough time to clean your plate before it's your turn."

That made Abby twist around to look up at her father, disappointment etched all over her precious face. "*My* turn? Aren't you going with me? I want both of us to be in the picture."

Aidan's bite of salad went down in a gulp. This one he hadn't expected. But knowing Abby, shouldn't he have?

"Don't you want it to be just you ladies?" he tried, knowing, even as he watched Abby give a vehement shake of her head, that he'd soon be sitting on a shell, posed beside Abby and a mermaid, also knowing that he'd never live down his brother's and his team's reaction when Abby flourished this photo before everyone's eyes.

"Please, Daddy?"

Two words. That's all it took.

"Okay, Princess Abby." He tousled her hair, which Emma had arranged for the occasion, but which had been wind-blown during her ride on the carousel. "I'll go up with you."

"Yay!"

Abby bolted through the rest of her food and was more than ready when the last child was finishing up. "C'mon, Daddy." She dragged Aidan up to the smiling mermaid and said, "Hi, Ariel. I'm Abby. My daddy wants to be in the picture, too." She turned to gaze up at Aidan. "Say hi to Ariel, Daddy," she instructed him in that parental tone that made Aidan wonder if they'd reversed roles.

"Hello, Ariel," he replied. "It's a pleasure to meet you."

Aidan caught the understanding glimpse in the mermaid's eyes. "Lovely to meet you, too." She wriggled her tail and scooted over a bit so that both Abby and Aidan could join her on her scalloped throne.

The photos and the visit were a rousing success.

The aftermath? Not so much. Even as they left Ariel's Grotto, Abby was already urging him to text a copy of the picture to her Uncle Marc.

Aidan had finally relented, and he and Abby were heading back to the hotel when the secure cell phone that connected Aidan to Vance Pennington rang.

"Give me one sec, sweetheart." Aidan gripped Abby's hand tightly in his as he reached for the phone.

"Okay, Daddy." Abby was sucking on a rainbow lollipop that was bigger than she was. "But just one."

"Promise." Aidan glanced down at his phone, frowning when he saw the number. It wasn't Vance. It was Susan.

"Yes," he answered.

"There's someone watching me, Aidan," she blurted out. "A man. He vanishes every time I look, but I've spotted him more than once and I know he's there. I'm petrified. What if they figured out that Vance isn't following their instructions?"

"That's not the case." Aidan kept his voice low and his words few. "Can you describe him?"

"He's Asian. Medium height and build. That's about all I can say. He disappears as soon as I turn in his direction, and I don't want him to suspect I see him so I look away quickly. But I'm not imagining things," she rushed on.

"I know you're not. But this scenario isn't new. A visual has been in place from the start."

"When will you be here?" Susan sounded as if she'd barely heard him. She was coming unglued—the last thing Aidan needed right now. He couldn't calm her down when he was standing in the middle of Disneyland with his all-too-curious daughter, who was already tugging at his hand.

"Vance is on the ski slopes with the kids," Susan raced on hysterically. "But I couldn't go. I just couldn't. I keep pressing Vance for details, but he only gives me the bare-bones facts. What specialized computer is he talking about? What if he can't use it? What if he says the wrong thing and they kill Lauren?"

"He can, and they won't. You have my word."

Mentally, Aidan moved up his flight time and canceled the drink he was going to have with Simone. He'd fly straight from Disney to Reno without making a stop at his hotel in Silicon Valley. Thank heavens he'd enjoyed his planned afternoon with Abby before Susan's meltdown.

"Hang out in your hotel room," he instructed her, knowing it was the only safe place for her when she was losing it like this. "Have a glass of wine. I'll move up my schedule and be there to meet with you in a few hours."

14

For the second time that day, Simone was escorted through the CEO's inner sanctum—this time to Zoe Pearson's office.

Zoe's door was ajar, an open invitation that she was expecting Simone. Still, she held up one finger as Simone entered the room and shut the door behind her. Zoe gestured at her phone, which was pressed to her ear, and mouthed the words: "Just finishing up."

Simone nodded, glancing around the office that, although smaller than Maxwell's, was decorated in a similar contemporary style and emanated class and style. The main difference was that Zoe's office was all business, with no personal touches at all—no family photos, no special knickknacks, only a few tasteful but impersonal pieces of Chinese objets d'art on her desk and hand-painted landscapes of rural China on the walls. An intriguing—or coincidental—choice of countries; China seemed to be very popular today. Alongside the paintings was a gold plaque announcing Zoe's fifteen-year anniversary at NanoUSA.

That told Simone not only the obvious—that family wasn't a key factor in Zoe's life—but that Zoe was a woman who was determined to be taken seriously. She'd made a visible decision not to water down her image by giving away anything personal about herself, including hobbies or outside interests. Nothing to display a softer side. It wasn't merely a classic show of a strong, cultured woman playing in a man's world—a battle Simone knew only too well. It was a definitive statement that Zoe was all Nano and nothing but.

Simone took a seat in one of the leather chairs across from Zoe's desk, using the opportunity to subtly assess Robert Maxwell's PA herself and noting the details that no dossier could provide.

Zoe Pearson was more attractive and put-together than she was pretty. She looked younger than her mid-forties, partially because she was so petite. She overcame that with an air of utter confidence—a combination Simone was all too familiar with, since she herself was "small but mighty." Zoe's straight, black, shoulder-length hair was fashionably cut and styled and her makeup was perfectly applied and expensive, as was her Hugo Boss heather-gray sheath dress and jacket. She was tan and toned, a clear sign that she visited the company gym on a regular basis, probably daily. Her dark brown eyes were sharp and intelligent, and her voice as she wrapped up her business call rang with authority.

A formidable businesswoman and an ostensibly loyal Nano employee.

In the final seconds before Zoe disconnected the call, Simone made a quick jewelry scan. Not that there was much to see. Zoe wore only a single silver pendant around her neck, although that pendant did scream money. No wedding band. And no tan line that might indicate a one-time presence of a discarded wedding band.

Unmarried to a man. Married to a job. Much like the dossier had suggested.

Zoe put down her phone and rose, reaching across the desk to shake Simone's hand. "Ms. Martin," she greeted her. "I apologize for holding you up. Unfortunately, that call was important and ran longer than I expected."

"No need to apologize." Simone met her handshake and then sat back down. "I've been in the same situation more times than I can count. And, please, call me Simone."

"And I'm Zoe." She gestured at her coffee station. "What can I offer you?"

"Nothing, thanks." Simone waved away the gracious offer. "Given all the meetings I've conducted today and how much coffee and water I've consumed, I think I'm about to drown."

Zoe smiled, a practiced smile worthy of those Simone had seen on Hollywood faces. "I can imagine." She reseated herself, her back ramrod straight, her fingers interlaced on the desk. Although she made comfortable, direct eye contact, she made no move to walk around and sit in the chair adjacent to Simone, or to suggest they move to the sitting area of her office.

Zoe Pearson was intent on making a point. The semicircular desk was an orchestrated barrier between her and Simone, and her body language said she was determined to stay in charge.

Simone had her work cut out for her.

"I was just admiring your pieces of art," she said. "Where did you get them?"

"Robert Maxwell travels to China frequently on business. He knows I have a weakness for Chinese art and would often bring home a gift for me." Zoe paused. "And just for the record, he never charged any of them to his company expense account. I would know; I file all of his reports. The gifts were a gesture of kindness and appreciation—something Robert is well-known for."

Defensive. Not about herself but about Robert. What was *that* about?

"Zoe, please relax." Simone went straight to the heart of things. If she couldn't lower the wall Zoe had erected, she'd never get anywhere.

"I've heard nothing but glowing praise when it comes to you and to Robert Maxwell, and I'm only here to pick your brain and see if you can shed some insight on how I can improve the manufacturing division. I have no ulterior motive and no hatchet to bury in anyone's back." Simone paused, seeing the skeptical look in Zoe's eyes.

Ah, another indicator of how close Zoe and her boss were.

"I'm sure you've spoken with Robert." Again, Simone went for the direct approach. "And I'm sure he's clued you in on the fact that, as part of my job, I'm checking out any potentially problematic dynamics between departments that might interfere with the proper functioning of the manufacturing division."

Zoe's brows rose slightly, but she neither confirmed nor denied Simone's statement.

"I take that to mean a yes," Simone said. "I'm glad he shared that with you, because it saves me the trouble of doing so. This isn't a witch hunt. It's information gathering. I realize Robert is uncomfortable with it, given how protective he is about his employees. But it's just a small part of my assessment, and a necessary one. He has nothing to be concerned about."

"Do you have reason to believe our employees are not team players?" Zoe asked bluntly.

"If I did, I'd be discussing that with Robert. And I'm sure he'd be passing that information on to you. So I think you know the answer to that question already."

"I only know that you're still pursuing that path."

"Along with any other applicable ones. Would you mind if I ask why you're so defensive?"

Zoe drew in a breath. "Nano is more than my place of employment. It's a huge chunk of my life. The staff here is more like a professional family than a bunch of co-workers. So, yes, I get defensive when I feel as if our integrity is being questioned."

"Point well taken." Simone nodded. "I've seen the teamwork you're describing firsthand. It's more than impressive, and equally rare. I'm not expecting to find anything to dispute that."

Zoe seemed to thaw a bit, although her body language remained guarded. "What questions do you have for me?"

"Ones you could most likely answer in your sleep." Simone crossed one leg over the other, intentionally opting against taking notes, just as she had with Ethan. Zoe wouldn't squirm the way Ethan would have. She would just shut down. After that, all she'd give Simone was one party line after another—a total waste of time, especially when Zoe could be a valuable ally.

"Robert made it very clear to me that you're far more than an extraordinary PA," Simone began. "He said you're more like an executive, with a keen knowledge of business transactions and emerging technology. You're highly educated. You attend and participate in high-level meetings. Yet you're also Robert's right hand. That's a unique combination."

"I like to think so."

"As a result, you have a unique view of your boss and how he interacts with everyone in his world. You know his most significant time challenges and his main conflicts. You also have a unique overview of Nano as a whole. I need that perspective to help me do my job. So, from where you sit, are there any weak links in the manufacturing department? Not employees," Simone added hastily. "Processes. Things that could run more smoothly so as to better the company."

Zoe shook her head. "From my vantage point, Vance is a fine leader and a smart man. After all these years, he runs his department like clockwork. He and Robert work closely together, so there are no communication gaps that would slow things down. If anything, I'd say that Vance eases Robert's challenges. In fact, I'm not even certain why Vance hired McKinsey to evaluate the effectiveness of his department."

"Vance is a perfectionist," Simone replied. "Also, with a revolutionary new technology about to be released, he wants to ensure that everyone and everything in his department is up for what lies ahead. It's a common practice for executives to employ under these circumstances."

"I'll take your word for it." Zoe tilted her head and waited.

Simone cut down on her list of routine questions, asking only the bare-bones ones. Zoe was well aware that Simone had gotten most of these answers already and was just seeking confirmation. It was time to ask for her help.

"Zoe, I'll be frank with you. Everyone I interview is going to give me the answers they know I want to hear. Very few employees in a tight-knit group like yours are going to say derogatory things about the company or their co-workers. You're firmly committed to your career here. If I sense a problem, may I come to you to discuss it? I think you're the right person to shed light on whatever issues I have or perceptions I get. And if that means setting me straight, all the better."

Zoe looked a bit surprised but not displeased. "I can do that. Just remember that my loyalties lie with Nano."

"And my job is to improve Nano. So our goals are the same. I need you to be straightforward and objective. That's not always easy. But given your company loyalty and your broad knowledge of everything that goes on here, I'm counting on you to be both. Can you?"

For the first time, Zoe looked at Simone as if she might not be the enemy.

"Yes. I can."

"Good. Now I'm going to broach a topic that won't be in your comfort zone, but that is necessary. And that's the future leadership of Nano."

Again, Zoe looked unfazed, as if she'd been anticipating this question. Maybe Robert had prepped her for this one, as well. As true as that might be, he couldn't have prepped her for the personal angle Simone was about to take.

"The future leadership of Nano?" Zoe repeated. "I'm not sure I understand what you're asking."

And I'm sure you do, Simone thought. "Then I'll be frank. More than one person I've interviewed has implied that Robert plans to retire after the big technology release. From what I'm gathering, it sounds as if Vance has the inside track to becoming the new CEO. That promotion would be a powerful reason for him to be committed to getting his department in top-notch shape so his successor could step in. Which, to my way of thinking, would be a very good reason to hire me to do exactly what I'm doing."

Zoe didn't dispute the point. "Assuming you're right, what exactly is your question?"

"Vance and Ethan seem to be a very tight team. Therefore, if Vance becomes CEO, I'm assuming Ethan would move up with him. That's a game-changer for everyone, including you. So I guess I'm asking how all that would affect your position at Nano?"

Two angry spots of color tinged Zoe's cheeks. "I'm not at liberty to discuss Robert's plans," she stated flatly. "But how would my future here relate to what you're hoping to accomplish? Is my integrity being questioned?"

"Absolutely not." Simone gave an adamant shake of her head. "I'm just trying to understand what your role might be during the transition and afterwards."

The anger abated. "I see. Well, as I said, I'm not at liberty to discuss Robert's plans. But I'll be frank with you about mine—as long as this is on a confidential basis."

"It is."

"Then, regardless of any transition that might or might not be occurring, Robert and I are in the process of exploring my moving up to an executive position. He's considering something in the HR department, possibly Director of Human Capital."

"Congratulations," Simone replied. "So, should Robert be retiring, he'd make sure to enact that change before he turned over the reins to his successor?"

"Absolutely. Robert takes care of his employees. So, yes, he'd see me settled in before he made any personal change of his own."

Simone pursed her lips. "And what if you were unhappy with the new leadership? Would that impact your decision to remain at Nano?"

Zoe's brows rose. "It would take a lot for me to leave Nano. But if you're asking if I have options, of course I do. I'd be a stupid businesswoman if I isolated myself. I've been in this business for fifteen years. I have more contacts in the industry than I can count. In addition, Robert would give me a glowing recommendation. So I feel very secure, regardless of what the future should hold."

"I'm glad—although I doubt it would come to that. You seem to have a very positive opinion of Vance."

"I do. We also have a solid working relationship, as do Ethan and I. It's going to be very hard for you, or me, to find gaps in their department that need filling, either with additional or better personnel."

Simone pushed back her chair and rose. "Then my job here will be easier than even I expected." She gave Zoe a sunny smile. "Thank you for your time."

Zoe plucked her card from her desk and handed it to Simone. "I'll be available to you all week," she said. "This is my direct contact information. It'll help you bypass the various assistants in order to reach me. Any questions or concerns that I can help you with, I will. Like you, I want Nano to be the best it can be."

West Coast Bar & Grill
San Jose, California
27 February
Tuesday, 7:15 p.m. local time

June Morris leaned one hip against a barstool, her fingers interlaced on the counter. She angled her head long enough to give the room a quick once-over before ordering her glass of merlot and ensuring that her gift box was propped up against her handbag at the edge of the counter.

Polished wooden tables and chairs. Comfy leather couches. Decent music. And a crowd that was definitely comprised of business professionals. As a well-dressed, forty-one-year-old "corporate" type, she fit right in.

It was a funny thing. She'd been to so many different bars that were fifteen or more miles from Nano and that were similar to this one that they'd actually started to look alike. Then again, she'd specifically chosen bars that catered to professionals so she would fit in and, at the same time, go unnoticed. Occasionally, a guy would try to hit on her—until her date arrived. Then they took the hint and their attentions elsewhere. She'd never spotted a Nano employee at any of her drinking holes, thank goodness. Given the gridlocked drive from Santa Clara, the Nano team would naturally choose to stay closer to home for their after-work drinks. And "after-work" was still an hour or more away for most of them.

She wasn't the only workaholic Robert employed. Although she was up there with the most intense of them. The only days she left this early were the ones on which she visited her elderly mother in a senior facility—a fact that was well-known and understood by the Nano team.

What they didn't know was that she always made this critical stopover on the way.

The infrequent days she left earlier than nine p.m. didn't matter. She always took work home with her. Becoming CFO in a cutting-edge technology company like Nano had taken her down routes she'd never expected to go. Holding on to what she'd achieved took every drop of her mental acuity and then some. Her days were long, her nights were a continuation of her days, and the competition out there was fierce. She was good, and she knew it, but that didn't mean there weren't stronger candidates out there who could do her job if she missed a step. Loyalty, even to Robert, would only go so far. She was well aware that she wasn't a frontrunner for the future CEO position, and quite frankly, that made her feel relieved rather than resentful. She had all she could handle on her plate as it was. And the screws only turned tighter as the workload increased.

What she needed was a clone.

What she was getting was as close as it got.

"Here ya go, ma'am." The mid-twenties bartender placed the glass of merlot in front of her.

"Thank you." She paid him, took her drink, gift box, and purse, and headed over to one of the vacant couches.

Ma'am? When had she become that? She was barely out of her thirties and—with the help of expensive makeup—still pretty. She used to be what people called cute. But all that fresh-faced, Midwestern youthfulness had faded. The strain was starting to show in the lines of tension around her mouth and the pallor that even makeup couldn't disguise.

Okay, so she wouldn't be winning any Miss USA pageants. That part of her career rise was over anyway. It wasn't her game plan any longer.

She sank down on the leather cushion, twisting around to glance at the front door. Impatiently, she checked her watch.

Ethan was late.

She hoped like hell he hadn't been called into an unscheduled meeting. With Vance on vacation, that seemed unlikely.

Her heart rate began to accelerate and her hands began to shake. Cold sweat broke out on her forehead. Quickly, she set her drink down on the glass side table. She couldn't let herself fall apart. Not here and not now. She was in public. She had to keep it together. That was becoming harder and harder these days thanks to the side effects. But the alternative to riding those out was unthinkable.

In answer to her prayers, the door swung open and Ethan strolled into the bar, his messenger bag slung over his shoulder. He scanned the room briefly, his gaze finding her. He smiled in her direction, then went up to the bar and ordered his glass of scotch. Three minutes later, he sat down beside her, placed his bag on the floor and his drink on the glass table. As always, they gave each other a huge hug. It was clear they were tight, but whether it was as friends or lovers, that was unclear. It didn't matter. As long as they weren't obvious enough to be a spectacle, let the patrons think what they wanted—if they cared enough to think about them at all.

"Hey," he greeted her. "Sorry I'm late. I got stuck behind a landscaping truck doing twenty-five in a forty."

"It doesn't matter." June willed her hands to stop shaking, and when they cooperated, she picked up her glass of merlot and took a long sip. "You're here now." Her gaze flickered to the messenger bag.

"Sure am." He took a swallow of scotch, then turned his attention back to her.

"How did *your* interview go?" June asked.

"Just fine." Ethan spoke very quietly. "She asked mostly about Vance, routine stuff that I could field no problem. A few red flags, but nothing to do with you. She barely skimmed over your name. Just whether or not you'd jump on the idea of becoming the new CEO. I told her I had no idea since we didn't interact one-on-one, only through channels."

"Good." That was one big relief. Even though June's meeting with Simone had gone smoothly, she was still terrified that Ethan would inadvertently say something—anything—that would raise Ms. Martin's antenna. The woman was smart and incredibly shrewd. And June couldn't risk giving her fodder for a more thorough personal investigation.

"You look pretty strung out," Ethan said, scrutinizing her expression and her mannerisms.

"All the better for you."

"Hey." He looked hurt. "Business arrangement or not, I'm still concerned."

June blew out a breath, nodding as she did. "I know that. I didn't mean to snap at you. I'm just having a really hard time. It's bad enough that the tension at work is in the stratosphere. But adding a McKinsey consultant to the mix is the last thing I needed. I'm freaking out."

"When was the last time you slept?" Ethan asked.

"Sleep? What's that?" June gave a humorless laugh. "That word's not in my vocabulary these days."

"Well, it should be." Ethan lowered his voice even further. "I brought you something to take care of that. You need a balance if you want to perform at the level you're aiming for."

"I didn't bring enough…"

"Forget it. Consider it a gift. Which reminds me…" He reached into his messenger bag and extracted a bracelet-sized Tiffany box. "Happy belated birthday." He spoke in a normal tone now, handing her the box and leaning forward to kiss her cheek. "I know you have to run, so open it at home. But text and let me know how you like it."

June took the box, a smile on her lips and relief in her heart. "Thank you. That was so sweet. I'm sure I'll love it." She picked up the box she'd propped next to her purse. "Happy belated birthday right back at you." Her eyes twinkled—something she was capable of now that she had what she needed. "It's great that we share a birthday month. It helps make sure you don't forget."

"Works for me." Ethan took the box and grinned widely. "Thanks a lot. I bet I know what it is."

"I bet you do. And I wish I could stay and watch your face when you see it. Unfortunately, I can't." She drank the rest of her wine and rose. "I'm running late to my dinner meeting. But I'll text you right after—once I've admired my gift." She waited until he stood and then gave him another hug. "You're the best."

"Don't let so much time pass next time," he replied, returning her hug. "You know how important you are to me."

15

Three days left…

Aidan sat up in a wing-backed chair in Simone's hotel room. Dressed in the hotel's bathrobe, he sipped his coffee and watched Simone sleep, her breathing even and relaxed.

He was anything but.

While their lovemaking had been a welcome diversion, it hadn't come close to calming Aidan's adrenaline rush enough to let him rest.

Last night had started out for him in Lake Tahoe with getting Susan Pennington's meltdown under control followed by the arrival of his package and a closed-door computer lesson and prep time meeting with Vance—one Aidan had promised to drill home again at six a.m. this morning, just prior to Vance's first—and obviously emotional—communication with Lauren.

That done, Aidan had jetted back to Palo Alto, given Simone the school ring, and jumped right into the lengthy videoconference between him, Simone, and Ryan.

Simone had listened intently and absorbed everything Ryan explained to her in painstaking detail. Their discussion had included Aidan cluing Ryan in on the tweaks they'd made to his plan. Since the ring had originally been designed for a man—with the idea that Vance would be handling this data transfer—a little improvising had been necessary. The new plan was that Simone would wear the ring around her neck on a silver chain Aidan had purchased. If anyone asked, she'd say it was her boyfriend's pride and joy and that he'd given it to her to wear as a prelude to a future commitment. Since she'd already told Lawrence Blockman she had a boyfriend, this would be no great revelation. Aidan had made sure the chain had an easy-open clasp so Simone wouldn't be slowed down in her efforts. *If* everything went as planned, the Chinese would have what they wanted and the necessary time would be bought.

But Aidan wasn't a fan of *ifs*.

He saw that Simone was outwardly calm and prepared. But he also knew her too well. The task ahead would be pushing her way out of her comfort zone. She was a consultant, not a technology specialist or a thief. Plus, this involved a whole new heightened type of pressure. The security of a human life, not a corporate entity, was planted solely in her hands. How could she not be a bundle of nerves?

So on two separate fronts, today's events would be not only challenging but critical to the assurance of Lauren's well-being.

Aidan checked his watch. Time to shower and get dressed. Soon, he'd be hopping on the Gulfstream and heading back to Lake Tahoe. He'd be way earlier than six. But it was imperative that he make sure Vance was both mentally and psychologically ready. Everything hinged on how Vance handled this call and the information he extracted.

Once the call was complete, Aidan would be on high alert as he waited for Simone's call, announcing that she'd successfully completed her mission, that she was now outside Nano's impenetrable walls, and that she was ready to transmit the sample of the stolen technology, as promised.

It was going to be a hell of a morning.

As if sensing Aidan's scrutiny, Simone stirred, blinked, and opened her eyes, her gaze finding Aidan's shadowy form even in the darkened room.

"I'll be fine, *chéri*," she said without preamble. Pulling the sheet up around her, she propped her pillows against the headboard and hoisted herself into a half-sitting position. "Stop worrying."

"Not going to happen," Aidan replied, standing to pour Simone a cup of the steaming coffee he'd ordered from room service and adding both cream and sugar to the cup so she could enjoy her coffee just the way she liked it.

He handed her the cup and gave her a quick kiss.

"You're getting ready early." Simone glanced at the clock. "Whose performance are you obsessing over—Vance's or mine?"

"Both." Aidan was as honest with her as always. "Vance is a novice at using our specialized computer and a nervous wreck about the conversation he's about to have with Lauren. Not a reassuring combo. As for you, I'm not doubting you can pull this off. I'm just concerned about the unknowns, the things Ryan can't prep us for. You have to double- and triple-check to make sure that Lawrence Blockman and his PA are away from their desks. You have to play the part of a burglar and an escape artist. All this while executing a challenging and delicate task."

"Only that?" Simone teased, sipping at her coffee. She set down the cup, a small smile curving her lips. "You forget that my father is a magician. I learned quite a bit from him."

"I haven't forgotten." Aidan still had to grin at the thought that Simone, the consummate corporate professional, had a successful French magician for a father. Jacques Martin might not be a household name like Houdini, but he was well-established and constantly employed. And, yes, Simone occasionally showed off the tricks he'd taught her when she was growing up.

"Honestly," Aidan added, "what you learned from your father, not to mention my faith in you, are probably the only things keeping me sane enough to let you do this."

"Good. Then stay sane." Simone waved him off. "You go handle Vance. As you Americans say, *I've got this.*"

Aidan hesitated for a brief second, then nodded. "Call me the minute you're outside Nano and can get a signal."

Simone snapped off a salute. "Sir, yes, sir."

Farmhouse
Slavonia, Croatia
28 February
Wednesday, 3:15 p.m. local time

Lauren was burrowed under the covers of her bed, trembling with an internal chill that had nothing to do with the weather. This morning things had been different. Rather than staying scarce when she was around, her kidnappers had been having a heated conversation right out in the open—in the dining area, directly attached to the tiny kitchen, where she was forcing down breakfast. Their backs were to her, but their words were fast, furious, and urgent. The fact that she couldn't understand a word of what they were saying made it even worse. In addition, Bashkim was visibly tense and watchful as he stood beside her while she ate her meal, his gaze boring through her. The whole scenario was panic-inducing. And it made her imagination go wild.

Something was happening. Something that involved her. Had a ransom arrangement been made with her father? Or had they reached an impasse and now planned to kill her?

Their voices had eventually quieted, and Lauren had choked down the rest of her food, escaping as quickly as she could to her bedroom. Bashkim didn't say a word, just strode along beside her, waiting until she was inside before shutting the door and leaving her.

An eerie silence had ensued. No voices. No footsteps. Nothing.

Lauren's fear had mounted steadily, until now, when she was strung so tight she was prepared to snap.

A firm knock sounded at the door—and she nearly jumped out of her skin.

Jolting upright, she gathered the blankets around her in some ridiculous show of self-protection. "Yes?" she managed. She sounded half-dead, even to her own ears.

"You're awake?" Bashkim asked from the other side of the door. What he really wanted to know was if she was decent. Quite the paradox—a respectful killer.

"I'm fully dressed," she replied. *And about as far from sleep as one can get.*

The door swung open. Bashkim entered, carrying a tray of food. "You didn't come out for lunch. You must eat."

Why? So I'll be a plumper corpse?

"Thank you," she said aloud. She slid farther up on the bed and accepted the tray of food. There was no point in antagonizing him. And maybe if she asked in a respectful but tearful way, he'd fill in a few blanks for her. Whether or not she wanted the answers she sought remained to be seen.

"Bread and soup," Bashkim supplied, still wearing that sober expression. "And a plate of *kulen*. You seemed to like it yesterday."

Yes, she had. The spicy slices of sausage were the first thing she'd eaten all week that wasn't bland and that had a pleasant bite to it. It wasn't a pepperoni pizza with her family, but it would suffice—normally. Not today. And not now. She didn't want food. All she wanted was answers.

She opened her mouth to speak, and then, seeing the hard set of Bashkim's jaw, changed her mind. Refusing to eat would only piss him off and she wanted him as amenable as possible when she questioned him.

She had a little bread and soup and then chewed and swallowed three slices of *kulen*. It was all she could hold down. And it seemed to be enough for Bashkim, because he nodded, although his posture remained rigid, his mouth set in a thin, tight line.

"Very good," he said, his tone belying his praise. He remained at her bedside, clearing his throat before he next spoke. And suddenly Lauren realized she wasn't going to have to ask anything. Bashkim was about to fill in the blanks on his own.

Her heart began hammering in her chest.

"I'm going to leave you now," he said. "Take a shower. Get dressed. Be ready."

"Ready?" Lauren croaked out the word. "I don't understand."

"I'll be back to get you in a half hour. You'll come with me. And you'll do as I say if you want to live."

Lauren's insides turned to ice. "Please, Bashkim, tell me what's happening. Please."

"You're going to talk to your father. On the computer. You'll see him. He'll see you. For five minutes only."

Lauren started, stunned by this development, which was the last thing she'd expected. A videoconference. Her father had somehow managed to arrange a videoconference with her. How, she had no idea. But the very thought of seeing his face and hearing his voice made tears well up in her eyes.

"Thank you," she whispered.

Bashkim frowned. "Don't thank me. This is not a reunion. It's an arrangement we made—for our purposes. There are rules. You'll follow them. I don't want to kill you. But I will—right in front of your father's eyes—if I have to."

Lauren didn't doubt his claim for a moment. "What are the rules?"

"I'll tell you when it's time. Your job is to convince your father that he should give us what we're asking for."

"I don't know what you're asking him for. So how can I…?" The question slipped out before Lauren could stop it—and, seeing the thunderclouds now gathering in Baskhim's eyes, she wished to God that she had.

"You don't need to know." His tone was as ominous as his expression—a further reminder to Lauren of what he was capable of. "Your father knows. Don't ask any questions—or I'll slit your throat."

Lauren squeezed her eyes shut at the horrifying image, tears seeping out from between her closed lids. "I'm so sorry. I won't ask anything. I'll do whatever you say. Please, Bashkim, you've been so kind to me. I wouldn't have survived this long without your decency and compassion. Please don't hurt me. I'll follow your rules exactly. I promise."

The thunderclouds abated. "Good." Bashkim took her tray and turned toward the door. "Thirty minutes."

Starbucks
Northstar Drive, Lake Tahoe
28 February
Wednesday, 6:33 a.m. local time

Vance arrived early in order to stake out the table at Starbucks with the best Wi-Fi connection. He was desperately trying to find a semblance of control over a situation where none existed. Control was what he did best. But this wasn't a business transaction. Lauren's life was in his hands. Against his nature, he had to rely on Aidan and his team to take the lead, and do exactly what he was told.

After careful inspection, he selected the table near the back room and closest to the Wi-Fi access point. The door was labeled: *Employees Only*. Which meant he'd have the fast Internet connection and the privacy he needed. During the morning rush, Starbucks would be all hands on deck. None of the employees would be going anywhere other than to their stations to meet the needs of their coffee-craving patrons.

Vance got himself settled, then took a deep breath and fired up the special laptop that Ryan had prepared for this situation. He didn't know the technical details, other than the fact that it wasn't the normal Windows machine it appeared to be. Something about special keylogging and screen capture software that would secretly stream all data that came across the laptop back to the server belonging to Aidan's team so they could see and hear everything that was going on.

He plugged in his headphones and waited for 7:10 to arrive.

It seemed to take forever.

Farmhouse
Slavonia, Croatia
28 February
Wednesday, 4:05 p.m. local time

Lauren swallowed hard as she settled herself behind the simple wooden table that served as a desk.

She was in an empty bedroom that she'd never seen before. The entire room was bare—walls, floor, and ceiling. The only items present were the desk, a wooden chair for her to sit on, and a laptop computer.

Bashkim was standing just off to her left, positioned where he couldn't be seen on camera but where he could reach her in two long strides. He gripped the handle of a frighteningly long knife—one that could slit her throat in a heartbeat, and the tightness of his grasp was a reminder that he would do just that if provoked.

Lauren had now been given the precise details of what she must say. She must assure her father that she was being well-cared for by informing him that she was provided with three meals a day, with her own bedroom, use of a bathroom, and with the freedom to move about as she pleased. Not a word about the dwelling she was in, how many people might be here, or what language they might be speaking. Just her care and comfort—and the most imperative part—a plea for her father to supply whatever he was being asked for. If he didn't cooperate, she was to assure him that she'd be killed.

She interlaced her fingers tightly in front of her, chilled despite the royal blue turtleneck sweater she was wearing. She'd chosen it carefully, hoping she looked as much like her usual self as possible. Sweater and jeans, her customary winter attire.

But no sweater could alleviate this internal chill.

"Just a few more minutes," Bashkim told her. "The computer is on. Now we wait."

Starbucks
Northstar Drive, Lake Tahoe
28 February
Wednesday, 7:10 a.m. local time

Vance connected to the videoconference using the link he'd been provided.

The next few seconds felt like an eternity.

Abruptly, he could see himself in the large window in the center of his screen. Thirty endless seconds later, another window appeared, replacing his larger image and reducing his to a smaller one in the lower right-hand corner. As the new center screen image took form, he could make out Lauren's face and the bright blue sweater she was wearing. The vibrant color did nothing to ease his pain or his worry. Because what he saw wasn't the exuberant, vivacious daughter he loved. It was a shell of her—a terrified young woman with an ashen, haunted look on her face and an equally determined attempt to conceal her fear.

Vance's throat clogged up. But he knew better than to make reference to her deteriorated condition. "Hi, honey," he began, fighting to keep his voice steady as he mentally counted down the few precious minutes he had.

"Daddy?" Lauren's voice was high and thin. She hadn't called him Daddy in years.

"Yes, Lauren, it's me. We only have five minutes. So tell me how you are. I need to know. I'm sick with worry."

"I'm okay." The words were forced, and she tightened the grip of her interlaced fingers as if to anchor herself for the façade of a conversation they were about to have.

"They haven't hurt you?"

She shook her head. "Not at all." She sounded like a parrot, reciting a memorized speech. "They've been very respectful. I have my own room, I'm offered three meals a day, and I'm allowed to walk around"—a brief pause as she searched for the acceptable phrase—"inside the place where I'm being held."

Fully aware of what Aidan wanted him to do, Vance jumped on his opportunity. "*Offered* three meals a day?" he reiterated. "Or *eaten* three meals a day?"

Lauren's gaze darted quickly to her left. Vance didn't have to guess why. One of the kidnappers, no doubt armed, was monitoring her every word and providing her with instructions on what she could and could not say.

Evidently, her eating habits was a safe topic, because Lauren replied, "I eat all my meals."

Vance leaned forward, knowing that his daughter's claim was pure bullshit. "You know how much I worry about your eating—specifically your *non-eating* when you're under stress. I have to be sure you're not starving yourself. So tell me what you mean by 'all your meals.' What have you eaten today?"

Lauren drew in a sharp breath and then continued with her recitation. "A hot roll and coffee for breakfast, and bread, soup, and *kulen* for lunch. It's not dinnertime here yet, but last night I ate pasta and tomato sauce."

Abruptly, her shoulders began shaking with sobs, as if the burden of all the pretense was too much for her. "They haven't hurt me, Daddy," she wept. "Not yet. But they will if you don't cooperate. They said so. Whatever they want, please just give it to them. Please."

She broke down completely, lowering her head and twisting a knife in Vance's heart as he saw the streams of tears falling onto her clasped hands. "I want to come home. I don't want to die. Please, please, make this nightmare end. Do what they ask. Give them anything. Bring me home."

Vance's soul was splintering into nothingness and he could barely breathe. "I will, baby," he vowed hoarsely. "I'm giving them exactly what they want. You'll be home with us soon. I promise. It'll be okay." His voice broke. "I love you, Lauren."

"I love you, too," she wept. "But I'm so afraid. Please, Daddy—"

The screen went dark.

16

Aidan was hunched over his computer in the living room of the Penningtons' suite, rapidly Googling for information on what he'd just heard, when Terri called.

"*Kulen* is a smoked sausage, spiced with paprika, and prepared primarily in the Slavonian region of Croatia," she said, answering his unspoken question. "Slavonia is in the northeast corner of the country. Its size is four thousand eight hundred forty-eight square miles, and it's approximately one hundred seventy-five miles east of Zagreb. Population-wise, it's just over eight hundred thousand people. Osijek—which is its main city—is the fourth largest city in Croatia with an approximate population of one hundred and eight thousand. Having said that, Slavonia is predominantly agricultural, consisting of vast farmlands, which would lend themselves perfectly to holding a kidnapping victim. Those are the basic specs. Give me fifteen minutes and I'll have a fully detailed dossier for the entire team."

"I'll give Philip and Marc a heads-up," Aidan replied. "I'm calling them now and alerting them to the direction they'll be taking."

The Westin Zagreb
Zagreb, Croatia
28 February
Wednesday, 4:21 p.m. local time

Philip and Marc were seated around the coffee table in the living room of Philip's suite, rereading and discussing the notes they'd compiled after the first two meetings with Danijel's CIs. Marc had handled the first meeting, and Philip the second.

Danijel had provided them both with the names of the three Albanian organized crime groups who were still operational—to varying degrees—in Croatia. One group could be immediately eliminated, given that its leader was presently spending time in prison and his whole organization was in disarray. That left two plausible groups. Marc and Philip had used that knowledge as a foundation when they questioned the CIs and had managed to pick up a few enlightening details.

Now Marc spoke up first. "After what we've heard so far, my instincts tell me that the Sallaku OC family is the most likely to be involved in this. From what the CIs leaked, they have the greatest interest in increasing their criminal reach throughout Europe and perhaps even beyond. In addition to drug trafficking, human trafficking is high up on their list of specialties. And they're smart, so it's no surprise that they've been linked to other dealings with the Chinese."

Philip's brow was furrowed and he looked distinctly unhappy. "I agree with your assessment. And if that's the group we're looking at, there's another ugly, unpleasant factor we need to address."

"That they're also the most violent of the three groups," Marc supplied.

"Yes, with a total disregard for human life."

"You don't think the payment they're receiving from the Chinese will be enough."

"No, I don't. Experience tells me that Albanian OC groups like this won't be satisfied by just quietly collecting their money and handing over the victim. I'm willing to bet that the bloodshed has already begun. Their guy who hit on Lauren and was therefore a known commodity? I'm sure he was a cutout and is already dead. Anyone and everyone who's a threat to them, they'll slaughter."

"Including Lauren," Marc added, his expression grim. "Which blows Aidan's theory to hell. He's been focusing on the Chinese angle, knowing that it's in their best interests to get Lauren home alive. But the Albanians are ruthless and don't give a shit what the Chinese want. They'll get their money and still slit Lauren's throat, claiming she was trying to escape and they had no choice. The way they see it, the Chinese will have gotten what they wanted, which is all their next employer will focus on. Shit, Philip, we need to bring Aidan up to speed on this because this is going to clock him cold."

Philip nodded. "We'll call him in ten. First, let's brainstorm tonight's meeting, which you'll be handling. That way we can give him a comprehensive overview."

"Okay." Marc agreed because the logic made sense. But he knew his brother—and his brother's soft spot. A young woman—someone's daughter. The very thought that Lauren could be collateral damage in all this rather than just a bargaining chip? This was going to be a train wreck of a conversation.

Philip was already strategizing aloud. "Danijel says that the CI you're meeting with tonight knows a hell of a lot and has the potential motive to share it. It's up to you to convince him to do just that. To my way of thinking, we can't keep soft-pedaling it the way Danijel wants, just handing over money and keeping it friendly. We've got to find a way to push this guy hard without shutting him down."

"I totally agree." A corner of Marc's mouth lifted. "You know that big Rambo knife I have?"

"Actually, I was curious what that was for."

"Just this type of situation. While Danijel is doing the questioning and translating, and before I pay the guy off, I'll just stare him down, silently sharpening my blade with a stone. It never fails to loosen tongues. We already know this guy has info and motive, both of which might cause him to talk. I'll help tilt the scales in our favor. Money is one incentive. Fear is another. Together, they're lethal."

Philip smiled. "So to hell with diplomacy alone. I agree. These informants are afraid to talk. They've got to be more afraid of us than they are of the people they know."

At that moment, Philip's secure cell phone rang. He scooped it up. "Yes?"

"It's me," Aidan said.

Instantly, Philip set down the phone and pressed the speaker button. "Marc and I were on the verge of calling you. Do you have something for us?"

"Oh, yeah," Aidan replied. "Terri's about to send you a private chat message with a link to a mini-dossier detailing what I'm about to briefly relay." Aidan proceeded to tell them what Vance's conversation with Lauren had yielded.

Philip whistled. "The timing of this information couldn't have been better." He proceeded to tell Aidan about the CI Marc would be meeting with that night. "We'll talk to Danijel about this *kulen* and see if he can use it to narrow the field of questioning and steer it in the direction of operations in Slavonia. We'll move from there, hopefully armed with more ammunition."

"Good. Were you calling to give me an update at your end?"

Marc and Philip exchanged glances, and Philip gestured for Marc to take the lead.

It was probably best that way.

"Aidan." Marc kept it factual, laying out the realities and waiting to deal with the fallout. "Our investigation here suggests that the Sallaku OC family is likely behind the kidnapping. Unfortunately, they have a reputation for killing victims despite monetary compensation. They have their own set of rules and wouldn't think twice about screwing over the Chinese once they've been paid." A heartbeat of a pause. "Which makes it all the more crucial that Philip and I get to Lauren."

There was dead silence at the other end of the phone.

"Aidan?"

"I'm still here." Aidan sounded as thrown as Marc had expected. "I've been promising the Penningtons that Lauren would be returned safely if they followed our lead. I don't break promises. Plus, I'm a father. How can I tell another father that, not only have I misled him, but that his daughter's life is in even greater jeopardy than we all thought? Vance is already at the breaking point. I already need him to play his part without wavering. Based on what you're telling me, that's even more essential. "

"I know this puts you in a terrible position," Marc replied quietly. "But principles or not, candor has to take a back seat here. You can't tell them; Vance will definitely blow it, from what you've said. The bottom line is that we'll be bringing Lauren home, alive and unharmed. Her father never has to know more than that."

"There's no other way. I get it." Aidan gave the only answer he could, then quickly switched gears to avoid dwelling on the subject. "Anything I should know about your upcoming meeting? Same MO?"

"Nope." Marc knew that if anything would lighten Aidan's mood, it was this. "I need to really pressure this CI, put him in a talkative mood. So Big Rambo is coming along with me."

As expected, Aidan started to chuckle. "You still have that stupid knife from high school?"

"Laugh all you want. I can't tell you how many meetings I've had with CIs where, once they see Big Rambo, they shit themselves and can't stop talking."

"Well then, who am I to stand in the way? Happy hunting. Now go read Terri's mini-dossier."

NanoUSA
28 February
Wednesday, 9:38 a.m. local time

Simone sequestered herself in the small office she'd been provided for her week's assignment at Nano. With the door shut and locked, she removed the chain from around her neck and placed the ring on the Qi wireless charger sitting on the desk. She noted the current time—nine forty a.m. In thirty minutes, the device would be fully charged and ready.

She'd already done her morning homework, confirming what she'd skillfully coaxed out of Lilah Mathers, Lawrence Blockman's chatty, newly divorced PA, yesterday as she and Simone had reapplied their makeup at the ladies' room sink. As Lilah had mentioned, Blockman was in his nine thirty meeting with Robert Maxwell in the CEO's office. And Lilah herself was on her regular early-morning coffee break, gossiping with other female employees in the break room.

This would be Simone's only chance at getting inside Blockman's office and extracting the drawings from his drawing cabinet—exactly where Vance had told her the VP Engineering kept them.

* * *

Promptly at ten past ten, Simone was outside Blockman's door, pleased but unsurprised to find it unlocked. As Vance had explained, given the extreme security measures taken by Nano, very few executives locked their doors until they went home at night. Thankfully, Blockman was no exception. However, if he had been, Simone would have used her skills to get in anyway.

She paused in the corridor, glanced to her left and right, then let herself inside, shutting the door quietly behind her. As she crossed over to the large steel drawing cabinet, she removed the decorative barrette from her chignon, letting her hair tumble to her shoulders. She'd make the necessary repairs later.

By the time she'd reached the cabinet, she'd separated the pin from the hair accessory. Vance had emphasized that Blockman's cabinet would definitely be locked at all times, given the sensitive nature of what was inside. Well, Simone could take care of that. In a few quick twists, she used the pin to pick the lock on the cabinet and slid open the top drawer. Just as Vance had said, inside were production drawings of the factory floor layout, including machine settings and specifications that were an integral part of Nano's manufacturing breakthrough. There were too many drawings for the small camera to capture, but Vance had said the drawings marked "DRAFT" were the ones she was looking for. And since the goal was to make sure the images were real but not complete, she chose the first five—the exact number of shots that Ryan's mini ring camera would allow before power would be exhausted.

She placed the drawings on the floor to take pictures and proceeded to aim the ring at her quarry. Bridging double zeroes in the middle of the year on the high school ring with the metallic nail polish on her middle finger, she closed the circuit on the charged capacitor, enabling the embedded image sensor to photograph the drawing. Without a view finder, there was no way for her to be sure if she was aiming the camera accurately. But Ryan's genius camera design had anticipated that.

She repeated the process four more times.

Carefully she placed the drawings back in the drawer just as she'd found them, relocked the cabinet, and placed the ring and chain around her neck, tucking it neatly inside her blouse. She redid her chignon as she walked, pausing to open the door a crack—just enough to ensure that Lilah was still away from her desk.

There was no sign of anyone.

Ten minutes later, Simone drove through Nano's gates.

Houdini couldn't have made a better escape.

Her father would be proud.

17

Damn the traffic.

Simone burst into her hotel room and rushed over to the desk, not even bothering to take off her coat. She had no time to read Terri's mini-dossier. It would have to wait. She had twenty-five minutes to make the kidnappers' noon deadline. Everything else would have to be put on hold.

Aidan knew where things stood. The two of them had brought each other up to speed via secure cell phone on her drive over. Now she had work to do—fast.

Reaching around with both hands, she unclasped the chain from around her neck, then quickly slid off the ring. She placed it in a special dongle that Ryan had engineered. Once the black cable was attached to the ring, she plugged the other end into an available USB port on her laptop. The whole process made her think of how she connected her Fitbit to its charger. She'd be sure not to mention that to Ryan; somehow she doubted he'd appreciate the mundane analogy.

Task complete, she launched the custom file transfer program Ryan had written to extract the image files from the ring itself and store them on her own laptop. Then she closed the application and removed the ring and its dongle.

Immediately, Simone initiated a videoconference with Terri.

"It's done," she said.

"And not a moment too soon." Immediately, Terri assumed control of Simone's laptop and began the process of downloading and checking the images taken of the engineering drawings.

"Nice work," she said. "From what I can tell, these will clearly show the kidnappers and their overlords that the drawings are real and that we're not bullshitting them. That said, the content is interesting but not sufficient for them to take the technology and run with it. There's much more needed to make that happen."

"So which ones should I send to the kidnappers?" Simone asked.

"I would send numbers two, three, and five. Those should suffice for now."

"Terri, since you're already in control of my computer, can you do this for me?" Simone was looking at her watch. "We've only got twelve minutes to meet the kidnappers' deadline and you're the expert at this, not I. Plus I've got to get back to Nano before anyone becomes suspicious."

"Done." Terri was already at work as Simone rose to dash to the bathroom before returning to Nano for her next round of interviews.

Terri fired up a virtual Linux machine on Simone's laptop, giving her a sandboxed area from which to conduct her clandestine work. Inside the VM, she started a Tor browser, which would mask her identity from prying eyes. She followed the kidnappers' instructions verbatim, typing their assigned link in the address bar. She then logged in using the code name *baba*. Once inside, she efficiently uploaded files two, three, and five. She then terminated her Tor browser session and closed the Linux VM, restoring Simone's computer to its previous state.

All with six minutes to spare.

Terri picked up her phone to call Aidan.

Franklin Wales Executive Recruiting
San Mateo, California
28 February
Wednesday, 12:25 p.m. local time

David Cheng had just ground out his cigarette and was about to reenter the building when his current burner phone rang.

"Cheng here."

"We've received the drawings," the voice at the other end of the phone told him in perfect, almost indiscernibly accented English. "My experts are examining them now to ensure they're legitimate and to determine how much information we can extract from them and use toward completion."

Cheng sagged with relief. True, he'd had no influence on whether or not this portion of his employer's plan would be successful. But had it failed, his role would have become obsolete—as would he.

"I'm very pleased to hear that," he replied, then waited. His employer was a busy man, seated in a CEO chair halfway across the globe. He didn't waste words.

"However, my experts did say that the photos were clearly taken with a specialized camera. Pennington would have to know someone to get this technology. That suggests he's brought someone else into the equation—a complication that would require action on our part."

"I've seen no indication that law enforcement is involved."

"Then find out who is. I expect answers from you. Tonight."

NanoUSA
28 February
Wednesday, 12:45 p.m. local time

Zoe was nibbling at her chicken salad sandwich and mentally preparing herself for her one o'clock meeting when Jen buzzed her.

"A David Cheng is on the line for you," she said. "Do you want me to take a message?"

"No." Zoe was already dabbing at her mouth with a napkin. "I'll take the call. Go ahead and put him through."

"No problem."

An instant later, David's upbeat, executive-recruiter voice greeted her. "Hi, Zoe. I haven't heard from you, so I thought I'd give you a shout."

"No problem. I was actually going to give you a call after I finished wolfing down my sandwich. Olivia got back to me this morning." Olivia Stack was Nano's VP of Human Resources. "She can set something up for Friday at ten o'clock if that works for you."

The barest hint of a pause. "That would be great," David replied. "Thanks. But I was really calling about you. Have you made any decisions?"

"Decisions?" Zoe's brows rose. "It's been less than two days since we spoke, David. I need more time than that. As I told you, I'm confident there's something in the works for me here. And if that's the case…"

"You still won't be making the kind of money you'll be pulling in here," he finished for her.

"Yes, you made that abundantly clear."

"Look, Zoe, let me be blunt. My partners and I would like to know if you're considering pursuing the opportunity we discussed." David pushed only as hard as his instincts told him he could. If he overshot, he'd lose her, and they both knew it. "If you are, let's grab a drink after work today and I can share the details of our offer with you."

"I just can't talk right now," Zoe said. "I'll call you in an hour."

David accepted the slight delay without question. "I'll be here."

Zoe hung up and sat back in her chair, feeling that same surge of professional excitement she'd felt when she'd first met David Cheng. She'd been having a solo drink at Jake's, a bar that was frequented primarily by tech company people. She was ordinarily closemouthed about her work, but David had caught her in a vulnerable moment, a moment when she was wondering if Robert would really come through for her and ensure she got that promotion before he retired.

Well-dressed in a way that screamed success and smelling faintly of cigarette smoke, David had sought her out the moment she'd gotten settled at her table. He'd made a beeline in her direction, greeted her by name, and introduced himself as an executive recruiter for Franklin Wales. He'd gone on to say that he'd read her LinkedIn profile, done some heavy-duty research on her, and was planning on reaching out to her tomorrow—so he was delighted to run into her tonight. Zoe had glanced down at the business card he'd proffered, more than familiar with the prestigious firm name and very curious about why he was so eager to make contact with her. Obviously, he had an agenda. Everyone in Corporate America did.

One thing was for sure, and that was that this was no attempted pickup. Zoe knew those signs only too well. No, this was business through and through. But to what end? That she intended to find out. So she'd asked him to join her.

David hadn't wasted time. Within a minute, he'd made it clear that besides what he'd read on LinkedIn, he had an astonishingly accurate handle on what she did—not just her PA role but the full extent of her accomplishments and aptitude.

"You're executive material," he'd stated flatly. "So why are you still a personal assistant—even if it is to the CEO?"

"I have a promotion on the horizon," she'd replied, pausing and ultimately deciding there was no point in closing off her options. "As it happens, it's in the human resources department. I've always had aspirations of going in that direction."

"And you're more than qualified to do so." David hadn't looked surprised. He'd looked like he was about to pitch something.

Zoe waited.

David had indeed wanted to pitch something, but it was not at all what Zoe had been expecting. Rather than presenting a potential career opportunity at another company, he'd flatly asked if she'd be interested in coming on board at Franklin Wales—not as an employee but as a full partner.

"We're actively pursuing qualified people who can bring with them a substantial network of tech contacts and do a buy-in into our company."

Zoe had felt the wind go out of her sails. She knew exactly what a buy-in would mean. "I don't have the kind of capital to invest that you'd require," she'd said. "But I'm flattered that Franklin Wales would consider me."

David had waved away her obviously anticipated objection. "Given your income range, we assumed the monetary investment would be a no-go. But there are other perks you bring with you. For example, you know a large number of high-level executives, both inside and outside NanoUSA—executives we'd love to have access to."

Access to? That triggered warning bells in Zoe's head. "What exactly is it we're talking about here?"

"Nothing unethical," David had reassured her with a hint of a smile. "Although I do admire your loyalty. I'm just saying that your value-add is that you'd open a lot of doors for us if you joined our team. Yes, we do have clients who are interested in recruiting people out of Nano—but only if those people are equally interested in moving. But the same applies to executives at the many other companies you deal with. You're in a unique position to match the right people with the right opportunities—and to know which executives and which companies to approach."

Zoe had sipped her wine. She couldn't argue that point.

David went the next step—one that was the very Achilles heel she'd been contemplating when he'd approached her. "You said you have a promotion on the horizon. Just beware that as you walk, the horizon always recedes—you rarely actually get to it."

"I recognize that. But I work for a very honorable company."

"Company dynamics change—especially when the CEO is in his sixties and about to reach the pinnacle of his career by releasing cutting-edge, game-changing technology. Sounds like a great swan song to me."

Zoe pressed her lips together and said nothing.

"Look," David had said. "Franklin Wales doesn't need to solicit employees, much less partners. I wouldn't be approaching you if I didn't think this would be a great fit. You know the industry. You know the players. You have the connections. And—speaking on a strictly professional basis—you're an attractive woman in a male-dominated field. Much as we all try to pretend that doesn't matter, it does. It's a reality and a plus."

That was one of Zoe's hot buttons. But she couldn't say he was wrong. He wasn't.

"Let's say I'm interested," she said. "What would be the next step—interviews with the other senior partners?"

"Not necessary, not in your case. My partners are comfortable with my making the right call. But we have aggressive financial targets and we need to get started on achieving them. So we need to know in short order if you're game."

"I see."

"If you do join us, we'd want you to recruit at Nano and other tech companies right away. And—on a separate note, and not a caveat to the job—I'd appreciate if you could get me a meeting with Olivia Stack. Striking up a relationship with Nano's VP of Human Resources would be a coup for me and an in to a new corporate client—an in that you can nurture if you choose to come aboard."

Nothing David had said was sleazy. He wanted resolution. He wanted contacts. And as an ambitious guy, he wanted to connect with a VP who could make things happen for him.

"Fair enough," Zoe had replied. "You've given me a lot to think about. And while I appreciate your sense of urgency, I do need some time to consider my options. I've worked at Nano for fifteen years. This would be a major change for me. And I want to make sure it's the right one. I don't want to waste either Franklin Wales' time or my own. As for Olivia, I'll talk to her tomorrow. I'm sure she'll agree to a meeting."

That was a day and a half ago.

And here was David, following up like a good executive recruiter—one who smelled victory.

She still didn't know whether that victory was in the cards. But she'd done enough research on Franklin Wales to know that opportunities like this didn't come along often. And as for her future at Nano—she was about to walk into the meeting she'd set up with Robert to discuss that very thing.

On that thought, she pushed aside the rest of her sandwich and rose, head held high.

Time to take her future into her own hands.

18

Zoe didn't need Jen, or anyone else, to escort her into Robert's office.

She simply knocked, waited for his "come in," and when it came, entered with confidence, shutting the door firmly behind her.

Robert rose from behind his desk, gesturing for her to join him in the sitting area.

"I'd rather talk at your desk," Zoe replied, lowering herself into one of the cushioned seats across from his executive chair. Setting the tone she wanted, she smoothed down her pencil skirt below her knee before crossing one leg over the other. This meeting was going to be all business and all about her future at Nano. No corporate discussion. No technology updates. And certainly nothing that smacked of personal.

"All right." Robert looked puzzled, but sank back down into his chair, studying Zoe as if trying to figure out what was going on in her mind and what this meeting would entail.

He was about to find out.

"Robert, this follow-up conversation is long overdue," she began. "I don't need to remind you yet again what a loyal, committed member of the Nano team I've been for over fifteen years. I've devoted my entire life to this company, and to you."

"No one knows that better than I do," Robert replied. "Just as you know how much I value you."

She sidestepped that one. "You've told me in confidence that you'll be retiring even sooner than the rumor mill expects—probably in May. You've also told me that Vance will be your appointed successor. It doesn't take a brain surgeon to figure out that that means a big promotion for Ethan."

Robert's brows knit. "None of this is news to you, Zoe. I've been completely up front with you from the start. In fact, you're the only person at Nano who knows my timeline."

"Yes, and also the reason for your timeline."

Tight lines formed around Robert's mouth. "Now you're out of line."

"*I'm* out of line?" Zoe felt a surge of anger. She'd thought she'd long since let this go, but clearly it was a wound not so easily closed.

Forcibly, she shut the door on her emotions. To rehash this was useless. What was done was done. The important thing here was her promotion.

"I didn't come in here to argue, Robert. I came to discuss my future at Nano."

Some of the tension left Robert's body. He leaned forward, resting his elbows on the desk and interlacing his fingers. "I haven't forgotten my promise. Shortly, I'll be analyzing the composite of the HR department. That will be a key step in finding a way to seamlessly fit you in."

"What does *shortly* mean?" Zoe asked. "It's been two months since we first discussed this."

"I understand your impatience." Robert's voice was both sincere and reassuring. "You know me better than to think I'm blowing you off. But you also know how consumed I am with the release of our new technology. That takes priority over everything. Even you. Please have patience with me. I won't leave you hanging."

Zoe sighed. "I don't doubt your good intentions, Robert. I, better than anyone, know how much Nano means to you as well as how important the release of our new technology is. It will revolutionize the industry, change the balance of power, and create thousands of American jobs. But I have to be a little selfish. I have a career to protect. I'm very upset that we're no further along in securing my future here than we were two months ago. And now you have a McKinsey consultant sniffing around, one who could suggest any number of changes or streamlining—all of which could wind up screwing me."

Leaning back in his chair, Robert rubbed his eyes. "I'm truly sorry, Zoe. I mean it. But I'm stretched way too thin to promise you an immediate response. I fully intend to promote you to a position worthy of your talents. And, yes, I'd like it to be in human resources, just as you've requested. It's just going to take some time for me to figure out the best way to make this happen without ruffling everyone's feathers."

"How much time?" she asked quietly.

Zoe's tone must have struck home, because Robert straightened in his chair and stared directly into her eyes, searching for something and finding it.

"Is this your way of telling me that you have some personal deadline after which you start checking out opportunities outside of Nano?" he asked bluntly.

Zoe didn't look away, nor did she lie. "It means I can't live on somedays. I've told you that in the past. And, no, I haven't put myself out there yet. That doesn't mean I haven't been approached."

"I see." Rather than pissed off, Robert looked sad. "I'd hate for Nano to lose you. *I'd* hate to lose you. You're very important to me—you always have been, both professionally and personally. I want you to be happy. I hope I can make that happen right here at Nano. But if something extraordinary comes along sooner than I can come through for you, I'll understand. I'll hate it, but I'll understand." He searched her face. "Is that what you wanted to hear?"

To Zoe's own dismay, a shimmer of tears glistened in her eyes. At the same time, she felt vindicated about the decision she was about to make, and the necessary actions that would accompany it.

"Not really," she replied. "What I wanted to hear was that you'd found the ideal executive position for me. Instead, what I'm hearing is that I'm not high up on your to-do list right now, but that I have your blessing to resign."

He rose, reaching across the desk to take her hand. "That's not what I'm saying."

She pulled her hand away and then came to her feet. "Actually it is. What's more, down deep I guess I expected just this response. That doesn't mean it hurts any less." She blinked away her tears, more set than ever on her course and unwilling to ever let this man make her cry again. Too many years, too many tears.

"We understand each other, Robert. Just as we always have. I've given you my all. Now it's time for me to take care of me."

* * *

Zoe marched straight back to her office, any indecision having evaporated.

She picked up her phone and called David Cheng.

"Hi, David, it's Zoe. I'm ready to hear your offer."

"Great." He sounded more than pleased. "Let's meet for a drink at Jake's. What time is good for you?"

"There's no time like the present. How about three o'clock?"

"Done. I'll bring our offer in writing. You'll see firsthand how much we value our partners. In anticipation of us striking a deal, why don't you bring a copy of Nano's org charts? That way, we can start making money together sooner."

"That works for me. See you at three."

Zoe disconnected the call and dialed Jen's extension.

"Can you sit at my desk for the rest of the afternoon?" Zoe almost smiled as she asked. Jen would jump at this chance. She might be just a seat-holder. But she'd relish any interaction with their CEO.

Sure enough, Jen sounded delighted. "No problem, Zoe. Is everything okay?"

"I just have a splitting migraine. Tell that to Robert if he asks."

Sava Bridge, Zagreb
28 February
Wednesday, 11:25 p.m. local time

The night was winter cold, with only a few pedestrians making their way across the arched bridge that spanned the old and new sections of Zagreb. There was a second bridge a short distance away, where a small stream of cars was moving in both directions, but the bridge on which Marc waited was solely a pedestrian bridge, where walkers, joggers, and bikers were free to travel without vehicle interference. Tonight, few of them were taking advantage of that opportunity, given the dipping temperatures and the lateness of the hour.

Marc leaned against the railing of the bridge, staring out across the smooth, dark waters of the Sava. The lights cast by the occasional streetlamps flickered off the river surface, reflecting off the snow-covered trees and making them glisten. A picture-perfect postcard, were Marc here for the scenery. But he was not.

He knew he was early. A quick glance at his watch confirmed that fact. Ten minutes to go. He pushed away from the railing, instinctively glancing to his left and to his right before reaching down his shirt, feeling for the slide switch on the transmitter, and moving it to the on position. A couple of seconds later, he could hear the sounds of Philip's voice coming through his earpiece.

Speaking at a normal volume, he sought the verification he needed. "Philip, can you hear me?"

"Loud and clear," Philip replied in Marc's earpiece. "At your end?"

"Crystal."

"Good." A pause, during which Marc could visualize Philip scanning the area.

"No sign of them yet," Philip reported. "But it shouldn't be long now. Sorry you don't have your Rambo knife to play with while you wait."

Marc didn't smile. "Evidently, that's for the best," he replied. When he'd spoken with Danijel a short while ago, he'd felt obligated to be forthcoming. And Danijel had told him—no, *ordered* him was more like it—to leave the knife behind.

"This is a key contact I'm setting you up with," he'd said in a tone that shut the door on any argument. "I've worked with him before and kept him out of prison more than once. But feel lucky that he agreed to talk to you. He's not a big talker. You won't get a second chance. So use this one wisely. Know who you're dealing with. This is not a violent man. Let's say he arranges shipments for a competing Albanian group."

Okay, drugs. Marc got it. "So he's doing this because he owes you?" he'd asked.

"Partly. But also because the Sallaku family was responsible for killing his brother. His desire for vengeance is great. But his fear is greater. If you show up with a weapon, he'll bolt. Leave the knife at the hotel, or I'm calling off this meeting."

Marc had instantly agreed.

Now he walked over to the nearby bench and sat at the edge, legs spread apart, hands gripping his knees, ready to snap into action at the first sign of Danijel and his CI. He breathed deeply, watching his exhales emerge in clouds of icy mist. As always, he was outwardly calm, internally coiled to strike. It was the Navy SEAL in him, a quality that was as much a part of him as breathing.

"Your guests have arrived," Philip announced.

"So I see." Marc had spotted them approaching out of the corner of his eye. He rose, wishing he'd worn his damned gloves. It was freezing, but given what Danijel had said, there was no way Marc was shoving his hands into the pockets of his parka. Too much of a risk that the informant would think he was reaching for a weapon. He just turned to face them, arms at his sides, putting on his let's-do-business rather than his intimidating expression.

"Good evening," Danijel greeted him, purposely avoiding the mention of his name.

"Chief Inspector Horvat," Marc replied with a nod. "Thank you for meeting with me tonight. And please thank your contact."

While Danijel was doing just that, Marc gave the anonymous CI a quick once-over. He was short and stocky, wearing a heavy work coat with the hood pulled as far over his face as possible. All Marc could make out was a long face with a shock of black hair, a large nose, and a stubble of beard. And the guy was a nervous wreck, shifting from one foot to the other and gazing furtively around as if he expected to be shot dead at any given moment.

Marc was glad he'd listened to Danijel about the weapon.

"In English, tell me exactly what you want him to know," Danijel instructed. "I haven't told him anything other than you're American, that you're trustworthy and in trouble, and that you require his help. I want to be sure I convey as much or as little as you choose. But be as detailed as you're able. It's the only way we can find out how much help he can and will offer you."

Marc cleared his throat, keeping his gaze on Danijel as he spoke—and not only because it would be Danijel who did the interpreting but because a direct stare could freak this quaking CI out and send him running. Which was the last thing Marc wanted, not when his gut instincts were telling him that this liaison could yield major results.

"Please let him know this situation is urgent," he responded to Danijel's request. "We're looking for a kidnapped young woman. She's an American college student and we have reason to believe she's being held in Croatia by an Albanian crime group. If he can do anything to help us—and fast—we'd be very grateful. Assure him that this is a low-risk, high-reward arrangement for him. For the right information, he stays nameless and safe and also receives a large cash payment."

Danijel turned and spoke to the man in rapid Croatian, clearly saying a whole lot more than Marc's tersely worded statement. The CI listened intently, spitting on the ground when the name Sallaku was introduced.

Derica spoke up in Marc's ear. "Chief Inspector Horvat is saying that he is certain the Sallaku family is behind this kidnapping and that he knows about this man's personal vendetta against them," she said. "He expressed sympathy about the murder of his brother. He also assured him that this conversation would be completely confidential on the law enforcement front—no official reports filed or red flags raised. And he gave his word that you can be trusted and talked to."

The man hesitated for a few seconds, and then fired back a reply to Danijel.

"He's frightened," Derica translated. "He says they'll slit his throat if they find out he talked to you at all, much less gave you damning information. He wants certain reassurances in advance—more than just Danijel's word that you can be trusted."

Even as Derica spoke, Danijel was turning to Marc. "I think an incentive might be in order."

Marc had already figured that one out and was reaching into his pocket. He waited only until the chief police inspector had averted his gaze.

"This is for you," Marc said directly to the informant, handing over some folded bills. He knew it didn't matter that his words couldn't be understood. He was speaking the universal language of cash.

Even though the man's face was partly covered, Marc could see the look of surprised pleasure that lifted the corners of his mouth. One thousand American dollars wasn't something he was offered every day.

He stuffed the money in his pocket, then said something to Danijel's averted profile.

"Chief Inspector," Marc murmured to Horvat. "Why don't you rejoin the conversation."

Danijel complied, turning to Marc. "It seems that my contact is willing to help you—given your offers for now and for later."

Marc stifled a chuckle. The guy was making sure there was more cash to come.

This time he looked directly at the CI and nodded.

Satisfied, the man glanced back at Danijel and resumed speaking.

"He's saying that Croatia is too broad an area for the kind of time frame you're talking about," Danijel told Marc. "He's sure you have a more specific location in mind. And he wants to know what that is."

"Slavonia," Marc replied without hesitation. "She was taken there less than a week ago. We need specifics about where to look. And just so your informant knows, all we want is her safe return. We have no interest in anything or anyone else."

Danijel again rattled off something in Croatian, and a brief back-and-forth ensued.

"Danijel just repeated what you said and then reminded his informant that he owes him a favor," Derica reported. "The informant hedged, saying he's based in Zagreb and knows nothing about Slavonia. Danijel jogged his memory, commenting that the CI has a well-connected uncle in Slavonia—one whose hatred for his nephew's killers is equally powerful."

Marc absorbed all that information, watching as the nervous man fingered the cash in his pocket. Apparently, it reassured him, because he nodded again.

There was another brief round of conversation between him and Danijel.

"The informant asked for a few days," Derica said. "Danijel refused. He said that time is of the essence and he expected a meeting with the informant and his uncle by early morning. He said that you and he would meet them in Osijek at the location of their choice."

Marc knew from Terri's report that Osijek was the capital and largest city in Slavonia, and that it was less than a three-hour drive from Zagreb. Of course, there was also a forty-five minute direct plane flight between the two cities, but that might be tricky to pull off without producing proper ID—something that would be an impossibility for both Danijel and the informant, each with different needs for anonymity.

"I'm a fast driver," Philip said in Marc's ear. "Even dawn is more than doable."

Inwardly, Marc nodded. Outwardly, he stood quietly as the informant responded to Danijel.

The chief inspector inclined his head at Marc. "I'll hear from him within the hour," he reported. "I don't expect any complications. As for the rest of my conversation, I'm sure you already heard all the details from your interpreter. So go back to the hotel and wait for my call. Be ready to drive."

19

Simone was standing at Jen's desk, waiting to determine Robert's calendar for the end of the week, when Jen got the call from Zoe.

"Excuse me," Jen said to her. "Hi, Zoe, what do you need?"

A minute later she was all smiles, coming to her feet and scooping up her handbag. Clearly, she'd received some happy news.

"Can we go over Robert's schedule later?" she asked Simone, although it really wasn't a question. "I have to cover Zoe's desk."

Something about Jen's overly enthusiastic response gave Simone pause. She glanced at the flowers on Jen's desk, took in her radiant expression, and a realization clicked into place.

"No problem," she assured the young woman. "What time will Zoe's meeting be over?"

"Oh, she isn't going into a meeting, not this time. She's heading home—splitting migraine. I'm just manning her desk to field any problems that might come up to the best of my ability."

Even as Jen spoke, Zoe exited her office, carrying a slim file folder and her purse. She looked more like a woman on a mission than a woman with a headache. And leaving the office in the middle of the day? Zoe, who lived for and at Nano? Not likely.

Zoe nodded as she passed Jen, walking by Simone without really seeing her. Clearly, her mind was locked onto something. The question was: what?

Simone waited until Zoe had left the executive suite, her heels clicking purposefully on the marble floor as she headed toward the outside doors.

Then she followed her.

Jake's Bar & Cocktail Lounge
28 February
Wednesday, 2:55 p.m. local time

David was waiting for Zoe in the lounge area when she arrived. He rose from behind one of the red leather couches that catty-cornered a second one, both clustered around a polished oak table, and waved her over.

She acknowledged that she'd seen him with a responding wave, then bypassed the bar and made her way over to him.

"It's great to see you," David said, gesturing at the adjacent couch. "Please, sit."

Zoe complied, her brows lifting as she saw the bottle of champagne chilling on ice. "Confident, aren't we?"

"Actually, yes," he replied. "And not because I'm arrogant. Because I know you'll make the ideal addition to Franklin Wales. You'll see that for yourself once you've read over our offer."

He opened a manila folder and handed her the pages inside.

Zoe read through them, her eyes widening despite her best attempts to maintain a poker face. The bonuses alone were more than her annual salary at Nano. And the rest—it was a dream job, and not just because of the money. She'd be the one controlling her own future, contributing to the company while spreading her wings. She'd be able to implement all the creativity, the business savvy, and the experience she had to offer. She'd be recruiting and placing top-level executives in the technology field, and she'd be one of a half dozen partners—all heavy hitters she could learn from. This offer made her aspirations at Nano look like child's play.

"I take it you're satisfied?" David asked, having watched her expression like a hawk.

Zoe lifted her gaze to meet his. "I'd be a fool to say otherwise. Obviously, I have a few questions—which I prepared in advance, given you said that time is of the essence."

"Shoot."

Quickly and efficiently, Zoe ran through those items that weren't covered in the agreement. Just as quickly, David answered them all, agreeing to put his promises in writing as an addendum to the proposal.

"Then I'm fine." Zoe nodded, her eyes glittering with anticipation.

David extended his hand. "Welcome aboard."

Zoe met his handshake firmly. "I look forward to a successful partnership."

"As do I." David reached for the bottle of champagne and popped the cork. He filled each of their waiting flutes to the brim. "To the future," he said, raising his glass.

"To the future," Zoe echoed.

As they sealed their new partnership with the first sips of bubbly, David's gaze shifted to the folder Zoe had placed beside her on the couch. "Why don't we take a quick scan of the org chart you brought? We can order some appetizers and brainstorm ideas while we enjoy?"

"Good idea." Zoe pulled out the copy of Nano's organizational chart, listing everyone's name, title, and contact information, department by department. She slid it across the table, waiting as David ordered some spicy wings and jalapeno poppers.

A few minutes later, they were eating, drinking, and poring over the org chart, chatting about the Nano team.

David played his part perfectly. He feigned interest in all the right places and adhered to a verbal analysis that made sense for an executive recruiter—all without making Zoe suspicious. The truth was, the course he was taking would help him figure out who was providing Vance Pennington with the technical help he needed to transmit the technology. And the more he analyzed the chart and listened to Zoe's explanations of the various people's roles and backgrounds, the more certain he was of the best direction to take.

He went straight for it.

"I assume Robert Maxwell's retirement will be by year's end?" he asked, knowing full well that Zoe was going to evade the question. "Never mind," he said quickly, waving away the need for an answer. "I don't expect you to confirm that. You're still a Nano employee. I won't compromise your integrity. But *if* that's the case, and *if* you were to guess, who do you think Maxwell's slotted for the CEO position? My money's on Vance Pennington."

Zoe pressed her lips together, then clearly decided to go for the supposition. "I think your money is safe."

David nodded. "Ethan Gallagher." He pointed at the name. "He's Pennington's PA. Is he a good one?"

"He's exceptional," Zoe replied. "He's also very tight with Vance. So if your supposition includes wondering about whether or not Vance would take Ethan with him to the executive suite, the answer is, yes, he definitely would."

"Is he qualified?"

"More than qualified." Zoe gave David a brief overview of Ethan's educational background and skills, as well as his solid years of training under Vance's tutelage. "If one of your—*our*—" she amended, smiling, "clients is looking for a new PA, Ethan is about as good as they come.

Other than me, of course." Her eyes twinkled. "But it would take a lot to pry him away from Vance. As I said, he's definitely his golden boy."

"By a lot, you mean money?"

"Money, growth potential—the works."

"I know Nano's pay scale," David said. "It's better than competitive. But it's not off the charts. And if Ethan is as good as you say he is, he's probably nearing the top of his salary grade range. So why hasn't he pressed for a promotion? Maxwell hasn't been on a retirement track until now, so Ethan would have no way of knowing his boss was slated to be the new CEO. I guess he isn't as hungry as I'd imagine."

Zoe shrugged. "Judging from the car he drives and the kind of friends and fun he describes, I don't think he's hurting."

"Meaning?"

"He bought an obscenely expensive Porsche a few months ago. And he hangs out with an executive crowd that is major pay grades higher than he is and enjoys the good life."

"How does he pull all that off?"

Another shrug. "Truthfully, I never asked. I hear what I hear in the break room and from other employees who like to gossip. But Ethan and I are colleagues, not friends. He's probably either up to his neck in credit card debt or he's got rich parents subsidizing him."

Or he's getting payoffs from Pennington to do a little off-the-books work, David thought.

He'd found the probable candidate to be helping Pennington. Ethan Gallagher's educational background had no doubt given him the technical skills he needed. And he was glued to Vance's side and willing to do anything to make his boss happy and to boost his own income in the process.

"David?" Zoe was calling for his attention, and David mentally kicked himself for zoning out on her.

"Sorry, Zoe." He gave her a sheepish look. "The truth is, I'm desperate for a cigarette. I've been trying to quit, but without much luck so far. Would you mind if I stepped outside for a minute?"

"No problem." Zoe was already reaching for the proposal he'd given her. "I'll do a little rereading while you're out."

"Great."

* * *

By the time Zoe's companion rose from his seat, Simone had taken half a dozen photos of him from her hidden stool at the end of the bar. She'd also been able to make out the logo at the top of whatever papers he was handing Zoe. Franklin Wales. Big-time headhunters. She wished she could have caught snippets of their conversation, but she couldn't risk moving closer. The exchange of papers and the intensity of the conversation told her that this was serious business. And the champagne toast? Clearly a deal being sealed. But what kind of deal? Was Zoe making a career move? Or was the whole scenario, including the document exchange, a cover? Interesting that Zoe's companion was Chinese.

That could be sheer coincidence. On the other hand, it could mean that Zoe was the mole that Zermatt was searching for.

Simone used this break in the action to open the browser on her cell phone and check out the Franklin Wales website. She went straight to the "members of our team" link and ran through the names and faces.

It didn't take her long to find this guy. David Cheng. Impressive bio. Contacts all over the globe. Fluent in Mandarin.

Quickly, she forwarded a brief summary of what was going on right now, along with the photos she'd taken and the link to Cheng's page on the Franklin Wales website, to Terri. "See what you can dig up," she typed. She made sure to cc Aidan.

Then she waited patiently for Cheng to return.

* * *

Jítuán Headquarters
Shenzhen, China

Xu Wei, the CEO of Jítuán, disconnected the call with Cheng and contacted his head of security, simultaneously texting him all the pertinent information about Ethan Gallagher he'd just heard.

"Send our people to this man's apartment tonight," he instructed in Mandarin. "Find out everything about him." A pause. "Yes. Tonight. Pay them whatever is necessary."

20

Aidan had been in the Penningtons' hotel suite all day and had no immediate plans to leave—not with the instability of things at this end.

He resettled himself on the sofa, quickly firing off a Daddy text to Abby, promising that when his work in Santa Clara was done, he'd join her for a full day in Disneyland before they all flew home to New York. It was a promise he was determined to keep—not only because he loved spending time with Abby but because the fact that he'd be able to do so meant that Lauren Pennington would be safely reunited with her family, and he'd have a clear mind to spend time with his daughter.

But first he had to bring the Penningtons' daughter home.

He glanced up, seeing the same scene he'd seen all day.

Vance was standing like a statue at the panoramic window. He hadn't moved in hours, and he was wound so tight that he was about to erupt. And Susan had been crying and walking the floors all day. Between the two of them, Aidan was gravely concerned that someone might do something stupid, something that would endanger Lauren's life.

Sure enough, Vance's head snapped around and he stared at Aidan. "If we don't hear back soon, maybe I should reconsider and contact the FBI."

Aidan kept his demeanor calm. "That would be foolish, Vance, and I think you know it. You're panicking. I understand. But you learned a great deal from one conversation with Lauren. Based on her diet, we've narrowed down our search to Slavonia, which is a small region of Croatia. My team members are meeting with informants who will narrow down that area even further. We'll get locations and answers. We'll bring Lauren home safely. You have my word."

The vow tasted bitter on Aidan's tongue, especially after his conversation with Marc. But he had to shove his fears aside and go with his instincts. And his instincts screamed that his team *would* rescue Lauren in time.

"Your word is wearing thin," Vance snapped. "We have less than three days left. Did you see Lauren's face? How pale and terrified she is? She's a young girl, Aidan. Her life has barely begun. And here I am, sitting on my hands when I should be doing something to bring her home safely."

"You *are* doing something," Aidan replied. "Lauren's continued safety relies on her kidnappers' belief that you're following their orders and not contacting law enforcement. The Albanian organized crime groups are not known for their tolerance. You've had faith in me up until now. Hold on for a little while longer."

Susan stopped pacing long enough to plant herself in front of Aidan. "Vance sent them a portion of what they want. So why haven't they contacted him yet? Outlined their next step?"

Aidan responded with composure and logic. "I'm sure they're having their experts review the drawings to make sure they're legitimate. That takes time. By tomorrow, you'll be hearing from them with further instructions. Vance will also have seen and talked to Lauren again. This will all come together—and well before their deadline."

"You're that certain?" Vance asked, searching Aidan's face.

"Yes." Aidan didn't blink, having successfully squelched his own fears. "I'm that certain."

At that moment, Aidan's cell phone buzzed. He glanced down at it and then rose. "I need to make a quick phone call. I'll be back shortly."

Susan jumped all over that: "Is it about Lauren?"

"It's not from my overseas team members, so no," Aidan hedged carefully. Now was definitely not the time for full disclosure—even after he'd read Simone's email. Given the Penningtons' state of mind, he was determined to keep them on a need-to-know basis. The investigation was too fluid and escalating too rapidly to provide a blow-by-blow update to his emotionally distraught clients.

He was already headed for the door, intending to read and respond to the email alone in his hotel room. "Once I've handled this business matter, I'll be back."

Simone had used the emergency code; he didn't have time for niceties or explanations.

* * *

Aidan sat down at the hotel desk and opened Simone's email. He read the contents and studied the photos before calling her.

"Yes?"

"It's me," Aidan said. "Are you able to talk?"

"I'm still at the bar," Simone answered quietly. "But Zoe just went to the ladies' room and her friend is outside, presumably smoking, according to what he told her. It looks like they're wrapping up, so I'll slip out now and call you in five minutes."

Simone was true to her word. Aidan's cell phone rang four-and-a-half minutes later.

"I'm in the car," she said. "This is an interesting twist, no?"

"More than interesting. Has Terri gotten back to you yet?"

"Only to say that she's on the verge of hacking into the Franklin Wales servers so she can find the specifics of whatever company agreement Cheng is signing with Zoe. The rest—finding out if Cheng is merely an executive recruiter or something more—that will take longer. It's not like that will be written out anywhere."

"Yeah, same for determining if Zoe is merely jumping ship or working with Cheng as an inside agent for the Chinese."

Simone's pause was thoughtful. "Something about that last part just doesn't feel right. Zoe might be leaving Nano—and I have a pretty good idea why—but I don't think she'd be vindictive enough to turn her back on fifteen years of loyal service and participate in something criminal. For what? Money? Intuition tells me that that's not an incentive for her."

Aidan hadn't missed out on Simone's inference. "Why *do* you think Zoe is considering leaving Nano?"

"Aside from the fact that she's an ambitious woman who's going nowhere in a hurry? Because she's in love with Robert Maxwell. Because they had an affair that I'm guessing was long-term and serious—at least to Zoe. And because he's turning his attentions elsewhere these days. Elsewher*es*—I don't place much credence in him being a one-woman man."

These were the areas where Simone's people-whisperer skills shined through. "I'll bite," Aidan said. "Where is he turning his attention, and what makes you think he's a player?"

"I have no doubt that he's sleeping with his receptionist, Jen. She's young, pretty, and positively radiant at the thought of being near him. She has an expensive fresh floral arrangement on her desk as well as that new-lover look—a look she keeps aiming at the door to Robert's office. As for the others, I noted a few women—Nano's CFO, June Morris, in particular—who I suspect are Robert Maxwell discards. They're all at least a decade older than Jen, and they share a few other things in common: rapid succession up the corporate ladder and utter exhaustion from the major struggle they're enduring to stay on top of their current positions."

Aidan processed that thoughtfully. "So Maxwell does have a chink in his armor. And I suspect that none of the women in question would consider filing sexual harassment charges."

"It would come down to a he-said-she-said," Simone agreed. "A battle that would end up destroying their careers. Maxwell is way too smart to leave breadcrumbs. Whatever promises he made to get them into bed would fall by the wayside because these women are probably still half in love with him. He's incredibly charismatic. You should have seen the once-over he gave me when we had our first meeting. He's quite the charmer, wedding band and family photos or not."

Aidan's brows drew together in a frown. "Does that mean that, when this case is resolved, I should beat the shit out of him?"

Simone laughed. "Don't waste your energy, *mon amour*. You have no competition."

"That's just what I wanted to hear." Aidan's frown vanished as quickly as it had appeared. "You mentioned Zoe's ambition. So you do think that's, at least in part, a reason for her meeting with Cheng?"

"Yes. I managed a quick glance at Jen's calendar before Zoe left. Zoe and Robert had just finished up a meeting of their own before she made her unprecedented midday departure. I'd be willing to bet she gave him a career ultimatum, one he didn't meet."

"Okay, so she's a woman scorned both professionally and personally. That gives her motive to seek employment elsewhere. And Franklin Wales is a well-respected executive recruiting firm. But David Cheng in particular—is the fact that he's of Chinese descent just a coincidence or is there more to it? When and under what circumstances did the two of them meet? And is a career move the totality of their association? Even if Zoe is innocent of anything criminal, does Cheng have his own one-sided industrial espionage agenda?"

"I'm sure Terri will find answers to all those questions."

"I'm sure she will," Aidan replied. "The problem is, even though Terri's a wizard, we don't know what we're up against, so we have no clue how long she'll need. And timewise, we're up against a wall. We've got to take a risk."

"What kind of a risk?" Simone asked.

"One that involves my making some fast arrangements. I'll call you back."

Aidan disconnected the call only to make another.

Mickey's Toontown
Disneyland, Anaheim, CA
28 February
Wednesday, 4:35 p.m. local time

"Hello?" Emma's voice was breathless, as it always was when Aidan called her these days. His nonstop Abby was a little hurricane to survive, even for someone with Emma's high energy levels.

"Bad time again," Aidan deduced. "Sorry. Couldn't be helped."

"One sec," Emma replied. Her next words were muted enough to indicate she was talking to someone other than him. "Joyce, could you just hang out with her for a little while?"

Joyce agreed at once, and Aidan could hear Emma's breathing as she covered enough distance so that Abby would have no idea it was her daddy at the other end of the line.

"Okay, I can talk," Emma said. "We've been character hunting for the past hour and Abby finally spotted Rapunzel. They're in animated conversation. And they're standing still, so Joyce can handle it alone. Which buys me some time." A pause. "You don't normally call in the middle of the day. What's up?"

"What's your schedule with Abby for tonight?"

Emma must have picked up on the urgency of his tone, because she got right to the point. "A five-thirty character dinner and then some souvenir shopping before we go back to the hotel and crash. Abby's wiped. We've been racing around all day."

"Good. Then Joyce can handle things there alone."

"Alone? Where will I be?"

"Here, with me." He continued, putting a lid on the onslaught of questions he knew was about to start. "I know I said I didn't need you to do any investigative work. I lied. I'm sending the private jet for you. It should be there within an hour. Tell Abby you're meeting a friend, but that you'll be back at the hotel late tonight. Then pack an outfit—nice jeans and a blouse—and grab a taxi to the airport. I'll meet you when you land."

"I... Okay." Emma sounded as if she'd been hit by a truck. "I'll be there. But I don't have the kind of clothes you're talking about. All I've got is Disney T-shirts, shorts, and bathing suits."

"What size are you?"

"Four."

"I'll take care of it. And, Emma, thanks."

* * *

There was one more step to Aidan's plan, a hunch he had to play. It would push the boundaries of his need-to-know philosophy with regard to his clients and elicit a slew of questions. But it was the only way he could ascertain if his hunch had merit.

When he returned to the Penningtons' hotel room, it was armed with his laptop, which now contained the photos he'd emailed himself.

Susan opened the door. The dubious expression on her face told him she hadn't believed a word he'd said about the communication he'd received not being related to Lauren's kidnapping.

There was nothing like a mother's instinct.

"Did you take care of your *business matter*?" she inquired, shutting the door behind him.

"Yes." Aidan neither averted his gaze nor lied. "I didn't think it would relate to Lauren's kidnapping, but it might. I need *you* to tell *me*."

"What does that mean?" Vance demanded. "How can we—"

"Not *we*," Aidan corrected. "Susan."

Susan's brows drew together. "I don't understand."

"Let's you and I sit down." Aidan was already striding into the living area. He perched at the edge of the sofa and fired up his laptop, simultaneously gesturing for Susan to join him.

She did, and a few moments later, the photos of David Cheng appeared. Aidan zoomed in as close as he could without distorting the images.

"Look closely," he instructed Susan. "Have you ever seen this man before?"

Susan peered intently at the screen, and the color began to drain from her face. "I think that's the man who's been watching us," she whispered. "I can't swear to it, but aside from the obvious fact that he's Asian, there's a certain tilt to his head and the way his hair hangs over his forehead… As I said, I can't swear to it, but I think it's him."

Vance was beside them in a minute, searching the screen. "Who is he?"

"Right now, just a suspect," Aidan replied. "If he's the person who's been watching you, then he's probably working for the Chinese company that's trying to steal your technology."

"So what do we do with this information?"

"We exploit it, full force. I'll be taking care of that tonight." Aidan gave Vance a warning look. "You'll be doing nothing with this. We're close, Vance. Leave it to me and my team. No detrimental heroics. Lauren's life is at stake. And figuring out which company—and who at that company—is orchestrating this industrial espionage can help lead us to the kidnappers."

"And to Lauren," Susan breathed.

"Yes. And to Lauren." Aidan looked at Vance, a hard, penetrating look.

Briefly, Vance shut his eyes. Then he opened them and nodded. "Get us answers."

21

The two-story apartment complex was new, sleek, and über-pricey. As if it deserved its own elite domain, it was tucked away on a private, tree-lined street, traversed only by a sidewalk where a few evening bicyclists pedaled past, lost in the music coming through their headphones or texting with one hand as they maneuvered along.

It was easy for the two men to slip in and out of Gallagher's apartment, timing their entry and exit to the moments when the sidewalk was deserted. They knew they had time to do their job; Cheng was taking care of that right now.

They moved from room to room, checking both the accessible and the inaccessible areas, being careful to return things to their previous state so as not to clue Gallagher in to the fact that they had been there.

Mostly, everything was out in the open and contained nothing of interest. But in the spare bedroom, they encountered a locked drawer, which a knife blade took care of quickly. In the back of the bottom drawer, there was a surprising, if not directly relevant, discovery. The men took some photos. They then rearranged things and relocked the desk.

A half hour later, they were gone.

Once in the car, the taller man texted the photos to Xu Wei. He waited a few minutes and then followed up with a phone call.

"Did you receive the photographs I sent you?" he asked in Mandarin.

"I'm looking at them now," Xu Wei replied, also in Mandarin.

"We found nothing to directly tie Gallagher to Pennington's activities regarding the Nano technology, but, as you can see, Gallagher has a very lucrative side job."

"Indeed." Xu Wei studied the photos more closely. A strongbox that contained numerous stacks of cash, all neatly rubber-banded together, along with dozens of plastic bags containing everything from pills to powder. "So Gallagher is a drug dealer," he said. "And a man of so little character and conscience would have no trouble committing industrial espionage for the right price. He could be our proverbial fly in the ointment, and we cannot risk him interfering. I'll call Cheng immediately and alert him to what we've found. The conversation he's currently having will be moving in a less ambiguous direction."

Jake's Bar & Cocktail Lounge
28 February
Wednesday, 8:30 p.m. local time

Aidan parked his car in an alley just two blocks away from Jake's. He flipped off the ignition and turned to Emma, who was wearing the dark-washed jeans and green silk blouse that one of Aidan's female contacts had picked up for her.

"Let's review this again," he instructed her now. "I've shown you photos, so you know what our target looks like and you know he's inside that bar, probably talking to a bunch of his tech friends."

Emma nodded impatiently. "And for whatever reason you won't tell me, this guy carries both a regular cell and a burner phone. Fine. I get it. I'm supposed to get close to him, and one of your team is going to dial his regular number. How do you know he'll answer?"

"Once he sees the Caller ID, he'll answer," Aidan replied tersely. He had no intention of telling Emma that Terri had done her magic to ensure that the Caller ID would register as NanoUSA. But Aidan knew that once David saw that and assumed it was Zoe, he'd grab the call in a New York minute. "Watch carefully to see where he pulls his cell phone from. After that..."

With the confidence of a pro, Emma waved away the rest of Aidan's sentence. "I don't need to watch carefully. No one wears jackets out here. Which means he'll either go for his shirt pocket or one of his front pants pockets. If he goes for the pants, I'm gold and can just target the pocket he doesn't go for. If he goes for the shirt, I'll have to check out which hand he holds his phone in, so I'll know whether he's right- or left-handed, at which point I can figure out which of the front pockets is where he keeps his burner. I'll then borrow it."

Aidan opened his mouth and then shut it again, giving a bemused shake of his head.

Emma shot him an impish grin. "You seem to have forgotten just how good at this I am. So I figured I'd remind you." With that, she plucked something off the seat beside her and tossed it at Aidan. "I think that's yours."

Aidan caught the wallet and turned it over in his hands. "Shit," he muttered. "You're scary."

"Scary *good*." She turned to look in the direction of the bar. "So now that your worries are over, let's deal with mine. We've established that I can steal anything from anybody. But what's a Bluejack and how do I work it?"

Aidan handed over his cell phone and pointed at the icon for the Bluejack app. "Once you get the burner in your possession, open this app and make sure to keep my phone near his. Press the app's red start button and the icon will start spinning. That tells you that it's working. It shouldn't take more than a few minutes. When it's finished, you'll see a big green check mark across the screen. Wipe your prints off his phone and slip it back in his pocket. Then you're outta there."

"I'll be meeting you back here?" Emma confirmed, sticking Aidan's phone into the pocket of her jeans.

"I won't budge."

With a nod, Emma reached for the door handle. "Now?"

"Now."

* * *

Inside Jake's, David was following orders.

Perched at a table, he was talking business with Ethan Gallagher. Despite Gallagher's loyalty to Vance Pennington, it had been easy for David to set up this meeting. Gallagher was an upwardly mobile guy whose affinity for the finer things in life was consistent with his willingness to keep all his options open. All David had to do was give him a call, say he had a few high-paying clients who were looking for people with Gallagher's experience for newly created executive positions, and *poof!* Gallagher appeared at the bar.

David had already run through a few fictitious opportunities, elaborating on the salaries and growth potential. He balanced out the career talk by engaging Ethan in personal conversation, feigning the desire to get to know his interests outside of work. His job was to pace himself to buy as much time as possible for Xu Wei's people to complete their task.

Ethan was just describing his last ski trip to Aspen when David's burner phone rang.

"Just give me one minute," he said to Ethan. "I've got an urgent client call I've been waiting for."

He stepped away, turned his back, and took the call, speaking very quietly in Mandarin, his voice swallowed up by the talking, laughter, and music of the bar.

"Yes." He absorbed the information that was given to him. "Now *that* I wasn't expecting. It's not a direct link, but it's an indicator. Let me see if I can learn anything more."

He disconnected the call, slipped the burner back into the right front pocket of his jeans, and turned back to Ethan.

He'd barely opened his mouth when his regular cell phone rang.

* * *

Emma ordered herself a drink at the bar, watching as her target disconnected whatever call he was already on, pocketed the phone, and prepared to resume a conversation with the guy at his table. Abruptly, he paused, holding up one finger and plucking a different phone out of his shirt pocket.

This was the call that would be her cue.

She put down her drink, pleased to see that her target was standing. It would make her job a hell of a lot easier. Slowly, she weaved her way over, timing her approach as her target glanced at his Caller ID and immediately took the call.

"Hello?" He frowned. "Hello? Anyone there?"

With a frustrated shake of his head, he disconnected the call and dropped the phone back into his shirt pocket.

"Wrong number, I guess," he told his friend.

Okay, Emma thought, lifting Aidan's cell phone to her ear and pretending she was chatting with someone as she closed in on her prey. *Time to get into the target's right front pocket.*

"…get their hands on the industry-changing technology that NanoUSA is about to release…" the target was saying. "…must be even higher levels of security to prevent leaks…"

The other guy seemed to tense up, but Emma didn't dwell on it. She had one focus and one focus alone.

She eased her way behind the target, making her fictitious telephone conversation seem more and more intense.

"I told you, I was working," she said into the phone, stopping just behind the target's left shoulder. "There is *no one* else."

Automatically, he averted his head toward the sound of the distressed woman's voice.

"Sorry," Emma murmured with an apologetic look. *Boyfriend,* she mouthed and pretended to shoot herself in the head.

The target gave her an understanding smile.

By the time he turned back to his friend, Emma was palming the burner phone. She walked a short distance away and then, with seeming annoyance, hung up on her boyfriend.

Fast as lightning, she opened Aidan's Bluejack app and pressed the red start button. The icon started spinning. Holding the two phones low and close together, she waited.

A minute and a half later, she got the big green check mark she'd been waiting for. Whatever syncing Aidan wanted was done.

She pocketed Aidan's phone, reaching over to pick up a cocktail napkin. She wiped her prints off the target's phone, carrying it that way as she retraced her steps to his table.

"...hard to believe the whole company is so loyal that no one would be tempted to work with any of the entities who are dying to steal the technology before it's released..." the target was saying.

Emma bent down to adjust the strap of her sandal.

She slipped the phone back into the target's pocket as she rose.

Discarding the cocktail napkin, she walked toward the entrance. Abruptly, she paused. Working at Forensic Instincts had honed her budding investigative skills. The snippets of conversation that were just now sinking in seemed like they might be of interest to Aidan.

Also, if the guy whose pocket she'd just picked was important, maybe his friend was, too.

She wriggled Aidan's phone out of her pocket and took a few unobtrusive photos of the men.

Hey, she thought, *you can't have too much information.*

* * *

Aidan's brows rose as Emma got back into the car and handed him his phone.

"Mission accomplished," she said.

"And in record time," he replied. "Any problems?"

"Nope." Emma shook her head. "Your app worked great. As did I."

He chuckled. "No self-esteem issues, huh?"

"Not when it comes to this, no." Emma turned to face him. "There were a few additional perks I brought to the table. They could mean nothing or they could mean something. I'm just the uninformed messenger."

"Meaning?"

"Mr. No-name wasn't with a bunch of guys, just one. They were definitely talking tech. It was about some company called NanoUSA and the chance that someone could be trying to steal new technology."

Aidan's eyes narrowed. "Tell me exactly what you heard."

Emma did just that.

"Damn," Aidan muttered. "I wish I knew who the other guy was."

"Check the new photos on your phone. They might answer that question."

Without a word, Aidan opened his photos and checked out the zoomed-in shots Emma had taken. Given that Simone had provided him with full bios, photos, and background data on all the key players, he instantly recognized Ethan Gallagher.

He raised his gaze to meet Emma's. "You're a real asset, Artful Dodger. Casey is lucky to have you."

"Promise to tell her that?" Emma asked with a smile.

"You couldn't stop me."

Four Seasons Hotel, Palo Alto
28 February
Wednesday, 10:15 p.m. local time

Aidan let himself into Simone's hotel room after putting Emma back on the plane to Disneyland and calling their usual pricy but lightning-fast courier service. This package had to go out tonight.

He could hear the shower water running and Simone singing a lovely song in French as he walked in. As much as he would have loved to join her, he had urgent work to take care of first.

He locked the hotel room door and headed straight for the desk, whipping out his cell phone as he did.

"Yes?" Terri answered his call.

"I've got what we need off David Cheng's phone," Aidan said without preamble. "The courier service is on its way. You'll have the copied phone first thing tomorrow morning."

"I'll begin the analysis as soon as it arrives."

"I also need you to find out whatever you can on Ethan Gallagher."

"Pennington's assistant?"

"Yup. He was talking Nano business at the bar with Cheng. Could be a coincidence. Could be more."

"I'll start that process now."

"Thanks, Terri."

Disconnecting the call, Aidan sat down and took out a black box with two wires hanging out of it. He set it on the desk. First, he plugged the red wire into the phone he'd given Emma. Next he plugged the black wire into a new phone that Terri had provided for this purpose.

He pressed the button on the machine. It came to life, the status light flashing orange. Fifteen minutes passed.

The status light turned green.

Aidan turned off the unit, disconnected the phones, and packed it up.

The courier service would be arriving shortly.

22

Two days left...

This high-traffic location was their designated meeting spot.

A horde of people already swarmed the crowded market, weaving their way around Marc, Danijel, and Danijel's informant, Valmir—whose name Danijel had provided after getting his permission during the long car ride from Zagreb. The offering of a name, plus the fact that the CI had dropped the hood of his work coat and exposed his face, were two key signs that the guy was starting to trust Marc.

Of course, the additional five hundred American dollars Marc had given him in the car hadn't hurt.

As they waited for Valmir's uncle to arrive, Marc surveyed the area, duly impressed by the volume of people and the extensive size of the market. All around them were tables with overhanging umbrellas, and despite the winter weather, the tables featured an astonishing array of fresh fruits such as apples, oranges, grapefruits, and pears, as well as imported bananas, pineapple, mangos, avocados, and coconuts. There were also fresh vegetables on display—spinach, carrots, potatoes, sweet potatoes, and many types of local salads—not to mention goat's and sheep's cheese, homemade jams, and on the periphery in refrigerated cases, cured meats and fresh poultry. The wares spread out in a kaleidoscope of color, texture, and eye appeal, and the loud voices of the salespeople beckoning the shoppers to their wooden tables to taste and to buy were interspersed with conversations of friends who clearly met here on a regular basis, mothers with their children in tow, shoppers bargaining for a better price, and tourists who'd come to visit this regaled Osijek stopping point.

It was easy to remain invisible in a place like this.

"May I ask Valmir what to call his uncle?" Marc asked Danijel. "All I need is a first name. Since this man will be taking over from here, it sure beats 'hey you.'"

Danijel's lips twitched. He relayed Marc's request to Valmir, who hesitated, then said, "Jozef."

Marc nodded. "*Hvala.*"

Danijel's brows rose as Marc thanked Valmir in Croatian. "Picking up the language, are we?"

"Trying my best." Marc touched his ear. "But I still need the benefit of a pro on anything more than a few words."

This time the pro involved was Ellie, their second translator, who'd accompanied Philip to this meeting and would be talking in Marc's ear. Despite the fact that Derica had more experience in undercover operations, Ellie spoke fluent Albanian as well as Croatian—an asset that Marc and Philip had agreed would be crucial given the players involved and the potential strategy that lay ahead.

Marc was keenly aware of the moment when Valmir's chin came up, his gaze finding someone in the crowd.

"I think we're on," he murmured.

"Indeed," Danijel concurred.

The men waited as Jozef zigzagged his way through the sea of shoppers and made his way over. Marc noted the family resemblance at once. Jozef had the same long face and prominent features as his nephew, although he wasn't as stocky and his shock of black hair was turning gray.

He reached the group, glancing quickly around as he did a once-over scan of the area. He then hugged his nephew and turned to the other two men, greeting them with a nod.

Valmir spoke to him in rapid Albanian.

Ellie's voice sounded in Marc's ear. "Valmir is explaining which of you is which and reminding him that neither of you speak Albanian so they can talk freely to each other during this meeting without either of you understanding. Otherwise, they plan to use Croatian, for obvious reasons." She gave a whisper of a laugh. "Valmir also told his uncle that you gave him five hundred American dollars in the car in addition to the thousand you handed him last night, and that there's even more to come. He said they could both make out quite nicely from helping you out—not to mention avenging Valmir's brother's death in the process."

Jozef was replying to his nephew, and Marc distinguished the name "Sallaku" in his response.

"Jozef is asking if Valmir is sure Zarik Sallaku's people are responsible for the kidnapping," Ellie translated. "He's also making sure you specifically mentioned Slavonia as the region where the girl is being held."

"*Po*," Jozef replied with a nod. Marc didn't need Ellie's skills to figure out that meant yes.

Jozef's eyes hardened and he turned to face Danijel, switching over to Croatian.

"I loathe Sallaku and wish him dead." Ellie's voice resounded in Marc's ear. "It's the main reason I agreed to help you. The other reason is the generous payment I expect to be offered."

Jozef waited for Danijel to translate and for Marc to nod his head in agreement.

"Good," he said. "I reached out to my contacts after Valmir called and received information in return. Your friend here will need to come with me to the town of Ðakovo. He'll have to find a woman to go with him. Everyone there knows everyone, and a man who's alone and who looks like a federal agent will— to use an American expression—stick out like a sore thumb. I have friends. They tell me there's talk of strangers in the area. My friends are willing to help—also for the right monetary compensation. There are many abandoned farmhouses they can take you to."

Danijel turned to look at Marc. "I assume you got all that, so I'll just pretend I'm translating for you. Ðakovo is about a forty-minute drive from Osijek. Can you arrange for a female teammate to accompany you? Hopefully, one who speaks both Croatian and Albanian, since this is where I must step out of things. I've pushed my boundaries as far as I'm able."

"I know." Marc was well aware of how far out on a limb Danijel had gone for them. He was also aware that they were about to move into criminal territory, a reality they'd all known would ultimately be necessary in order to rescue Lauren.

"I'll go," Ellie volunteered in Marc's ear at once.

"So will I," Philip echoed. "It's time for me to do recon."

"My female translator just agreed to help us," Marc told Danijel. "The one additional change is that Philip, not I, will be the one to accompany her. His background is best suited for this portion of the investigation."

"His work in covert recon," Danijel remembered Philip's dossier aloud.

"Exactly. I know that neither Valmir nor Jozef have met Philip, so I'll be here when we reconvene to make the introductions. After that, you and I will leave. I'll be staying in Osijek, but you go ahead and return to Zagreb. We owe you a huge debt of thanks."

"No thanks are necessary." A corner of Danijel's mouth lifted. "I'm pleased that it's now Aidan who owes a favor to me."

With that, he turned and explained the situation to Jozef and Valmir.

The men exchanged glances, and Jozef gave a quick nod of agreement. He then ascertained in Croatian that, once their business today was over, Valmir could ride back to Zagreb with Danijel, after which he'd be free to go. Danijel provided that reassurance.

"Very well," Jozef continued in Croatian. "Valmir can come home with me for breakfast. Meet us back at this same spot with your two new people in an hour. They'll receive their instructions as we drive to Đakovo."

"We'll be here," Danijel replied.

Palo Alto, California
1 March
Thursday, 12:05 a.m. local time

Jia li Sung was lying, weak-limbed, in bed, still shivering with the aftermath of her climax, when the arrival tone of a text message sounded on her cell phone.

Reluctantly, she rolled away from her lover, propped herself up on one elbow, and plucked her phone off her nightstand.

"It's Xu Wei's private line," she murmured.

"He's too smart to call from Jítuán," the man beside her replied, hoisting himself into a sitting position and tucking a pillow behind his head. "There can be no corporate record of this."

Jia li nodded and then opened the text, quickly scanning to make sure that what she'd received were indeed the anticipated photos. She didn't pause to study them more closely, given that she had no training in this area. Instead, her gaze dropped to the accompanying message.

Our experts have examined these and found them to be genuine. Please verify.

"I believe these are what you've been waiting for," she said, handing over the phone.

He scrolled through the photos, his brows knit in concentration as he did. "These appear to be authentic. But I'll need a while to study the details a little more closely. If I'm satisfied, you can text Xu back and tell him we need the rest immediately."

With that, he turned and gave her an intimate smile, tucking a strand of hair behind her ear. "After that, I'm all yours."

Four Seasons Hotel, Palo Alto
1 March
Thursday, 12:32 a.m. local time

Aidan and Simone were just finishing up room service and reviewing the day's events when Aidan's cell phone rang. He grabbed it on the first ring.

"Yes."

"It's me," Marc replied.

"Where are you?"

"Hotel Osijek. I've got to be on the move again soon."

"Then talk to me."

Marc didn't waste time. He swiftly filled Aidan in on the rapidly escalating activity at the Croatian end of the investigation.

"This guy Jozef is homed in," he concluded. "When he heard what I had to say, he zeroed right in on Đakovo. I think he knows exactly where he's sending us and who can take us there."

"Not a surprise. These three OC groups probably keep a watchful eye on each other's activities and locations. That's how they survive."

"Yeah, well, my gut is telling me we're coiled to strike."

"So does mine."

Aidan slid back his chair and walked over to grab a duffel bag, tossing articles of clothing into it as he spoke. "I'm hanging up and alerting my pilot. It'll take me thirteen flying hours to get to Osijek, not to mention the bullshit at either end. So I'm outta here ASAP. Do you have all the gear we need?"

"Yes," Marc confirmed. "Philip took care of that in Germany. We're armed and ready to move as soon as Philip locates the right place, completes his recon, and you and I come up with our tactical plan."

"Okay. I've got a shitload to tell you at this end, but I'll call you when I'm airborne—right after I talk to Abby and let her and Emma know I'll be away for a day or two."

"Where are you now?"

"Palo Alto with Simone."

"How are you going to handle Vance's morning call with Lauren?"

"I'm not. Simone is. She's going to have to be my stand-in babysit-ter. Susan and Vance are coming apart at the seams. I can't count on them to be rational."

"Go call your pilot and get your ass here. I'm about to head back to the farmers market with Danijel. After that, Philip and Ellie will go with Jozef to Đakovo, and Danijel will return to Zagreb. I'll be here at the hotel, waiting for Philip's updates. I'll pass all his recon on to you during your flight so we can formulate our tactical plan. I'll meet the Gulfstream when it lands in Osijek, and we'll drive straight to Đakovo."

"Sounds like a plan."

Aidan hung up and turned to Simone, who was just disconnecting her own phone call.

"I spoke with Stanley," she said, referring to Stan Trumble, the Zermatt pilot. "He's taking care of the flight plan and assorted details as we speak. You should be ready for takeoff by the time you finish briefing me and arrive at the airport."

A corner of Aidan's mouth lifted. "You've developed quite the rapport with Stan. He used to take his orders directly from me. That's twice now you've broken that chain of command."

"And I always make sure he knows I'm calling on your behalf," Simone said with a smile. "Since you're the one traveling, he can verify his information when you get there. But since time is of the essence, I took the liberty of overstepping. Is an apology in order?"

"Nope." Aidan tossed a few toiletries into the duffel bag. "A thank you is. And as for briefing, we need to talk—fast." He repeated all the information that Marc had passed along. Then, he glanced at his watch. "There aren't any commercial flights from here to Reno-Tahoe until morning. You can't wait that long."

"I'll call right now and arrange for car service. It's a four-hour drive. I'll leave when you do. I'll be there well ahead of Vance's scheduled videoconference." She paused. "What else do you need?"

"For you to be with the Penningtons as much as possible."

"That's not a problem. I'll dress in business attire and bring my briefcase. I can fly to and from Nano with Vance today. It will look like we're wrapping up a hectic week of work for McKinsey." She rose and walked over to the wardrobe closet, selecting her clothes as she spoke. "And don't worry about explanations. Once I tell Vance that you're flying to Croatia because Lauren's rescue is imminent, he'll behave. He and his wife will be understandably frantic, but I can handle that. You just take care of business at your end. And Aidan?"

"Hmm?"

"Be safe."

23

Đakovo, Slavonia
1 March
Thursday, 10:08 a.m. local time

Philip and Ellie sat in the rear seat of Jozef's 2005 VW Golf, each one of them taking in their surroundings as they drove through the suburbs of Đakovo.

Side-by-side rows of compact houses lined both sides of the street, most of them made entirely of brick, although a few had painted, plaster-covered fronts and brick sides. The wooden-shingled roofs were green-tinged from the moss growing on them, and patches of grass and squares of concrete that served as driveways were the only things dividing one house from another.

The road continued that way, pretty much a straightaway, until Jozef slowed down, turned the steering wheel, and pulled onto the concrete pad of an all-brick house, parking alongside an old-model Audi A4 sedan.

"We're here," he said in Croatian, unbuckling his seat belt as he did.

Ellie and Philip followed suit, climbing out of the car and waiting politely for Jozef to precede them.

Ellie translated as he spoke.

"My dear friends, Ivan and Helena Flego, live here. They are also Croatians with a proud Albanian heritage, but they are not part of my world. Do you understand?"

Philip waited for the translation. Once it came, he easily read between the lines. "They have no ties to organized crime and you want to keep it that way," he deduced.

Jozef watched Ellie carefully as she supplied Philip's reply. He was visibly pleased by what he heard. "That's right. So here's how things will go. You will hear the explanation I give them and what I'm asking them to do. You will act accordingly. You will do what you're told and not ask questions or offer information. Is that clear?"

Ellie relayed that to Philip, who nodded again.

Satisfied, Jozef led the way to the door, which was opened by a round-faced woman in her late forties wearing a white blouse, dark, slim-fitting jeans, and a scarf wrapped decoratively around her neck. She greeted Jozef with a kiss on each cheek, then beckoned them inside and introduced herself to Philp and Ellie as Helena Flego. Ellie followed suit, providing the introductions for both herself and Philp. Handshakes followed.

A murmur of voices made Philip glance inside. Two teenage girls were seated at a table in the adjoining room, heads bent over what appeared to be their schoolwork. In between reading their textbooks and jotting down notes, they paused to point out paragraphs to a man who was obviously their father. When the girls spoke to each other, Philip could make out phrases of English, and he realized the girls were conversant in the language.

Ellie obviously heard them, as well, because, speaking in Croatian, she asked Helena if she and Ivan also spoke English.

A rueful look crossed Helena's face and she answered Ellie's question. At the end of her explanation, she angled her head to gaze proudly at her children.

Ellie turned to Philip. "In a nutshell, Helena said that she and Ivan know only what they've picked up from their girls. Only half of Slavonians speak English—the younger half of the population. Her girls are being taught English in school and are now fluent in both languages. They also know some Albanian."

"That's very impressive," Philip replied.

Hearing the sound of voices coming from the entranceway, Ivan Flego looked over and realized that Jozef and their guests had arrived. He said something to his daughters and then rose, walking over to join the group. He wore dark jeans, a striped button-down shirt, and leather shoes, rather than the informal American sneakers.

He gave Jozef a hug and then turned and extended his hand to Philip and Ellie.

Once again, Ellie introduced herself and Philip and then explained that she was multilingual and spoke both Croatian and Albanian, so the choice of language was theirs.

"And Philip?" Ivan inquired in Croatian.

A small smile played on Ellie's lips. "He speaks only English. So I'll be the communicator."

Ivan nodded his understanding.

"These are the people I told you about," Jozef interjected, switching to Albanian. "They're friends of my nephew and they need your help. Please let them stay with you today and overnight. As soon as possible, drive them to the two deserted farmhouses I referred to in our conversation so that they can get a good look at them—but from enough of a distance so you won't be seen. Philip will probably need to return to the area on his own. I want you to have no part in that. He'll have to arrange for a rental car."

Once again, Philip was following the conversation via Ellie's translation. And once again, he remembered Marc's gut feeling that Jozef knew exactly where he was sending them. At this moment, he had to agree. The two deserted farmhouses had to be safe houses used by Sallaku's men—something Jozef had clearly learned from the information-gathering of his own organized crime family.

"I'll make sure to keep this initial trip short, but it won't be a quick drive-by," Philip qualified to Jozef. "We'll need a few hours at those two farmhouses. Then we leave and it becomes my problem."

"I understand," Jozef responded to Ellie's translation, meeting Philip's eye with an awareness that said he did. "Just so you know, Đakovo isn't large. You'll get to the farmhouses you're looking for in twenty minutes. Once you figure out your target location, Ivan will drive you to Osijek to collect your rental. You'll be back in position soon after."

Philip nodded, waiting while Jozef made his requests to Ivan and Helena.

"What is it they're looking for?" Ivan asked.

"Neither you or I need to concern ourselves with that," Jozef assured him.

Ivan's dark brows rose. "And the reason you can't do this yourself is because you might be recognized in this particular section of abandoned farmhouses."

A quick nod. "You're very shrewd, my friend. I'm asking you to be a host and a guide. What this couple is looking for and why they want it is their business, not ours. We'll be well paid for our help."

"You'll want this arrangement to remain private," Ivan said. "That will be a problem. Everyone here knows everyone else. Newcomers, especially ones who look like tourists, are instantly recognized as such."

Clearly, Jozef had thought that one through in advance. "You're right that no one can know why they're here. So if anyone asks, the woman is your cousin from Germany, visiting with her British husband."

Ivan glanced from Philip to Ellie and back again. "I suppose that would work."

"Do whatever is necessary to make them fit in."

"We will. And you'll stay in contact?"

"Of course."

Jozef turned to Ellie and Philip, intentionally dropping his voice so only they could hear as he did. "As I'm sure you've guessed, I've gotten the information I need to narrow down the search for you. Two farmhouses. Both Sallaku's safe houses. Like all the farmhouses in the area, they have roughly the same layout." He took a folded sheet of paper out of his pocket, then paused. "You have something for me?"

Ellie passed along Jozef's pointed demand—one that Philip had already figured out, given the expectant look on Jozef's face.

He reached into his pocket and pulled out twenty one-hundred-dollar bills, subtly tucking them into Jozef's hand. Sifting through them long enough to determine the amount, Jozef's eyes glittered with approval and he handed over the folded page.

"I drew you a diagram to ease your way, including the points where you can get in and out. Doors are rarely locked. And the people inside get lazy and relaxed. Use that to your advantage. I hope you find the girl and kill everyone in Zarik Sallaku's family."

Philip took the diagram without responding to Jozef's words. He skimmed the layout, which was simple and straightforward—a one-story building containing a kitchen with an attached dining area, two or three bedrooms, and a single bathroom. A front door and a back door. No side entrances. Pretty much what he'd expected.

"Thank you for this," he said.

"You can thank me when you've avenged my nephew's death."

* * *

Forty-five minutes after Jozef had driven away, Ivan's sedan backed off the patch of concrete and into the street. Helena sat beside him, with Philip and Ellie in the back. To the average onlooker, they appeared to be two couples, out for a ride.

With the Flegos' assistance, Philip and Ellie had changed clothes to modify their appearance. Gone were Philip's silk shirt, designer sports coat, and Patek Philippe watch. Now, along with his tight-fitting dark-wash jeans, he wore a modest cotton button-down shirt and equally modest sports jacket beneath a plain wool overcoat and a matching scarf wrapped around his neck for warmth. He carried a long, black canvas duffel bag containing Jozef's hand-drawn maps of the farms in the area and his own surveillance gear. And Ellie wore a cotton blouse with her jeans, together with a similar wool coat and multicolored print scarf that was pulled down just enough to show off her Croatian silver filigreed earrings. They might not fool the locals, but at least they didn't stick out like sore thumbs.

Ivan drove for a short while, then veered left off the main road. Immediately, the road transformed into a rutted dirt path, making the ride bumpy and rough. The suburban houses disappeared, replaced by acres of undeveloped land—endless stretches of green with patches of snow, punctuated by brown underbrush and leafless trees made naked by winter. Watching intently, Philip spotted more than one neglected farmhouse, set far back from the road. Their exteriors were rotted, their shutters were hanging, and their windows were cracked and falling apart.

He reached for his bag, ready to grab his binoculars and begin his surveillance the moment Ivan stopped. The Audi A4 sedan had enough windows to give him multiple angles from which to view the buildings and any visible occupants. His job right now was to find the precise farmhouse he was seeking and scope it out. After that, he'd return to do static recon at the site.

To his surprise, Ivan stopped at none of the passing farmhouses. He just continued along, ignoring the structures entirely, never slowing down or even glancing around.

Philip remained quiet. But he eased forward on his seat, keeping his hand on his duffle bag, studying everything they passed.

A minute later, Ivan made another left-hand turn, saying the last thing Philip wanted to hear Ellie translate but knew he couldn't argue with.

"Before we go on, I want to show you something. I'm a proud Croatian, and I want you to see the best of Đakovo before I show you the worst."

As he spoke, a cluster of buildings appeared—not a tiny farmhouse like the one Jozef had drawn, and certainly not a replica of the ramshackle buildings they'd just passed—but a veritable compound that covered both sides of the road. On one side was the main house and a large barn, surrounded by multi-acres, with a dirt driveway on which several parked cars stood. Inside the barn's open door, Philip could see a good-sized silver tank, clearly a storage tank of some sort.

On the other side of the road, a Claas tractor roared along, pulling agricultural machinery in its wake. Men in work pants, winter jackets, and baseball caps called out to one another as they made their way about—some of them weaving their way through pens where cows were grazing and others walking in and out of adjacent outbuildings, at least one of those buildings giving the appearance of an additional barn or stable. There were women working, too, and children—some young ones who stayed close to their mothers' sides, others older and working right along with the adults. And three dogs—the size and shape of sheepdogs but with fur that was jet-black, curly, and silky-looking—who were literally herding people along.

"What breed of dogs are those?" Ellie asked in Croatian, clearly sharing none of Philip's urgency. "I've never seen ones quite like them."

"And you won't outside of my country," Ivan replied. "They're Croatian sheepdogs, unique to here. They herd animals and people as well." His eyes twinkled. "Everyone here is hardworking, even the dogs."

"This place looks huge." Ellie was looking around, taking everything in.

"It's one of Đakovo's larger dairy farms," Ivan explained, pointing to the side of the road where the action was taking place. "The dairy operations are underway. The stables are where the cows are kept. And that large tank inside the barn is where the milk is stored." He raised his voice as the roaring of machinery got louder. "The process becomes very loud. The family can barely hear one another, even if they yell."

"The family?" Ellie asked.

Ivan nodded. "The farm is family owned and operated. The husband and wife live and work here with their children and grandchildren. I think there are about twenty people in all."

Despite Philip's urgency, his curiosity was aroused. "Is there particular training they have to go through, or do they just learn from each other?"

After hearing the question in Croatian, Ivan smiled. "I think I'm going to surprise you. The owner of the farm graduated from Osijek University with an agricultural degree, as did his wife. His children are studying to do the same. This is a very common path to follow here. As for their food production, the farmer supplies milk commercially and meat for McDonald's."

Philip blinked, realizing he'd been put in his place—and rightfully so. "I apologize. Thank you for setting me straight." He glanced down at his Urban Watch—a uniquely Croatian brand that Ivan had loaned him.

Okay, it had only been a ten-minute setback.

As if reading his mind, Ivan made a quick swerve around and reversed his path. "I apologize for the brief detour, but as I said, I wanted you to see the best of my town, not just the worst." He turned onto the road and continued along toward their destination. "We'll reach the farms you're interested in seeing in five minutes."

24

Jítuán Headquarters
Shenzhen, China
1 March
Thursday, 6:35 p.m. local time

The view from the CEO's office in the towering modern skyscraper was striking, overlooking a city now often referred to as China's Silicon Valley.

New technology companies were popping up everywhere, and overseas companies were building subsidiary offices here. Jítuán was one of the original entities, headquartered right here in Shenzhen and having grown from a small business to a thriving corporation.

With the addition of this new, industry-changing acquisition, they would become a corporate giant.

Xu Wei sat at his desk, his fingers steepled in front of him and his mind rapidly assessing his options based on what he'd learned.

He was a hard man who had no tolerance for disobedience. However, he was also a practical man—one who knew that achieving the ultimate goal was all that mattered. There was a great deal at stake here, a groundbreaking technology to acquire and to release prior to any further announcements from NanoUSA. So he had to rapidly assess any potential threats and to deal with them accordingly.

Pennington had involved someone else in the process. By doing so, he had violated his instructions.

That angered Xu—but in this case punishment would do more harm than good. He was well aware that, were he to communicate the situation to the Albanians, they'd kill Pennington's daughter on the spot. That was not Xu's intention. He wanted no blood on his hands. He'd made that clear from the onset. Partly because he wasn't a man who achieved his goals through violence, and partly because, should Lauren Pennington be killed, there was every chance the international investigation might find its way to his company and to him.

No, that was untenable. Which meant another direction needed to be taken—one he would have to determine on his own.

True, Pennington had sought assistance. But the man was desperate. His daughter's life was on the line. And the help he'd solicited hadn't been law enforcement. It had been his most trusted corporate source—his personal assistant. Gallagher had the skills required to transmit the photos they'd demanded. And he'd have the skills to complete the job in the requisite amount of time. It was the least egregious violation Pennington could have made—a logical solution to a near-impossible task.

As for Gallagher, the man was being paid for his work and for his silence. He was greedy and he was smart. He'd stay quiet as long as he was receiving his money. He'd gain nothing by alerting anyone else to his actions. And once the transfer of data was complete, he no longer represented a threat. Anything he decided to share with law enforcement would only serve to implicate him.

Time was short. Pennington had under two days to deliver the remainder of the technology. Given that, Xu decided, a mild but outright threat would be enough to frighten Pennington into unassisted and immediate compliance.

Xu reached for his private cell phone.

He had to act now.

The next communication between father and daughter was just a few hours away.

Đakovo, Slavonia
1 March
Thursday, 12:45 p.m. local time

Ivan drove his now filthy car up the rutted dirt road and parked behind a stand of trees. An acre of land wrapped around what was ostensibly a deserted farmhouse, surrounded by nothing but soggy ground dotted with an occasional ice patch, all with a perimeter of unkempt brush and a crumbling stone wall. In the distance, there was the outline of a second farmhouse.

Instantly, Philip whipped out his binoculars and did an overall scan of the area.

"Where does this road ultimately lead to?" he asked. "And are there other ways to get in and out?"

Ellie's answer to the first question was: "to a dead end" and to the second question: "no."

Philip grabbed his Nikon D-850, removed the AF-S FX Nikkor eight-hundred-millimeter lens from its protective case, and attached the massive lens to the camera body. He'd be able to see a fly's nostril hairs from a hundred meters with this thing—or so the salesman had said.

At the time, he'd wondered if a fly even had nostril hairs.

Quickly, he took a few shots. The place was a ramshackle structure that looked like it would collapse to the ground if given a hard shove. There was a barn outside but no animals in sight. Given the house dimensions, window placement, and one-story height, Philip suspected that what Jozef had said was true—this farm had the same layout as the one he'd provided in his sketch.

Long minutes passed as Philip continued his scrutiny. There were absolutely no signs of life and no sense that anyone had been here in months, maybe more.

Philip's gut told him they should move on, making sure to stop a substantial distance away from the farmhouse. The deserted, barren road would make it far too easy to spot an approaching vehicle.

He made the request through Ellie, and Ivan nodded, pulling back onto the road and traveling closer to where the second farmhouse was located. Once again, he pulled his car behind a stand of trees, keeping it hidden from view.

Philip repeated his procedure. This farmhouse could have been cloned from the first. Same surroundings—unkempt brush, soggy ground, and crumbling stone fence. Same dilapidated appearance. Same construction. Same dimensions and exterior appearance. Same barn—or not.

Philip's gaze locked on the side of the barn closest to the house, and he peered intently through his camera lens, moving from the barn to the house and focusing on an overhang of naked trees. Parked against the building—length-wise, headlights facing out—was a black sedan. The combination of its proximity to the house and the shadows cast by the tree branches—black on black—made it practically invisible, unless someone was looking hard.

Which Philip was.

He took some photos, then picked up his binoculars and resumed his surveillance, studying the house from different angles, making mental notes of concealment spots for the team to use during the rescue, and ultimately waiting to see what comings and goings might take place.

It took a while, but eventually his patience paid off. One muscular guy who had to be over six feet tall left through the back door, got into the black sedan, and pulled out.

As the car passed their secluded location, Philip had a good view of its driver, even without his binoculars.

"Is there anything distinguishable about him that suggests he's of Albanian descent?" he asked Ivan.

"Tan skin, dark features aren't just Albanian," Ellie translated Ivan's reply. "But he's tall. That's a trait of Albanian men."

As she fell silent, the front door opened and a second guy sauntered out. Leaning against the side of the building, he lit up a cigarette and began to smoke. As soon as the butt became too small, he tossed it to the grass, ground it under his heel, and lit up another.

A chain smoker. Good. It meant the guy would make frequent trips outdoors to light up. And if he was a creature of habit, he'd probably choose the same spot to enjoy his cigarette. Which told Philip that he needed to time the cigarette breaks. That information could be crucial to their tactical plan.

It had been quiet for a while, so whoever else was inside with Lauren was either guarding her or otherwise occupied.

More waiting ensued.

Forty-five minutes later, the tall guy returned, parking in the exact same spot he'd left from. He opened the back door of the car and pulled out a few bags—bags that, upon closer scrutiny of Philip's zoom lens—contained food and household supplies.

Okay, so the tall guy was the worker bee. And even though he used the back door for his comings and goings, he wouldn't be a permanent fixture there. Plus he wouldn't be going out for supplies more than once a day, and certainly not in the middle of the night or the wee hours of dawn.

That suggested that the back door was a weak point—making it a strong point of entry for the team.

That was all Philip was going to get for this quick go-round. Time to head back, collect his rental car, and return on his own. In truth, he could have used several days to get the full picture of arrivals and departures. But the team didn't have the luxury of time. So he had to make a quick determination of the number of kidnappers and their routines.

Marc had already taken care of the rental arrangements. He'd gotten two dark Peugeot 5008s at the closest place in Osijek. Philip would pick up one, Marc the other. The first would get Philip back to the farmhouse for recon. The second would get Marc to the airport to collect Aidan, after which he'd drive them both out to join Philip at the rescue site.

Sitting back now, Philip dismantled his camera and lens and shoved his equipment into the duffel bag. "I'm finished for now," he told Ivan via Ellie. "I'd like to drive directly to Osijek so I can pick up my rental car."

"Fine," Ivan said. "I'll leave you there and drive home with the women. Will you be returning tonight?"

"No." Philip was peeling off two thousand dollars, holding the twenty hundred-dollar bills visibly in his hand. "Once we reach Osijek, I'll be thanking you for your help and hospitality." He added another ten hundred-dollar bills. "And asking that you pass this along to Jozef with my thanks. I'm sure he'll exchange all this for Croatian kuna without a problem. Ellie will be spending the night. Please drive her to the Hotel Osijek in the morning."

He turned to Ellie and spoke in a low tone. "You and Derica have successfully completed your assignments. Payment will be wired to you ASAP. You can both return to Germany."

Ellie smiled and extended her hand, shaking Philip's. "It's been a pleasure working with you."

Zermatt Group Offices
West 75th Street, Manhattan, New York
1 March
Thursday, 7:55 a.m. local time

Inside the Cage, Terri sat back in her desk chair, a smug smile on her face as she studied her laptop screen. After long hours, she'd cracked David Cheng wide open, uncovering every facet of his life and, in the process, discovering a whole lot more.

For starters, Cheng was receiving monthly wire transfers of twenty thousand dollars, deposited into his account on the first of every month just like an employee's salary or an outside consultant's retainer. Each wire transfer had the same SWIFT code—SZDBCNBSOSA.

Terri quickly identified that code.

It belonged to a Chinese bank—specifically, Ping An Bank. Located in the city of Shenzhen, the code indicated that it originated at headquarters, the offshore banking department. And the originator? Jítuán, a large electronics assembling company that employed tens of thousands of people.

A company that would be crippled by the success of Nano's new technology and that would thrive if it were able to control and exploit it against competitors.

So now Terri knew what entity Cheng was working for. All she needed was the duplicate cell phone Aidan had overnighted her to find Cheng's contact at Jítuán and to figure out how high up this went.

She glanced at her watch.

The courier service should be here soon.

Starbucks
Northstar Drive, Lake Tahoe
1 March
Thursday, 7:10 a.m. local time

Vance was even more distraught going into today's videoconference with Lauren than he had been yesterday.

Simone Martin had showed up at his and Susan's hotel room door before dawn, explaining that, even though the entire team, including

Aidan, would be listening to and observing the videoconference at the same time that Vance was having it, it was she who would be here as a stand-in for Aidan. And when she'd told them why—because Aidan was on his way to Croatia—he'd started to weep, holding his sobbing wife in his arms. They both knew that meant there was a rescue mission in place. Aidan's on-the-ground team had summoned him. It was time.

And while this entire week had been hell, just knowing that this life-or-death moment was upon them had pushed both Vance and Susan over the edge.

Simone had spent several hours with them, talking calmly and reassuringly. But the fact was, she could offer them no promises. All they could do was to trust in Aidan and the team, follow their own game plan.

And pray.

Now, his laptop ready, Vance tried to calm his breathing as he prepared to give the performance of his life.

He couldn't so much as hint to what was going on, nor could he act any differently than he had yesterday. As Simone had said, it was imperative that the kidnappers be totally unaware that a rescue mission was in the works.

His heart thundering in his chest, he typed in the new link the kidnappers had provided for today's use.

The screen opened, and Vance's face appeared. Seconds later, the second window opened with Lauren's face in it, reducing Vance to a small image in the lower right-hand corner of the screen. The effect was one of bringing Lauren that much clearer and that much closer.

Again, Lauren was wearing a bright sweater that was clearly meant to make her appear hale and hardy. The attempt failed miserably. If anything, she looked more drawn, her eyes more haunted than they had yesterday. In his heart, Vance knew that Lauren was not only wearing down, she was giving up.

It took all his willpower not to tell her that help was on its way and that she'd soon be home with her family.

Instead, he just greeted her as he had before. "Hi, honey." He knew his voice sounded shaky. But as Aidan had told him, the kidnappers would not only expect but welcome his fear. They'd feel that much closer to victory.

"Hi, Daddy." Lauren was fighting for control, for her life.

"Tell me how you are. Are you eating? Sleeping? No one has hurt you, have they?"

"I'm fine." She gave him the same staccato answers that she had yesterday. "I've eaten and I've slept. My privacy has been respected and I'm unharmed." She ran through her food intake, her activities, and her continued good health.

Abruptly, she broke off, her gaze darting to her left. Then, her shoulders began to shake and tears poured down her cheeks. "Daddy, I have to give you a message: *Stop asking others for help, including your most trusted associates at Nano. The people who have me said they'd kill me on the spot if you refuse to comply.*" She buried her face in her hands. "Please, Daddy, don't let them kill me."

Oh dear God.

Everything inside Vance turned to ice.

"Lauren, honey, don't cry. I don't know what they're talking about. Of course I won't tell anyone at Nano. No one even has any idea you're missing, much less kidnapped." His eyes darted around the screen, knowing the kidnappers were right there beside her. "Whoever's listening, please don't hurt my daughter. I'm following your instructions. I'd never risk her life. I've told no one at NanoUSA that my child has been kidnapped. No one. I swear it. Please..." Now Vance was the one who broke down and started to cry. "I'll get you the rest of the drawings you want. Before the deadline. I promise. I love you, Lauren…"

The screen went blank.

25

Zermatt jet
1 March
Thursday, 3472 nm to OSI
10:11 a.m. EST

"*Shit.*"

Thirty thousand feet in the air, his private jet en route to Osijek, Aidan had been on his laptop, watching and listening to the video feed that was being relayed from Vance's computer through Terri's server and out to the Zermatt team members. When the screen went black, he slammed his fist against the arm of his cream-colored leather seat.

"*Shit. Shit. Shit.*" He didn't wait for Simone to initiate an emergency videoconference. He did it himself. Rapidly scanning through his contacts, he clicked on Marc, Simone, and Terri. Their names went green, at which time he clicked on the connect button at the bottom of the screen. He watched as his team members appeared.

"What was *that* about?" Marc asked, his tone grim.

"I don't know," Aidan said. "But that message clearly came from the Chinese, not the Albanians. The sophisticated phraseology, the careful choice of words… This came from the top."

"Gentlemen, Susan is right outside this bedroom door." Simone's voice was hushed and she looked shaken, a rarity for her. "And Vance is going to be storming into the hotel room in about ten minutes demanding answers, so I better have some to offer. Do you think the Chinese know about me? That I'm the insider at Nano who's assisting Vance? Do you think I was somehow careless and that someone saw me go into Blockman's office?"

"No on all counts." Aidan gave an adamant shake of his head. "They carefully chose the phrase *trusted associate*. You're hardly that. You're a consultant, working at Nano for a week. I think they have reason to believe that an insider—other than their mole—is now in the mix. The questions are what made them believe that and which of Vance's associates is the suspect?"

"I've got a good guess as to the first part of your question," Terri said. "The photos. I didn't think of it before, but the technology and the skill set required to send them was sophisticated—maybe too sophisticated for Vance's capabilities. If the Chinese tried to figure out where and how the pictures were taken, they would get nowhere. Ryan told me that the ring camera would strip out all Exif data, which normally indicates the type of camera, the exposure details, even GPS coordinates showing where the picture was taken."

"Good points." Aidan picked up on the particular note of urgency in Terri's voice—a note that meant she had something substantial of her own to report. But whatever it was, it would have to wait. Right now their focus had to be on the immediate crisis.

"Let's shelve the brainstorming," he said pointedly. "We need to give Simone the ammunition she needs to handle Vance and Susan. She's about to have to sign off. Whatever else we discuss, I can pass along when she gets in touch with me afterwards."

"I'd focus on the reality of the message itself, not the words," Marc said to Simone. Formerly with the FBI's Behavioral Analysis Unit, he was a pro at assessing and managing people. "The fact that the kidnappers are warning Vance means they've chosen to scare the shit out of him, not to kill Lauren. If the opposite were the case, she'd be dead and the message would be moot. All that's a good sign. They want to up the pressure in order to eliminate interference and to get what they want. And what they want is a technology, not a corpse, just as you surmised from the beginning, Aidan."

"That makes sense." Simone was calming down. "I'll make sure to stress that point to Vance. But I'll also be honest with him about the transference of the photos being the possible red flag that led the Chinese to suspect another Nano employee is involved. I must be honest with him. He'll know if he's being played."

"I totally agree." Marc's response was instantaneous and adamant. "You need to maintain their trust. Bullshitting them with half-truths is a surefire way to break that trust, at which point we'll lose them entirely."

"Vance is going to ask who at Nano we believe the kidnappers are referring to."

"Again, be honest," Marc replied. "Tell them we're working on figuring that out now. But also tell them it's not a bad thing that the Chinese are pursuing a dead end. It'll keep them occupied while we carry out our rescue mission."

Simone nodded. "Good point. I'll make sure Vance and Susan understand that."

"So we've given Simone a Band-Aid for dealing with the Penningtons," Terri interjected. "But I have a lot going on at my end that I need to share with the team."

"I guessed as much." Aidan was watching Simone, who'd turned to look over her shoulder. He knew exactly what that meant.

Vance had just arrived.

"Go do your damage control, Simone," he said. "No one does it better than you. In the meantime, Marc and I will get Terri's briefing and fill you and Philip in later."

* * *

As soon as Simone's face disappeared from the screen, both Aidan and Marc looked expectantly at Terri.

"Go," Aidan said.

Terri didn't waste an instant. First, she filled them in on what she'd dug up on David Cheng. Then she went on to the rest.

"I analyzed the data from Cheng's burner phone."

"Any contact with someone who works at Nano?" Aidan demanded. "Someone who could be our mole?"

"Nope. But I have one better. Cheng's contact at Jítuán is Xu Wei, the company's CEO."

There was a heartbeat of silence.

"So the CEO himself orchestrated Lauren's kidnapping to steal Nano's technology." Aidan digested that piece of information. "How much do we have to go on?"

"More than a dozen phone calls to and from Xu's private cell phone."

"That's not enough."

"Then I'll give you more. There's another person Cheng's been in frequent contact with—a young woman named Jia li Sung. She's a graduate student at Stanford Business School with an outstanding GPA and a background check that's impeccable. From her photos I can also tell you that she's quite lovely. She lives in a garden apartment in Palo Alto and drives a nice, pricey BMW. Between the rent she pays and the car she drives—she's definitely not hurting."

"It can't be Cheng's girlfriend," Marc surmised. "He wouldn't be contacting her on a burner phone. Not unless there's some connection to Xu?"

"Don't steal my thunder." Terri sounded as revved up as she always did when she was on the brink of some major revelation. "When I went on to do my due diligence on Xu, I hacked into US Customs and discovered that he'd visited the Silicon Valley area just last month, from January thirtieth to February first. From there I went on to dig up Xu's credit card and see where he stayed, which was the Nobu Hotel Epiphany Palo Alto. I then tapped into the hotel security tapes for those dates in particular. And you'll never guess who met Xu outside the hotel on two separate occasions."

"Jia li Sung." Aidan leaned forward, his mind racing. "Did they embrace? Kiss?"

"Handshakes. Formal ones. Nothing even hinting at an affair."

"So she's working for Xu in some capacity. And whatever that role is, it's lucrative. It also requires her to talk to David Cheng—and, ultimately, to meet with Xu in person." Aidan leaned back, steepling his fingers. "It sounds as if she's a more significant player in all this than Cheng is."

"I agree," Terri replied. "I'm willing to bet that she knows—and is in communication with—whomever our mole at Nano is."

"And I bet you're right." Again, Aidan could tell from Terri's tone that she had an idea to run with. "You want to go out on a limb with something. Let's hear it."

"It's a risk. But it's one I think will pay off. I'll send a text message to Jia li from Xu Wei by hacking into his cell phone carrier and pretending to be him. The text message will be sent at a specific time this evening. Jia li will be on or near the Stanford University campus, based on her typical schedule and tracking her routine. He'll tell her that he's in Palo Alto because his security team turned up a classified leak that requires an urgent person-to-person meeting between the two of them and their Nano contact. He'll tell her to set it up at her apartment—where they won't be seen or recognized—to take place a half hour after the text is sent. She'll take the bait."

"And what will happen during that half hour?"

"*Before* that half hour," Terri qualified. "What I have in mind will take place in two parts—the first, before Jia li goes out, and the second, while she's gone. The text will come last."

"Fine. What will happen *before* that half hour?" Aidan amended.

"An unexpected visit to Stanford Business School. And an equally unexpected visit to Jia li's apartment."

"Explain."

"If you recall, I included a few other items when I overnighted you the specialized computer for Vance. One of those things is an IMSI-catcher, complete with some special software I added. It's a black metal box with a plug. I labeled it Windsor, after my dog. Once it's been appropriately planted in the right room at the Business School, it will be near enough to Jia li for me to embargo her incoming text messages and calls."

"Preventing any surprise communications from Xu Wei that would screw up your plan."

"Uh-huh." Aidan could hear Terri frowning through the phone. "It's not foolproof. Once Jia li leaves the building, there'll be a twenty-to-thirty-minute period of time when Xu can reach her. We have to take that risk. His calls to her aren't that frequent."

"And during that twenty-to-thirty-minute period of time, you—as Xu—will be texting her about the emergency meeting."

"Yes. That's why I'm capping it at a half hour. Less time, less risk."

"And the break-in at her apartment?"

"Another device I sent you is an electronic bug Ryan designed—one that needs to be planted in Jia li's apartment. Quite impressive, it looks like an electronic key fob, so that, even if Jia li were to find it, she'd merely assume that one of her friends left it there. In reality, it's a one-way microphone that will transmit the conversation in the apartment over an encrypted channel linked to one of our cell phones that's in close range. Using the Donovan app that I've installed on every team member's cell phone, I'll be able to listen in on the conversation and record it for evidentiary purposes."

"By one of our cell phones being in close proximity, you mean Simone's," Aidan deduced aloud. "You want Simone to carry out these assignments."

"Yes. I know what you're thinking. Unfortunately, there's no time to call in one of our experienced operatives and bring them up to speed. Plus, I don't think it's necessary. The Stanford part will be easy and low risk. The apartment break-in will obviously be a little trickier, but Simone is well-trained to handle it. And that's where the major impasse lies—if you stick to your decision about her remaining with the Penningtons."

"I'll talk to her—and to Vance," Aidan responded. "They'll be flying into Santa Clara from Tahoe in an hour or two. It'll be my job to make Vance realize that babysitting him won't accomplish what we need to in the next twenty-four hours. Knowing that we're about to choke off the head of the monster who ordered Lauren's kidnapping might even pump him up about the imminent success of our mission."

With that, Aidan paused, mentally assessing the delicate timing taking place in both Silicon Valley and Croatia. "Terri, do the physical setups. But wait to hear from me before you send the text and set the wheels in motion. I'll tell the same to Simone. I know that will cause you angst because it potentially lengthens the vulnerable time frame when Xu and Jia li could be in contact. But once this arranged meeting happens and Xu doesn't show up, Jia li and her Nano co-conspirator will realize they've been set up, which will set off alarm bells reaching from Santa Clara to Shenzhen. That can't occur until we've pulled off our direct attack and Lauren is safe. She's our number one priority."

"Understood. I'll delay things any way I need to, even if it means filling up Jia li's voice mailbox and flooding her with junk texts. No matter what, I'll wait for the go-ahead from you."

Nodding, Aidan shifted his gaze to Marc. "Any news from Philip?"

"He's in Đakovo with Ellie and the couple the CI put them in touch with. Recon is well underway."

"Good. Because regardless of how well I manage Vance, there's no way we can count on him getting through another videoconference with Lauren, not after what just happened and not when he's painfully aware that he'll be down to the final day. Between that and Terri's plan, we've got to move now and get Lauren out of there and headed home before dawn."

Marc didn't flinch. "Philip is checking in with me in a matter of hours, after doing as much static recon as he can manage, given our urgent time frame. You and I will use the information he gives us to devise a tactical plan. How long before you land in Osijek?"

"About seven hours."

"I'll be waiting at the airport. Đakovo is a quick drive from there. What else did you need to fill me in on?"

"Actually, Terri covered the David Cheng angle for me. The rest—Ethan Gallagher is now in our sights as a potential piece of the puzzle." Aidan gave Marc a quick rundown on the data that was leading them in that direction, reminding him of the fact that, on top of all the other hints of his involvement, Ethan also spoke fluent Mandarin. "Oh, and I'll be giving Casey a call later to thank her."

"You lost me."

Aidan explained Emma's role in Operation Bluejack.

Marc began to chuckle. "She must have loved every minute of that. Oh, man, we'll never hear the end of it."

"Yeah, well, my jaw was hanging when she brought me the cell phone that fast, together with incriminating info on Gallagher."

"Don't ever be fooled into thinking that Emma is a rookie. She's quite the pro, in her own way."

"Let's get back to the message Vance just got from the Chinese." Aidan brought a close to the brief moment of levity. "With this new verbal threat comes a new possibility. Do the Chinese suspect Ethan of aiding Vance? Is that the close associate they're referring to? He certainly has the skills to send those photos. *We* know he didn't, but *they* don't. And based on what Simone reported, he's certainly living a lifestyle that would suggest he's getting some extra income. Maybe that's why Cheng was with him, not to collaborate but to probe. And if that's the case, then he's not being paid by the Chinese and he's definitely not our mole. Simone doesn't believe that Zoe is either, and I tend to agree with her."

"And Blockman is clean," Terri added. "I ran his expense data through the prison algorithm. The only thing he's guilty of is cheating on his wife by having a girlfriend on the side."

"Which brings us back to square one," Aidan said.

"Hopefully, Terri's bug will give us the answers we need," Marc responded. "Till that happens, there's no point in speculating."

"I agree." Aidan's focus returned to the life-or-death mission ahead. "Call me the minute Philip is in contact."

Abandoned farmhouse
Đakovo, Slavonia
Thursday, 7:10 p.m. local time

Patience was the mark of a good operative, and Philip had been exhibiting the necessary amount of it over the past few hours.

He'd been at the farmhouse since five fifteen, having stashed the gun-metal gray SUV behind a stand of bare-limbed trees and then hunkering down against it with his recon gear. Binoculars. Nikon D-850. Attached AF-S FX Nikkor eight-hundred-millimeter lens.

All was quiet on the grounds. The black sedan was parked in its customary spot. And no other vehicles had arrived, which told Philip that these Albanians had no backup. It was just the handful of them.

There were a few low lights on inside the house, enough to allow Philip to make out a modicum of activity. From the blur of motion he'd seen from the dining area fifty minutes ago, the kidnappers had taken their evening meal. With any luck, it had been accompanied by a few bottles of rakia—enough so they'd be tired, their senses would be dulled, and their awareness of their surroundings would be compromised for the night.

In concurrence with that theory, Mr. Smoker had seemed a little unsteady on his feet when he'd stumbled out to take his last cigarette break—which he did every hour on the hour. There'd been no sign of Mr. Worker Bee since he'd taken out some trash after dinner. Whoever else was in there was a huge question mark. Philip had yet to see anyone who resembled the guy who'd chatted Lauren up at Hofbräuhaus and then physically abducted her. It made him even more convinced that what he'd told Marc was true—that the scumbag had been a cutout—a middleman whose face they realized was likely captured on camera and who'd have to be disposed of to avoid being ID'd.

Still, theories, no matter how compelling, were just that: theories. It was possible he could be inside the farmhouse with an unknown number of others.

Philip had hours to figure it out.

He continued to watch and wait.

26

Simone left Vance's office, fairly secure that, between the phone call Aidan had had with Vance and her own calming techniques, they'd gotten both him and Susan under control. At Simone's urging, Susan had agreed to stay inside her hotel room in Tahoe today, feigning a migraine to her kids, since she was in no shape to pull off acting normal. And Vance was going to apply himself to task-oriented work at Nano for another hour and then fly back to join his wife. Aidan had bluntly told him that if either he or Susan deviated from this hunkering-down plan, they'd run the risk of compromising the rescue mission—and of further endangering Lauren's life.

Love for their daughter had kept them in check—that and Aidan's promise that either he or Simone would keep them in the loop every step of the way.

Simone was about to leave the building and check in with Aidan when she reached Ethan Gallagher's office, which was adjacent to his boss's. A woman was just walking in, and Simone caught her profile as she disappeared into the room and shut the door behind her.

June Morris.

Now *that* was interesting. Ethan had claimed to scarcely interact with the woman, and here she was going into his office for a closed-door meeting.

Simone glanced around. The hall was empty.

Fortunately, Nano was sleek and modern, with lots of chrome and glass. Using that to her advantage, Simone flattened herself against the wall adjoining the large office window. Glass was much easier to hear through than a solid wall. It also had the advantage of allowing Simone a view of what was taking place.

To an outsider, June was invisible. Which meant she'd pressed herself against the back of the door to avoid being seen. Ethan, on the other hand, was pacing around the room, alternately rubbing the back of his neck and dragging a shaky hand through his hair. Perspiration was beading up on his forehead.

Definitely not the composed Ethan Gallagher who Simone was used to seeing.

"Someone broke into my apartment last night," he was saying.

"Oh no." June's two-word response was low, but not so low that Simone couldn't tell that she was strung tight. "What did they take?"

"Nothing," he replied, stopping in his tracks. "That's what's got me scared shitless. Stuff was moved around and then put back as carefully as possible. And, June, whoever it was got inside my desk and to my stash." He paused, staring at the door—and obviously at June—like a terrified rabbit. "My cash and pills were rearranged. Not stolen, just askew. Which means they didn't want to take them. They either wanted evidence, blackmail ammunition, or I don't know what. But whatever it was, they got it."

June was silent for a minute, and Simone strained her ears to hear her response.

"Did you have a client list in there?" she asked tentatively.

"What? No," Ethan snapped. "My records are all stored electronically, and encrypted. Happy?"

"Of course not." A tinge of relief, but still a shaky voice. "No one's contacted you?"

"Not yet, no." Ethan was pacing again. "But it's just a matter of time. They didn't go through all that for nothing. Photos have probably been circulated to whoever's behind this. I don't know what to do."

He looked like a small child about to cry.

"Sit tight." June sounded so tightly wound that her calming words were almost laughable. "There's nothing you *can* do until you're approached."

"How cavalier." Now Ethan was visibly pissed. "May I remind you that if my ass is fried, your deliveries dry up?"

"You don't need to remind me," June choked out. "But we have to find out what they want. What else can we do but wait?"

"Right. Great. So it's business as usual around here until a bomb goes off in my face." Ethan sucked in his breath, striving desperately for control. "I've got to pull myself together. I can't look or act weird, not when I'm holding down the fort for Vance while he's in Lake Tahoe." He ran a palm over his face. "You'd better get out of here," he said. "The last thing we need is for anyone to make a connection between us. We're screwed enough as it is."

Simone shrunk against the wall as Ethan walked over to the window and peered out, perceiving what he believed to be a deserted hallway.

"Go now," he told June.

"You'll keep me updated?"

Ethan was nodding, but Simone didn't wait to hear anything else. She couldn't risk the door opening and June finding her eavesdropping.

She slid along the wall until she was back outside Vance's office. There, she paused, opening a file folder and relaxing her stance as she seemingly studied the folder's contents.

When enough time had passed, she slipped the file folder back in her briefcase and continued on her way.

The area near Ethan's office was deserted.

* * *

As soon as she'd driven beyond Nano's gates, Simone called Aidan and filled him in.

"A drug dealer. Nice." Aidan was still sitting in the same seat on the Gulfstream that he'd been occupying since the team videoconference. "So the Chinese were checking Gallagher out after Cheng reported in. They wanted to know where he was getting his spare change. And what they found will lead them to assume he's also immoral enough to commit industrial espionage. That only confirms what we already guessed—that Ethan Gallagher is *not* our mole."

"It also explains why June Morris is so strung out." Simone was driving as she spoke. "Sleeping with Robert helped get her the CFO spot. But holding on to that position is another matter entirely. It's gotten bigger and more overwhelming as Nano has grown. And she no longer has the perk of sharing Robert's bed to get his support."

Aidan tapped his pen thoughtfully against his leg. "We've got tons of corporate drama going on at Nano and no clue as to who the insider is. Lots of suspects, not a single damn lead." He blew out his breath, clearly wrestling with the situation. "Our mission is to rescue Lauren," he stated flatly.

"But you also want the whole case wrapped up and all the involved parties punished." Simone's assessment was matter-of-fact. She knew Aidan only too well.

"Yeah, I do. But my attention needs to be focused on where I'm going, what Philip, Marc, and I are planning, and how we're carrying it all out successfully. I need you to spearhead the other parts of the investigation, Simone—you and Terri. When all this is over, I want everyone who's guilty to pay for his or her crime, one way or another."

"Which brings us to this young woman you briefly mentioned—Jia li Sung."

"I couldn't get into detail, not with Vance still a loose cannon. Now I can. Because it's the reason I asked you to drop everything and leave Nano once Vance was settled in."

Aidan went on to explain everything to Simone—Terri's findings, her plans, and their hold-back-but-coiled-to-strike timetable.

Simone listened intently, then said, "The plan is strong and may very well hand us our mole. And while it's necessary that we wait to initiate the text, I want to maximize my time. I'm supposedly heading back to my hotel to compile a comprehensive report on Vance's department in preparation for my meeting with Robert and Vance tomorrow. No one expects me to be on-site. Once I'm in my room, I'll call Terri and get briefed on the details of my job and drive to Stanford Business School right away. As for the electronic devices I'll be using, you left the package Terri sent you in my hotel room for security purposes, locked in my safe."

Aidan stated the obvious: "Clearly, you're all in."

"Did you doubt it?"

"No. But I'm not happy. Ideally, I'd call in one of our contacts and have him or her do the dirty work."

"I'm sure you would," Simone said defensively. "But we don't have the luxury of time, and I'm perfectly capable of handling this. Plus, I'm as vested as you are in bringing down the insiders who had a hand in Lauren's kidnapping. A college girl was taken—a vulnerable young woman who's barely more than a kid. I intend to take an active role in closing this case."

"And I respect that. But, Simone, planting the bug could be dangerous. You'll have to work fast and get out of there in a hurry."

"I'll be fine, *chéri*." Simone's voice softened as she heard the deep concern in Aidan's voice. "I managed just fine in Blockman's office, no?"

"Yes." Aidan blew out a breath. "But in this case, you're invading someone's home. And given the players involved, you're putting yourself in harm's way. Remember: in America, people can have guns in their homes. So, yeah, I'm worried."

"You, who are about to put your life on the line by attacking violent killers, are worried about a little breaking and entering?"

The irony of Simone's words wasn't lost on Aidan. "Guilty as charged. But we're talking about you, not me."

"And I thank you for that. But I'll take every precaution. You just concentrate on your mission. Terri and I will take care of the rest."

"Terri's in New York. You're the one in Silicon Valley." Aidan wasn't ready to wrap up this conversation. "Not only am I worried about you planting the bug, I'm even more worried about what happens afterward. If things go as planned, you're going to be alone in the car outside the apartment when two desperate people figure out they've been played. If I were them, I'd hop the first flight I could out of the country to a place with no extradition. And knowing you, you'd be in hot pursuit to prevent that from happening."

"You're right. I would."

"I'm going to talk to Terri. Once Lauren is safe, I want her to hack into the TSA and place everyone we suspect on the No Fly List. They'll be stuck in the US until law enforcement picks them up. And if they try to head to Mexico by car, California traffic will prevent them from getting very far."

"Fine. So there's no reason for me to follow them. But just in case I'm spotted, I plan on being armed. You have several guns locked in my hotel room safe. One of them is a Glock 27. I'm trained to use that pistol, and you know it."

"You've never shot anyone."

"And hopefully I won't have to this time. These are white-collar criminals, not violent offenders. But if one of them has a gun and tries to use it, they'll be dead before they can pull the trigger. Count on it."

After they hung up, Aidan looked down to where he was gripping his pen more tightly than he'd realized. He'd never been able to talk

Simone out of anything once she made up her stubborn mind. This time had been no different.

Four Seasons Hotel, Palo Alto
1 March
Thursday, 12:05 p.m. local time

Terri answered on the first ring. "Yes?"

"I'm at my hotel," Simone began without prelude. She was squatting in front of her room safe, removing the package she needed while simultaneously locating her pistol and ammunition. Those she set aside for the moment.

"I'm holding the electronic gift box you sent Aidan."

"Good. You know what you're looking for?"

"Aidan told me." Simone was already rummaging around. "I've got the key fob," she said, extracting the item. "How does it work?"

"Think of it as a really small cell phone." Terri explained the device in the simplest terms possible to Simone. "The difference is, there's no speaker in the key fob, so no one can hear your side of the conversation. Only you can hear what's going on in their location. The microphone is optimized to be very sensitive and to pick up sounds in all directions."

Simone nodded, pursing her lips as she turned the device over in her hands. It looked totally innocuous. "So the conversations going on in Jia li's apartment will be transmitted to my cell phone. I'll have conferenced you in so you can listen and record what's being said."

"Exactly. Also, you and I can talk to one another without being heard, just as if we've placed them on mute."

"Okay." Simone looked inside the package and extracted the black box labelled: *Windsor*. "I've got the cell phone interceptor gadget."

"The IMSI-catcher," Terri clarified. She then went on to explain how it functioned.

"And I'm planting this exactly where at the Business School?"

Terri gave her a building and room number. "Just put it in the closet there. That's all the proximity I need."

"I can do this any time?"

"Sometime between now and four p.m."

Simone blew out a breath. "Let's get into the specifics of this two-sided plan. For starters, how do we know Jia li will be away from her apartment when we want her to be? Especially since we don't know for certain when Aidan will give us the go-ahead?"

"The Gulfstream should be landing in Osijek at one a.m. Croatian time, which is still four p.m. PST," Terri reported. "Aidan and the team will already have their plan in place. The strike will be imminent."

"That still doesn't pinpoint the time."

"Agreed. So I've isolated our window of opportunity. Jia li is registered for the winter session at Stanford Business School. She has no classes today, but she does have a seven p.m. meeting of her business club—a meeting that generally runs a minimum of an hour and a half and often as long as two."

"In the room you just gave me."

"Yes. According to her credit card receipts, she eats at the same off-campus café every Thursday evening at six. It's a twelve-minute drive from her apartment to campus. Which means you can park outside her building and watch her leave, probably between five thirty and five forty-five."

"Then our start time is pretty well set," Simone replied. "But what about our end time? It's possible we won't hear from Aidan until dawn, Croatian time, which is about nine tonight, PST. That's tight."

"After her club meetings, Jia li and a few of her friends hang around and have a few pizzas delivered. It appears to be their weekly ritual. She stays in the same classroom for at least an hour, which gives us extra padding. It should be enough. You're correct that there will be pressure. But you stand up well to that."

Simone smiled at Terri's typically brusque compliment. "I appreciate your vote of confidence. I got your specs on Jia li's car. I know I'm looking for a BMW M4 blue metallic convertible—which should be more than easy to spot, just in case she's already exiting the apartment complex when I see her. Now, what other details do I need to know up front?"

"I texted you Jia li's photo and address."

"I have both. Pretty girl. Nice garden apartments from the photos I saw online."

"Nice but understated. No doorman or front desk—handy for someone who wants to keep a low profile and entertain visitors who prefer to remain anonymous. Jia li's unit is on the first floor—apartment five, to the left of the lobby—so you won't have stairs to navigate. On the other hand, it's bound to be a higher-traffic area. Plus, you'll have to find a way to get into the building itself, which will require a key card to gain entrance."

"Understood. I'll handle it."

"Call me after you've left the school and again when you're situated at the apartment," Terri said. "I have my own homework to do in the meantime. Plus, Aidan already gave me his instructions about hacking into the TSA. I'll penetrate their firewall and be ready to add the suspects to the No Fly List when Aidan gives me the go-ahead."

27

Eighteen hours left...

Abandoned farmhouse
Đakovo, Croatia
2 March
Friday, 2:25 a.m. local time

Everything was in place.

The Zermatt jet had landed on schedule. Aidan had jumped into the passenger seat of the black SUV, and Marc had peeled off, heading for the rescue site, where Philip was waiting for them.

Marc parked behind the stand of trees adjacent to Philip's vehicle.

"Give me an update," Aidan instructed Philip, vaulting out of the car and tossing his ski jacket into the back seat. As he spoke, he zipped open his gear bag and removed all the necessary equipment. He pulled on his bulletproof, standard military-issue vest—which he loaded with two flash grenades and extra ammo—and shoved his Glock 27 nine-millimeter pistol into his thigh holster. He then collected his Peltor headset, which would block out the deafening noise created by their flash grenades, and his flashbang-proof goggles.

Last, he readied his H&K nine-millimeter MP5 submachine gun and yanked on his Nomex gloves. Marc had hopped out of the SUV and was going through the identical process.

Philip was already in full gear, so he used those precious minutes to give Aidan a full report.

"Mr. Smoker had his last cigarette break twenty minutes ago. He should be doing a repeat performance in another forty. The others are inside. There's been no outdoor activity and no visible indoor activity since my earlier report to Marc."

"So we progress to our attack position now," Aidan said, referring to the barn, where they'd be launching their assault of the house. "We'll move from point to point based on Philip's recon—first the stone wall, then the drainage ditch, then the trees, then the barn. We wait for Mr. Smoker to come out and light up. Then we go."

Both Marc and Philip nodded. The tactical plan had been finalized as Aidan's plane was nearing Osijek. All three men were ready to act.

On Aidan's signal, they moved.

Silently, using only hand and arm signals to communicate with one another, they made their way forward, stopping at each designated point and squatting down low for concealment and assessment. Once assured that they were undetected, they continued to advance, sidestepping all icy patches so their athletic boots didn't make the slightest crunching sounds on the otherwise soggy ground.

They didn't stop until they were secure in the shelter of the barn.

Anchoring their helmets, goggles, and radio microphones in place, they hunkered down and waited.

Crescent Woods Garden Apartments
Palo Alto, California
1 March
Thursday, 5:32 p.m. local time

Simone had parked on the tree-lined street directly across from Jia li's apartment complex. Hers was one of a line of cars parked along the curb, so it blended in nicely, inconspicuously.

She was hopeful that this second part of the plan would go as smoothly as the first. The only potential obstacle she'd come up against at the Business School was a tired custodian whose cart was propping open the outside door. The cart itself was a blessing in disguise, as it had allowed Simone easy access to the building. The custodian was the sticky part. Using her best damsel in distress techniques, she'd managed to convince him that she'd left her iPad in a particular room and prevailed upon him to let her in to find it. He hemmed and hawed for maybe two minutes, during which time he'd checked out her legs twice and her breasts three times. All part of her plan; he let her in.

The custodian waited outside the room, giving Simone plenty of opportunity to plant the device, slide her iPad out of her tote bag, and pretend to find it again. Exiting quickly, she'd thanked him profusely, clutching her iPad like a priceless treasure, and scooted out the door.

Success.

She'd reported in to Terri, who was concentrating hard on whatever she was working on and who sounded totally revved up by the results.

"I need you to make a quick stop at Fry's," she said. "There's one right there in Palo Alto. Pick up a small USB drive, a name brand, not a generic, and one that's easy to open."

"How large a capacity should it have?" Simone asked.

"Anything sixteen gigabytes or bigger should be fine. And get some anti-static gloves in your size. Also, a padded manila envelope. Pay cash so there's no electronic trail."

"Of course."

"One last thing. Make sure you have your laptop with you when you head out to Jia li's apartment."

"I already have it. It's in my tote bag."

"Good."

Simone had squelched her curiosity. She'd get her answers when she needed them.

Now, she turned off her ignition and called Terri again, this time not only to check in but to fit in. She looked like yet another driver, parked and waiting for someone and, in the interim, chatting on her cell phone.

"I'm in position," she said as soon as Terri was on the line.

"Good." Terri had been quite pleased with Simone's results thus far. "You took care of the errand?"

"I have everything you asked for, and my laptop is ready and waiting for your instructions."

"Do you have a visual on Jia li's apartment unit?"

"Yes. I'm parked directly across the street from the apartment and the covered parking area. I'll be able to see her leave and to make sure she doesn't make a surprise return. You haven't heard from Aidan, have you?"

"Not yet."

"Neither have I." Simone's forehead creased with worry. "I know this is business-as-usual for him, but I'm on edge anyway. Unrealistic as it is, there's a part of me that was hoping the mission was already completed and that the team was on their way home with Lauren."

"I understand." Terri sounded concerned, too, at least for Terri. "I half expected to have gotten the thumbs-up from Aidan by now. That having been said…" She continued, back to her get-it-done self. "You and I must compartmentalize so we can be effective at our part in this investigation."

"Agreed." Simone glanced up as a runner jogged by—a tanned California girl with a blonde ponytail. Definitely not Jia li.

"Do you have all your tools ready?" Terri asked.

"Um-hum—along with my gun."

"I see." Terri didn't sound surprised. "I'm sure Aidan wasn't happy about that."

"No, he wasn't. But it's a necessary precaution, especially once you fire off that text. Who knows whether either the mole or Jia li will turn violent once they realize they've been compromised. The mole will likely recognize me from Nano, and I need to be prepared."

"Of course."

"Are you going to tell me what I'm downloading onto this USB drive?"

"Later. Time's too tight right now. Jia li will be leaving for her club meeting any minute."

Abruptly, Simone sat up in her seat. "Sooner than that," she said as a blue BMW exited from the enclosed lot. The driver signaled right and pulled out, at which point Simone got an excellent view of her. "Jia li is on her way."

Simone waited five minutes to make sure her target didn't return unexpectedly for some forgotten item. Then she grabbed her purse— complete with everything she and Terri had discussed—got out of her car, and calmly strolled across the street.

The garden apartment complex was three stories high, charming in an outdoorsy, California kind of way. Each unit had a private wooden terrace wrapped around it, with a broad window that overlooked either the landscaped grounds or the outdoor pool. Lots of palm trees and lush greenery lined the stone path that Simone walked up as she made her way to the quiet entranceway door.

There she paused, taking out her cell phone and, brows drawn together in feigned frustration, seemingly checked and rechecked her text messages.

It took less than ten minutes for a young couple—holding hands and gazing intimately at each other while laughing at some private joke—to exit the building. They moseyed their way out, letting the door swing shut behind them, barely missing Simone as they did. They moved on, oblivious to Simone and the whole damned world.

Simone caught the handle just before the door shut completely, the hint of a smile at her lips. Nothing like twentysomething lovers to give her the unnoticed entry she sought.

The lobby was nothing more than a polished oak floor, two tufted armchairs, and some striking potted plants. No front desk. No front doorman. As always, Terri was spot-on with her research.

Simone turned left and headed down the deserted hallway to apartment five. She paused, listening for approaching footsteps and simultaneously scrutinizing the hallway. So far, so good.

She took out her lock-picking tools and went to work.

Three minutes later she was inside, ready to go.

The living room was straight ahead, decorated with a matching sofa and love seat and two accent chairs, all done in muted shades of turquoise and pink. Peaceful watercolor artwork hung on the walls, and there was a simple glass coffee table in the center of the furniture grouping. All very feminine and tasteful. More mature than youthful, but that was no surprise, given Jia li was far from the average grad student. She played in the sophisticated big leagues and her decorating tastes reflected that.

Simone didn't waste a second. She crossed over to the sofa, took out the key fob, and knelt down, sliding it across the carpeted floor just beneath the center section of the sofa. Out of sight. Out of reach. But so innocuous that, if and when found, it would seem insignificant.

In a heartbeat, Simone snapped her purse shut and retraced her steps, then hovered with her ear against the front door. She heard a bunch of footsteps accompanied by laughing voices as a group of people made their way down the hall, passing Jia Li's apartment, their voices fading away as they neared the lobby.

There were no other sounds alerting her to further activity, but Simone still waited a good few minutes longer. She wasn't taking any chances. Jia li's apartment door was visible from the lobby. She had to make doubly sure that whoever had passed had also left the building.

Utter silence endured.

Carefully, Simone opened the door a crack and peered both ways. No one.

She slipped out of the apartment, reengaged the lock, and walked out of the building with the same easygoing veneer with which she'd arrived.

Abandoned farmhouse
Đakovo, Croatia
2 March
Friday, 3:07 a.m. local time

Aidan's adrenaline was pumping.

Mr. Smoker had just sauntered out of the house and was now leaning against the porch post, taking long, leisurely drags of his cigarette.

One minute. Two minutes.

The kidnapper flicked an ash and shifted position so that his back was to them.

"Now," Aidan ordered between gritted teeth.

They all moved at once.

Philip raced to the front door, Aidan and Marc to the back.

Before Mr. Smoker had lifted the cigarette back to his lips, Philip was on him, cracking the butt of his MP5 over the guy's head, fracturing his skull in one motion. He crumpled to the ground. Philip dealt a second blow to the already-dead man, then checked for vitals. None.

"One down," he said into his microphone.

Aidan and Marc had reached the back door. Contrary to expectation, it was locked. Marc put the heel of his boot alongside the doorknob and kicked it in. Aidan pulled the pin out of the flashbang, turned his head away, and tossed the grenade inside the farmhouse on the floor.

A deafening bang and blinding strobe lights exploded through the house. Piercing screams echoed as loss of sight, hearing, and balance seized whomever was in range.

Aidan and Marc burst in. In direct sight was one powerful guy who'd been sitting in front of the TV and who'd now dropped to his knees, howling in agony. His eyes were squeezed shut, and his hands were clapped over his ears.

Aidan raised his MP5 and double-tapped him, delivering two shots to the chest. He followed up with one quick shot to the head. The man fell like a stone.

A second guy came screaming out of one of the bedrooms, unaffected by the grenade but scared shitless by the explosion and gunshots.

Marc swerved around, MP5 raised, and took him out, also going for center mass and firing two shots to his chest and a final one to the head.

Two dead bodies. No further activity.

"Two men down," Aidan said into his microphone. "Room clearing."

Aidan and Marc did a sweep of the farmhouse, finding all the rooms empty except one.

In the center bedroom, curled up in a ball on the bed and frozen with terror, was Lauren Pennington. She whimpered when she saw them, looking frantically around for a means to escape.

"We're the good guys, Lauren," Aidan said gently, purposely staying still and not advancing toward her until she understood. "We work for your father. We're here to take you home."

"Home?" Lauren stared at them for a moment and then burst into tears. "But Bashkim… he's out there. And the others…"

"They're all dead. You're safe."

"Safe," Lauren repeated, shock making it almost impossible for her to absorb anything.

"Yes, safe." Aidan felt that tightening in his chest, the one that reminded him he'd saved the life of someone's daughter.

"Oh my God." Lauren covered her face, uncontrollable sobs shaking her body as she rocked back and forth on her heels. "Thank you. Thank you."

This time it was Marc who spoke into the microphone. "All secure. We've got the hostage."

"All clear in front," Philip replied.

Aidan moved forward, squatting beside Lauren. "Are you hurt?"

She shook her head.

"Then let's get you out of here." He scooped her up in his arms and turned to go. "Coming out with Lauren," he said.

"I'll do a tech sweep," Marc told him.

Nodding, Aidan went to plan, heading for the front door since it was the shortest distant back to their SUVs. "Confiscate any computers," he called over his shoulder.

"Yup." Marc did that by rote. He moved quickly, retrieving the kidnappers' cell phones, grinding them beneath his heels so they couldn't be tracked. "Did you take care of Mr. Smoker's cell phone?" he asked Philip into the microphone.

"Crushed," was the reply.

The only other electronic device in the house was a laptop—clearly the one they'd used for Lauren's videoconferences with her father. That, Marc took with him, striding forward to join Aidan.

Philip was waiting and they all raced for where the cars were hidden. Lauren was softly weeping, her face buried against Aidan's vest, her body quaking with the aftereffects of her ordeal.

They reached the SUVs, where Aidan wrapped Lauren in warm blankets and settled her on the back seat.

Marc held out the laptop, and Aidan gestured for him to put it in Philip's car, which Marc did.

"Please deliver that to Danijel in Zagreb," Aidan requested of Philip as they all shed their gear. "Besides the usual porn, games, and sports stuff, I'm sure he'll find a gold mine of data, like other operations in Croatia that this scumbag Albanian OC group is running. Tell him I hope it helps, and thanks. Oh, and tell him there'll be a case of Blanton's coming his way. Fine bourbon is Danijel's Achilles' heel. I'll have Terri get on it ASAP."

"Done." A corner of Philip's mouth lifted. "Then I'm heading back to the UK for some much-needed rest and recreation."

Aidan chuckled, shaking his colleague's hand. "Enjoy both, particularly the latter. You've earned it."

Philip snapped off a salute to Marc, who'd hopped into the back seat of the SUV next to Lauren, both to offer her any reassurances she might need and to make certain she did nothing to distract Aidan while he drove.

Settling himself behind the wheel of the other SUV, Philip pulled the door shut and flipped on the ignition. Then, he waited, per Zermatt protocol, until all team members were ready to go.

Minutes later, both SUVs rolled out, Philip en route to Zagreb, Aidan and Marc en route to Osijek Airport.

Lauren's nightmare was at an end.

28

Simone shifted in the driver's seat of her car, itching to enact the plan to trap the mole.

It had been almost two hours since she'd planted the bug in Jia li's apartment. Since then, she'd been holed up in her car, cell phone on the seat beside her. Her Bluetooth-ed headset in place, she remained connected to Terri.

This was the waiting part.

The fun part had been when she first returned to her car.

Terri hadn't wasted a minute.

"I need you to put on those anti-static gloves now."

"Why?" Simone couldn't help but ask.

"Because you and I both know that Aidan is going to want everyone involved to be brought to justice. And that means supplying the authorities with proof—anonymous proof. We can't have your fingerprints on the USB drive with all the evidence I'm about to place on it for the benefit of the FBI."

"So that's what you were working on earlier. Don't keep me in suspense—what proof did you find?"

"I hacked into Xu Wei's cell phone carrier." Terri sounded like the proverbial cat who'd swallowed the canary. "The images of the stolen technology were sent from Xu's cell phone to Jia li's. Also sent from his cell phone were numerous calls to Croatia."

"*Bon.*" Simone was both excited and impressed. She reached for the gloves and wriggled her fingers into them. "Gloves are on."

"Now remove the USB drive from the package and insert it into your laptop. Let me know when you're done."

A few minutes of struggling with the packaging and the drive came loose. Simone inserted it into a spare USB port.

"All ready."

Terri took over from there.

She switched to the remote window where she could see and control Simone's laptop. She copied the phone logs and images of the Nano confidential drawings that Xu had stolen. Then, she ejected the drive. "Simone, please remove and reinsert the drive so I can test it."

Simone complied quickly.

Terri saw the drive reactivate. Then she double-clicked on each file to make sure they were readable. Satisfied with her workmanship, she ejected the drive. "Success. Now place the drive inside the padded manila envelope and seal it."

Simone dropped the drive into the envelope, removed the self-sealing strip, and closed the envelope. "All done," she replied.

"Great. We'll be getting that to the FBI as soon as we're done here. I'm sorry you're stuck outside the apartment complex, but transmitters have a limited range and you need to be in close proximity to pick up their conversation."

"I expected that. But there's another reason I'm still here. While it's likely that things will go as planned, it's always possible that Jia li and the mole will leave the apartment without revealing what we hope to hear, in which case I'll have to see who the mole is with my own eyes."

After that, neither of them had much to say. The sense of accomplishment they'd experienced soon ebbed, and tension crackled cross-country, as they waited for news and waited to act.

"It's been hours, Terri," Simone said, speaking their concerns aloud. "I'm worried. I know Aidan. And so do you. He wouldn't wait. He'd move in the moment the opportunity presented itself."

"Which it might not have." Terri was trying to be the voice of reason. "There's a young woman's life on the line. Aidan is strategic, highly intelligent, and well-trained. He'll do this and do it right."

"I know. I just…" Simone's mouth snapped shut. Who was this apprehensive woman? She always kept it together. Being cool under pressure was essential, both at Zermatt and at McKinsey. Yet here she was, seized by raw nerves and acting like a rookie.

"I apologize, Terri. Let's chalk it up to the fact that I'm not good surveillance material. I'm too type A proactive."

"Sitting on my hands and waiting is tough for me, too," Terri replied. "And like you, I'm not ordinarily a worrier." A discreet cough. "Plus, it's worse for you. I'm not emotionally involved."

"You're right." Simone didn't pretend to misunderstand what Terri was saying. Despite the total professionalism she and Aidan exhibited when doing Zermatt business, their personal relationship was hardly a secret to the team. "This investigation is high stakes, just like all of ours. But now we're talking about a life-or-death mission."

"Aidan's a survivor. He'll be fine."

As she spoke, there was a beep on the line, followed by the audio announcement: "*Joining conference call…*" and then their team leader's familiar voice: "Aidan."

Osijek Airport
Osijek, Croatia
2 March
Friday, 4:38 a.m. local time

"Hello, ladies." Aidan's voice was laced with satisfaction and still thrumming from his adrenaline high. "Just wanted to let you know we're airborne. Marc and I should be landing with Lauren at twenty-one hundred hours—nine o'clock Pacific Standard Time—give or take air traffic and customs."

"You're all safe?" Simone demanded.

"All except the Albanians. They won't be sending out Christmas cards this year—or any other year."

A chuckle from Terri's end. "A shame."

"Yeah, life sucks."

Amusement gone. Urgency back.

"We're wrapped up at this end," Aidan said. "Is the bug in place?"

"Ready and waiting," Simone replied.

"Good. You're out of harm's way?"

"Yes, and in record time. The magician's daughter hasn't lost her lock-picking talent."

"Never doubted it. Terri, send that text."

"Already composed."

A second passed as Terri hit the send button. "Gone."

"Terri, now that Lauren is safe, it's time to bring down the remaining people involved. Add all the suspects to the TSA's No Fly List."

"Will do. We should see action very soon, followed by audio confirmation of who at Nano we're dealing with. Once that happens, I'll add the mole to the No Fly List, as well."

"Nice work, both of you," Aidan praised. He paused, his mind veering to his immediate concern. "Simone, stay in that car. And don't use your weapon unless it's absolutely necessary. In America, civilians have an obligation to attempt to flee from danger rather than standing their ground. You're not in your home, where those laws are different. I don't want you in danger. Nor do we want the fallout if you have to defend yourself."

"Fine."

Aidan ignored the patronizing tone of Simone's reply. "I'm texting you contact information on a pal of Marc's who handles industrial espionage at the FBI San Francisco field office—Special Agent Jeffrey Albertson. Without providing specific details, Marc's asked him to hang out in Palo Alto tonight. He got him a reservation at Sundance the Steakhouse and bought him a prime rib dinner with all the trimmings in exchange for his availability. So he'll be close by."

"Sundance the Steakhouse?"

"Yup. Odd name, but the best steakhouse in Palo Alto. If push comes to shove, don't hesitate to reach out to him."

"Push won't come to shove. But having his nearby presence will make you feel better." Simone went on to fill Aidan in on what Terri had found and what they'd done.

Aidan let out a low whistle. "Terri, have I told you lately how indispensable you are?"

"Not often enough." Terri's voice was filled with smug satisfaction.

"Well, you are. After you wrap up there, Simone can deliver the evidence to the maître d' at the restaurant and ensure that he passes it along to SA Albertson."

"I'll do that," Simone said.

Simone's terse answers finally elicited a response from Aidan. "Don't be a cowboy, Simone. I mean it."

"*Bon*. Besides, I am French, not American. We don't have cowboys in France. And if we did, I'd be a cowgirl, *n'est ce pas*?"

Aidan rolled his eyes, realizing it was pointless. Simone was going to do things her way.

"Changing topics," Simone said, "thank Marc for taking care of you by addressing your unnecessary concerns. Now, can you fill us in on the rescue mission?"

"I'll conference back in a few minutes. Right now, I'm setting Lauren up for a videoconference with her parents. I called them on our way to the airport, so they know she's safe. But they need to hear and see their daughter." A pause. "And I need to call mine."

"Of course you do." Simone didn't need an explanation. "Tell Abby I want a stuffed Disney Princess. Her choice. It's unfair that I should fly all the way from Lyon and not get the chance to see the original Disneyland."

"Will do." This time there was a smile in Aidan's voice. "Knowing Abby and her enthusiasm, she'll have Emma buy you one that's taller than you are. Be glad you're flying home on the Zermatt plane."

Stanford Business School
Palo Alto, California
1 March
Thursday, 7:40 p.m. local time

Jia li went sheet white when she read the cryptic text.

Xu Wei was here?

A classified leak. One that was serious enough for him to fly to Palo Alto for an urgent person-to-person meeting with all parties. And not at his hotel. At her apartment, where they wouldn't be seen or recognized. In a half hour.

Something had gone very, very wrong.

She stood up and mumbled something to excuse herself from her meeting. Grabbing her things, she tripped and nearly fell in her haste to get out the door.

She made her phone call the moment she stepped outside the building.

The person at the other end listened intently, as freaked out by all this as she was—and with a lot more to lose. "I'm on my way."

Crescent Woods Garden Apartments
Palo Alto, California
1 March
Thursday, 7:55 p.m. local time

Simone watched as Jia li's BMW came tearing down the street and veered into the development until it disappeared into the underground parking.

"Well, your text certainly worked," she announced to Terri. "Jia li just broke every speed limit and nearly hit a tree on her way in."

"I expected no less." Once again, Terri sounded both smug and pleased.

"Our mole should be here soon."

"Yes, but don't expect to spot him or her, not unless things go wrong and you have to relocate your car. Whoever it is will definitely not want to be seen. They'll drive around back and tuck their car in an unobtrusive spot. Jia li will let them in via the back door. I'm sure that's how they arranged any previous meetings they held here—assuming there were any."

"My guess is, there were," Simone replied, her gaze darting everywhere just in case their mole was sloppier than Terri expected. "Jia li is an unknown chess piece to everyone but us. Her apartment would be the best choice for face-to-face interaction. Public places would be risky, and anything closer to Nano would be riskier still. So I think your theory is a sound one."

"I'm glad we're in agreement." Terri sounded as revved up as Simone felt. They were on the brink of a major discovery and they both knew it.

A few more minutes ticked by, during which time they heard the muffled sounds of Jia li letting herself into her apartment, tossing down whatever things she'd been carrying, and then hurrying back out the door.

Silence.

"She's on her way to let her colleague in." Terri stated the obvious. "The back door is at the other end of the corridor and around the bend from Jia li's apartment. I'm sure she's running. But it'll still take a couple of minutes. Let's sit tight and take some deep breaths."

"Right." Simone knew far better than to think Terri was either sitting tight or breathing deeply. She herself was perched so rigidly at the edge of her seat that her breasts were being flattened by the steering wheel.

At last the apartment door opened with a whoosh, followed by some hurried footsteps and the door being shut.

"Xu Wei will be here in less than five minutes." Jia li's hysterical voice came through Simone's headset, clear and strong. "I'm frightened. I don't even understand what's happening. Or why."

"Neither do I," came the reply. "But whatever it is, we have to fix it. Fast. My entire future is on the line."

Simone's jaw dropped as she recognized the voice of the other person in Jia li's apartment.

"Terri," she said in shock. "That's Robert Maxwell."

29

Crescent Woods Garden Apartments
Palo Alto, California
1 March
Thursday, 8:05 p.m. local time

"Holy shit," Terri exclaimed. Her fingers were already flying across the keyboard. "This is a game changer. We've been looking for a mole. But Robert Maxwell? If he's the insider, then he's the *kingpin*, not a mole."

"But why would he sabotage his own company?" Simone asked, her head still reeling. "Do you think the technology doesn't work?"

"I don't know. I'm digging while we're listening."

From inside the apartment, there was the sound of rhythmic pacing, followed by Robert's muttered, "Where the hell is he? What could have backfired? Everything was on track—at least that's what he said. The first set of drawings were the real deal—I checked them myself. Nano is set to go into production. We have to beat that deadline. *Dammit!*"

Simone recognized the clinking sounds of ice and the slamming of a bottle that followed. Robert was pouring himself a drink.

"What if someone from inside Jítuán figured out what Xu Wei is doing?" Jia li asked.

Silence.

"Robert, talk to me. I'm not an idiot or a child."

"I think my actions have shown that I regard you as neither."

"Then stop trying to protect me. From the minute I agreed to fly to Shenzhen and talk to Jítuán's CEO on behalf of a mysterious friend of yours seeking VC funding, I knew something was up. No one invests millions to create a competitor to NanoUSA without knowing the people and the technology involved. And after your dinner with Xu Wei over the summer and my subsequent meeting with him last month, I became certain that my role as a go-between was part of a much larger scenario."

Robert was pacing again. "That's more than you need to know. Leave it, Jia li. If anything goes wrong, I don't want you in trouble."

More silence.

"I didn't do this for the finder's fee or even the VP position at your new company. I did it because I love you." Jia li's voice broke. "I don't want you to go to prison."

New company?

"So there's nothing wrong with the technology," Terri muttered, the clicking of her keyboard momentarily at a pause. "Abandoning that search." She resumed typing.

Simone was mentally processing what she was hearing, simultaneously integrating it with what she knew about Robert.

Figuring out where he'd met Jia li was easy. It had to have been during one of his speaking engagements at Stanford's Business School. He would have handpicked her. She fit the mold—young, beautiful, ambitious—the quintessential Robert Maxwell sexual acquisition. And he'd needed her to make his agenda a reality. Not only was she bright enough for the challenge, she had the language skills to cross a cultural barrier that was in the way. So he'd promised her everything she wanted—including himself—in exchange for her help.

But why would he want to steal his own technology and start a new company when his *current* one was about to make groundbreaking history?

"Okay." Terri's voice sounded in Simone's ears. "Nothing suspect on Robert's corporate credit card. But I just ran his personal credit card receipts from last summer. July eighteenth, he paid for an extravagant dinner at an out-of-town restaurant. That would be the dinner Jia li is talking about."

"Are you crosschecking that with the initial press coverage of Nano's breakthrough?"

"Already done. What I'm finding is inconclusive, because the rumor mill was at it long before legitimate sources started reporting." Terri was still typing. "But there's a more interesting connection. The dinner took place two weeks after Nano held its quarterly board meeting."

"How is that significant?"

"Because the corporate minutes show that that's when the subject of Robert's early retirement was finalized." A pause. "*Finalized* being the key word here. It indicates that his stepping down was under discussion before that." Another pause. "Months before that, given the dates I'm reading. And not just under discussion. There was a heated debate over the urgency of his exit."

Simone's brows drew together. "So much for our theory that Robert chose to go out with a bang—commercialize the technology and step aside when he was at the pinnacle of his success."

"So much for our theory that he *chose* at all."

"He's being forced out."

"Looks that way. Maybe his leadership isn't as extraordinary as it appears to be."

"Uh-uh." Simone's people-whisperer skills kicked in. "He's an extraordinary leader. His employees think he walks on water, at least most of them do. Terri, this isn't about Robert's abilities. It's about him. If his retirement was a board decision and not his own, it's because of sexual misconduct. I picked up on it from the onset, and given the ages of the women he's discarded, this has been going on for years. Even though none of the women involved has filed an official complaint, it doesn't mean the board is unaware or that settlements weren't made wrapped neatly behind ironclad confidentiality agreements."

"And if they are, they'd politely ask for his resignation with the implied threat of something ugly if he refused." Terri let out a low whistle. "If we're right, he sure as hell found a great way to exact his revenge—and to stay rich and relevant. He'd be taking himself out of the equation and taking the technology along with him."

"What about *how* he orchestrated the theft of Nano's IP?" Simone demanded. She felt like throwing up. "He planned out Lauren's kidnapping to force Vance's hand so he could get what he needed to start over. My God, he has children and grandchildren of his own. What kind of monster is he?"

Simultaneously, the reality of the situation hit Simone like a ton of bricks. There was no point in adding Robert's name to the TSA No Fly List. He and his corporate jet would be disappearing along with his girlfriend before the FBI could sort everything out. She and Terri had anticipated everything, except for Robert.

Terri's mind was clearly on the same wavelength. "We're screwed," she said. "Right now, all we have are theories and speculation. Nothing the FBI could go after Robert for and certainly not before he would escape. We need concrete evidence."

"I'll get it."

"Wait," Terri interrupted her quickly. "Simone, we're playing by different rules now. If Robert is the brains behind Lauren's kidnapping, he's a lot more dangerous than a mole. You can't just march in there and confront him—not without reinforcements."

"What are you talking about?" Simone demanded. "We can't notify law enforcement. Zermatt doesn't officially exist. Plus, everything we're doing here is way outside the law."

"There will be no interaction or visual sightings." Terri's tone was factual but adamant. "I'm calling Marc, having him amend the plan he has with SA Albertson. I want the Feds on-site just in case."

"I can't meet with an FBI agent."

"You won't. I'd never compromise either your or Zermatt's anonymity. Get Robert's confession and I'll record it as planned. I'll upload it onto a secure drop box so the FBI will have the evidence it needs. And to protect your identity, I'm going to have Donovan alter your female voice into a male voice. 'Simone' will become 'Simon' on the recording. It doesn't matter if Robert or Jia li uses your name, because the pronunciations in French sound very much alike. Donovan will also convert all female pronouns to male pronouns. In the meantime, do you have that extra phone I sent you?"

"Yes. You told me to keep it on hand."

"I'll call you and pretend I'm SA Albertson. In reality, I'll be notifying you when Marc tells me that Albertson has left the restaurant. That'll be your five-minute warning to get out. Albertson will take over from there on."

"He'll have no grounds to take over—at least not yet. He won't have instant access to Robert's confession, nor will he have the manila envelope I'm getting to him to implicate Xu Wei. He doesn't have a clue what's transpiring, and even if he did, his hands would be tied."

"That will all be fixed."

"How?"

"Trust me. Do you have your anti-static gloves?"

"Of course. I wouldn't handle the envelope without them."

"Also have a pen on hand. We're going to add a note to Agent Albertson's delivery, providing him with the location of the drop box."

"All of which I'm delivering *where*, if Agent Albertson is leaving the steakhouse? No matter what, he won't have it in time for him to go in and arrest Robert now—"

"Simone, listen to me because we're running out of time. You just get that confession. I'll work with Marc and provide you with an action plan when you and I talk on the burner phone. We'll make this as seamless as possible, given that Robert is a flight risk. But you're right—the order of things is backwards and Albertson isn't about to storm the place without evidence, warrants, and all the other legal crap our team bypasses. So we'll move as fast as we can to rectify that. In the meantime, we're already breaking protocol. Aidan will be livid. And we are *not* jeopardizing your life."

Before Simone could respond, a muffled oath came from inside the apartment.

"Goddammit, that's it." Robert's tone said he'd reached his limit. "We've waited long enough. Text Xu Wei. Find out where he is. Better still, give me your phone. I'll call him."

"That's my cue," Simone announced. She was already in motion, grabbing her tote bag, which contained her gun, burner phone, gloves, writing essentials, and the manila envelope. She pulled off her headset, placed her current cell phone on the console, and reached for the door handle. "Do what you have to. I'm going in."

Zermatt jet
2 March
Friday, 5103 nm to SFO
5:30 a.m. CET

Aidan's voice had a definite edge to it when he answered the phone, as if he knew he wasn't going to like what he heard. "Yes."

"It's me," Terri said. "Conference Marc in."

Aidan called out to Marc, then did as Terri asked. "Problem?" Aidan pressed her in that same edgy tone.

"Complication." Terri filled the two of them in with a few quick sentences.

It was enough.

"Maxwell. Shit. I never saw that coming," Aidan said, his jaw clenched. "And Simone's in there with him?"

"She just went in. You can ream us out later. Marc, I need you to contact your FBI buddy. Offer him a rain check for *two* steak dinners.

Just get him to Jia li's apartment complex *now*. Once he's there, ask him to park and wait. I'll call you the instant Simone has what she needs and is leaving the apartment. At that point, get the make and model of his car and find out where he's parked. Request that he take a short walk away from his hopefully unlocked vehicle. He'll understand why when he gets back."

"That last part will never fly, but I'm on it." Marc had his cell phone in his hand. "The steakhouse is five minutes from the apartment. I'll get Jeff there. Call you right back."

Three minutes later they were back on the phone.

"Jeff is en route," Marc told Terri. "I lit a fire under his ass by telling him—off the record—that the crime going down falls under his FBI industrial espionage division. He'll play by our rules that he received an anonymous tip."

"Which he will."

"FYI, he's driving his personal vehicle, a silver Honda Civic. He'll give me an exact location of where he's parked once he's in place. Forget the unlocked car. It's a no-go given the weaponry carried by a special agent. What I got him to agree to is to leave the passenger window cracked open an inch so that Simone can slide the manila envelope in."

"That'll have to be good enough," Terri replied. "I'll relay all that to Simone when she calls."

"Let me know the minute that is," Aidan told her, his anger barely contained. "I want to hear she's safe."

Crescent Woods Garden Apartments
Palo Alto, California
1 March
Thursday, 8:25 p.m. local time

The apartment complex was busier than it had been earlier, with tenants arriving home from work or heading out for a late dinner. It was easy for Simone to slip inside by appending herself to a small group of students who were complaining about their workload while carrying in plastic bags filled with cartons of Chinese takeout.

Once inside, she veered down the hall and made a beeline for Jia li's unit.

As she raised her hand to knock, she heard Robert's muffled voice saying, "I don't know what kind of game Xu is playing, but that voice mail ought to get his butt in gear."

"I don't understand it," Jia li replied. "His text was urgent."

Simone knocked.

"Finally." Robert was clearly beyond worrying about staying hidden, because he strode across the room and yanked open the door. "Where the hell have you been…?" His mouth snapped shut and his entire body went into startled red alert when he saw Simone standing there.

"Simone?" He uttered her name inanely as if trying to connect the dots.

"Hello, Robert," she replied. "Aren't you going to invite me in?" She didn't wait for an invitation, just walked around him and made her way into the living room, where Jia li was standing looking totally baffled and equally unnerved.

"Have we met?" she asked, on some level realizing that this woman Robert obviously knew had just invaded *her* apartment.

"No, but we're about to." Simone had angled herself in such a way that she could keep both of them in her sights. Robert was still standing at the open door, staring at her.

"Close it and come in," Simone instructed, her fingers inching to the closure on her tote bag. She had a feeling she'd be needing her Glock, even if it was just to keep them in line and get them to talk.

Robert complied on autopilot, simultaneously finding his tongue. "What are you doing here? How did you even know how to find me? Is this some Nano emergency?"

"Oh, it's a Nano emergency all right. But not the kind you're thinking of." Simone kept her tone calm and even. What she really wanted was to kick Robert in a very vulnerable part of his anatomy. "As for how I found you and what I'm doing here, why don't you and Jia li have a seat on the sofa and we'll talk."

Despite the fact that Robert was looking a little green around the gills, he planted his feet where he was. "I'm not going anywhere until you tell me what this is about."

"Have it your way." Simone pulled out her pistol and calmly aimed it at Robert, who did a double-take, his gaze moving from the gun to Simone's face and back. Jia li clapped a hand over her mouth to silence her scream.

"Sit," Simone commanded.

"Robert, please, do whatever she says." Jia li had already darted over to the sofa and perched herself at the edge, looking like a terrified mouse about to be devoured by a feral cat.

Robert gave one last glance at the door.

"Xu Wei's not coming," Simone said, properly reading his mind. "He never left Shenzhen."

Now Simone got the reaction she'd been waiting for. Robert literally lurched with shock, his eyebrows shooting up so high they practically disappeared into his hairline. His mouth opened and closed several times, but nothing came out. On stilted legs, he went to the sofa and lowered himself to the cushion beside Jia li.

"Good," Simone said. "Now here's how this is going to work. I'll lay out the scenario. After that, you'll fill in the blanks."

"Who are you *really*?" Robert finally demanded.

"The person who's running this conversation," she replied. "A conversation that could take a very ugly turn if you don't do as I ask. Understood?"

She didn't wait for them to acknowledge that they did. She just stared Robert down and began laying out the facts.

"You're using Jítuán's resources to start up and run a whole new subsidiary company in Shenzhen. You're colluding with their CEO,

Xu Wei, as we speak, to steal Nano's technology in order to beat out Nano's rollout of its new manufacturing process. This way, you can introduce it yourself in your new capacity—as CEO of the newly formed company. Anything you want to amend thus far?"

You could have heard a pin drop in the room.

"Very well, then I'll go on as to why this is happening." Simone shot Jia li a quick glance. "You might want to cover your ears for this part, you foolish little girl. Otherwise, you're going to find out exactly who the love of your life really is."

"Robert?" Jia li murmured, slanting an uneasy look in his direction.

Robert didn't respond, his gaze locked on Simone.

Simone turned her attention back to him. "You've had sexual relationships with far too many of your female employees while promising them career advancements along the way. As far as your board of directors is concerned, your libido supersedes your accomplishments at last. You're no longer an asset. You're an unacceptable liability. They're forcing you out—now."

At that provocation, Simone got the reaction—and the outpouring of words—that she needed.

Robert jerked forward on the sofa cushion, fury flashing in his eyes. "An *asset*? I *am* NanoUSA. I founded it, made it the electronics giant it is today. And the new breakthrough manufacturing technology that will turn the electronics industry upside down? I created it. *Me!* It's mine. If I go, it goes with me. Screw the board. Screw the whole damn company."

"And screw your country in the process," Simone added icily. "Aren't you the diehard patriot who was going to revolutionize the industry by bringing tens of thousands of jobs back to the US? Wasn't that the reason behind all your efforts? Or was that politically correct bullshit and this was always all about your ego?"

"Not my ego," he corrected. "My relevance. I have more to offer the world than all the thirty-year-old millionaire kids combined. I'm not walking off into the sunset, not by a long shot. As for my country..." A flash of regret crossed his face. "Yes, that was the plan. Unfortunately, that's not the way it's going to play out. You can thank the narrow-minded board for that."

"And the women you took advantage of? Are they just collateral damage?"

Tears were trickling down Jia li's cheeks.

"I've never assaulted a woman in my life," Robert replied. "Whatever decisions they made, they made of their own free will."

Simone shook her head in utter disbelief. "You take no responsibility for your actions, do you?"

"Only those I'm guilty of."

At that, Simone's fingers tightened reflexively on her pistol. "You mean things like putting an innocent girl's life on the line in the most horrific way possible?"

Robert heard Jia li's quiet weeping, but he was totally focused on Simone's accusation. "What are you talking about? Jia li is in no danger. She's establishing her professional future."

Simone raised her pistol. "No games, Robert. You know damn well I'm not talking about Jia li."

He spread his hands wide, shaking his head at the same time. "Then who are you talking about? Whose life is in danger?"

"Lauren Pennington. Or did you think I didn't know?"

His brow furrowed. "Lauren—Vance's *daughter*? What does she have to do with anything?"

Simone studied him for a long moment before realization exploded in her head like fireworks. "You really don't know, do you?"

"Know what, for God's sake?"

Simone answered with a question of her own. "What's your arrangement with Xu Wei? How is he getting your technology, given Nano's impenetrable security? Clearly not directly from you. And clearly not with the help of anyone at Nano, for the same reason. So who in the US is working with him?"

"I have no idea. Nor do I care. The security measures at Nano apply to everyone, including me. I'm not a spy and I wasn't about to jeopardize my career at Nano by stealing trade secrets. That was what Xu Wei was for. Our agreement was that he steal the technology. That was his buy-in. Once that was done, we'd move forward. However he accomplished that was his problem, not mine. And you haven't answered my question—what does Lauren Pennington have to do with this?"

Simone laid it out in several tersely worded sentences, so as to gauge Robert's reaction.

"She's the bargaining chip Xu Wei played to gain access to the technology when other methods failed. Xu hired a brutally violent Albanian organized crime group. They kidnapped Lauren, snatched her off the streets of Munich, and took her to a remote farmhouse in Croatia, where she's been held hostage. The instructions to Vance were to get them the drawings they wanted in seven days or his daughter would die. That's the nightmare your friend has been living while you've been plotting your professional future."

For a long moment, Robert simply gaped at her, as non-comprehension transformed into agonized awareness.

"Oh my God." His entire body recoiled, his pupils dilated with shock—a reaction that left no doubt as to his obliviousness over Xu's methods. "Oh dear God."

Sweat broke out on his forehead, trickling down onto his face, and Simone wondered if he was going to be sick. He swallowed convulsively, and his hands shook as he gripped his knees, leaning forward to scrutinize Simone's expression. "Is Lauren... Is she... Did they...?"

Part of Simone wanted to prolong his fear, to remind him that he could be facing another charge—accessory to murder. But the man was in obvious torment, his features twisted with panic and anguish, his breathing coming so fast that Simone feared he'd have a heart attack. Human decency prevailed and she went on to end his suffering.

"Lauren was rescued a few hours ago," she told him. "She's alive, traumatized but physically unharmed, and on her way home to her parents."

"Thank the Lord." Robert sagged into the sofa cushion, covering his face with his palms. "Poor Vance. And Susan, my God, Susan. What they must have been through."

"I think you know the answer to that." Simone had everything she needed. Time to wrap this up and get the wheels of justice in motion.

"It's over, Robert. Now it's time to do the right thing—actually, the *only* thing, given that an FBI agent is arriving on the scene as we speak and that our entire conversation here has been recorded. They'll be receiving the recording of this conversation, along with all the evidence we've compiled against Xu Wei—enough to implicate him and to link him to Jia li. Which makes her an accessory—an accessory who I'm sure will be more than willing to cut a deal, now that she knows how meaningless your love affair is."

Jia li nodded vigorously, anger and betrayal stemming her flow of tears. "I knew nothing about this," she stated flatly. "Only that Robert was being wronged by NanoUSA and that he was negotiating with Xu Wei to take his technology with him and use it to start a new company. The rest…" She shuddered. "Violence? Kidnapping? Organized crime? I had no idea." Her lips thinned. "Nor did I know anything about the women—about there being so many others before me and how my future would be when I'm no longer as young and fresh. He told me it was his age, that they didn't want a sixty-three-year-old man running their company when there was so much young blood out there. Clearly, I was a gullible fool. I won't make that mistake again. Anything the FBI wants to know, I'll tell them."

"None of this is necessary." Robert spoke quietly, his shoulders slumped in defeat. "I'll voluntarily talk to the FBI myself. I'll admit to my crimes. But I swear those crimes were limited to conspiring to commit industrial espionage. I would never… never…" He broke off, tears shimmering in his eyes. "I have to face Vance, to explain, to apologize, to…"

"I doubt he'll want to hear your explanations. Instead, I suggest you contact your attorney." Simone took out her extra phone and made her call. "Yes, Agent Albertson. As you heard, Robert Maxwell has agreed to come in willingly. As has Jia li Sung."

"Yup, I heard it loud and clear," Terri replied. "That works out perfectly." She gave Simone the necessary information Marc had provided, together with the details of the plan. "By the time Albertson returns from his stroll, you'll be gone. Time to make a graceful exit. Tell Robert you're meeting up with Agent Albertson outside for a quick, private briefing and that he'll be coming in shortly to take them into custody. As soon as you're out the door, get those gloves on, get out that pen, and scribble the drop box link I'll give you on the outside of the envelope. Then slide it through the open window in Albertson's car. Between the contents of the USB drive and what I'm uploading to the drop box, the FBI will know about everyone, from Robert Maxwell down to David Cheng."

"I understand."

"Aidan was worried, to say the least," Terri added. "I'll let him know you're okay."

"I appreciate that." Simone disconnected the call.

"I'm meeting Agent Albertson outside to tie up loose ends," she told Robert and Jia li. "I'll stress the fact that you're both eager to cooperate. The rest is up to him."

"Thank you," Robert said.

"It's a fact, not a favor. Frankly, you make me sick," she replied, leaving without a backward glance.

* * *

The Zermatt Group Offices
West 75th Street, Manhattan, New York
1 March
Thursday, 11:55 p.m. local time

Terri turned her attention to the large wall of computer displays in front of her. It was time to wrap up the one loose end that was still a thorn in her side: Xu Wei. While the evidence implicated everyone, the FBI had no jurisdiction in China, so to nail Xu's ass to the wall, she needed to commit a crime in his name in China.

Resorting to her favorite game, Terri made a few tweaks and created Wheel of Fortune, the Macau edition. So instead of spinning for dollars, she was spinning for renminbi. When she didn't like the amount the wheel stopped on, she rounded up generously. After three spins, she had the three amounts she was going to wire out of Xu Wei's personal account and into the pockets of some crooked government officials. While corruption was nothing new, blatant greed and overt displays of corruption were not tolerated.

Terri made sure to make the bribes highly embarrassing to Communist Party officials, leaving them no choice but to take care of the problem.

She smiled at the thought of Xu Wei rotting in a Chinese jail.

30

Los Altos Hills, California
2 March
Friday, 9:45 p.m. local time

Lauren was out of the town car the instant it stopped in front of the brick staircase leading to her family's house. Simultaneously, the front door burst open and Susan, Vance, and their two older children all raced out. Like a true mother, Susan was half a step ahead of the rest of the family, her arms outstretched as she hurried down the front steps to snatch her daughter in her arms.

"Lauren, oh, Lauren," she sobbed, rocking her from side to side as if she were a small child. "Thank God. Oh, thank God. You're home. You're alive. You're safe."

"I'm okay, Mom—really I am." Lauren's choked-up words were meant to be reassuring, but she was clinging to her mother as tightly as her mother was clinging to her, and the aftermath of shaking and weeping began all over again. "I was so scared," she whispered. "I thought they'd kill me. I never thought I'd see you again. I'd given up…" Her gaze met her father's over her mother's shoulder. Tears were seeping down his cheeks and he moved in, wrapping his arms around both his wife and his daughter and hugging them close.

"Baby..." he managed. "Welcome home."

Lauren swallowed hard. "I never thought I'd hear those words, not ever. Thank you for sending Aidan and his team. They saved my life, Daddy. They were *amazing*."

"I know." Vance's gaze flickered to the town car. Aidan was standing outside it, hip planted against the open rear door, genuine pleasure glinting in his eyes as he watched the joyous reunion.

By this time, Lauren's two siblings had joined their parents, grabbing Lauren to kiss and hug her. They themselves were still in shock over the gruesome situation they'd only just learned about and were weak with relief that their baby sister was home safe and sound.

Gently, Vance disengaged himself from the group, murmuring, "I need to talk to Aidan." He kissed his daughter's forehead. "You all go inside and get settled. Dr. Flecker will be here soon to check you out. I'll be right in." He waved away his daughter's upcoming objection. "I know Aidan's pilot has medical training from his army days and that he examined you and gave us a thumbs-up. I know that *you've* told me a half dozen times that you're fine. But I need to hear it from our family physician."

Lauren nodded, a new maturity and understanding underlying her response. She'd been through hell, but so had her parents. "Okay."

Vance glanced at Susan, who was looking directly at Aidan and mouthing, *Thank you. Bless you.*

Aidan smiled, giving her a nod of understanding.

Vance watched his family escort Lauren inside. Then he walked over, pausing in front of Aidan as he struggled for the right words. "I don't know how to express my gratitude. You did everything you said you'd do and more. Your team... your guidance... your skills... without them, Lauren wouldn't be here. She wouldn't be alive."

"But she is," Aidan replied.

"Yes, thank God." Vance reached into his back pocket and extracted his checkbook and a pen. "I'll write you whatever fee you name. There's no amount too great for what you've given me."

Aidan waved away the offer. "Not necessary. Watching your family reunion is all the gratitude I need."

Vance looked startled. "Is it the anonymity? I can pay you in cash."

"We're more than solvent. No financial payment is needed." Aidan changed the subject to one that was in the forefront of his mind. "Lauren is a lovely young woman, strong and courageous. And, yes, physically, she's fine. Still, there's bound to be some degree of post-traumatic stress following an ordeal like the one she suffered. I'd suggest you get her into counseling right away. You and Susan would benefit from some, too."

Vance nodded. "Susan suggested family counseling. She already got recommendations for a few highly rated therapists." He swallowed hard. "I couldn't bring myself to help her. I was afraid to think that far ahead."

"Completely understandable. But now you can." A contemplative pause. "The FBI is already starting to conduct a full investigation. Given the size of the two companies involved, plus the inevitable leak of Lauren's kidnapping, there's no way you'll escape an onslaught of media coverage. All the more reason Lauren will need counseling. This is going to be tough on her, even if she refuses to comment."

"I know. I've already contacted our attorney. We'll protect her any way we can. But you're right. Every news station will be running with this. Social media will be flooded. Lauren's friends, professors, everyone will want to know what happened. She's going to need a lot of support. And she'll have it." Vance locked gazes with Aidan. "What about you and your team? How will you retain your anonymity?"

A corner of Aidan's mouth lifted. "I'll hand that problem over to Marc. He's former FBI. He'll know what to do. Not to worry. What about you? Have you decided whether or not you'll speak with Robert Maxwell? As I understand it, he's frantic to talk to you."

Vance stared at the ground. "I'm not ready to make that decision. I'm not even ready to think about whether or not I want to stay on at Nano. Industrial espionage, a link to organized crime, and a corrupt CEO will result in irrevocable damage—the kind I'm not at all sure I want to ride out. As for Robert, on some rational level, I realize he didn't have a hand in Lauren's kidnapping. But his actions and decisions precipitated it." Vance raised his gaze to meet Aidan's. "He was my mentor and my friend, one of the most honorable people I've ever met. Or so I thought. Now…" Vance gave a baffled shake of his head. "I don't even know the man. Maybe I never did. Seeing or even talking to him right now would be a bad idea. He's trying to purge, but I'm trying to recover. I'm going to need time."

"That's very decent of you," Aidan replied. "Not many people would even consider speaking to him. From what I'm hearing, he's a broken man. Everything he cares about is gone—his job, his reputation, his freedom. And, if rumor has it correctly, his wife. Looking away from indiscretions is a far cry from having them splashed all over the Internet. That, together with having her husband facing federal charges and an almost certain lengthy prison term, is more than she's willing to endure."

"His poor children and grandchildren," Vance murmured. "The impact on them is going to be very hard. For that reason alone I might agree to speak with Robert. I know his family. Maybe I can help in some way." Once again, tears glistened in Vance's eyes. "I have my daughter back, alive and well. I feel very blessed—blessed enough to be compassionate about Robert's kids and grandkids, if not Robert himself."

"I understand." And he did, more than Vance could ever know. Even as they stood there, finishing up, all Aidan could think about was Abby. He couldn't wait to get to Disneyland and hold his little girl.

He extended his hand, clasping Vance's in a firm handshake. "Go inside and enjoy your family."

"I will." With a grateful glance over his shoulder, Vance nodded. He turned back to Aidan a different man than he'd been a week ago—one who'd come close to enduring an unthinkable loss and whose priorities would be forever changed. "Again, you have my eternal gratitude."

"Semper Fi," Aidan replied, repeating the same Marine motto he'd uttered in Vance's office a week ago.

"Semper Fi."

Marc scrutinized Aidan once he was back in the town car and their driver had started on the return trip to San Jose International Airport. "That looked intense."

"Yup." Aidan rubbed his eyes with his thumb and forefinger. "No surprise there."

"You okay?"

"Just wiped. The adrenaline rush is giving way to major exhaustion."

"You're full of it. You're thinking about Abby. So am I." Marc blew out a breath, leaning his head back against the headrest. "I can't wait to see the little tyrant. Even if it is only long enough for us all to catch a few hours of sleep, after which she and I will share a quick carousel ride and a ginormous breakfast before I pack Emma and Joyce up and the three of us fly back to New York."

"I hope you understand," Aidan said. "I just want a few fun days alone with her—just to be Daddy. I need that after this one."

"I know you do." Marc needed no explanation. "Besides, I have my work cut out for me—dealing with the Bureau and keeping Zermatt a secret." He grinned. "Hey, if push comes to shove, I'll credit Forensic Instincts with Lauren's rescue."

Aidan grinned back. "Feel free."

"I appreciate the use of your plane. But how's Simone getting home?"

"She's flying commercial, and she's already airborne. But she's not going straight home. She's going to spend a week of vacation time in Manhattan."

"Ah, so the two of you kissed and made up via phone."

"If that's what you want to call it." Aidan rolled his eyes. "I reamed her out for breaking protocol and putting herself in danger. She reamed me out for being too rigid and for letting my personal feelings cloud my vision. Robert's appearance at Jia li's apartment, and his guilt, came out of the blue and we'd had no plan in place for dealing with that. She went on to remind me that I would have done just what she did under the circumstances. And she's right; I would have."

Marc nodded, hiding his smile. "You can't argue with success."

"Yeah, I get it. Don't sound so smug." Aidan shot his brother a sideways look. "So to answer your question, yes, she and I are good."

"And you'll get to explore just *how* good since she'll be waiting in New York when you and Abby return."

"Exactly." Aidan's grin was back. "Nothing beats make-up sex. I'm a lucky guy. Which reminds me, does Maddy know you'll be home tomorrow? Or are you surprising her?"

"Oh, she knows. She's preparing a welcome home celebration—just the two of us. I wouldn't want to deprive her of that."

"Of course not."

Both men laughed.

Abruptly, Aidan sobered, and he put a hard hand on Marc's shoulder. "It was great working with you, Frogman. I might have to call on you again some time."

Marc sobered, as well. "Sounds good, Leatherneck. I've got your back."

"I know. And I've got yours."

EPILOGUE

Offices of Forensic Instincts
Tribeca, Manhattan, New York
4 March
Monday, 9:00 a.m. local time

For the first time in ten days, the entire Forensic Instincts team was reunited, gathered around the conference room table.

"Nice tan," Casey said to Emma, sipping her coffee and going for the weakest link to try and get some inside info.

With that, both Claire Hedgleigh, FI's claircognizant, and Patrick Lynch, the team's security expert, leaned forward. Besides Casey, they were the only two team members who'd played no part in the past week's adventure. Now they were eager for intel.

"Thanks," Emma replied, grinning like a Cheshire cat. "But don't waste your time pumping me. I only know the Bluejacking part Aidan already told you, plus every ride and attraction at Disneyland. Other than that, I'm clueless. And exhausted. Running after Abby helped me lose three pounds in spite of all the junk I ate."

The team chuckled.

"Okay," Patrick interceded. "Ryan? Spend any quality time in your lair last week?"

Ryan leaned back in his chair, bending his leg at the knee and resting it on top of the other. "It was an interesting week." With that, he popped a piece of blueberry muffin in his mouth.

"That's it?" Claire demanded. Other than the cryptic conversation Ryan and Marc had had while she was in Ryan's bed, she'd learned nothing from him. "You must have something to toot your own horn about. You always do."

A corner of his mouth lifted and he continued to chew. "I've been told by the best that I'm brilliant. That's all I have to say."

"By the best, do you mean Aidan?" Casey asked.

"C'mon, boss. You know you're the best." Another bite of muffin, chewed slowly, then swallowed. "Too bad I missed the great weather Emma soaked up. I had to brave the New York winter and miss out on Cali by working long distance. Sucks for me. But no complaints. Life is good."

Casey rolled her eyes, turning to her last—and most unlikely— source. "Marc?"

"Nope." He barely lifted his lips from his coffee cup to utter the word. "Nothing to say," he finally added.

"Really." Casey put down her coffee cup, interlacing her fingers on the table and giving Marc a penetrating stare. "I've been watching this weekend's breaking news. Specifically, that industrial espionage story involving NanoUSA—you know, that mega-giant in Silicon Valley where Emma did her Bluejacking—and Jítuán in Shenzhen. Both CEOs are implicated. And, apparently, it goes deeper than that. Phrases like *Albanian organized crime* and *overseas kidnapping of a NanoUSA executive's daughter* are gathering speed."

"Are they." Marc didn't blink.

"Funny thing," Casey continued. "I did a lot of digging—on my own, since Ryan seemed reluctant to help—and there doesn't seem to be a shred of information on how that young woman was safely rescued. It's almost as if a ghost SWAT team blew in and out, leaving no trace of themselves behind."

Marc kept his same look without reply.

Casey arched a brow. "Thanks for the confirmation. Your silence says it all."

"I did a little poking around of my own—on the inside," Patrick added. As a retired FBI agent, he had many contacts still with the Bureau. "It seems there's a former FBI agent, now living and working in the Big Apple, who's been acting as a go-between between the Bureau and a confidential informant who was privy to details of the rescue. A field operative with those kind of resources—pretty amazing, huh? Having someone of that caliber right here in the city? Maybe we should hire him."

At that, Marc's lips twitched. "Maybe we should. I bet he's worth double what they're paying him wherever he works."

"So are the other pros who assisted him," Ryan said.

"Aha, now we're getting somewhere." Claire gave Ryan a sweet smile. "Any pros you want to name? Like Ryan McKay, perhaps?"

Ryan averted his gaze, clearly annoyed at himself for speaking up.

Emma had no such reservations. "Also a pro who can use her awesome pickpocketing skills to Bluejack a phone that yields mission-critical information to… well, to her temporary employer."

Casey was about to burst out laughing. "And here I thought *I* was your employer."

"You are," Emma added hastily. "You know what I mean. Aidan said he'd called you to brag about me."

"Actually, he called to commend you and to warn me that *you'd* be bragging about you." Satisfied, she sat back in her chair, tucking a loose strand of red hair behind her ear. "I think we've tortured the three of you enough. You gave Aidan your word. We'll honor that—to a point. If the questions from the Bureau start to penetrate FI's walls, then we're involved. Fair enough?"

"Yup." Marc pushed aside his empty coffee cup. "More than fair."

"Not to sound patronizing, but I'm very proud of the three of you," Casey said. "Just don't get any ideas of leaving FI to go work for Aidan."

"Not to worry," Marc replied. "Aidan is doing just fine on his own. And so are we."

"But you'd like to work with him again," Casey astutely deduced. "Well, so would I. The couple of times he helped us out on cases, he was extraordinary. And that was just him. I now realize he has his own team—unnamed but stellar in capabilities. Imagine what our two teams could do together."

"Yeah, just imagine." Marc smiled. "There'd be no stopping us."

* * *

ACKNOWLEDGEMENTS

Angela Bell, FBI Office of Public Affairs—always my first and foremost. Angela, you're the glue who holds it all together—including me!

James McNamara, FBI Supervisory Special Agent (retired), FBI Behavioral Analysis Unit, and former Captain of Marines—Jim, you're my quintessential source, my true go-to guy. If there is a Superman, you're it.

FBI Unit Chief Joseph Gillespie, Balkan/Eurasian Operations Unit, BU Criminal Division—my deep appreciation for your time and detailed explanations. This was a whole new and exciting realm for me.

Amy L. Shuman, FBI Legal Attaché – Vienna—Amy, I don't know where to begin. You literally brought Croatia to me, introduced me to the country, its law enforcement, its traditions, and its wonderful people. To say you went above and beyond would be a gross understatement. I can't thank you enough.

The following list of professionals and people of Croatia, who gave of their time, their expertise, and their food and drink! I can't wait for my next taste of *kulen*!:

Toni Škrinjar
General Police Directorate
Criminal Police Department
International Police Cooperation

Rudolf Kolarić
Chief of Police
Đakovo, Croatia

Branko and Marija Kolak – dairy farm owners and producers of artisanal *kulen*

Krešimir Kovačićek
General Police Directorate
Criminal Police Department
Police Liaison Officer

Anita Kovačićek
General Police Directorate
Criminal Police Department
International Police Cooperation

Ladislav Bece
Commander
Osijek, Croatia

A few addition personal acknowledgements:

Sally Dedecker—my longstanding friend, cheerleader, and advisor. You are deeply missed.

Jerry the Jeweler—thank you for allowing me a "tour" of your space. It helped me bring an important scene to life.

Ted Polakowski—nothing gets by your analytical eagle-eye!

LP a.k.a. MOE—you're, in a word, indispensable.

My family—you're the reason I get up each morning. You fill my heart and my life, always!

We hope you enjoyed this book from Bonnie Meadow Publishing.

Connect with us on BonnieMeadowPublishing.com for more information on our new releases!

Other ways to keep in touch with Andrea Kane:

 andreakane.com

 facebook.com/AuthorAndreaKane/

 @andrea_kane

 goodreads.com/AKane